I0675498

Legend

Spirian Saga Book 3

Rowena Portch

Legend

Originally published in America by Rowena Portch, in
2010 as *Legend*

FIRST AEON ENTERPRISES EDITION,
JANUARY 2013

Copyright © 2013 by Rowena Portch
All rights reserved. No part of this publication may be
reproduced, stored in a retrieval system or transmitted in
any form by any means, electronic, mechanical, photocopy,
recording, or otherwise, without the prior permission of
the publisher, except as provided by USA copyright law.

www.Aeon-Enterprises.us
Cover illustration and book design by
Aeon Enterprises

ISBN-978-0-9886275-2-9
V2.0_r2
Printed in the U.S.A.

This is a work of fiction. The events and characters
described herein are imaginary and are not intended to
refer to specific places or living persons. The opinions
expressed in this manuscript are solely the opinions
of the author and do not represent the opinions or
thoughts of the publisher. The author has represented
and warranted full ownership and/or legal right to publish
all the materials in this book.

ACKNOWLEDGMENTS

Gregg, you are a wonderful mate. Thank you for sticking with me through all my adventures in life. I know it's hard to be married to a female with a gypsy soul. God bless you, my angel. You are and always will be my best friend.

Daughter, Erika. Your skill of storytelling inspires me to continue writing. I know your own novels will be a huge success. Thanks for your undying support and cheerful spirit. Most of all, thank you for my wonderful grandchildren who make me smile.

Nick, Andrew, and Zach, you are the most gifted sons a mother could ask for. Not only do you encourage me to continue pursuing my dreams, you call when I need to hear the words, "I love you, Mim." Thank you.

To the females in my life, Mum, Evelyn, and Georgian, bless you for the girl time, the laughs, your support, and most of all, your unconditional love. I couldn't make it without you.

To my fans, thank God for you all. You inspire me to continue pursuing my passion.

Prelude

*To journey means to be present in the moment, gain wisdom
from the past, and release expectations for the future.*

IT HAD BEEN FOUR MONTHS since the Spirian clan leaders
had met on an island off the coast of Brazil. Despite the
Shadows' rebuttals, it had been decided upon to return to the
Father's law. Territories were to be respected by all Spirians
and the act of taking another's mate resulted in death. Each
Spirian was to have only one mate of pure blood, and all
other mates, humans, and halflings were to be set free. An
exception was granted to Spirian/human unions that were
already established.

The risk of my pregnancy with twins was vastly becoming
apparent. I was large, uncomfortable, and still had six months
left of my term. My mate, Khalen, worried that I would not
survive the birthing. In the dark shadows of my mind, I was
too, but I would not reveal it to anyone, not even Khalen.

The issue of Aidan and Sunjia had yet to be resolved. Her
templar, Dirk, wanted her back, which meant Aidan could

not claim her. It was clear to me, however, that Aidan and Sunjia were perfect for each other. If Khalen would just feel the same, I knew he could change Dirk's mind, but Khalen was stubborn and still believed that Sunjia, his late brother's mate, was a threat to the clan.

Khalen, was designated to head the North American Continent and become the regional leader of the Pacific Northwest. It was his duty to ensure that his clan members selected the proper mate. Despite Aidan's feelings for Sunjia, he would not be able to go against Khalen's decision without severe repercussion.

The Shadow clans had been warned that if they did not heed the new laws, Khalen would personally see to the release of their women and halflings. It was time to follow up on his decree.

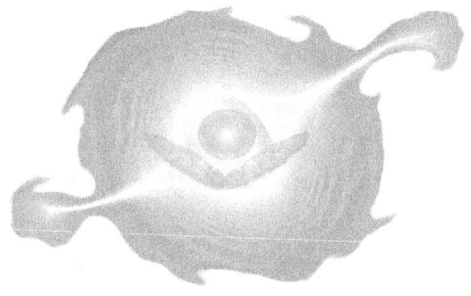

Chapter 1

Even the darkest clouds cannot shadow the brilliance of the sun.

IN ACCORDANCE WITH THE NEW order, Spirian mates had been paired with single men of the Shadow clan—haphazardly, no doubt. Khalen admitted that acquiring my ability to read intention had proven to be quite useful when dealing with the Shadows.

He had approached Sage, the Shadow leader of Washington, but the spineless bugger had no intention of enforcing the new law completely. There were still halflings and human females that had not been released. Sage's father, Victor, was sure to catch wind of it after Khalen took action, he assured me.

"What will you do with the captives?" I asked, as Khalen quietly reflected over a cup of coffee. He had been silent for most of the morning, keeping his thoughts to himself.

"Without a clan, they will be vulnerable," he admitted.

"What are their choices?"

He looked at me with soft golden eyes and I could feel the pain in them. "The humans are a danger, Skye. The females have had a taste of Spirian affection and will crave it. That cannot happen any longer. The humans will not understand. They will continue their destructive patterns, despite the tragic outcome."

"Destructive patterns?" I asked, confused.

He raised his brow as if curious about my confusion. "You have loved both a Spirian and a human. You know the difference now. Could you ever go back to loving a human and be completely satisfied?"

"No, but I'm a Spirian. Surely it is different for humans. You said so yourself that they would not be able to survive the full power of a Spirian lover."

"This is true. Perhaps you should ask Eve or Ember what their feelings are on the matter?"

My face grew warm with the thought. I sipped my coffee in silence.

He chuckled in response. "God, I love your innocence."

"So, to humans, Spirians could be like an addiction that was difficult but not impossible to ignore?"

"Yes, a very strong addiction. It would be like gorging on fine wine, and then forced to endure grape juice in its stead."

I smiled. "Fine wine, huh? Is that how you describe your lovemaking skills?"

Now it was his turn to blush. I could not see it, of course, but his silence and sudden draw of energy was proof enough.

"How would you describe it?" he cleverly countered.

I set my coffee down and thought for a moment. "I suppose I would compare it to a lavish meal with several fine wines, all carefully selected to compliment each course with perfect balance. And just when you believe the meal is over, and you're satisfied, dessert arrives, accompanied by a twenty-year tawny port. When you take your first bite, the dark chocolate coats your tongue like a soft blanket of rich and delicate flavor. The port adds to the sensation, and your mouth explodes with ecstasy as the combination slides down your throat to tantalize your stomach."

He laughed. "And how would you describe loving a human in comparison?"

I cleared my throat. "Aside from my late husband, Derrick, of course, I would describe it as a happy meal with cold, soggy fries, a flat soda, and no surprise."

His laugh deepened. "Now you understand."

I didn't completely understand but was ready to let the matter go. "What about the halflings?"

"Without the support of a clan, they will soon perish like any Spirian. Unfortunately, any clan who harbors a human or halfling female that is not mated will be breaking the Spirian law." He lowered his head. "Gregg and Ro are fortunate to have found one another. They are both halflings with a good clan to live under. Though they are sterile, they have a good chance at having a long life together."

My stomach lurched. "What will happen to Ember and her sisters?"

He sipped his coffee. "They must leave, Skye."

"No," I cried. "They can't, Khalen, there must be another way."

His shoulders dropped and slumped forward. "Are you going to find them a human mate?"

"If I must."

His eyes turned hard. "You cannot save the world, Skye. The clan must remain pure. We made some horrid mistakes in the past and have left damage in our wake. Now is the time to change, difficult as it is."

"We will figure something out."

He stood from his chair and set his mug on the counter. "This burden is mine to bear. The law must be enforced."

"Khalen, this is wrong, and you know it. Spirians created the halflings and now they want to leave them for dead? Halflings or no, they are people, not just the spoils of a bad idea."

His eyes were closed when he turned to face me. I knew he was keeping his anger in check and that I was stepping over a volatile line. "As my mate, Skye, I'm asking for your support. If you cannot offer it, I understand, but I really could use it now."

Slowly I wrapped my arms around his waist and laid my head against his warm chest. It was obvious that he did not agree with the humans' and halflings' fate, but he also had obligations to the clans and the Spirian law.

He kissed the top of my head. "Thank you," he whispered against my hair. "If we could form a commune for the halflings, they might stand a chance. Those who are mated will be able to join a Spirian clan."

I nodded. "I like that plan."

"I'm taking Aidan and Ian with me. We'll be back by nightfall."

I kissed him softly. "Stay safe."

He squeezed me tight then grabbed his keys from the

counter and left. I watched as the three men climbed into our new silver Escalade. Maiyun pressed against my leg and released a low howl. I scratched behind her ears. A long walk was in order for both of us, I thought.

The twins were growing swiftly in my belly and I could feel their every move. My term with them was half over. In six more months, I would be able to hold them both. The discomfort of carrying them made me wonder how I would ever survive the remaining months. I grabbed my coat from the peg by the door and headed out for the day.

Eve met me near the first fire between our yurts. The dusting of flour that scented her face and shirt indicated that she had been busy baking for the evening meal. She carried an air of sadness about her as she warmed her hands by the glowing coals that lingered throughout the day.

I stood beside her, waiting for her to speak first. When she didn't take the hint, I bumped into her and smiled. "What has you so glum, Eve?"

A small smile tugged at her lips. "Are you going for your walk?"

I nodded, and then glanced up at the cloud-covered sky. "Yeah. I was kind of hoping the sun would be out, though. It was earlier this morning."

"Typical fall weather," she said. "Mind if I join you?"

The request caught me off guard. Eve rarely joined me for my walks. She preferred working in the garden over traversing the woods. "Not at all. I would love to have your company."

Eve dusted herself off before approaching my right side. "Where to?"

Maiyun and I lead her toward the north side of camp. She intended to talk, that much was clear, but what about was a mystery I was sure would unfold in a flash flood of emotion.

"Are your pains easing at all?" she asked. Her weak attempt at small talk did not escape my notice. Her thoughts were a trap of pain, frustration, and yearning all wrapped up in a bundle of confusion.

I shook my head. "Not at all. Khalen is concerned with their rapid growth, but that's expected with how much food he expects me to eat at each meal."

More silence followed as we took the right trail that bordered the small lake. The scent of rain lingered in the air. Bright maple leaves that marked the middle of fall cushioned my bare feet, their coolness a welcoming comfort. Instinctively knowing that my vision was weak in this light, Maiyun stayed close by my side and guided me over and around the many obstacles that littered the path.

"It's important for you to stay strong," Eve finally said, though her words were distant.

I finally touched her shoulder and led her to one of the many logs that overlooked the lake. I laid down my coat and urged her to sit, thinking that stillness would encourage her to reveal what weighed upon her mind like wet sand.

"What's on your mind, Eve?" I asked. "Your heart and mind are far too heavy."

"Case wants us to return home."

"Home?"

She twisted her hands together. "Yes, to England. He is worried about the clan."

My close-knitted brows marked my confusion. "Why?"

"Tetris, the man he left in charge, has not responded to any of Case's messages. The clan has been out of touch for several weeks now—very unusual."

I studied her expression. It was not one of concern, but one of sadness. "And you don't want to leave?"

"No, I don't. Our clan in England lives in houses; together yet separate from one another. I feel my family is here."

"Perhaps once Case sees that all is well with his clan, he will choose to return?"

She shook her head. "No, he believes that our place is in Europe, not here. This is Khalen's domain now."

I wrapped her hand in mine. "Khalen wants me to birth the twins in Scotland."

Her eyes widened with surprise and perhaps a bit of hope. "Shanuk's place?"

"Yes, he thinks it would honor the old man."

"That it would," said Eve. She laughed a bit. "Darius will be thrilled to see his brother again."

"Brother?"

"Darius is Shanuk's first grandson and Dirk's older brother. He and Khalen grew up together. They were inseparable until each of them left for college." A smile stretched across her face and her eyes regained their sparkle. A quiet chuckle escaped her throat as she slowly shook her head with remembrance. "Lord, those two knew how to find trouble."

With sadness, I realized there was so much about my mate I had yet to learn. Khalen rarely talked about his past. Oddly enough, nor did I. In that respect, we were very much alike. "Does Khalen keep in touch with him?"

"Oh yes, frequently. Darius' mate, Lenore, is a midwife.

Khalen has been asking her many questions about pregnancy and the birthing process. He wants her to be there when you are ready to give birth."

I felt a cold rush wash over me. "So the real reason for going to Scotland has nothing to do with honoring Shanuk?"

"I think it has a lot to do with it, Skye. Khalen would never tell you something that was untrue. It would be just as easy for Darius and Lenore to come here as it would be for you to travel, would it not?"

I smiled and rubbed Maiyun behind her soft ears. She placed her huge head on my thigh. "Yes, it would." I paused in thought for a moment. "I certainly hope he doesn't plan to allow Lenore to deliver the girls."

"Khalen is not schooled in midwifery. I'm sure he feels uneasy about your request."

I glanced at her, firm in my decision. "I will not reconsider it, unless our daughters' lives are in danger."

"It is not your daughters that worry him, my dear. It is you."

"He worries too much about me. For pity's sake, it's nearly stifling."

"To me, it is refreshing." Her eyes sparkled again. "I have not seen him care for anyone for such a long time, this is a true delight, I assure you."

"Will you be there?" I asked. "For the birth?"

She swallowed hard, opened her mouth as if to speak then swallowed again. Her dark eyes glimmered like polished obsidian as she met my gaze. "You would allow that?"

I squeezed her hand. "Absolutely. I cannot imagine doing this without you."

Eve half laughed and half cried, making a sound that resembled an excited chipmunk. "I would be honored." Whatever sadness that had followed her here had quickly turned tail and ran away. I hoped it would stay away for quite some time. Seeing her so hollow was nothing I wanted to experience again.

I stood and offered her a hand up. "Come, it's getting chilly."

She placed her hand in mine and we continued our walk with idle chatter. "I will miss you when you go," I said, staring down at the ground.

I heard the subtle flutter of Eve's lashes and the slight constriction in her sinuses. She was holding back the tears that wanted so badly to flow. "Ro said she and Gregg would stay here more often, and you have Dania, Caleb's mate to talk to."

"Oh, I have many females to talk to, Eve, but none of them are you."

She squeezed my hand.

Since Khalen banned all Shadows from the island, it was refreshing to be able to walk outside the camp and not be on high alert.

One of the twins kicked my ribs, nearly dropping me to my knees. "Oh!" I yelped as a sharp pain ripped at my side.

Eve supported my arm. "Skye, are you all right?"

I nodded and clenched my teeth while trying to encourage the little tyke to shift her position. "Honestly, I cannot imagine another six months with these two inside me."

"Now you know why it is so dangerous for you to carry twins."

The babe moved and I was able to stand up straight again and continue walking. "My decision to keep them both was the right one," I assured her.

Her silence and lowered head revealed her doubts, but I was not in the mood to discuss the issue.

Chapter 2

Under the warm blanket of night lies the promise of dawn.

~ K h a l e n ~

As expected, Traeger's clan was dissolved. The members had either joined with neighboring clans, or they were waiting for Traeger's successor to be determined. The area was free of all Shadows, yet the house was clean—not a speck of dust anywhere.

I looked at Aidan, who walked through the corridors on full alert. Ian had disappeared into the basement where the females had been chambered. In thought, I asked Aidan if this was an illusion. He shook his head.

I can sense them, he said in thought. There are Shadows here.

Yes, I confirmed. Their coldness was unmistakable. It was the kind that stung clear to your bones.

Ian telepathically called out. Get down here.

Aidan and I hurried through the mansion's corridors and ran downstairs. When we reached the commons' kitchen area, Aidan stopped dead. Bloody hell, there were fifteen of them—all males.

Ian held them trapped in an illusion. They all stood in what looked like wavering water, dazed, confused, and subdued. No doubt they would come out fighting once he released them.

"Get ready," said Aidan.

Ian released the illusion.

I recognized the big man dressed in black leather. His skin was dark enough that his eyes and teeth looked horribly out of place as he hissed. He was crouched in a fighting stance. He was a member of Damon's clan and a loyal warrior of the dark arts. The energy that emanated from his hands felt like stinging daggers against my shield.

I held my hand up. "Easy Pyro, we're not here for you or your blokes."

Another man lurched forward from behind Pyro. I passed enough energy through him to daze an elephant. He dropped to the ground, twitching. A few more of the Shadows stepped back, rethinking their intention to attack us all at once.

Pyro reigned in his power. I was familiar with his gifts. He could stop a freight train dead on its tracks and could crush a boulder to powder. He was an energy bender and very lethal. "I was told you killed your twin," he said with a thick Jamaican accent. "How is it then, that you stand before me now?"

"We've come to free his women," I said, avoiding his question. Revealing how Traeger's mate had helped save my life after I killed her mate would not be wise and would no doubt make her a target of the Shadows.

Pyro looked at me with curiosity and challenge in his dark, narrow eyes. "The women are gone."

"Where were they taken?" I asked.

"We break no laws, Khalen. The mandate you had threatened to endorse has been fulfilled. The Shadow males have one purebred mate, the halflings are gone, and there is nothing left that should concern you."

He was telling the truth, but there was something underlying that truth—something not quite right. "And the halflings?" I prodded.

A sinister smile stretched across his face. "We sold them."

I narrowed my eyes. My anger hummed in my veins. "To whom?"

Aidan placed his hand on my shoulder then jumped back with a curse. He knew better than to touch me when I was amped up, but his intention to bring me back to neutral had worked. The hum around me calmed and my thoughts were clearing. "Whom did you sell them to?"

"It does not matter," Pyro said with indifference. "They are no longer your concern."

I knew there would be no leaving this situation without a fight. In truth, I was looking forward to it. I needed some way to vent my anger, and pounding these Shadow blokes was as good a way as any. Pyro advanced first, followed by the others. Ian and Aidan flanked my sides. Holding the Shadows off provided a challenge. They did not fight honorably. Objects could come flying at you from all angles.

The dilemma with fighting so many gifted beings was

that it took concentration to manifest your gifts. That inner concentration opened the door for your opponent's attack. You had to stay alert and in the present moment at all times. Your feelers had to be out and seeking potential threats. One mistake would render you helpless in a fraction of a second, and God forbid if you were to be knocked out.

The Shadows moved closer. I cleared my mind, formed my shield, and prepared for the onslaught of attacks. Standing on the loose rug was a danger. I silently warned Ian and Aidan to move back until our feet were off the rug. As expected, the Shadows came forward, stepping on the rug we had just cleared. When all of them occupied the volatile footing, I willed it out from under them. They toppled to the ground like wooden soldiers in a shoebox. Before they could regain their wits, we moved in.

Our goal, of course, was not to kill them, just render them unconscious. Pyro reformed his switchblade into a sword then swung it toward my chest. I deflected the blow then pounded my fist across his face. Another quick blow to the side of his neck dropped him like a rag doll. When Drew taught me to fight, he stressed the fact that you never wasted energy. Each blow had to count.

The next attack came from the side. I turned to deflect a piercing blow of energy. The man lunged at me with a knife, while his buddy attempted to sweep my legs. When he made contact, he cursed as if he had just struck solid steel. I grabbed the hand with the knife, twisted it up until the knife dropped, and then locked his wrist joint. The man dropped to his knees. One solid energy blow rendered him unconscious.

The one who attempted to sweep me stared with wide

eyes, backing away slowly. The other five who stayed out of the fight stood behind him confused and dazed. To leave, they would have to pass the three of us, something they obviously felt uncomfortable doing.

A line of blood dripped down Aidan's arm where he had been slashed. He didn't seem too interested in stemming the flow. His eyes were dark and focused, his body tense. Ian looked pumped and ready for more action. He always enjoyed a good fight, unlike his brother, who despised any form of violence.

"Where are the halflings?" I calmly asked.

The one rubbing his leg looked up. "Some of them were taken to Sean's clan. The others were sent overseas, I'm not sure where."

"Sold as slaves, no doubt," Ian spat.

The blood stopped flowing from Aidan's arm and his gash slowly fused. The observing Shadows stared in disbelief. They'd likely never seen a man who possessed the gift to heal. Skye had obviously tapped my thoughts and did a quick assessment of the damage. I could feel her disappointment with the demise of the women. I assured her I would pay Sean a visit.

"Who is your clan leader?" I asked.

"Seth, Traeger's son, but none of us can find him."

"Find another leader," I decreed. "I am claiming this county as Protected territory. Warn the others."

The Shadow nodded then looked down at his incapacitated cohorts. Ian, Aidan, and I left. My sympathy for the Shadows' weaknesses did not concern me so much as how it affected the balance of all Spirians. As in all of life, when the balance shifts, changes automatically occur to restore symmetry. The void of the Shadows would be quickly filled. The smart choice would be to set up Protected clans in every city to ensure purity. As it stood, King County would be the next Shadow dominion in Washington.

Aidan placed his large hand on my shoulder. "Your thoughts are heavy and guarded, my brother. What occupies you?" He was not my brother by blood, but he was as close as any brother I could ever have.

I gently broke away from him to hoist myself into the driver's seat of the Escalade. Aidan sat shotgun while Ian sat in back. I revved the engine, glancing over at Aidan who waited for an answer. He knew better than to push me. "We have just claimed the county," I explained. "Sean will not back down lightly."

Ian cleared his throat. "He has no interest in claiming the peninsula, why would he care?"

"We just dissolved Traeger's clan and pushed them from the area. Sean will feel the aftermath. He will not be pleased. Sean had high hopes for Seth. Losing him to the Protected would be a hearty blow to his overinflated ego."

"So, what is your plan?" asked Aidan.

"We need to grow our clan and distribute them throughout the county."

Both Ian and Aidan remained silent. I could feel their inner turmoil bubbling like the Sol Duc Hot springs. Neither of them wanted the clan to separate. We had resided in close proximity for many years. Having it split was like watching members of a very close family sprout their wings and fly away.

Aidan was the first to speak. "It's a solid plan." His words did not match his emotions. Loyal as he was, he trusted my decision. The nice thing about Aidan, though, was that he would challenge me when he felt it was absolutely necessary. He provided a good counterweight to my occasional reckless will.

I looked at Ian's reflection in the mirror. "You still have connections with the King County clans?"

He nodded. "Are you thinking about relocating them?"

"I am. Sean's strength is in numbers, while ours lies in gifts. The more consolidated we are, the better we stand in defeating them. Unlike most Shadows, Sean is a strategist and a manipulative one at that. If we are not careful, he will encroach upon us like lava beneath the earth's surface. We won't feel the heat until the ground crumbles and we lay open like helpless clams engulfed in steam."

Aidan's expression changed to amusement. "Colorful analogy."

"We should alert the clans in Port Townsend and Port Angeles as well," Ian added. If the Protected claims Mason County, you can bet that the Shadows will want to claim the neighboring borders."

I glanced into the mirror. "I want to drive them from the entire peninsula and create a safe place for the Protected to dwell."

"A castle surrounded by a very large moat," said Aidan. "Brilliant."

Now it was time to pay Sean a visit in Seattle. The I-5 was slammed when we entered Tacoma. How anyone could tolerate living in the city or surrounding metropolitan areas astounded me. I felt as if I stood among cattle crammed into a small pen awaiting slaughter. My hands gripped the steering wheel.

"We really need to find a way to project ourselves through space," said Aidan, noticing my discomfort and frustration. There were some energy benders known to dematerialize and suddenly reappear miles away but they were rare and the act had proven to be dangerous on several levels. Those who were able to do it never lived for very long. Wizards who were at least second-generation alchemists were the only ones who could transport without repercussion.

"Yes," I said. "I can see how that could be very useful— dangerous, but useful." I crept the car forward a few more feet then stared at the clock. It was already two in the afternoon. At this rate, we would roll into Seattle at three or three-thirty. My stomach roared, reminding me that its last meal had been breakfast. My hunger would have to wait. I wanted this day to be over with and return to my mate. My next meal would be with her.

My love, I called to Skye in my mind. *I'm afraid we will not make it home by nightfall.*

I figured as much, she responded. *We will have dinner when you return.*

No, please eat without me. I'm not sure when I will be home.

I will not eat without you. She responded.

I don't want you to wait.

Tough.

I drew my lips back into a tight line and shook my head. Stubborn. *How are you feeling?*

Her reply was slow and calculated. *The girls are very active. I feel good.*

You're a horrible liar, Skye. I want you to rest.

Stay safe.

Rest. I demanded

I love you.

I pounded the steering wheel. "Women can be so difficult."

"I'm sure she thinks the same about you," said Ian with a knowing grin.

"I do not like her with twins."

Aidan looked at me. "Then why did you not take one of them away?"

I met his stare. "Could you?"

"It's not one of my gifts."

My expression reflected his sarcasm. "If it were, could you take one of the girls from her?"

He pursed his lips as if weighing his answer. "No, I don't believe I could."

I raised my hands. "Now you understand."

"She's a strong woman, Khalen."

"Strong, but not immortal. The girls are big and are growing too fast."

Aidan looked out the window, fighting his own fears. He tried to hide his feelings from me but I sensed them all the same. He loved Skye almost as much as I did.

"You two are pathetic," said Ian. "Skye will be fine. She has a great doctor and Shanuk protects her from the other side. What could go wrong?"

Aidan turned back to him sharply. "Have you no fear of anything, brother?"

Ian held up his hand. "Whoa, sorry."

Aidan turned back around, his fists were tight and his eyes focused on nothing particular out the window. I had chosen Skye's templar wisely. Aidan would lay his life down for her, I was certain. I felt the pain in his heart, though, and that concerned me. Perhaps Sunjia would be good for him. If there were only some way to convince Dirk to release her to him. The thought of it churned my stomach like tainted meat. Good as she was, she was still a Shadow.

Two hours later, we rolled into Seattle and parked in front of Sean's mansion. As I discovered several months ago when Skye was abducted, he had more than one residence. It was anyone's guess where he might be staying. I was counting on reading his servant's mind if Sean was not staying here. I reached out the window and rang the buzzer.

"Welcome to Bayer Manor, how may I help you?" a frail voice poured from the speaker.

"We're here to see Sean."

"Master Sean is not available, Sir. May I tell him who came to call?"

"Khalen Dunning."

A long pause filled the silence then the gate's buzzer sounded. The large black wrought iron gate slowly pulled aside. "Please, come through," said the voice.

I glanced over at Aidan, who had his feelers out for any illusionists that might be around. Sean's clan was littered with them. Most of them were young and careless, but under Sean's guidance, they would soon be dangerously efficient. Sean had strong mind skills and could easily get into your head if given half a chance.

The butler met us at the door with a broad smile. His billowing sleeves and satin cummerbund looked oddly out of place. He stepped aside and gestured us into the house. The ambient hum grew louder as Sean met us in the foyer. He was testing our boundaries, which was typical when two opposing forces shared the same space.

"Khalen, to what do I owe this unannounced visit?"

I felt Ian fall into an illusion. His intent was to do some investigating of the premises. Aidan stayed behind to mask the illusion with one of his own. Nested illusions were difficult to master, but incredibly effective when used in the company of other illusionists. When Sean became suspicious of Ian's quiet stance, Aidan mocked a quiet conversation with his brother, something that cannot be done in a typical illusion. It was enough to curb Sean's suspicion for now.

"Where are the halflings?" I asked. I tried probing his thoughts, but it was like sifting through a sandstorm to find a grain of truth.

Sean's smile broadened. "They have been released from our care." His red eyes glistened against the light from the crystal chandelier. It was unknown why the irises of a bloodsucker turned red after several months of being part of the clan. The tradition of drinking the blood of a gifted soul originated hundreds of years ago by a band of gypsies that roamed through Europe. The priest of the tribe believed that the blood of the gifted blessed and strengthened the one who consumed it. Some believed that gifts were passed from one individual to another by sharing blood. That belief was never confirmed.

It was an odd practice, but one that spawned a new breed

of Spirian. The bloodsuckers were cunning by nature, with strong manipulation skills. They tended to band only with their own kind, reaching out to others only for personal gain. They absolutely despised humans. The only thing they could possibly want from the halflings was enslavement. They would become the clan's minions—disposable slaves.

Ian returned with nothing to report. The manor was void of occupants, other than staff. If Sean did stay here, it was short term only.

"I am claiming the entire peninsula, Sean. Shadows are no longer permitted on our territory."

His eyes narrowed and the hum in the room grew louder. I felt the presence of others in the room, closing the distance.

"Your clan is too small to back that claim, Khalen. Jarel has assumed Traeger's lot, including his property."

"Not without Seth's release of it all."

"Seth," Sean laughed. "That spineless buck couldn't lead a parched herd to water. Let him try to stop us."

"Seth is backed by my clan. I assure you, Jarel and his lot will not succeed with their unjustified acquisition."

Although he tried to hide his shock of the news, Sean was truly shaken. His energy drew inward and I could smell his anxiety. Its pungent aroma made my nose sting with the scent of salt water. He took a deep breath and raised his chin. With his guard momentarily down, I saw snippets of his thoughts and knew that his plan had been to take us over, and not the other way around. He was not counting on my aggressive ruling.

"Be careful you do not bite off more than you can chew, Khalen, lest things get caught in your throat."

"I will back up my claim, Sean, I assure you. If I knew that wiping out your kind would benefit the Father, I would do so. But we both know that voids are quickly filled. I believe that territories must be established to ensure peace among the clans. I will meet with Victor and seal a treaty with him. He will be responsible for ensuring that treaty is withheld."

"The clans have always run independently within the region. Getting Victor involved will do nothing."

"Then he will be removed, according to the Spirian laws."

Sean clenched his fists. He was clearly uninformed of the outcome of the meeting we had in Brazil. Victor will not have a choice but to assume responsibility for the clans in his region. Until now, clan leaders made up their own rules. Now, they would have to conform to the rulings of the regional leader. The plan was a good one, and was intended to restore some semblance of order and accountability.

"The clans will have to relocate."

I nodded.

"Where will they go?"

His concern of losing his hold and power consumed him. I could sense his panic now. Strong leaders would be forced to migrate into his territory and he lacked the power to thwart them. It would take nothing for them to overpower his clan and consume them.

"I assume they will take over most of King County."

Sean's nostrils flared. "The numbers of our kind dwindle, Khalen. You know what will happen if the Shadow clans darken this city."

Sean never saw his kind as Shadows. He saw them as something better, more prestigious and civil.

"I understand there are many of your kind in Europe. Perhaps you could return to your homeland?"

Sean turned away. "That is not an option for me." He tapped his lower lip with his finger then trained his eyes on me. "I understand your mate carries twins?"

The sudden change in subject was Sean's way of saying this battle was not over with. Skye was the weak link in my armor and he was testing it now.

"She is not your concern, Sean. I suggest you focus your energy on more personal matters. Your first matter, of course, are the slaves you have sold. Victor will be interested in their fate, I'm sure."

Sean's face paled. "I carry your mate's blood in me," he seethed. "I will find her."

Without any coaxing, the energy I had built up released and slammed Sean against the wall. His minions closed in. I turned toward the closest one and blocked a metal staff he swung toward my head. The crack against my bones stung clear into my chest. My hand went numb. The other men closed the distance and attacked the three of us with such force and numbers it was impossible to hold them back.

Sean weakened my shield. If I didn't do something fast, we would be overtaken. The minions dropped one by one, their life zapped with only my will.

"Stop!" Sean shouted. "Enough. You made your point, Khalen, now leave." The pain in his ruby eyes was enough to convince me that he understood where things had fallen.

My body shook with my rage and it was hard to gear it down. Aidan gripped my shoulder. "My brother, let's take our leave." I knew that he felt pain in his hand, yet he held firm, grounding me.

My eyes locked on Sean's as we walked toward the door. "Skye is mine," I said. "Understand?"

Sean nodded.

Chapter 3

*When lightning strikes, does it do so with the intent to harm
or is it merely seeking ground?*

~ S k y e ~

SOMETHING WAS WRONG. I TRIED to contact Khalen, but
all I received was this raging headache and a strange urge
to slam my fist into the wall. I paced the circular space of
our yurt, feeling the warmth of the tigerwood beneath my
feet. The fire crackled as it warmed the space. I left the lights
turned off because my eyes needed the rest. My vision was
fading lately and I wanted to preserve what little sight I had
left. With any luck at all, I would be able to see the faces of my
young after they were born.

Sam and Karin were planning to visit tomorrow and stay
for a week or so before leaving for Virginia. I was excited to
see them again. I walked over to my nightstand where my
iPhone rested. I pressed my finger over the screen. A pleasant

British female's voice announced the time, "Eight, forty-two pm" *Khalen, where are you?* I thought, hoping he would respond.

I'm coming home, he answered. *See you soon.*

His thoughts were short and tense. I decided not to probe him, my head was aching far too much. I wandered toward the kitchen and increased the flame under the pan of vegetable soup I had made. My stomach growled, anticipating its long-awaited meal. I wrapped the bread that Eve had made in foil then placed it in the oven. I rotated the dial to 200 degrees to keep the loaf warm. The tactile dots that Khalen had placed on the dials made it much easier to set the temperature. I guess he got tired of me burning our meals.

Shortly after we returned from Brazil, he had hired Drew to remodel the yurt. It now had Wolfe ranges and cobalt-blue Silestone counters. The simple pine cupboard had been replaced with solid cherry wood. Khalen's wardrobe had plenty of room in the new closets he had constructed. Brazilian tigerwood floors replaced the laminate flooring that came standard with the yurt. He even replaced the bed with an oversized King, complete with ample blankets that were both soft and purple.

I made my way to the fire pit in the center of our room. Focusing my weak vision on anything was near to impossible anymore, even in good lighting. Khalen thought that maybe the pregnancy had something to do with the sudden decline in my vision, but I doubted that theory. I knew that it was only a matter of time before my vision would fade completely. I reached into the wood stash for another log and laid it upon the embers.

I heard Maiyun gnaw on a bone in her bed. I lowered myself beside her and laid my head against her strong shoulders. My fingers combed through her thick fur. She smelled like bay rum, the soap Khalen used to bathe her in. I felt his presence as the Escalade rolled up the driveway.

The door opened as I pried my arm out from under Maiyun. My extended belly made it difficult to stand. Khalen was by my side, offering a hand. He pulled me up as if I weighed no more than a mere child, embracing me as if we had been apart for days instead of hours.

"How did it go?"

He stepped away from me and walked toward the wet bar to pour himself a brandy. "I will need to request council with Victor."

Shivers ran down my spine. "Victor? Why?"

He took a long, slow sip of his brandy then turned to face me. I imagined his face was long and sullen. "The halflings were sold as slaves. Sage knows about it but refuses to issue any sort of reprimand."

I sat down on the bed with a heaviness in my heart that settled like molten lead. "Slaves? Good Lord, why?"

"Personal gain," he said, taking another sip before joining me on the bed. His warm arm slipped around my waist and pulled me against him. "I intend to remove all Shadows from the peninsula. This will force them to condense in King County."

"Has it become that desperate then?"

"Yes, it has. I will meet with Victor next week."

I sighed. "Will you be gone long?"

"Only a night or two." He placed his hand over my swollen

belly. "They grow so fast, Skye." His hand jumped as one of the girls gave a good kick.

I groaned. "Well, there is no doubt about their strength."

"None at all," he agreed, forcing a smile. "How are you feeling these days?"

He knew the answer already. I was surprised he had to ask it. "Tired, uncomfortable."

"Aye," he said, slipping back to his native tongue. "The next six months will prove challenging at best."

"When should we leave for Scotland?"

"Three months. I have already arranged for our tickets."

I bit back the wave of panic that threatened to rise. "Are you hungry?"

"Starved. I haven't eaten a thing since breakfast."

"Let's get you fed then." I stood and headed toward the kitchen. I tripped over the stool Khalen had slid out while pouring his drink. His strong hands gripped my arm before I could fall.

"Damn my negligence," he cursed, slamming his drink on the counter.

"Not your fault," I said. "I heard you slide the stool out and simply forgot to be careful."

"Your vision is getting worse then?"

I nodded. "No worries, Khalen. I knew this day would soon come and so did you."

"It will improve once the twins are born," he said, but there was doubt lacing his voice.

"Perhaps," I said, doing my best to appease him. I rubbed my sore arm where he had gripped me and willed the pain away before retrieving a hot pad from the drawer. He took it from my hands.

"Let me get this. I want you to rest. He led me to the counter and pulled out a chair. "Sit."

"Khalen, I am capable."

"No doubt," he said, "but you will sit, anyway."

"You have become quite bossy lately."

He did not reply, but I could imagine his expression; narrowed eyes, firm lips, and jaw clenched. Ladling us both a bowl of soup, he spoke in a firm voice that offered no room for rebuttal. "I have asked Gregg and Ro to clear your schedule until further notice." He slid my bowl before me.

My first inclination was to toss it right back at him, but my stomach overruled that intention. "Why?" I kept my voice calm, which was completely opposite from how I felt on the inside.

He sliced up the bread, placed it in a basket then came to sit beside me. I allowed him to take my hands in his and say a prayer before demanding his answer. He took time gathering his thoughts—too much time for the violent emotions slamming around in my brain.

"Eat," he said, gesturing to my bowl.

"Not until you explain why you took liberties with my schedule."

"I believe the reasons are obvious, Skye."

I pushed my bowl away and started to stand. He gripped my arm, keeping me in my seat. There were dark stains on his shirt. I smelled the faint coppery hints of blood. Probing his thoughts provided the details I would have preferred not to experience. I sat back down, dizzy from the sudden images that flooded my mind. "I don't like this," I said, shaking my head. "So much violence."

"I'm sorry," he said. "I didn't want to show you, but you did make me promise to keep my thoughts open."

"Whose blood is it?"

He spread a thin bit of coconut oil on a piece of warm bread, and then placed it on my plate before preparing his own slice. When he didn't answer me, I pulled his sleeve up. My hand brushed the many scars along his arm, swollen and crusted with blood. I wasted no time in healing them all.

"I didn't see these," I said, slightly confused. "I saw Aidan's injuries but not yours."

"They happened later, during our visit with Sean. They were too minor to concern you over."

I scanned his body with my failing eyes. "Are there anymore?" Judging by the energy his body emitted, there was a sizable bruise on his left lower leg. I healed that then scanned him again. He brought my chin up and his golden eyes glowed.

"Skye, I'm fine. It is you I worry about. If you do anything at all for me, heal your own pain. By taking care of you, you care for me."

I frowned. "Can I ask you to do the same? Care for yourself?"

"My role as regional leader is difficult for you?"

"You know it is, but I would never ask you to stand down. Leadership is in your blood. What I ask of you is to stop worrying about me so much. You feed the reality that you don't want and starve the outcome you really do want. Why? You of all people understand that truth, do you not?"

He held both my hands in his as if I would fall away

should his grip falter. His breath deepened and the golden glow of his irises dimmed beneath the lids that now cloaked them.

"You've had visions," I said. He was keeping them out of my reach.

"You needn't know about them." His voice was low and gruff.

"If it concerns me and our daughters, I most certainly do need to know."

He slid my bowl of soup before me. "Eat, Skye, please."

Again, I probed his thoughts and found nothing. He released my hands. I felt as if my emotions were locked in a cold, dark cave, surrounded by heavy dampness. The bowl of soup was cooler now, nearly too cold. I ate it anyway.

When our meal was done, Khalen led me over to the bed, before returning to the kitchen to wash dishes. The silence was discomforting, but I wanted him to speak first. I rose to add another log to the fire. It was far too cold in this yurt tonight and it had little to do with the weather.

I padded my way toward Maiyun who lay sleeping in her bed. Using her belly as a pillow, I snuggled up next to her. The scent of her filled my nose with musky familiarity. I found it comforting along with her soft fur sifting through my fingers.

I listened as Khalen continued to clean the kitchen and put things away—his thoughts still closed to me. I couldn't help but feel the edge of trepidation coursing through my mind, fearing the unknown. Would something happen to the girls? To me? If something were to happen, could fate be changed? I reminded myself that God was in control, not us. All the worrying and planning in the world would not alter the path of what was meant to be.

I heard Khalen approach then stand quietly beside me. With little effort, he lifted me into his arms to carry me to our bed. Without releasing his hold, he lay beside me, burying his face in my hair. Still I waited for him to speak.

He rose, laid his hand upon my belly, eyes glowing. The girls responded in kind. I felt them move and shift beneath his loving touch.

"Let me see what you see," I whispered.

An image of the girls filled my mind as if I had been granted a magic window through which my vision was flawless. I saw every detail of their delicate faces, the dark orbs of their eyes, their tiny beating hearts. A sob escaped me and my eyes filled with warm tears. "God, they're beautiful."

Khalen gently brushed the tears from my cheek. "I love you Skye Dunning, more than life itself."

I pulled him closer to me and closed my eyes. "Then don't hide from me, my love. Whatever you go through, allow me to journey that path by your side, no matter how horrible you think it is."

I felt his breath deepen and a low growl rumbled the bed. "I cannot show you what I've seen."

"Why?"

"Because it won't happen. I won't allow it to."

I leaned up on one elbow and stared down at him. "You are strong, Khalen, but hardly a match for our Father."

"My visions are possible fates, not absolutes. The Father has blessed me with foresight so that I can choose an alternate outcome."

I closed my eyes and shook my head. "You are a stubborn

man, Khalen Dunning."

"Yes, when you unite with another soul, you tend to pick up a trait or two of theirs."

I looked at him skeptically. "And what, pray tell, have I acquired from you, Sir?"

"Strength and wisdom, of course."

I laughed. "Of course."

That night, he made love to me for the first time in several weeks. I could sense the apprehension in his movements, but also the relief in his body. He slept soundly now, barely moving except to breathe. I felt more relaxed than I had in the past few weeks, but my mind was an electrical storm of thoughts. The remembered images of the girls soothed me. My eyes remained open, yet consumed with darkness. Perhaps if my vision failed me completely before the twins were born, I could see them through their father's eyes. I was tickled with the thought. A painful kick quickly replaced it. I stifled my groan so I would not awaken Khalen.

I placed my hand on my ever-growing belly to calm the young. Once settled, I rolled onto my side and allowed the beat of Khalen's heart to sooth me to sleep.

The dream that consumed me was not a typical one. I was weightless like moisture in a cloud colored in various hues of blues and greens. Shanuk appeared before me, dressed in a beige cotton robe that was rather plain compared to the vibrant colors that surrounded us. Concern dulled his vivid-blue eyes.

"Skye," he said, extending his hands toward me in greeting. "You are radiant."

I took his ethereal hands in mine and lowered my head.

"Shanuk. How I have missed you." We remained that way for some time, simply enjoying each other's presence.

"Listen to me, Skye. What I tell you is imperative to your life and the life of your young. Sunjia will instruct Khalen on what to do when the time comes. He will not trust her. You must convince him to do so, understand?"

I shook my head. "No, I don't. Why not just tell me?"

"The information is not for your ears."

I wanted to scream but instantly knew it would do me no good. It was oddly difficult to accept and trust without knowing the hows or whys of it all.

"Do not ponder this now, Skye. Your answers will be revealed in good time."

I nodded, while biting back the nagging urge to question him further. If Shanuk had information for me, he would reveal it without my asking. His image started to fade. The hands that fit so protectively over mine lost their mass and faded into the mist that now surrounded me. I wanted to call out his name, but I had no voice.

"Remember, Skye. You must convince Khalen to trust Sunjia's words." His voice was hollow.

I felt my body being shaken. "Skye, wake up. You're dreaming."

Khalen leaned over me, brushing the damp hair from my forehead. "I saw Shanuk," I said in a groggy voice.

"I know. You were calling his name."

"He told me to tell you something."

"What?"

"He wants you to listen to Sunjia and do what she tells you to do."

He leaned back. "You were dreaming, Skye. Shanuk would not ask such a thing."

"He said her instructions would save my life and those of our young. You must listen to her."

"Shh," he hissed. "Sleep now. We'll talk about this tomorrow."

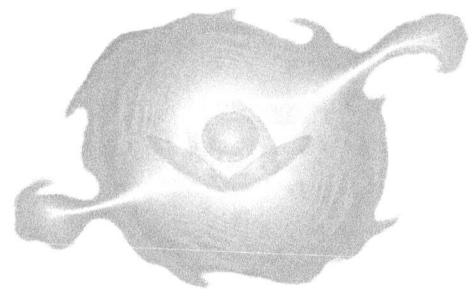

Chapter 4

The tide follows the subtle draw and pull of the sun and moon, and yields to the power of a storm. Through its humbleness, it draws a strength of its own.

I AWOKE NESTLED WITHIN KHALEN'S warm embrace. The sun flooded in through the windows, revealing the vast pasture where the animals fed. I turned my head to find him staring at me, a tender smile curling his lips.

"Good morning," he said, brushing my cheek with this thumb.

"Well, it certainly is a bright one," I replied, blinking against the sunlight. Khalen pressed a button near his nightstand and the sheer shades wound down over the windows.

"Better?"

I nodded. "Yes, much. Thank you."

"You want some coffee?"

"What time is it?"

He glanced over his shoulder at the clock on his

nightstand. "Eight o'clock."

I sat up. "That late?"

"Late?" he laughed. "Skye, most people sleep in on their days off until nine or ten—eight is hardly late."

"Sam and Karin will be here at any moment for breakfast."

He swung his legs out of bed. "I thought they weren't due to arrive until nine or ten?"

"Sam is always early," I explained. "Especially when a meal is involved."

He combed his long fingers through his thick hair and growled. "Today, he will have to wait until I am ready to share you." He leaned over and planted a firm kiss on my lips before heading into the kitchen.

"Always the commander, eh?"

He glanced back over his shoulder. "Blame it on the natural leader in me, my love."

I scooted up into a sitting position and settled against the backboard that Khalen had designed to mimic the back of a very comfortable recliner. No pillows were necessary to find comfort. The morning provided the best vision for me before my eyes became too tired, so I reached for my journal and began recording the dream I had last night. Soon, I would have to record my thoughts on my phone where they could be read back to me. I inwardly sighed at the thought.

There was something very therapeutic about writing my thoughts with a pen onto paper. It wasn't the same speaking them into an electronic device. I was not too excited about technology, even if there were some definite advantages to it at times.

"What are you writing?" Khalen asked, bringing his

coffee and joining me on the bed. There he sat in all his naked glory, bronzed skin glinting against the sunlight that gently filtered through the sheers.

"My dream that I had last night."

He sipped his coffee. "Well, don't take it too seriously."

I looked up at him. "I'm taking it very seriously. Shanuk would not have come to me if it weren't important."

"Skye, it was a dream, not a vision."

I continued to write down the details before they were lost. "Either way, when the time comes, we will know for sure."

"When the time comes," he said, "we will be in Scotland and Sunjia will be in Brazil."

I stopped writing. "Unless you convince Dirk to release her to Aidan."

He growled, a habit he often applied when his will was challenged. "I have spoken to him about it and he is unmoved in his position. He intends to claim her in one month after he returns from New Zealand."

"That's it?" I questioned. "His word is final in this? I remember hearing that you had control of the entire North American continent, Khalen Dunning. Dirk has no territories save those his father oversees. I believe you have more pull than you choose to employ."

"Being a regional leader does not grant me privilege to stomp my feet to get my way, Skye. There are laws to abide by and govern. What kind of leader would I be if I did not uphold the law in my own clan?"

"Use discernment," I argued. "You know this match between Sunjia and Dirk is wrong. She belongs with us, with

Aidan."

"She belongs with her templar."

I closed my journal, and stood from the bed. Without another word, I began getting dressed.

Khalen, too, stood from the bed and walked around to my side. "Are you closed to me now?" He rubbed my arms with his hands.

"No," I said. "I need a hot shower and some time to think, that's all."

His hands dropped down to his sides. "Very well." He turned, picked up his robe and wrapped it around himself before heading back to the kitchen.

I finished gathering my toiletries and clean clothes as he began preparing breakfast. Maiyun followed me out of the yurt, eager to be free of the building tension between me and my mate. I understood Khalen's position, but did not agree with his easy acceptance. Until I could provide a better solution, it was no use arguing with him.

I passed Aidan and Sunjia as they stood by the lake. They were engaged in conversation and hardly noticed my presence. I continued on down to the showers. Eve and Ember tended the gardens. Though Ember was forced to move from the camp and live with her sister, she often returned for visits. She and Eve waved to me as I continued on by. The clan children laughed and played soccer while their older siblings stood on the sidelines and talked. The sun felt good on my skin as it took the edge off the cold morning. Maiyun stayed close by my side, though her interest honed in on the other dogs playing near the soccer field.

"Go on, girl," I said. "I'll be all right."

Maiyun jumped with anticipation, her ears pricked up as if needing confirmation. I waved my hand and said, "Go play." She launched sideways playfully then bound toward the other dogs. I continued my way toward the showers.

I had the small hut to myself. Khalen had the place equipped with propane water heaters and plumbing that provided a healthy pressure. I wondered if I could persuade him to install a good-sized bath as well. Perhaps Ian and Aidan could conjure a hot springs filled with minerals. I smiled at the thought.

As I stood under the steaming hot spray, I closed my eyes and immersed myself in the heat. The water stung against my skin and carried the sweet hint of minerals from the earth. There was nothing as pure as deep well water, I thought, allowing the sweet-tasting liquid to fall over my head and trickle into my mouth. The pleasure was short-lived when the girls decided to tumble around in my belly. I lurched forward and held onto the wall for support. For a moment, it was difficult to breathe. When they finally settled, I straightened and breathed deeply, sighing with relief.

I heard the door of the shower hut open and just assumed it was another lady coming to shower. It was not. Khalen captured my face in his hands and planted a warm kiss on my lips. He was naked. I smiled.

"Hmm, this is a pleasant surprise," I said between kisses. "I doubt the poor soul who walks in on us, though, will feel the same."

He waved his hand toward the entrance. "No one will enter," he said. His gift for creating boundaries was uncanny and very useful at times, as I could well attest. One of the girls kicked against him. He stepped back and placed his hand over my belly.

"Be calm," he said quietly then proceeded to love me. In his arms, I felt as precious as the rarest diamond on Earth. I was entranced with his touch and captured in his golden gaze. When we joined, I felt his breath, his blood, his very soul. Human love could not compare. I knew that now.

When we were satisfied, Khalen lathered a good amount of soap on a soft cloth and washed me down. He then shampooed my hair, and distributed a generous amount of conditioner into my scalp.

"I know you are disappointed about Sunjia," he said. "I have contacted Arcadie and plan to fly down to see him next week about the matter."

"I want to come with," I said.

He rinsed the conditioner from my hair then smoothed the strands back from my face. "As your doctor, I advise against it. As your mate, I forbid it."

"Forbid it?" I tried to step back, but his hands tightened around my arms. "Khalen, this is important to me. I would like to have a chance to speak my mind."

He growled in response. "Very well," he said between clenched teeth. "Dirk is due to claim Sunjia next month. I will talk to Arcadie to see what can be arranged."

"Thank you," I said, pressing my lips against his chest.

"Do you not know that you are everything to me, Skye?"

"Yes," I said. "You have a wonderful way of reminding me every time we make love."

He released a hearty roar as he lifted me into his arms and carried me to the benches where my clothes and towel were draped. His clothes hung neatly over the pegs, along with his towel. He dried my body then stood there looking at me. I felt strangely exposed as his golden eyes scanned me from head to foot.

"God, you're beautiful," he said.

I reached for my clothes. "You make me feel that way," I replied shyly. Remembering Kiara and the other women I had seen Khalen with, I felt horribly inadequate in comparison. He was never affectionate with those women after he had known me, but I was well-aware of his ability to attract the opposite sex. I couldn't help but wonder what it was that he saw in plain old me.

"I see everything in you," he replied, his brow knit with a frown. "I see your genuine heart, your integrity, your gifts, your loyalty, your tenderness. He pulled the clothes from my hands and laid them back down on the bench. His fingers traced a chilling line down my arms. "I see your beauty, Skye, inside and out. For me, there will never be another."

We arrived back at the yurt in time to greet a grumpy, hungry bear of a man—Sam, my dear friend and his sweet wife, Karin.

Chapter 5

An earthworm is warmed by the sun, but if it remains
exposed, it soon shrivels beneath the hypnotic rays.

KHALEN PREPARED BREAKFAST WHILE I attempted to dry my hair by the fire. I could feel Sam's eyes on me, no doubt trying to imagine what Khalen and I were doing at the shower hut.

"You're staring," I reminded him. "And I don't much care for your thoughts."

Sam smiled. "It's just nice to see you in love, Skye, that's all."

"Yes, well, try to close the damper on your imagination, if you don't mind."

"You read those, eh?"

I looked at him with an expression that didn't require words.

He laughed and shook his head as if struggling with the truth of my gifts. "I cannot tell you how much you have changed, Skye. It's like you're an entirely different person."

I pressed my lips together in thought before replying. "Good or bad?"

He laughed some more as if I were daft or something. "Well, I liked you before, of course, but you were always withdrawn and protective of your thoughts. Now, you're much more bold, happy, and confident with who you are. I like the new you, with the obvious exception of your mind reading abilities. That part is kind of creepy."

"Not as creepy as your thoughts," I added.

Karin walked in with a huge bunch of fresh-picked flowers. "Look what Eve gave me," she said, bounding toward Khalen. He reached into the lower cupboard to the right of the pantry and pulled out a cobalt-blue vase.

"Here," he said, handing it to her. "Place them in this and set it down there." He pointed to the far end of the counter.

Karin frowned, obviously not pleased with his choice of placement. "We can hardly enjoy them way over there."

From the strong aroma, I could tell there was a fair amount of lavender that Eve had kept in the greenhouse. The flowers were meant for me, I was sure. "He doesn't care for lavender," I explained. "The scent gives him a headache."

"That's odd," said Karin. "Eve specifically stated that they were meant for Khalen. She made that point very clear."

Eve must have read my thoughts on the way to the showers and knew that he had upset me, I deduced. A small smile formed.

"Nice," said Khalen. "Please, return them with my utmost gratitude and assure her that her intention is acknowledged."

Karin carried the colorful bouquet across the room toward the front door. "Okay," she said in a voice that clearly stated she did not want to enter into a match with my mate. I remembered all too well how intimidating he could be when he wanted his point heard as well as felt.

"What was all that about?" asked Sam.

Khalen chopped the top from a green bell pepper then glanced over at Sam. "Don't ask."

Sam looked over at me. I shrugged while running my fingers through my tangled strands.

"You're getting big," Sam commented then shrank back when Khalen growled. "Jeeze, he's kind of touchy this morning, ain't he?"

"Why limit it to this morning?" I added in jest. "He has a bit on his mind, that's all."

Karin returned with a handful of yellow lilies and bright red leaves. "Okay, before I place these in a vase, do you find them acceptable?"

"Yes, you'll find another vase down there," Khalen pointed to the cupboard by the pantry.

She knelt down, digging inside the cupboard to find the right one. "She told me to give you a message."

"No doubt," he said dryly.

"She said that a bee that tries to find pollen will not produce honey—whatever that means."

I smiled. "It means that if you want positive results, you must do—not try."

"Or that the pollen the bee seeks is right in front of him, and by trying to look elsewhere, he misses it," Khalen added.

Sam drew his palm over his head, indicating that the conversation had finally gone over the top for him. "Mind dumbing it down for us humans, here?" he said, his voice dripping with sarcasm.

"Yes," said Khalen, "I do mind." The edge in his voice was a warning that Sam did not leave unnoticed.

"Family business," I offered.

Khalen aggressively chopped the root from an onion, causing everyone to look up at him.

"I think I'll see if Eve needs help in the garden," Karin said while standing and heading for the front door. She made a gesture toward Sam to follow. He didn't take the hint.

"Sam," I said, "can you please ask Eve if she baked fresh pumpernickel that we can have this morning?"

"Karin can do that when she offers to help in the garden."

"I also need you to help me unload the car," Karin added, a hint of frustration sharpening her tone.

With hesitance, Sam stood from the couch with a groan. "Jeeze, we just got here and I'm expected to work without even enjoying a meal."

"Your meal will be done shortly, Sam. I promise," I assured him.

When the two of them left, I joined Khalen in the kitchen. "Calm your anger, my love. Sam means no harm."

He continued to dice the onion as if defeating a violent foe. "My mother, of all people, knows how challenging my role is, yet she sides with you."

I rested my hand on his upper arm. "Women stick together, Khalen, be it right or wrong. I know you are doing all that you can. I have faith in you and support your decisions."

He laid the knife down and turned to face me. "But you don't always agree with them."

I lowered my eyes. "Not always, no, but I do support

them."

He picked up the knife again. "She's right, you know."

"Your mum?"

"Yes. When I last spoke to Dirk, I honestly did not care about his decision. I simply accepted his choice."

"I see." I picked up another knife and began slicing the mushrooms. His anger made sense now. His mother had driven a painful point home and he felt it.

Khalen stirred the potatoes that were frying with pieces of bacon and spicy Italian sausage. He added the onions then spooned in three healthy tablespoons of garlic.

"I love you, Khalen, and believe you will do what is right."

"Don't," he said, a hard edge to his voice. "Not when it comes to my brother's mate. I may not do what you believe is right."

I matched his tone with an edge of my own. "Then I will stand by your side as you fight this unseeable dragon, Khalen. You have ill feelings for Treager, that much is clear, but they cloud your judgment. This anger you foster will be your undoing. At some point in time, you must sever the cord that binds that anchor, or drown trying to carry its weight."

We continued to cook in silence. I was okay with that, seeing the only words that poured from his mouth were laced with venom. He was a difficult man to be around sometimes, yet I felt compelled to stay beside him. Deep down, I knew that's what he needed, words or no.

Eve bound through the door carrying bread, butter, and freezer jam. She was alone. "Did you make enough for two more?"

"Of course," said Khalen. "I fully expected you and Father

to join us."

Sam and Karin are setting a table up outdoors. It's much too pretty to stay inside and it's bright enough for Skye to see our faces.

I didn't have the heart to tell her that my vision was fading and that even in bright light the details were lost to me.

"I'll set these outside and return for plates and such." She left, leaving the door open behind her.

"My father has wisdom to share with me, no doubt."

"It might be helpful to hear it," I said.

A low groan escaped him as he added the mushrooms, scrambled eggs, and Gorgonzola cheese to the potato mix.

I gathered some plates, utensils, and a stack of napkins to set on the counter for Eve. Sam came back in her stead, and grabbed them. He smelled awful. "Lord, Sam, what happened? You smell like a stagnant fish pond," I said.

"I found Maiyun with other dogs and we started wrestling."

I pinched my nostrils together. "Please tell me you have a change of clothing."

"Karin's getting something for me."

I took the plates from his hands. "Hmm, you best get cleaned up. I'll take these out."

Just then, Eve returned. "No you won't," she countered. "Be a dear and find me a clean cloth to cover the bread with."

Between her and Khalen, I was lucky to be able to walk myself to the shower hut without them making a fuss over me. I imagine they would, soon enough, when I could no longer see my own feet.

I retrieved a clean bread cloth from the drawer and

carried it out to the table. Khalen followed with the huge cast-iron pan containing breakfast, and a plate of sliced avocados. Karin came back for mugs and cream while Case brought two pots of coffee. What started out to be a simple meal turned out to be a fabulous feast.

Karin, Sam, Eve, and I sat at one end of the table, while Case sat with Khalen on the other end. Both of them were engaged in a serious discussion.

"You two are staying the night?" asked Eve, hope laced in her voice.

Sam started to say no then winced as Karin pegged him under the table. "We'd love to," she answered for him.

"Fabulous!" Eve exclaimed, clapping her hands together. "I'm roasting a leg of lamb and we have some fine beets and greens to go with it. I'll even bake a couple of yams for you, Sam."

"Throw in a berry cobbler and I'm definitely on board," he said, a smile in his voice.

Khalen and Case finished their meals and then retreated to the thinking log by the lake. I helped the others clear the table and planned to spend the day with Karin and Sam. Our original plan was to hike to Twin Falls, but my ever-growing condition curbed the idea. Kayaking was also out of the question. After much debate, we finally settled on driving to Port Townsend for the day. There was a bookstore I loved to frequent, and my favorite Chinese restaurant at the marina was there, overlooking the Puget Sound as it opened to the Straight of Juan De Fuca.

Khalen was not too keen on the idea of us heading into Shadow central, even though most of them should have packed up and left. He was sure there was still a clan or two left in that area.

"There are plenty of things for you to do here in town," he said. "I don't like the idea of you driving so far."

"I'm not driving," I clarified. "Sam is, and Maiyun is coming with us. She'll keep us safe."

"I should come with you."

I placed my hand over his. "Khalen, you cannot be with me all the time, and Case and Caleb need your help today. We will be back before five, I promise."

"If you have any troubles, you let me know, understand? We have clans in that area and I will get someone to you."

"Honestly, you sound paranoid. If I have an issue, I'll call Jacob myself. That is his territory, is it not?" I lifted my cell phone to prove I had it with me.

He held my face in his hands. "Not paranoid, my love, just cautious, and you know as well as I do that if a Shadow gets a hold of you, your cell phone will be an afterthought."

He bent down to kiss me then offered a constricting hug. "Take care and have fun."

"Thank you," I said, stepping back. "I'll keep my thoughts open."

"Me too," he said then turned to face Sam who was walking up wearing a bright orange shirt and army pants.

Khalen winced. "Criminy, who chooses your clothing?"

"I do," Sam responded with pride. "I didn't want to embarrass Skye, so I chose something more—casual."

"Thank God she's blind," Khalen retorted. "Take good care of her."

"I always do." He reached to open the back door for me,

but Khalen beat him to it.

Sam frowned. "I guess I'll load up Maiyun."

"He's just being polite," I reminded Khalen. "He is not a Spirian and doesn't fully understand our way of life, or how possessive a mate of a Spirian female can be," I added with a bitter tone.

"Then he'll learn," Khalen said, his voice huskier than usual. He leaned through the window and gave me a kiss. "Take care of yourself."

"I will," I assured him, lifting my brow for emphasis.

Karin ran toward us as Sam held her door open, tapping his boot-clad foot. "Come on, woman, we don't have all day."

"You should be more patient, like Khalen."

All of us laughed, including Khalen.

"Pray I am not," said Sam, smiling up at Khalen who towered above him by a good two feet. Khalen growled in response.

"Have her back by five," he warned.

"Or there abouts," I added.

Sam pursed his lips, "By five it is," he relented then skirted around to the driver's side. As we drove away, he glanced back in his rearview mirror. "I'm not sure I like your new husband."

"He's more than my husband, Sam. He is my mate, and he can still hear you."

"What's he going to do, deck me?"

Just then, the car sputtered then died.

"Ugh," I groaned. "Khalen!"

"Your mate has some real anger issues going on, ya know."

I chuckled. "He says to tell you that he's well aware of

that, and to check your fuel pump."

"My fuel pump. Perfect." Sam popped the hood then stepped out of the car.

"Does he even know what a fuel pump is?" I asked Karin.

She peeked between the gap in the hood and the car. "It doesn't appear so. He's just staring at the engine as if it were a book written in a foreign language. She opened her door. "Do you need some help?"

"I got it."

A few minutes later, Sam jumped back as if the car had sprouted tentacles. The engined had roared back to life. He slammed the hood then returned to the car without a word.

And you trust him to take care of you? Khalen asked me in thought, clearly disgusted by my friend's ignorance of cars.

You could be nicer, I replied.

I was.

"So what was it?" Karin asked, feigning innocence.

"The fuel pump. It must have come loose or something."

"Or something," Karin giggled.

The trip to Port Townsend went smooth and the weather cooperated quite nicely with patches of sunshine and dapples of fluffy white clouds. We spent some time at the Phoenix Rising bookstore where I purchased two massage wands carved from crystal, and a silver dragon charm that reminded me of Khalen.

Sam bought several books on alchemy, and two colorful shirts made from hemp. He frowned when Karin held up a "man bag," she called it. She bought a crystal nail file and some stones she found in a bin.

"What are you going to do with those?" Sam asked.

"I don't know," she said, still admiring their beauty. "Put them in my display box, I suppose."

"Great, more dust collectors."

We perused the other shops on Waterfront Street until it was nearly two o'clock. It was a good 15-minute walk to Shanghai Restaurant and we were all ready for some lunch. My young didn't seem to like all the walking about and didn't hesitate to let me know about it. I bit back the stabbing pain as they shuffled about and jabbed at my ribs.

We turned left at the marina when the hair on my neck stood up. Maiyun slowed and pressed against my leg. I saw two figures walking toward us. I was about to tell Sam and Karin not to look into their eyes, but it was too late. Both of them stood as if they were frozen in time—trapped in an illusion.

I tried to form a shield but had difficulty concentrating. My mind couldn't focus on a single thought.

"Well, well, what do we have here?" one of the Shadows stated. By the broken tone of his voice, I gauged him to be a young male. Another one stood beside him. Five others came around the corner. My heart beat so loud it was difficult to hear anything else. Again, I tried to form my shield but it felt weak and unstable as water on a feather.

"What is a lone female Spirian doing way out here with only two humans to accompany her?"

One of the men grabbed my arm and examined Khalen's mark. Maiyun growled, stepping between me and the man. He immediately let me go and stepped away.

"What?" another man said. "It's just a dog."

"She's Khalen's mate."

"So?"

The man shook his head and walked away. "Leave her be if you know what's good for you."

"Who the hell is Khalen?" one of them asked.

Another shrugged. "I say who cares and let's get on with it." He reached for my arm then dropped to the ground as if someone had ripped his heart out. The others stared on with shock, mouths hung open and frozen in stance.

The illusionist released his hold on Sam and Karin then followed the first man who left. Two more followed him.

Maiyun growled, and then lunged toward the man who had walked behind me. I dropped her leash and harness then focused my energy at his chest. He fell back then cast a blow toward Maiyun. She yelped but remained standing between me and the man. I could feel the pain coursing her body and felt her shake. I had felt those energetic blows before and knew how much they hurt. My shield grew strong around us.

"What the hell happened?" asked Sam, staring down at the man scrambling to regain his stance and my shaking dog. "He didn't even touch her."

The other three men remained and circled around us. I felt my shield quiver.

"You boys are on my turf."

I recognized Jacob's voice behind me. Khalen must have called him.

"Who are you?" asked Sam, still trying to grasp the situation. Karin just stared at the dead man in the street with shock.

Jacob had five others with him. "Take care of him," he addressed the younger two gesturing to the dead man. He ignored Sam's question. "The rest of you beat it. I will discuss this incident with your leader, Marlow, later." The boys did as he asked, quickly scampering away like cockroaches did when the lights were turned on.

The two young men who traveled with Jacob scorched the body until only a fine ash remained. With a wave of his hand, Jacob blew the ash away before the commotion and bright flames drew the attention of bystanders. Jacob quickly assured them that everything was fine.

"Where were you headed?" he asked me.

I pointed across the marina. "To the restaurant."

"We'll escort you there."

"I can handle it," Sam said, raising his stout chin. He looked ridiculously brave against Jacob who stood nearly as tall as Khalen.

"I'm sure you can, but I will escort you all the same."

"Spirians," Sam muttered, shaking his head, "stubborn and egotistical, the lot of you."

Karin squeezed his hand. "I'm happy they're here, so hush."

"Did Khalen take that man's life?" I asked Jacob, still a bit stunned.

"Yes. He read your thoughts, took the bastard's life, and then called me. You were lucky I was just across the street. Are you hurt?"

I shook my head. "No, just shaken. Who were they?"

"Marlow's clan; just a bunch of young teens looking for some excitement. The dead one is Marlow's son. He won't be pleased."

"Clearly they were out of line."

"Oh, very much so, yes. Marlow won't care. Fortunately, his clan is young and weak. He won't stand a chance against Khalen, even if Marlow can get others to back him, which he won't."

"You sound so certain."

"You saw what your mate is capable of. Few will stand against him."

We turned right at the end of the marina and headed straight for the coastline. A large cruise liner moved slowly on the horizon, toward Friday Harbor. Jacob held a vise-like grip on my arm as if I would fade from his grasp. Khalen must have given him strict orders to keep me safe.

Sam and Karin walked several paces behind us, and in front of the other five men traveling with Jacob. Judging by the sound of Sam and Karin's conversation, it was not going too well. Karin's voice was strained as if gripped by emotion, while Sam did his best to appear calm and in control.

"You shouldn't have come here," Jacob finally stated. "The Shadows are out of control and getting worse."

"I refuse to become a prisoner because of them."

"Then choose better escorts."

I prayed that Sam and Karin had not heard that statement. "These are my friends, Jacob. I would appreciate it if you could show them some respect."

"You are a legend, Skye. For the sake of our race, I hope you start taking your role more seriously."

I closed my eyes and fought the urge to rip my arm from his unyielding grasp. I could now see why Khalen was so fond of this man. He was just as arrogant and stubborn as my mate. My appetite had suddenly diminished, though I was almost certain that Sam's hadn't, which is the only reason I continued toward the restaurant.

"Would you like to sit with us?" I was hoping he'd decline the offer but knew better.

Jacob smiled, seeming to know what was on my mind, though I kept my thoughts closed to him. "We would be honored." His eyes narrowed.

He greeted the familiar waiter in Mandarin and led me to a large circular table in the corner. Maiyun dutifully laid behind me in the corner and out of everyone's way.

The waiter liked to be called Steve, but I was sure that was not his birth name. He laid his hand on my shoulder. "Skye, Khalen's mate, what an honor it is to serve you again."

"Thank you, Steve," I choked back, feeling everyone's eyes upon me.

"What can I start you with?"

"Just some hot tea, if you please."

"No pot stickers for you today?"

I shook my head no. "Not today, thanks."

He took the order from everyone, leaving Jacob for last. "I will have an order of pot stickers for the lady, and a jar of your mother's famous sauce for her mate. I will have your walnut prawns."

"Very good, my friend."

"I'm not hungry," I said.

"But, you will eat."

Now I knew what a pampered princess felt like with everyone telling her what she could and could not do. It was no wonder why Princess Di fell away from the royal life, no wonder at all. I folded my napkin and tucked it under my plate. "If you'll excuse me, I need to use the privy."

Jacob stood and held my chair out for me, and then reached for my arm.

I pulled it away. "I know where to find it, Jacob, thank you." I motioned for Skye and she obediently obeyed my hand signal. I heard Jacob follow me. "Do you intend to join me in the stall as well?" I asked him.

"There are no windows that pose a threat, so no, that will not be necessary."

I entered the bathroom, grateful for my temporary solitude. *Khalen*, I called out in thought. *Please call off your watchdog before I choose to castrate him and remove his tongue.*

No. He is to stay with you until you are safely out of town.

There was no use in arguing with the man. He would not budge on this especially after what happened today. When I exited the bathroom, I could almost feel Jacob smiling at me. Maiyun led me back to my seat then curled up behind me.

Sam was talking with one of the young men who incinerated the Shadow's body. He and Karin were fascinated with the process and wanted to know how the man and his brother managed to get the flames so hot without burning their surroundings to the ground.

"Your young have grown since I saw you last," Jacob said, taking his seat beside me.

"Babies tend to do that," I retorted.

"Skye, do not be cross with me for helping your mate as a willing favor."

"I do appreciate your help, Jacob. It is your suffocating guardianship that angers me. "And, you embarrassed my friends."

"They don't seem embarrassed."

Sam and Karin laughed as one of the men told a story. Good ol' Sam could make light of any situation. Karin, too, seemed to have forgotten the recent drama and death of a man, like it was nothing more than a scary movie. I, on the other hand, could not forget it. The man dropped so quickly—no fright, no flight, no nothing. One minute he was standing, the next he was down, like a puppet whose strings had been clipped.

"He severs their soul," said Jacob, reading my thoughts. "There is no pain or fear for the victim."

"Save for his soul," I added.

"Khalen does not take a life unless it is absolutely necessary."

"I know."

Steve returned with two pots of hot tea and several appetizers. Jacob placed two pot stickers onto my plate before adding a generous amount of sauce on the side. Khalen's instructions, no doubt. I wondered what else Jacob was instructed to do if I chose not to eat them.

Jacob leaned over and whispered into my ear. "I am to hurt your friends," he said.

"You wouldn't dare?"

He sat back up and said nothing. He most certainly would, and upon Khalen's request. My anger flared causing the twins to act accordingly with a good kick. I gripped my side and held my breath.

"Your anger makes them uneasy."

"If only it made you uneasy as well."

He shrugged. "Not in the least. Now, are you going to eat or shall I break your friend's fingers?"

Jacob was an energy bender. Even if he didn't actually break Sam's fingers, he could make Sam believe that he did, thus making the experience real. I picked up my knife and fork and ate what he placed on my plate. The food sat in my gut like molten lead, burning a hole in my stomach.

As promised, Jacob followed us out of town until we reached the Hood Canal bridge.

Chapter 6

Clouds drift upon the currents of air void of destination.
Without thought, they constantly change form and direction
before returning to their source.

HAVING NOT FELT RIGHT SINCE we left the restaurant, I curled up on the back seat. Maiyun whined and paced until I assured her I was all right. She finally settled down and fell asleep. The idea was not a bad one. I welcomed anything that would offer a hiatus from the day's events. The day began well and ended with sad deflation, despite Sam and Karin's claim to having a good time.

My attitude was all wrong and all I wanted to do was crawl into bed and forget about life for a while. I closed my eyes and ignored the building pain in my gut.

I didn't even remember arriving home, nor did I remember going to bed. I awoke with a number of people looking down at me, including Sam and Karin.

"Why's everyone here?" I groaned.

Eve brushed the hair from my forehead. "You gave us all

quite a scare, dear."

"What happened? Where's Khalen?"

"He's not far and will be back very soon. You hemorrhaged and nearly lost the twins."

I placed my hand over my belly. The girls were still there, but they were very quiet. I silently called to my mate, *Khalen? Where are you?*

There was no reply. Case entered the yurt. "He will be here soon, Skye. You need to rest now." He ushered everyone but Eve from the room, asking them to wait outside. He sat beside me on the bed. "How are you feeling?"

"Weak," I said. In truth, I felt more like an overcooked noodle teetering on the edge of disintegration. "Are the girls all right?"

"Their hearts are strong." Something in the tone of his voice raised alarm in my core. There was something he wasn't telling me. His intentions were wrong. He was trying to protect me from something. I tried to sit but couldn't. Dizziness overwhelmed me. Khalen was close, I could feel him. I needed to be near him. Again, I called out, but there was no answer.

"Skye, please, you must rest."

"Where is Khalen? I need him here, beside me."

"He is resting," said Case.

"I know you're trying to protect me, Case, but you can't. Your intentions are strong and noble, but completely unnecessary and destructive in ways that I can't describe. I cannot read your thoughts, but what I do read makes me want to run from this bed and search for my mate. Please tell me he's all right."

"He is fine. He is resting and didn't want to worry you."

I wanted so badly to sit up but my body did not comply. My limbs felt like taffy on a warm rock. "I'm already worried. Please, I need to see him."

Case sighed. "He said you would be like this. Try and rest, Skye. He will be beside you when you wake up." He stood and added something to the IV bottle hanging above the bed. Before I could protest, I drifted into the black pharmaceutical hole of no return.

This time, I awoke to Khalen's sweet, gentle caress. He smiled down at me. My IV had been removed, and my limbs were beginning to feel whole again. "Where were you?"

"Resting, like you should have been."

"How long have I been out?"

"Three days now, but you are much stronger for it. I want you to try eating today."

The sound of eating anything caused my stomach to turn and my head to ache. I struggled to sit. Khalen offered assistance then stuffed a pillow under my knees.

"I feel like an old woman."

"Just a very pregnant one who is now on bed rest until your due date."

"I'm not!"

His lips curled into a cruel smile. "Yes, you are."

"Khalen, if you intend to keep me in this bed for another six months, I assure you I will redefine the word regret in your personal dictionary. I will—"

"Shh," he hissed, holding my hands. "By bed rest, I mean that you will have limited time out of bed. I still intend to take you to Scotland, though, our date will occur much sooner than planned. Arcadie has offered to fly us there, himself."

There was a large bruise on the inside of his left forearm. I traced my finger over the puffiness of it then immediately healed it. He grabbed my hand and pulled it away, as if that would stop the healing. "What happened to you?" I asked.

"You needed blood. I gave you mine."

"How much?"

"Does it matter?"

I pressed my lips to his arm and closed my eyes. "It does to me. Is that why I couldn't reach you or hear your thoughts?"

He nodded. "Case stopped the flow, and then carried me back to his yurt to recover. Before we started, I had instructed him on what to do. He started fluids in me and then returned to your side. I told him you would try to find me."

I narrowed my eyes. "Yes, I remember that part. You also told him to knock me out."

"I know you too well, my love. You would not have rested."

"And what would have happened if I had awakened only to hear that you were too weak to recover?"

"What if those Shadows had killed you, Skye? What if Sam had driven the car off the Hood Canal Bridge? What if—"

"Okay, I interrupted. I get it. Nothing happened and we're both okay."

The door to the yurt opened and Sam peeked in with Karin close behind. "Is everyone decent?"

"Yes, Sam, come in," said Khalen.

I was a bit shocked to see the two of them. They had planned to leave the day after our little adventure. I had to admit, though, that having them here was a warming surprise.

"Our day in Port Townsend wasn't enough to convince you that I'm dangerous to hang around with, hmm?"

"Dangerous, no," said Sam. "Exciting, perhaps, but not dangerous."

"Exciting," I parroted. "Is that what you call it?"

"Well, you're definitely not boring, that's for sure. Each time we come to visit, we're not sure what to expect."

"Great," I groaned. "I'm an adventure waiting to happen for you."

Karin came to sit next to me on the bed. "Don't mind him. He's about as sensitive and charming as a riled badger."

Sam glared. "Actually," he added, "Karin and I wanted to see you faring well before we left. Now that you're conscious, Aidan and Ian should feel relieved."

"They were worried?"

"About you, of course, but not as worried as challenging me in a game of poker. Now that you're awake, we will have to save the game for our next visit."

"Why?"

Karin patted my hand. "We want to spend time with you. Besides, the game will hardly be fair. Sam competes online with some of the best poker players in the world. He's very good." She leaned in a bit closer. "And, he doesn't play nice."

I laughed. "And Ian and Aidan are worried?"

"A bit," said Sam, "but I assured them that I would play easy for the first few rounds."

"Hmm. Perhaps Khalen and I could play as well?"

"You play poker?" asked Sam, nearly laughing the words.

I pressed back a smile. "A bit."

Sam slapped his hands together and rubbed them

vigorously. "Great, I could use some competition."

"We can play by the fire outside," I suggested.

"No," Khalen commanded. "You stay in bed. We will play here."

I closed my eyes, knowing that my brewing argument would find a cold and bitter end.

He placed a cup of tea in my hands. "Good girl," he added.

I groaned in response. "Don't get used to it."

He laughed.

As everyone bustled around me getting setup for the game, I sipped the chamomile tea that Khalen made for me. I also tasted a bit of valerian root, a calming herb whose constituents made one drowsy. I stopped drinking and set the cup down on my end table. Tonight, I wanted to have fun, not fall asleep.

Khalen stoked the fire while Ian, Aidan, Karin, and Sam sat around a square table that Case had brought in. He intended to join us later. Eve brought in some fresh cookies that were still warm from the oven.

Sam examined the deck of Braille cards that Khalen handed him. "So, these dots tell you what card you're holding?"

"Yes," I said.

He paused for a moment, and I imagined him looking around the room with suspicion. "Does anyone else know how to read Braille?"

"Why would they?" I asked.

"It would be rather convenient, don't you think?"

I laughed. "You think they took the time to learn Braille just so they could cheat at poker?"

"It's possible."

"Well, they don't know Braille, and even if they did, the dots are much too difficult to see against the pattern of the cards."

I could hear him flip the cards this way and that, obviously testing my theory.

"Now," said Ian, "you're gonna take it easy on us the first few rounds, eh?"

"Yes, that is what I said. But, after that, you're on your own."

"And we're playing for money?" Aidan confirmed.

"Yes," Sam answered impatiently. "I promise I won't take too much from you—at first."

Case came in and took a seat at the foot of the bed.

"Best not sit there," warned Sam.

"Why's that?" asked Case.

"Skye can see what you hold in your hand."

"That would be a neat trick, considering I'm blind."

Quiet chuckles filled the room. Khalen poured himself a brandy, placed two warm cookies on my table then sat beside me.

"Okay then," said Sam, shuffling the deck one more time. By the sound of it, he was showing off.

Sam won the first few rounds, even though he had promised to play easy. Karin reminded everyone how good he was and asked if anyone wanted to gracefully bow out of the game. Everyone declined the offer.

Two hours later, Sam and Karin had managed to lose over 500 dollars. Karin folded after the first hour, but Sam continued to play as if his luck was just around the corner.

"One more game," he said, pulling another bill from his wallet.

"Enough," Case interjected with a chuckle. "Are you daft, man? By now, you ought to know better than to gamble with a clan of Spirians." He fumbled through his pile of cash and tossed two bills at Sam. "Aidan, Ian, Khalen, Skye, pay the man back."

We all reached into our piles and returned Sam's money.

"I don't understand." Sam was clearly perplexed.

Case tried to hide his amusement but finally lost it and roared with laughter. "Good God, man. You have two illusionists who can make you see what they want you to see, a woman who reads your intentions and knows exactly what you're going to do before you do it, and all of us can read your thoughts. Honestly, what did you expect would happen?"

"An honest game for starters."

"To Spirians, it was honest."

Sam looked at Ian and Aidan. "So, that whole innocent, don't know much about the game routine, was all just a rouse?"

"Not really," said Ian. "We don't know much about the game."

Sam changed his posture, a sly smile shaping his lips. "How would you boys like to come to Vegas with me?"

"Absolutely not," said Khalen.

"Why not?" Sam's tone was incredulous.

"Playing with you is one thing. Playing to help you cheat is quite another."

"I fail to see the difference."

"We gave your money back," Khalen reminded him. "Our

gifts are not to be used for personal gain."

"Great," Sam muttered. "I have gifted friends with inflexible moral fibers." His eyes focused on me, and then narrowed. "You knew all along I would lose, didn't you?"

"Of course. Someone had to pluck a few feathers from that plume you kept flaunting."

"It was still a fun game," Karin said, gathering her share. "We should probably get to bed. We have an early start tomorrow."

"You're leaving that soon?" I asked, feeling disappointed.

"Why?" said Sam in a clipped but playful tone. "Do you have plans for clipping my wings too?"

"No, my dear friend. You are free to fly wherever you choose. I'll just miss you is all."

He huffed. "Yeah, I'll bet. I'll just take my fluffy plumes and leave then."

"Not for good, I hope?" I knew his anger was in jest. Sam could never stay angry for long.

"Well, until next time, anyway."

"We'll look forward to it."

Sam came over and offered a big bear-like hug. "You take care of you and those girls, gal. You know I love you."

I smiled up at him. "Yes, I do."

Karin came to hug me next. "Call us when those babes make their appearance, okay?"

"Will do. Have a safe trip."

Everyone else helped to clear the room of the added chairs and table, and then quickly took their leave. It was very late and I was feeling more than tired.

Khalen set his brandy glass down beside me then brushed

his thumb under my eyes. "You're exhausted, Skye. You need some sleep."

I sighed. "I feel that's all I've been doing."

He handed me my cold cup of tea. "Drink this. It will help you sleep."

I quickly downed the contents, and then attempted to swing my legs out of bed.

"Where are you going?"

I glanced back at him. "The girls are on my bladder. I'll be right back."

He rushed over to my side of the bed and supported my arm. After realizing how weak I had become, I was genuinely grateful for the help. "Lord, my legs feel like lead."

"Yes, well, you lost a lot of blood and I only have so much to give." I detected a smile in his voice.

"You gave me too much, anyway." My feet felt numb and it took my legs awhile to support my weight. Khalen helped me to the privy he had added to the back of the yurt. When I came out, he was standing there, waiting to offer a hand.

"You're not going to hover around me for the next six months, are you?"

"If I have to, yes."

"You don't. I'll be fine."

He guided me back to the bed and lifted my legs onto the mattress. "I've heard that before."

I placed my hands over my belly, hoping the girls would offer some sign of movement. "They've been so still. It worries me a bit."

"They've been through a lot and are resting as their mother should be."

"Resting? Are you sure?"

He sat beside me and his eyes began to glow. "See for yourself." I saw the image that he projected and smiled. One of the girls was sucking her thumb. I could see both of their hearts beating steady and strong. The image faded much too quickly. I closed my eyes in hopes of retrieving the brief vision that Khalen had shared. It was gone. "You have a wonderful gift."

He lifted my chin with his finger. "Yes, I do." He then pressed his lips to mine in a slow and gentle kiss.

As he sat and read beside me, I sipped another cup of tea, thinking about the Shadows we had encountered in Port Townsend. I remembered how difficult it was to maintain my shield and how vulnerable I quickly became.

"What's on your mind, my love?" Khalen asked, laying the book down on his lap. His warm hand enveloped mine.

"When we ran into the Shadows, I tried to form my shield, but it wavered as if the energy I conjured was unstable. I've never felt that before."

"There were too many of them. They overpowered you and kept your mind from focusing. If Jacob hadn't have come, I would have had to kill them all if they chose to pursue you."

A chill shivered down my spine as he said that. I remembered just how easy he had taken that young man's life who tried to grab my hand.

"You understand I had to?" he said, reading my thoughts.

I nodded. "It just seems so final. Wouldn't your binding shield have protected me?"

"Not if they all decided to grab you at once. I was not about to let that happen. I wanted to assure them that you were off limits and that my mate was not something to play with."

"Jacob said that the boy's father would not be pleased."

"Marlow is not a threat to us. He will have to answer to Victor soon enough for his clan's uprising."

I laid my head against his broad chest, unable to fight the building fatigue any longer. My mate's gifts struck me both as frightening and comforting in the same breath. I remembered when he wanted to take one of the girls from me, and how very easy it would be for him to do so. I placed my hand over my belly.

"No, Skye, it would not be easy," he whispered. "Not at all." He kissed the top of my head.

Chapter 7

Health, wisdom, and peace always come from within. Love is merely our way of sharing it with one another and helping it thrive.

KHALEN LEFT EARLY THIS MORNING to meet with Victor. The thought of it didn't sit well with me. From what I had heard about Victor, he was a dangerous man with a very short fuse. Like Jacob, Victor was an energy bender and a portentous match for Khalen's gifts. Ian and Aidan had offered to accompany him, but he took Case, instead.

Eve, of course, was relieved because it delayed their departure for England. Arcadie offered to fly them there before taking Khalen and I to Scotland. Plans were falling into place nicely and I felt better about traveling on Arcadie's jet rather than taking the commercial route. Eve, too, felt better for it and seemed happy to be able to stick around here a bit longer. She was not looking forward to returning to England.

She and I sat quietly by the fire as the rest of the clan took care of daily chores. I felt completely helpless. Khalen gave strict orders for everyone to cater to my needs in his absence and I was rarely left alone. Eve made it her personal duty to ensure that I rested in bed at least one hour out of every three. If I didn't find something other than audio books to occupy my time soon, I would certainly go insane. I was able to see better with all the rest I was getting and decided to put my vision to good use by doing some writing.

Eve glanced up from the blanket she was crocheting for the twins and focused her attention on Aidan and Sunjia. I followed her gaze and saw the two of them standing by the lake, hand-in-hand and talking very close to one another. My heart sank with despair.

"They are good for one another," I said.

Eve returned her attention to the blanket. "It will do them no good to pursue their desires unless Khalen blesses the union."

"Which he won't," I sadly stated.

Her lips tightened. "No, he won't."

"Because of her templar?"

Eve rotated the blanket and continued the effortless dance of hook and yarn in her hands. She made it look so simple. "No, because she was Traeger's mate."

"Not by her choice."

"Khalen wants her gone, Skye, plain and simple. He does not want any part of his brother's life in this clan, now or ever."

"What about Seth?"

"Khalen has asked him to leave with me and Case. Tria will leave with Sunjia."

"He said he would talk with Arcadie."

"Yes," she said, pausing from her work and glancing up at the couple by the lake. "He will."

I tapped into her thoughts thinking it would be easier to get my answers. It wasn't. Her mind was on so many things, reading it was like looking at alphabet soup spinning in a violent vortex. "But?" I finally prompted.

"I wouldn't set your goals too high, my dear. Khalen does not trust Sunjia and truly believes that Aidan is blind to her motives."

"And what does Case think about that?"

She began crocheting again. "He's smart enough to stay out of it."

"What are your feelings?" I asked with some hesitance. Part of me wasn't sure I wanted to hear her answer.

She paused and glanced up at me. I could see a dullness in her eyes. "I trust Khalen's feelings, though Sunjia does have a way about her. Part of me wants to embrace her, while another feels rather leery."

"She helped save Khalen's life, Eve. Doesn't that account for anything?"

"The Shadows have a way about them, Skye. They scheme and plan in ways that are difficult to comprehend. They cannot be trusted. Sunjia has lived with them for over 20 years now, and that is more than enough time to absorb their ways and become loyal to their purpose. As you have already observed, she possesses some unique gifts. Do you not find it odd that her templar has not come for her yet? Perhaps there is a reason she wants Aidan. If she could convince him to claim her, think about the victory that would be for the

Shadows." I could tell that Eve felt uneasy about the situation, and she didn't like the two of them getting any closer than was already apparent. "If she truly has switched sides, she would be a rarity."

Great, now I was starting to doubt Sunjia's intentions. It did seem odd that her templar had not yet come to claim her. It was also strange to see Aidan so smitten with someone who posed such a threat. He had never gone against Khalen's wishes until Sunjia came. Now, it was as if Aidan and Khalen were constantly locking horns. Aidan complied simply because he had vowed to. Khalen trusted Aidan, but only on the surface. What had happened to them? I needed to speak with Ian. He would know.

I called to him in thought. He was in the pasture attending one of the goats who had managed to trap herself under the fence. He promised to come by when he was done.

Eve glanced up at the sky. "It's time for you to lie down, my dear."

There was no point in arguing. When Khalen issued an order, it was followed to the letter. There was simply no way around it. Truth be it, though, I was tired and ready to rest. "I just summoned Ian. Can you send him in when he comes?"

"Of course. I'll bring you some tea and brownies in a bit, all right?"

I smiled. Food was not high on my enthusiasm list, but Eve found such joy in bringing it to me, it was hard to say no. I gathered my journal and pen and headed back to our yurt. Maiyun was busy playing with the other dogs. With me being so bed-ridden lately, she needed something to occupy her time. I missed her company, but completely understood her need for stimulation. I was already feeling the effects of stagnation and it had only been a few days.

My thoughts about having another child right after the twins' birth were quickly changing course. Pregnancy, I decided, was an overrated experience. It was no wonder Spirians were becoming extinct. The long gestation period alone was a strong deterrent. With Khalen refusing to make love to me, the next six months were promising to drag with torturous delay.

I heard Ian come through the door and awoke from a deep and sudden sleep. I smelled fresh brownies on my end table, along with a cup of cold tea.

"I didn't mean to wake you, lass."

I pressed my brows together and struggled to sit up. "No, it's okay."

"I wanted to shower before coming to see you. If I left the stench of goat in your yurt, Khalen would have my jewels for certain."

I rubbed my eyes then patted the spot beside me on the bed. "Have a seat."

"Uh, oh. I know that tone in your voice." He sat beside me and his eyes glowed green. "What kind of information are you after?"

"I want your opinion, is all."

"About?"

"Sunjia."

He ran his fingers through his thick blond hair. "She has my brother duped for sure. There's no talking to the man these days. His armor is steel but his heart is sand when it comes to that woman, and she's about as lethal as wildfire in a windstorm."

"Do you trust her?"

He sat back as if weighing his answer. "Yes and no."

"Explain."

"She's a Shadow, Skye, through and through. They cannot be trusted."

"So I've heard." My voice reflected my frustration. "You want to trust her, though, don't you?"

"Oh, aye, I do. She's a unique woman, that one, and gifted to boot. She's not too hard on the eyes, either, if you know what I mean."

"Do you think she's a danger?"

"Without a doubt, she is, lass. Be assured of that."

"But, Aidan likes her."

Ian stood and walked toward the liquor cabinet to pour himself a glass of Irish whiskey. "He likes the idea of her."

I waited for him to return to his place beside me. "Meaning?"

He took a sip of the amber liquid, held it on his tongue then swallowed, relishing the taste. "He's transfixed, you see. Her beauty, gifts, and undeniable charm has him hooked. He can't see past the illusion."

"And you can?" I sipped my tea, weighing his response.

"No, I can't." He took a long sip then swallowed. "Honestly, if my brother wasn't so smitten with her, I would be tempted to claim her myself."

I set my cup down on the table beside me. "In your heart, Ian, do you think she's a threat?"

He thought about my question. I could see the inner turmoil clouding his answer. After a long pause, he closed his eyes. "That's the sting of it all, lass. My heart wants to believe she's good, but the core of my being warns me against her on every level. I'm not sure what to do with that."

"I don't think she's a threat, Ian."

"You can't be sure of that, Skye."

"If she were truly faithful to Treager and his lot, she would have warned him. She would not have helped me save Khalen, and I believe she would have allowed or persuaded Aidan to claim her by now."

He sipped his whiskey and thought about my words. His brows pressed together in concentration. "Perhaps, but Shadows are loyal to no one. She may have only her best interest in mind."

I groaned with frustration. "There must be some way for her to prove herself."

"Why is this so important to you?"

I thought of telling him about my dream with Shanuk, but then thought better of it. Like Khalen, Ian wouldn't take it seriously. I bit my lower lip and shrugged. "It just is."

He sat quietly for a moment and I could feel him probing my thoughts. I offered him images of the dream, but nothing more.

"Hmm," he said, taking another sip of his drink. "Nothing 'just is,' with you, lass. This little issue runs deep in your heart." Again, he tried to make sense of the images I offered. His confusion produced a long silence.

After I shared Shanuk's request to convince Khalen to trust Sunjia's instructions, Ian's expression grew grim. I gave him a moment to put the pieces together.

"Do you understand now?" I asked.

"Aye, I do, but it is Khalen's trust you must obtain, not mine."

"Ian, if you trust her, Khalen might follow suit."

He held up his hand, "I have a better idea." He finished the last of his drink before carrying the glass to the sink to wash it. A knock sounded on the door and Aidan walked in, followed by Sunjia.

Ian smiled. "Now, here are the two who will convince Khalen to trust the situation." He dried his glass then carefully returned it to the display in the liquor cabinet. He walked over to the side of the bed, lifted my hand and kissed the back of it. "Best of luck to you, lass."

"Thanks," I muttered, disappointment lacing my words. I looked over at Aidan and Sunjia then sighed.

"How much did Ian tell you?"

Aidan sat beside me. Sunjia stood with her hands on his shoulders. I couldn't read their expressions. "Let's start with your concerns, Skye, shall we?" His words had an angry edge to them, making me cringe. This is not what I wanted.

I told them about my dream, wringing my hands together until they ached with rawness. They both listened quietly but said nothing. "I'm confused," I added. "I'm not sure what to do or who to believe anymore."

"Always believe your heart," said Sunjia. "It knows the truth of all things."

"My heart says to trust you. I find it hard not to, yet the rest of the clan has raised some pretty disturbing facts."

"I'm aware of their concerns," she said, walking to fetch a chair. She swung it around, and then took a seat near the foot of the bed. "They are all very valid, Skye. My ability to persuade any of you to trust me is undeniable. I can do so with little effort. I also have a strong motive. My position in the Shadow community is one of status. The act of gaining your leader's trust is all I need to take him and his entire clan down. Be assured, I am a threat. Khalen is wise not to trust me."

My confusion deepened along with the crease between my brows. Her confession did little to ease my concerns. "Apparently Shanuk trusts you."

"And how do you know that your vision was not just a dream?" she asked.

Aidan noticed my tea was cold and left with it to the kitchen to warm it again.

"Shanuk does not come to me unless it's important."

"I could have manifested that dream; given it to you to gain your trust."

My eyes narrowed. "Why do you say these things?"

"Because you need to understand your mate's dilemma, Skye. I am fully capable of doing all the things he fears I will do."

"But you're not. I can feel it."

"How can you trust your feelings when I can easily manipulate them?"

"You cannot alter your intentions."

I saw a faded glimpse of her white teeth as she smiled. "No, I cannot."

"But, Khalen has the power of reading intentions. He would know."

"That gift is new to him, Skye. He must remember to use it, and then learn to trust it. You have had this gift your whole life. It is a part of you. Khalen is jaded by the Shadows. He has lost much because of them. He has every right to be wary of me."

Aidan returned with my hot tea. "The more you try to push Khalen, the harder he will resist," he added.

"You two seem rather calm about all this."

Aidan chuckled quietly. "About six months ago, I heard a very wise woman ask Case and Khalen where their faith was. That same woman reminded them that God was in control and not them."

I rolled my eyes, remembering the conversation well.

He wrapped his large, warm hands around mine. "Where is your faith, Skye? When the time comes, Khalen will see the truth of things."

"Well said," I admitted, closing my eyes. Somehow, the edge of my own sword used against me felt much too sharp.

Aidan looked over at Sunjia. "Give us a moment?"

Sunjia nodded, returned the chair to it's place by the fire then left the yurt with the grace and dignity of a seasoned diplomat.

"Despite everyone's opinion of her," he began, retaking his seat beside me. "Sunjia is not a Shadow, Skye."

"Then, according to Ian, she is a rarity."

"Aye, a rarity, indeed. I, too, suspected that she was playing on my heart until she refused my advances."

"Your advances?" I sipped my white tea with a hint of tarragon and nibbled on the brownie. I offered some to him, but he declined.

"I asked her to lie with me one night, but she refused. We have shared affections with one another, but she only allows it to go so far. She is adamant about keeping the law and will not go beyond the boundaries her templar will permit. She refuses to give him any means to penalize Khalen. So far, no law has been broken. I don't believe she would be so diligent if her intentions were dark."

"You aren't seriously thinking of breaching the law with her, are you?"

He shook his head. "No, Skye. I merely pretended to do so to gauge her reaction."

I looked at him speculatively. "And you don't think she saw that coming?"

"I do have a few gifts of my own, you know. I'm not some whelp stumbling my first steps out of the den."

"Hmm," I responded, sipping more of my tea.

"I know everyone thinks I'm smitten with her, and believe me, I am. But, I'm not a fool. Sunjia is genuine, Skye—a keeper. If it is meant to be, I believe the Father will find a way to make her mine."

I set my cup down and laid my hand over his arm. "I believe so too."

After a moment of silence, he pulled the covers up to my shoulders. "You need your rest, lass. We'll talk more later if you want, okay?"

I nodded and smiled. "Thank you, Aidan."

He walked to the door, and then hesitated. "I will not place you in danger, Skye, you know that."

"Yes, I do." I said confidently.

The door closed silently behind him.

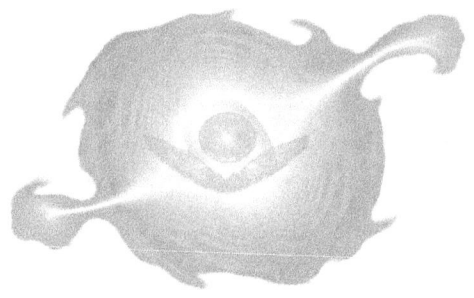

Chapter 8

A tree roots deep into the earth, as it stretches high toward the heavens. Its mighty trunk demonstrates a perfect display of balance, thus giving it strength, flexibility, and longevity.

~ K h a l e n ~

VICTOR SAT ACROSS FROM ME by his massive pool, martini in one hand, a voluptuous female in the other. My father and I met him at his mansion in Miami. It was far too hot for me here and dreadfully humid. His son, Sage, was due to arrive very soon. I was hoping to get on with our business so that we could return home soon after. I didn't like leaving Skye in such a delicate condition. Her recent scare with the twins had me on edge and the miles between us didn't help matters.

Another female, dark hair and eyes the color of seaweed, bent down to offer me the drink in her hand. I looked away from the goods she was obviously flaunting and declined the drink.

Victor laughed. "You don't like what you see, Khalen?"

I heard Case walk up from behind. He handed me a bottle of water he had taken from the cooler by the door. "There is nothing here that I want," I said, turning the cap of the bottle. A thready hiss escaped the seal.

"Except my attention," Victor added. He patted the woman beside him on the backside then gestured that she leave. She obeyed without a word. "So tell me what brings you to my humble home."

"Your lack of control on your clans," I blurted. Case pierced me with a stern warning. The sting of it lingered for quite some time.

"Insulting me, dear boy, will only produce disturbing results, I assure you."

I offered Case a chance to speak, but he chose to stay silent. I assumed it was because he didn't want to shadow my leadership. He was here for support only. This was my territory now and he wanted me to run it as I saw fit. I respected him for that, but also needed his council. I probed his thoughts. All I received was a sound warning to remain in control of my feelings—good advice.

I took a sip of my water and allowed the liquid to cool my tongue. "I'm not here to insult you, Victor. I'm here to inform you that your clan has chosen to ignore the laws. If they continue to do so, I am in my right to address the situation."

Victor leaned back and took a long draw from the thin black straw that pierced a colorfully-layered Drink. It resembled a sunset. I was surprised it didn't have a pink umbrella or some extravagant fruit ensemble hanging over the side. "And which laws are we referring to?" he drawled.

"Harassing another man's mate. Entering a home uninvited. Selling halflings as slaves instead of setting them free, and encroaching upon a territory that has been claimed."

Victor smiled. "I'm assuming you refer to the recent incident with your young mate, heavy with young? The inspection of Traeger's home after his death. The halflings he kept there, and the recent fact that you claimed the entire Olympic Peninsula?"

His response caught me off guard as he expected it would. I could see the glimmer in his dark eyes. "You are well-informed," I said.

"In time, young Khalen, you will know what it is to govern a region. Of course I am well-informed. It is my duty to be so."

"Being so diligent about your duty, I'm curious how you intend to address the issue."

"Just as Case has enabled you to handle your territories in the way that you see fit, I, too, intend to allow my son to handle his business his way."

"And if he chooses to do nothing?"

"That is his choice."

I sat back and thought about that for a moment. Using Skye's gift of intention, I concluded that he was trying to invoke my anger. Case also knew that as well, which is why he warned me to stay in control. Knowing all that, however, did not make it any easier to stay in control. If Sage chooses to ignore the situation, I did not have a good plan to implement. It was like telling an intelligent dog to stay when there was absolutely no way to enforce the command.

Victor, with his wry smile and casual demeanor, was enjoying this far too much. I tried probing Case's thoughts for direction and found none. He wanted me to figure this out on my own—bloody perfect.

There was some commotion at the back door of the house leading out to the patio. Sage came through with a female under each arm, and two drinks. The women looked tolerant, but not too thrilled to be his trophies. Both of them were human.

"Ease up, young Khalen. No law has been breeched. The humans are not mated when they are in season," Victor explained.

He spoke of the women as if they were animals, nothing more. Judging by the looks on the women's faces, they felt like animals as well. I wondered how they allowed themselves to get into such a predicament.

Sage smiled and waved his drink. "Once they have a Spirian male, there's no going back." He said it as if reading my thoughts, but I had kept them well hidden. Sage squeezed the young woman beside him, making her squeal. He then smacked her backside and gestured that she and the other woman leave.

"Young Khalen, here, wants to know what you intend to do about your unruly clansmen," Victor explained.

Sage laughed, snagged a carrot off the veggie tray beside his father then gestured for a female to bring him another drink. "What is it you expect from me, Khalen?"

"I expect you to enforce the Spirian laws that were established and agreed upon."

"And if I don't?"

There it was, the bluff called and displayed. I had to think of something and make it convincing or lose face and command of my territories. I took a deep breath and sat back, pressing the tips of my fingers together. "I will enforce the laws myself. Imagine what your clansmen will think of their leader when he does nothing about their demise."

"You think I'll do nothing?"

"If you try, you will fail. Your best option is to enforce the laws yourself and establish your position among them. No one will thwart you, but they will respect your commands."

I was trying to play upon his ego, inflate it a bit. The look in his eyes betrayed his lack of confidence against me. His powers were strong, but I knew they were no match for my own. He knew it as well.

"Very well, Khalen. I will deal with my clans and propose they move from the peninsula. I'm assuming King County is acceptable?"

I nodded. "And the slaves?"

"You know of their demise as well as I do. Slave or no slave, they have limited lifespans and are not worth the time and effort to save them. I can, however, ensure that no humans are bred, per the law." The glimmer in his eyes shone with some semblance of victory.

The law had mentioned that Spirians were not to meddle in the humans' lives, but the extents were not well defined. The Shadows had ensured that. In some respects, I did too, knowing that most of my clientele were human. If we were unable to interact with humans at all, my practice would cease.

"Good enough."

"You will see changes by next week," Sage announced, though I saw apprehension on his face."

Victor slapped his hand down on the arm of his lounger. "Fabulous! All is well then, we have reached an agreement."

Case and I stood. "Thank you for your time, gentlemen," I said.

"Surly you are not leaving so soon?" asked Victor, clearly disappointed.

"Our business is done here and I want to return home."

"Ah, yes, to your young mate. She is a beauty, and wonderfully gifted, or so I'm told."

"And well protected," Case added. The tone in his voice was a warning.

Victor tapped the side of his glass that glistened with sweat. "Understood," he said with a smile then nodded as we turned to leave.

Case and I headed straight for the airport, both of us anxious to return home. "You handled yourself quite well," said Case as we sat in the back of the cab.

"It is difficult to enforce the laws when there are no repercussions for breaking them."

"I believe you made your stance on the matter very clear. And I applaud your strategic use of swelling his ego—nice touch, surprisingly effective."

"I grow tired of their lack of respect and discipline,"

"It's all part of the balance, my son. Good cannot exist without the opposing evil."

I knew that to be true, but did not reply. There was no need for one.

~ S k y e ~

KHALEN CRAWLED BESIDE ME IN bed at two in the morning. His feet and legs were freezing. I moved in closer to warm him. "How did it go?" I asked, groggy from sleep.

He placed his hand on my belly and checked in on the girls. "Better than expected. How do you feel?"

"Perfect, now that you're home."

"Have you been resting?"

"Too much, thanks to you and your cursed orders to the clan. I was doted on so much, I felt I would soon suffocate."

"Good," he kissed my forehead then laid my head upon his chest. I relished in the feeling of his strong arms wrapped around me like a protective blanket. His breathing became slow and deep as he slipped into deep slumber. I had been sleeping so much during the day, I was only remotely tired. I remained still so I would not awaken my mate.

A loud knock rattled our door that morning. Khalen bolted up and drew in a deep breath as if awakening from a nightmare. "Come in," he said.

Aidan opened the door. "We have a situation," he said solemnly. My heart sank, thinking that he and Sunjia had gone too far.

Khalen swung his legs from under the covers then stood and grabbed a pair of jeans hanging over the chest at the foot of our bed. "What's the issue?" He picked up a long-sleeved shirt and started buttoning it as he followed Aidan outside. I could not hear Aidan's reply.

I, too, dressed quickly and followed them out. Case, Ian,

and Caleb stood against an angry Shadow mob. I did not recognize any of them, save one—the man in Port Townsend who had identified her as Khalen's mate. He was the one who had warned the others to walk away. Maiyun stayed close by my side as I made my way toward Eve and the other ladies.

Khalen approached the older man. "Marlow. What is this about?"

"You know damn well what this is about, Khalen Dunning, son of Damon."

Khalen stiffened but kept his anger in check. "Your son tried to harm my mate and paid the consequences."

"As will you for taking his life."

Aidan stepped between Khalen and Marlow, but Case waved him back. Khalen was honed in on Marlow's intentions, reading his energy and subtle body language. I, too, had focused in on the man. He was directing his thoughts toward me.

Before he cast a lethal blow in my direction, Khalen had him flying backward and on the ground, gripping his throat. "I understand your hunger for vengeance, Marlow, but God help you if you direct your sights upon my mate again." He released his hold on the older man and allowed him to stand, still gasping for air.

Another blow came toward Khalen from the right, but Case intervened. Aidan stopped another. Two Shadows circled around the back behind us women. I could hear them. Maiyun growled. Ian captured them in an illusion. I formed a shield, but it wavered against the Shadows' will.

"Stand down, Marlow, or we will take you down."

The old man's eyes glowed an eerie orange, like flames

in a vicious blaze. He assessed the situation and weighed his power against Khalen's clan. Once he realized that he would surly lose this battle, he held up his hand and settled his men. Ian released the two Shadows behind us, and the deafening hum in the air calmed to a tolerable level.

"This is not over," Marlow warned.

"You are trespassing on my territory, Marlow. I suggest you take your clan off this peninsula before your numbers start to dwindle," said Khalen, his voice deep and unquestionably calm.

"I don't answer to you."

Khalen directed his energy toward two Shadows in the back. They both dropped to the ground. Another fell shortly after.

"Enough!" Marlow roared. "You've made your point." His eyes focused on me and narrowed.

The hum surrounding us vibrated in my bones. Marlow dropped to the ground, gripping his belly. His groans were like that of a child who had eaten too many sweets.

"Focus your energy on my mate once more, Marlow, and I will cease your miserable life, consequences or no." Khalen was shaking, his powers clearly drained.

Marlow's men helped him stand and quickly stuffed him into the van in which they had arrived. Once they were out of sight and the dust from their tires settled, the humming vibrations calmed.

Khalen dropped to his knees. Case and Aidan were carrying him back to our yurt before I could reach him. He laid on the bed as I entered. Maiyun cautiously approached the three men, her nose stretched and gathering scent.

"Skye," Case called over his shoulder. "Come, give him your strength." He moved over and guided my hands to the souls of Khalen's bare feet. They were cold and shaking.

"What happened?" I asked.

"The lives of the men he took were very gifted. They drained him. The stronger the Spirian, the harder it is to take their life and the more life you must offer in return. Khalen must have believed that the men standing in the back were new and barely gifted, which is why he chose them. We are very lucky that Marlow didn't sense his weakness."

"How can you be sure?"

Case looked over at me. "Why do you ask?"

"When Marlow looked at me, I had the sense that he was observing—gathering information."

I could feel the warmth slowly returning to Khalen's feet, while I grew far more tired. Case removed my hands. "Enough, my dear. He will recover soon on his own. You must rest now." He guided me beside my mate and covered us both.

"Case? Why are my own gifts so weak these days? I couldn't even form a formidable shield."

"It's the babes, they weaken you. Typically, pregnant Spirian females are very strong, however, your pregnancy is a challenge and nearly unheard of. Few women survive the birthing of twins."

"I will survive it," I promised.

He squeezed my hand. "I pray you do, my dear. Now rest."

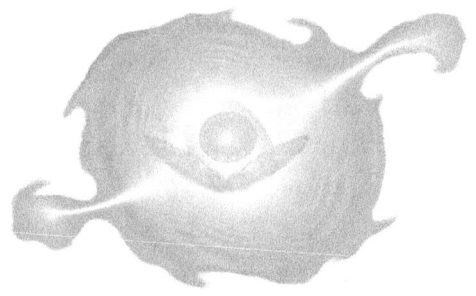

Chapter 9

Water does not gain its strength through mass, but through flexibility. Even a meek but persistent trickle can break down the toughest boulder.

I AWOKE TO THE ANGRY TONES of Case and Khalen arguing just outside our yurt. Neither of them held their thoughts open. Quietly, I donned my robe and walked closer to the door.

"You cannot protect her from this," Case said. "She is stronger than you give her credit for, but she cannot be allowed to go full term and you know it."

I could feel the turmoil in Khalen's chest. My own chest felt heavy and thick. It was hard to breathe. I held the wall, struggling to remain standing. The hum surrounding the two arguing men was deafening.

"I should have taken one of them."

"Yes, but you didn't and now it's too late." There was a long pause, and then tenderness in Case's words. "Son, you must act like a leader now. If the twins are strong, they will survive. You must convince Skye of this."

The men were silent for a moment, and I realized that they both knew I had been listening.

Their footsteps landed softly on the stairs leading to our front door. I opened it before they reached the landing.

"We need to talk," said Khalen, avoiding my eyes.

Case offered a half smile as he followed Khalen to the breakfast bar. I sat next to him as Khalen prepared three cups of joe.

"Arcadie will be here soon," Khalen began. "I want him to take us to Scotland within a week."

"What are the dangers of birthing the twins early?" I asked, not wanting to skirt around the subject any longer than necessary.

Case swallowed hard and glanced up at Khalen as he pushed a cup toward him then carried mine to me and placed it into my hands. I allowed him to formulate his answer without pressing. The coffee tasted bitter on my tongue. He had forgotten to add a bit of maple syrup to it.

"If the twins are too weak to survive the ordeal, they will die. We will wait as long as we can, of course, but you cannot go full term without irreparable complications."

I stood and walked around the counter to get the bottle of maple syrup. When Khalen realized what I was reaching for, he telekinetically pulled the bottle toward him and added the sweet contents to my coffee, stirring the drink without a spoon. "Come sit, Skye," he softly commanded.

I did as he asked then added a request of my own. "I want Sunjia to come with us."

I felt his body stiffen against me. "Why?"

"It will make me feel more comfortable having her there."

"Eve will be there with you."

"Yes," I acknowledged. "I want her there as well."

Khalen raked his fingers through his hair then walked around the counter to face me. "Sunjia has no business being there, Skye."

"Shanuk thinks she does."

The hum in the room increased. Case tapped his fingers against his lower lip. "Why?" he simply asked.

"It was a dream," Khalen growled, "nothing more."

"A dream?" Case asked, looking at me.

"It was more than a dream," I explained. "Shanuk came to me and said that Sunjia would play an important role in the twins' birth. She must be there."

Case looked over at Khalen. "Bring her along," he said matter-of-factly, as if there shouldn't be any question about it at all.

The hum in the room increased along with the cold draft emanating from my mate. Case stood and gestured to Khalen. "Walk with me," he said, turning toward the door.

Khalen dried his hands with a towel then slammed it upon the counter before following Case outside. He did not meet my eyes on his way to the door and his thoughts were closed.

Stubborn man, I thought to myself. While they were gone, I thought to take a long, hot shower and prepare for the day ahead. Eve and Case had invited Caleb and his clan over for dinner. I promised Eve I would help with the preparations.

I gathered my things and headed out the door with Maiyun close by my side. I urged her to play, but she persisted on staying beside me. The cold, late-morning air was pleasantly countered by the warmth of the sun. I loved fall days like this, cool, cloudless, and bright.

When I walked into the shower hut, one of the stalls was occupied. Maiyun laid down beside my things. I chose an open stall and started the water flowing before I stepped under the hot, inviting spray. I must have groaned with pleasure as the water drenched my scalp and body because there was a giggle in response.

"Good morning, Skye," a familiar voice called out. I could hear the smile in her tone.

"Good morning, Sunjia."

The water in the adjoining stall shut off. By the time I stepped out, she had gotten dressed and was brushing her wet hair. Maiyun continued to lay by my clothes. Sunjia's aura was brighter than usual today, and her eyes sparkled.

"What has you so chipper this morning?" I asked, drying my tangled hair with the towel.

"Aidan," she said.

My heart felt a pang. I wasn't sure if it was from regret or fear. I dressed without comment, hoping she would elaborate without prompting. She said nothing.

"You've fallen for him?" I asked, my voice barely audible and noticeably cracked.

"Completely," she said, smiling from ear to ear. I had never noticed how incredibly brilliant her teeth were until this moment. I was also not about to dampen that spirit of hers with regrettable facts. There was no need to ask if he felt the same toward her. That much had been clear from the start.

"Come, Skye, do not think for a moment that I don't know what battles your heart. Aidan and I both know that our attraction for one another is futile at best and may never result in a union. All we have is now. Tomorrow will take care of itself."

It was a beautiful way to look at it, I supposed, but still my heart ached for them. "It's nice to see you smile," I finally said.

"And what must I do to see you smile again?"

"For starters," I said, re-toweling my hair. "You could come with us to Scotland and assist with the birth of my twins."

"So, Khalen has agreed?"

"Not entirely," I admitted, "but Case is talking to him now."

The silence that spanned between us felt oddly uncomfortable. Her thoughts were scattered and withdrawn too much to make any sense. I bent my knees to gather my bag then doubled over in pain.

"Skye, what's wrong?" Sunjia rushed to my side.

I pressed my hand against my ribs and tried to breathe. It felt as if I was breaking inside. Maiyun pressed against me, panting heavily. I called out to Khalen.

Sunjia met them at the door. "Come quickly," she said, ushering them inside. With little effort, Khalen lifted me in his arms and carried me back to our yurt. Case reached for my bag, but Sunjia had already hoisted it onto her shoulder.

The pain in my belly deepened. My skin felt as if it were on fire. Both twins were active, kicking and pressing against my ribs as if trying to escape from a straight jacket.

Khalen lowered me onto the bed. My belly rose and fell

with the movement of our young. He placed his hand on my swelling flesh and whispered something in Gaelic. The girls calmed immediately. The pain eased a bit until I attempted a deep breath.

"Your rib is cracked," he said. "The babes have grown too large."

I began to heal myself. It took much longer than it should have. Khalen pulled my hand away before I felt I was done. "It's not healed yet," I said.

Khalen looked away, his hands were shaking.

"Arcadie has arrived," said Case, slipping his phone in his pocket. He flew into Bremerton. Ian and Aidan are bringing him home.

I finished the healing, grateful for the reprieve. "Hey," I said to Khalen, reaching out to take his hands. "I'm all right." Still, he would not look at me. Instead, his gaze fixed on Sunjia.

"Khalen, look at me," I said, gripping his fingers. "Please."

"Oh, Christ," Case mumbled.

Khalen's eyes were so gold they glowed, the flecks of green shimmering like emeralds. His thoughts were blocked. The hum in the room grew nearly deafening. Sunjia started to drop, but Case reached her before she fell to the ground. He lifted her in his arms and whisked her out of the yurt.

"What did you do?" I asked. When Khalen said nothing, I broke through his thoughts and ripped the veil he had placed around them. "Don't you block me, Khalen Dunning, not this time." He tried to pull away from me but I held firm.

Case returned. "Skye, let him go."

"Not until he talks to me."

"Listen to me. He's not in a good place right now."

"Neither am I." The words drifted out of my mouth as if someone else were speaking them. My limbs felt numb. I could hear Case speak, but his words were lost amidst the vibrating hum in my head. Darkness filled my eyes, my heart felt cold as if it pumped ice water instead of blood.

In the distance, I heard the commanding voice of Shanuk. "Stop!" His vice-like grip squeezed my arm, forcing my hands to surrender their hold. In his other hand was Khalen's arm, his golden eyes still glowing. Shanuk shook him hard then zapped him with a bolt of energy. I felt the sting clear to my gut. Khalen did not react.

"Khalen, look at me," he demanded.

Another shock vibrated through me. I refused to cry out. Shanuk held my arm so tight I felt as if my hand would drop like a wilted flower from its stem. The energy flowing from Shanuk felt painfully thick in my veins.

"Skye, you need to bring him back. Do it now."

I shook my head in confusion. "I don't know how. He won't listen to me."

"Make him listen."

"Khalen," I said, "look at me."

"No," said Shanuk. "Speak to his heart, not his mind."

I spoke in thought, straight from my heart. It wasn't hard. His distance frightened me and my heart ached with the emptiness and cold void that only he could fill.

Khalen, I thought. *Please, come back to me.* I reached out to him as if offering him my soul. It was akin to drowning and offering him my last breath.

I laid my hands over my belly. It was still and cold.

The twins weren't moving. I looked over at Shanuk. A tear streamed down his face.

"No," I shouted, not really caring if the word was spoken out loud. With all the force I could muster, I rooted my heels deep into the bowls of the earth, and allowed my spirit to peak the heavens. I felt the light of God fill my core and spread throughout my limbs. I imagined the light pooling around my young, giving them life. I was hollow now, nothing but a vessel of blue-white light. There was no thought, no feeling, no regret. Shanuk said something but I could not understand. It was as if he were speaking a foreign language. He waved his hands around me then sent me back with a bolt of energy so fierce, it stole my breath. Everything turned black.

I AWOKE TO THE NUMBING SOUND of jet engines. Everything was dark. My back was warm, and my chest felt constricted. Khalen's scent filled my nostrils. When I turned my head, the scent grew stronger—clove and cedar.

"Khalen," I voiced, my words gruff and scratchy. "Khalen!" This time, they sounded more desperate.

"Shh," he hissed. "I'm here."

"Where are we?"

"Arcadie's jet, heading for Scotland."

I tried to sit up. My head spun. Khalen pressed me back down against him. "Stay put," he grumbled.

My head felt as if it were caught between two powerful magnets. "What happened?"

"What do you remember?"

"You carried me back to our yurt after the twins broke my rib, and then Sunjia collapsed. You were catatonic. I was trying to bring you back. The rest is just jumbled fragments that don't make much sense."

He chuckled quietly, and then kissed the top of my head. I frowned in response. "Khalen, I hardly think it's funny. Is Sunjia okay?"

He gestured toward a chair where a dark figure slept. I swallowed hard. "Is she alive?"

"Yes," he said. "She's resting is all, which is what you should be doing."

I shifted, now aware of the hard surface beneath my aching hips. "Why are we on the floor?"

"You were thrashing around too much to sit you in a chair, and I didn't want you falling off the couch. I felt it was safer to just sit with you in my arms until you slept."

"Eve and Case, are—"

He squeezed me tight. "Shh, they're all here, Skye, relax."

"What happened between you and Sunjia? I saw her collapse and your eyes were glowing so bright. You didn't respond to me. God, I was so—."

"Skye," he whispered huskily, "please, stay calm."

"Your thoughts are closed. You promised to keep them open to me."

"They are open. You're too weak to read me now. You must rest—please."

I tried to turn and face him but his grip was too strong. "Please," I begged, "I need to know."

His deep growl vibrated against my chest. "I tapped Sunjia to read her true intentions," he finally said.

"What does that mean?"

"I placed her in a state that enabled me to tap her thoughts without her interception. I needed to know what she was about before I agreed to bring her along."

"I assume you were satisfied with what you discovered?"

"For now."

Now it was my turn to growl. "Meaning?"

He rested his hand over my forehead. Exhaustion suddenly consumed me and I fell limp against his chest.

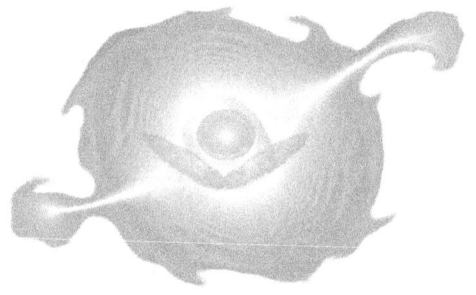

Chapter 10

Fire burns wild, but still knows boundaries. It tries to abide them, though its hunger for freedom makes it careless and unpredictable.

I SPENT THE NEXT FEW DAYS in and out of consciousness. Bright light pierced my eyes, forcing me to blink and squint.

"Khalen," I heard a strange voice call. It was a woman.

Khalen knelt beside me and brushed my cheek. "Hey," he said. "Welcome back."

My head felt as if it were being crushed. "How long have I been out?" My body was heavy and weak.

"Three days."

An IV hung above me with clear liquid. My hand instinctively moved over my belly, still very swollen with our young. "Are the girls all right?"

"Yes," he said. "For now."

I vaguely remembered having this conversation before, but could not make the memory stick. "Why am I so out of it?"

"I have kept you in a spiritual coma of sorts, to keep you calm."

I remembered his hand over my forehead, and then slipping into nothingness. "I don't want to be calm."

"I know," he chuckled.

"She's very weak," the woman said. I turned my head and saw a large-framed woman with a warm smile and deep-brown eyes. Her short wavy hair fell dark against the pale blue of her shirt. "I'm Lenore, dear, Darius' mate."

I nodded to her and smiled. I couldn't see her features but I immediately liked her and felt a bond between us. "I'm Skye."

She laughed. "Yes, I know who you are."

"Should we keep her conscious?" asked Khalen.

"Yes," I answered. "We most certainly should." I lifted his hand from my forehead and narrowed my eyes at him.

"It was for your own good, my love, trust me."

"Is this some new gift you've acquired?"

"One introduced by Sunjia, yes."

My interest was peaked. "Sunjia? Really?"

"Yes," he explained. "She happens to be a seer."

"Am I supposed to know what that means?"

He laughed quietly and then sat down beside me on the overly-plush bed that seemed three sizes too large. Lenore quietly left the room, gesturing that she would return shortly.

"She is able to see the gifts in others, even if they don't know about them."

"And she knew about this gift in you, and decided to share it?"

"Actually, I learned about it when I tapped her thoughts. I am finding it very useful."

"Hmm," I said, "I'm sure you have. Use it on me again, however, and I'll demonstrate the difference between a gift and a curse."

A playful smile stretched across his tired face. "Hmm, that sounds intriguing." When he moved his hand over my forehead, I slapped it away.

"Ah, a man's voice sounded from across the room. I see she's gotten her color back." Like Lenore, his Scottish accent was thick and charming.

"That," I said, "Would be from anger."

He laughed then handed Khalen a pint of beer. "Now, what would a fine lass like you be gettin' all blustered about?"

I looked at my mate and narrowed my eyes. "He knows."

The man's laugh deepened as he stretched his massive hand toward me. "I'm Darius."

I gripped his hand, trying to match his strength but sadly fell short of it. "I'm Skye."

Lenore returned with a steaming cup of tea in her hands. She looked at the two men and their pints of beer with distaste. "It's narly noon and you two are at it already?"

"Ah, now love, Khalen and I have a bit o'catchin' up to do, we have. It's been too long." He was a tall man with sparse black hair tied back. His hands were rough and strong like those of a construction worker.

Lenore handed me the cup of tea with a sweet smile. "Yes, well, you best be sober when these young start to stir." The bed squealed as she sat beside me. "How are ya feeling, dear?"

"Well rested," I lied. In truth, I felt as if I hadn't a moments rest, though I couldn't remember dreaming or even waking periodically. Fragments of memories littered my thoughts like confetti flittering in the air.

"That's good. We need to get some food in you and get some strength back."

At the moment, food was the farthest from my mind. I wanted to walk around and get a tour of this magnificent castle. I was told that it used to belong to Shanuk and I felt compelled to explore its many secrets. The large windows supplied ample sunlight to see by. The many days of rest had given my eyes new life and they felt fresh and clear. I wanted to take advantage of the temporary gift.

"Not for awhile," Khalen said. "I know what you're thinking."

"You can't expect me to stay in this bed for the next five months, Khalen. It won't happen."

Darius started to chuckle. "Oh, I like her fire." He nudged Khalen, nearly spilling his beer.

"I can always make it happen," he assured me.

"You wouldn't dare."

He arched his brow as if to say, "Watch me."

Lenore squeezed my arm. "Dun't worry, dear. I'll get ye strong enough to have a look around soon." She glanced over at Khalen with the expression of pleading him to be nice.

The next few days were spent regaining my strength. Khalen had slipped into an odd roll as if time had reversed several decades when he was young and reckless. He and Darius bantered like two close siblings with Lenore acting as the referee. Entertaining as it was, I saw a playful side of Khalen that I never would have guessed existed.

Eve and Case had left for England to check in with his native clan. They promised to return with Arcadie within the week. Sunjia had come to see me once then promptly left when Khalen entered the room. I didn't like the tension between them and wished there was some way to convince him she was good. For now, I was happy that he allowed her to come.

When I spoke with her, I could sense the intensity of how much she missed Aidan. I was sure that their separation was hard on him as well. We were too far away to speak telepathically, but a quick phone call to him yesterday was enough to convince me that he was miserable. He assured me that Maiyun was doing well and was enjoying the lamb bones he brought home for her each day.

I wanted Arcadie to return so that Khalen and I could speak with him together about Sunjia. I was sure that Case had filled him in during the trip to England. His reaction to hearing about his son agreeing to be the templar of a Shadow female was something I didn't want to miss. Then again, not seeing that reaction could be a blessing. I had a feeling that Arcadie could emit some potent energy when his anger flared.

Now that my strength was slowly returning, I felt anxious to be moving around. When I was alone, I contracted my muscles to keep them from atrophying. I even tried standing before Khalen came bursting into the room. His ability to read intentions was becoming annoying.

"Not yet, Skye," he said, leaving no room for argument.

"When then?" I asked. "Honestly, I feel like pond scum."

He assisted me back to bed. I crossed my legs and tucked

them beneath me. "I feel strong," I assured him, ignoring the pain stabbing my spine. The young were heavy in me and I felt close to bursting.

His golden eyes softened. "You are only seven months along, my love. Soon, we will have to induce labor. The young are premature and may not survive. My goal is not to drive you insane. It is to keep you from going into labor for as long as I can. I fear if you start walking, the young will drop and we will have no choice but to deliver them early."

I placed his hand over my belly. "Can I see them?"

His eyes began to glow as he peered into my swollen womb. I saw the same beautiful faces that appeared in my dream, though they were not as defined. One of the twins was clearly larger than the other and much more active. The vision of them faded.

"They look healthy," I said, hope etched in my voice.

He brought my hand to his lips, closed his eyes and brushed several soft kisses along my skin. "Tomorrow," he said. I will walk with you.

"Okay."

Lenore entered with a tray of food. "Are ye ready for lunch, dear?"

My stomach growled loudly in response. The smell of her cooking was an effective lure for my appetite. She had been bringing me several small meals each day. Most of them consisted of plenty of meat and vegetables. Two meals consisted of grains and veggies. Each day began with a bowl of fresh fruit and a hot cup of coffee.

She lifted the shiny lids and revealed a tender-looking lamb shank and steamed broccoli. A small glass of water accompanied the meal. I rarely finished everything on my plate, but this meal would be an exception, I was sure. She eyed Khalen as she set the platter down in front of me. "None for you, mister. Ye had yer share down in the kitchen. Dun't think I didn't see you."

"I nibbled," he said. "It was hardly worth a portion, Lenore."

"I'll share with you," I said.

"Oh, for Pete's sake," Lenore groaned. "You'll do no such thing. I'll bring another shank up for yer man."

Khalen's grin spread wide with victory. "Thank you, my lady," he mock bowed then winced as she smacked his head with a towel she had draped over her arm.

"Oh, Khalen Dunning. I had forgotten how truly annoying you can be." She winked at me then ticked her tongue as she left the room. "Ye got yerself a tightly-wound knot for a mate, lassie, that's for sure."

"Don't I know it," I replied.

Khalen narrowed his eyes at me. "A tightly-wound knot, eh?" he questioned.

"More like an explosive b-b bouncing about in a small jar."

"Hmph," he expressed then reached for my hands in prayer. "Lord," he said. "Put your hand on this woman you've blessed me with and bring forth our young in your care. Let your will be done."

"Amen," I said.

Lenore returned with another platter full of food and a carafe of red wine. "Is this to your likin' m'lord," she said with a graceful curtsy.

Khalen eyed the meal speculatively then grunted an approval. "It'll do, lass."

I nudged him in the ribs. "What my husband really means, is that he is very appreciative of your kind and overly-generous hospitality."

Lenore winked at me. "Aye, I thought that's what he meant."

Khalen bowed his head, this time with sincerity. "Lenore, my sister, thank you."

Her face turned red, obviously flustered with his compliment. She opened her mouth to speak, but nothing came out.

Khalen didn't help the situation with his boisterous laughter. He ducked as she tossed her towel at him.

"Khalen Dunning, you're a bloody arse." She turned and left the room.

"You have such a way with people," I said. "It's a wonder they remain your friends."

"She truly is more of a sister than a friend," he said between bites. "The three of us grew up together."

"Really? I would have never known." My sarcasm was not lost. He answered it by rolling his eyes.

He poured himself a glass of wine then offered me a sip. "Here, it'll do you some good."

"It won't hurt the girls?"

He shook his head. "No, but it will calm your belly and hopefully prevent early labor."

I took a long, slow sip and savored the first trace of wine I had the pleasure of tasting in several months. The flavors danced upon my tongue like a well-rehearsed ballet. A groan escaped my throat.

Khalen took the next sip. "Hmm," he said. "Not bad for a Bordeaux."

"To me, it tastes like heaven."

He handed me the glass and encouraged me to have another sip. I did, and enjoyed it as much as my first.

As expected, I finished the hearty meal, my stomach feeling ready to burst.

"I hope you saved room for dessert," he said.

I shook my head. "No, I most certainly did not."

"Too bad." He ticked his tongue. "Lenore makes a fabulous berry cobbler."

"Honestly, Khalen, I couldn't." My hand moved over my aching belly. One of the twins kicked in response, making me wince.

"They like your touch," he said. "I know how they feel." He lifted my hand and kissed the palm. "I cannot wait to make love to you again."

My face grew warm at the thought. It felt like years since we had last joined and my body ached to feel him again. Unfortunately, all the rest my body had during the last few days, only made it crave for more. I was drained and ready for sleep.

Khalen cleared the trays from the bed and urged me to lay down. He drew the soft blankets under my chin and laid beside me. "Rest," he whispered, brushing the loose hair from my forehead.

I dreamt deeply that night.

Shanuk gripped my hand solidly as if he were alive and standing by my side. I glanced down at my stomach. It was flat and void of the twins. Although I felt my feet press upon the warm stone floor with every step, my body felt as if it were floating alongside Shanuk.

His expression shone with such intensity, I could make out the details of it even in the darkness of the dimly-lit corridors. His blue eyes glowed, bright and surreal with flecks of silver. He smiled at me. "Remember," he said, gesturing toward the direction we headed.

I absorbed the character cracks in the walls, the furniture, rugs, and tapestries that littered the high walls. He led me down three long corridors then down a long and narrow set of stairs. At the bottom of the stairwell, he paused to reach for a key that lay hidden in a crack above the doorway. He made certain I saw where he placed it.

We walked into the dark space, lit only by the candles Shanuk had willed to life. I saw details I should have missed in this light. When he pointed at objects of importance, they glowed then dimmed with a wave of his hand. He pointed at a large chest. The key to open it was kept in a dusty jar on an impossibly-high bookshelf. He lowered the jar telekinetically then removed the key. It was unlike any key I had ever seen. Made of brass, it was shaped like that of a long dragon with talons that turned the tumblers in the lock. He opened the chest then handed me a large dusty book and a letter that was stuffed in the back cover.

Shanuk placed his hand over my forehead, his eyes still glowing a brilliant blue. "Remember," he said. Everything went black.

I AWOKE WITH A START, my hands tingling and warm.
"What is it?" Khalen asked, putting his book aside.
"What's wrong?"

I told him about the dream.

"I know of that room," he said. "The key has been lost for many years and we were told that nothing of importance was stored there."

"Well, Shanuk believes there is and he wants me to see it."

"Later," he said. "For now, get some rest."

I shook my head. "I'm not tired, Khalen. I need to know what's down there, please."

"Skye, it's not a good idea. The room is a fair distance away and you are in no cond—"

I flipped the covers off me and started to stand.

"Where are you going?" he asked.

"To find that room."

He growled, standing from the bed. With a snap, he whipped the shirt from a peg on the wall. "Damn your willfulness, woman. It will be the death of us both."

I pulled my nightgown over my head before heading for the door. I had a new-found strength in me tonight. The twins were heavy but not overbearing.

Khalen reached for my arm. When I turned to face him, he held out a robe. "You will need this," he said, his tone softer now. "If I sense fatigue or pain in you, we're heading back. Understood?"

I nodded, a bit apprehensively. I could not hide those feelings from him and he knew it. Reading my thoughts, he smiled, and then kissed my forehead.

"Come, my stubborn mate. Let's find your room."

He led me down the dark corridor. It was very early in the morning. Everyone was asleep. The castle offered an eerie silence as we padded our way down the hall. Khalen willed the lights on as we continued. I recognized the placement of tapestries and paintings but could not make out the details. As we rounded the second corner, I knew I would see an ornate bench on the left, and a tall skinny table supporting a crystal bowl. I was not disappointed.

The familiar stairwell was dark and much more narrow than I had remembered from my dream.

"Place your hand on my shoulder," said Khalen.

I followed him down the steep stairs until we came to a landing. "The key is in a crack above the doorway."

Khalen looked up. "There is no crack, Skye."

"It looks like this," I said, drawing the triangular shape of it on the dusty door. "Look above the door frame. Use your fingers if you must."

Khalen reached high above his head, feeling for the crack. Tall as he was, he had to stand on his toes. "I feel it," he said. "The key is stuck." He stood back then willed the key toward him. Dust and stone chards accompanied it. The long brass key shone in his hand, despite the many years of neglect. He slid it into the door lock and jiggled it open. With a firm push, he opened the narrow door. It creaked loudly, its old hinges complaining from having to wake after years of rest.

The room reeked of dust and mildew. There were no lights.

"Light the candles," I told him. "There." I pointed toward the direction where I had seen the candles lit.

Khalen willed one to light, and then the others. I could

feel him gazing down at me with apprehension. "What's next?"

"Look for a trunk." I gestured the approximate size with my hands and pointed to where it was. "It's behind a large table with ornate carvings." I added.

Khalen lit more candles and led me in the direction I pointed. "Stay here," he said, when there were too many objects for me to negotiate. He jiggled something solid. "It's locked."

"The key is up there," I pointed to a high shelf. "In a jar."

I could sense his hesitation. He reached up toward the shelf with his energy, connecting with the jar I had described. Carefully, he willed the jar down and into his hands. I could hear the key rattle as he struggled to open the lid.

"You must will it open," I said.

He did as I suggested. The top twisted open and he pulled the odd-looking dragon key out. I heard it slide into the lock on the trunk. A loud clank sounded as the chambers released the latch. Khalen peered inside.

"Look for a dusty book," I said.

"It is the only thing here." He pulled out a large, leather-cased book and blew the dust from its cover.

"There is a letter for me tucked inside the back cover."

He hesitated then flipped the book over to verify my belief. "It's here," he said.

"You sound surprised, my love."

"I am, actually, and a bit shocked."

"Let's bring it up to our room." I could feel my strength slipping away and did my best to hide it.

Khalen handed me the book then easily lifted me into his

arms. "You're weak," he said.

"And too heavy for you to carry," I added. "Please, put me down before you rupture a disk."

"Compared to the heaviness of my worries for you, my love, your weight is like that of a feather." He moved his hands from under me to prove his point, supporting me telekinetically.

"That's cheating," I said.

He smiled. "Not for me."

I tucked my head into his chest.

He lowered me onto our bed then took the book from my hands. "We'll have a look at this later. For now, I want you to rest."

I sat up. "Are you kidding me? Khalen, I cannot possibly rest now. I need to know what this is."

Groaning, he sat beside me, pulling the letter out that was tucked behind the back cover. His brows drew together in a frown.

"What?" I said. "What does it say?"

"It's written in an ancient style of Gaelic. I don't understand it."

"Are you sure?"

He opened the book. It, too, was unreadable.

"Can anyone read this?" I asked, desperation lacing my tone.

"Hmm," he said. "Arcadie, perhaps."

"Ugh, he won't be here for several days."

"Skye, relax. He'll be here this week."

I flipped through the pages of the old book and sighed. "Leave it to Shanuk to do this to me," I said.

Khalen laughed. "Perhaps he's trying to teach you patience?"

My eyes narrowed. "Do I need it?"

He raised his hands and stepped back. "Oh no, my love, not at all."

I flipped through the pages and gasped when something fell out from between the pages. It was a letter I had written when I was very young. The edges were worn and bent as if it had been read many times over. I could no longer read the writing, but I recognized the picture I had drawn and my handwriting.

Khalen pulled it from my shaking hands. With hesitance, he began reading it.

My Future

I want to be so pretty so that every man who looks at me craves to be near me. I want to help people heal, and be wise like my grandfather. I want to marry a man who cherishes me above everything else. My parents will be healthy and happy, and will have many grandchildren to love and spoil. I also want a pony with a very long tail that I can braid. A dog would be nice as well.

Skye Taylor — November 25, 1971

The picture that was drawn was that of a beautiful woman with long blonde hair, a dog by her side, and a horse with a very long tail. A tear burned my eyes before I allowed it to fall.

"What is this?" asked Khalen.

"Something I wrote when I was ten years old."

"Why is it here?"

"I don't know."

Chapter 11

When you are as hard as metal, you echo everything around you. The noise can make you insane.

THE NEXT FEW DAYS WERE trying. Despite Sunjia's gallant effort to calm my nerves, nothing seemed to work. Arcadie, Case, and Eve were delayed in England, and my patience was getting raw.

In my dreams and meditations, I ventured to contact Shanuk. I was not successful. It made no sense for him to elude me, seeing it was his idea that I find the items that he had stored in the cellar. I paced the deck, finding it difficult to rest in bed when my mind was flooded with speculation. It was obvious that Shanuk had known me as a young girl, or he wouldn't have had the paper I had written about my perceived future.

The wind brushed against my skin as if trying to carry my woes away. Khalen had gone hunting with Darius, and Sunjia offered to help Lenore in the kitchen. I, of course, was ordered to stay in my room. Given my present state of mind, Khalen did not trust me to stay out of the cellar. I had no doubt he bound me here. I was not too eager to test my theory.

Wise choice, he offered back to me in thought. His gift of telepathy was much stronger than mine. Then again, he had many more years of practice at it than I had.

Any word on Arcadie's arrival? I asked, hopeful.

There was a long pause before he answered. *They come tonight.* His thoughts were suddenly cut off. Perhaps they had spotted their prey? Khalen knew I didn't like the visions that often accompanied his hunting endeavors and politely kept them hidden from me.

The sixty-plus acres of forested land that surrounded Darius' home provided ample game. Khalen only used a bow and arrow to bring his prey down and he was deadly accurate. With his gifts, he really didn't need to use a weapon, but refrained from using his gifts when it came to hunting. He wanted to offer the animal every chance to survive. To hunt with a bow, one had to get very close and stay still and quiet. Its accuracy was only good within thirty yards. Khalen believed that the challenge offered a fair advantage to the beast in his sight.

I missed Maiyun terribly and wondered if she missed me as well. Ian and Aidan promised to take good care of her and I knew she was in good hands. Still, I missed the smell of her coat, the warmth of her body, and the penetrating inquiry of her eyes.

My hands were raw from rubbing them together. I did a quick healing on them then returned to the small tea table in our room to drink my coffee. Sunjia had brought me a dark-chocolate croissant to enjoy, but I hadn't touched it. She promised to return soon with a carafe of tea and a proper breakfast. I was sure that she and Lenore had received word of Arcadie's arrival, along with Case and Eve. They would be busy getting ready for our guest. I longed to help as well, despite my uncomfortable condition.

The twins sat heavy in my belly but remained alarmingly still. I was sure Khalen had something to do with that. He had a way of calming them with a touch. Eve had told me that when a clan leader issued a command, that command was obeyed. I guess that held true for the young as well—even the unborn ones.

I sipped my coffee. It had grown cold but remained delightfully fragrant. Per Khalen's request, Sunjia added stone-ground chocolate with a hint of cinnamon and cayenne pepper to discourage another hemorrhage.

The door opened, revealing Sunjia and Lenore's smiling faces. Lenore carried a large tray of food, while Sunjia had a tray of tea and cream.

"Good news," said Sunjia, her voice more jovial than I had ever imagined coming from her. Her black eyes sparkled like rainbow obsidian.

"I could use some good news about now. What is it?" I couldn't help but match her smile with one of my own.

"Arcadie, Case, and Eve come home tonight." She set the tray down. Sitting next to me she held both of my hands. "Aidan comes as well," she said in a hushed whisper as if she wanted no one else to hear. Seeing there was only the three of us in the room, I found it rather odd but cute just the same.

I could sense the joy in her heart and the pang in my own. If we couldn't convince Arcadie to break the templar bond between her and his son, Dirk, Aidan and Sunjia could not be together. At the moment, Sunjia did not act concerned.

Lenore served three plates of food—poached eggs with a layer of spinach and Brie on top, cheese biscuits, and sausage patties. "I have invited the neighboring clans to join us for dinner. It will be quite the feast." She took a seat beside me. "Lord, I do love a good celebration."

My mind was willing to partake in the meal, but my stomach had other ideas. The pungent aroma of caraway and aniseed spawned a bout of nausea. I stood from my chair and rushed to the washroom.

"Oh my," I heard Lenore say as I closed the door.

When I came out, both women were sitting at the table in quiet conversation. Neither of them looked too concerned, but both of them had waited for my return before eating.

I sat down and joined them in prayer before attempting my first bite.

"Start with the biscuit, dear. It'll calm your innards," said Lenore.

The sickness was a new development. Food had not been an issue until this morning.

"Yer body's preparin' for birth."

"So soon?" I asked.

"Yer body knows, as well as the rest of us that you won't go full term. The young will come soon enough. You've already begun droppin'." Her eyes focused on my protruding belly. She placed a hand on it then ticked her tongue. "I give ye less than a week, my dear."

My mouth suddenly felt dry and my appetite was gone. I pushed my plate away.

Lenore slid it back in front of me. "Eat. Yer gonna need yer strength."

"Think of it, Skye," Sunjia said with excitement. "Your going to be able to hold them in your arms soon. Isn't that wonderful?"

A smile soothed my features. How many times had I imagined them in my arms? "Yes," I said. It is."

"Has Khalen mentioned any names yet?" It was customary for the father to name the young.

"No. Khalen said that the names will come when he sees their faces."

"Ha," Lenore cackled. "That's what Darius said when our first was born. He stood there like a love-struck lad, void of thought and any ability to name the young. Poor Drew had no name for three days. Darius felt so bad, he had to make a ceremony out of the ordeal," she laughed.

"Well, I have some ideas of my own," I said "if Khalen isn't up for the task."

Sunjia waved her finger. "He won't allow it," she said. "It would dishonor him for you to name the young."

"We are united, are we not? How would my naming the young dishonor him when he and I are one?"

"Khalen is a clan leader. It is not only his right to name your young, it is his duty. Names are sacred for Spirians and must reflect their life contract," Sunjia explained.

I felt so ignorant still about the Spirian ways and customs and wondered if I would ever understand them all. I ate my biscuit in silence. The whole union thing was disturbingly one-sided and I had a hard time knowing that my independence was slowly slipping away. I was not okay with the man being in charge all the time. As a Spirian female, however, it was becoming increasingly apparent that my choice in the matter was irrelevant. The thought made my stomach churn.

"Khalen knows of your independent nature," Lenore intervened, having read my thoughts. "It is one of the things he loves most about you."

"Is that why he binds me in my room?" I gestured to the door.

"He does that to protect you, not to keep you confined, my dear."

"Perhaps the line is too fine for me to distinguish between the two," I said, tossing my napkin down beside my plate. The frustration of not knowing what Shanuk's letter read, my lack of sleep, and the recent confinement was ruling my emotions. My ever-changing hormones were also major players in fueling my foul mood.

"I'm sorry," I said. "I'm afraid I'm a bit of pill right now."

Lenore rose from her chair and smiled at me sweetly. "I have just the thing to set ye straight." She left the room.

When I glanced over at Sunjia, she looked away and sipped her tea as if to say, "I'm not saying a word."

"I'm glad that Aidan is coming," I said, trying to break the uncomfortable silence.

Sunjia smiled. "He loves you, you know."

"In a templar sort of way," I clarified.

"No," she shook her head. "In a lover sort of way. He confessed that bit of truth to me early on."

My heart felt suddenly heavy. "I'm sorry," I said, having no idea what else to say. To her ears, the news must have been devastating.

"Don't be," she said. "I honor his feelings and integrity to tell me the truth. You will always be his primary concern, even after he takes a mate."

"If he does take a mate," I said, picking at my food. "I pray it is you."

I felt her smile. "Thank you," she said, though the tone of her voice betrayed her doubt of any possible union with Aidan.

Lenore returned with three small cordial glasses, a bottle, and shallow container. "Yer going to like this, ye are." She opened the bottle and poured three portions of amber liquid into each glass. She then placed a thick piece of dark chocolate fudge on each of our plates.

"Um," I hummed. "I'm pregnant, and it is only 10am in the morning."

"Yer pregnant," she said, "not dead. A bit of vermouth won't do you or your young any harm. At present, I think a bit of liqueur will do us all a bit of good."

"And the fact that it is not even noon?"

"Time is merely an illusion, my dear, nothing more." She pinched a corner of the dark, thick fudge on her plate, carefully placed it on her tongue then sipped the tawny liquid. The ecstasy on her face was all the reason I needed to give it a try.

The rich, dark chocolate instantly began melting on my tongue, smooth as butter and thick as cream. I waited a brief moment before sipping the vermouth. The moment it coated my tongue, I was launched into a state of bliss that I had not felt for many months. The sweet taste of carmel, clove, and bitter chocolate excited my taste buds in a way that could only be described with pure expression. My woes, frustration, and petty attitude quickly parted in the wake of pure and instant gratification.

"Ah," Lenore exclaimed. "That be more like it, love. The sparkle in you eyes is one that would make yer own mate writhe with jealousy."

Sunjia's response sent her nearly-swallowed vermouth straight through her nose with a snort of laughter. Her napkin was her only saving grace. "Seriously, Lenore. Can you not wait for the rest of us to enjoy our pleasure before stating such a comment."

"Sorry, love," she said, between roars.

I, too, could not stop laughing. Whatever foul mood had shadowed me moments before, was gone completely.

We finished our delightful treat with laughter and stories of long-past events. Before we knew it, three hours had passed.

"We have many guests coming this eve," said Lenore. "We'd best stop all this lolly gagging and get to work."

"I want to help," I said, helping Sunjia stack the plates and cups onto the trays.

"If ye can find a way past Khalen's boundary, I'd say ye've earned that right. For now, love, I suggest ye get some rest. Khalen and Darius will be home soon. Ye can work things out with yer mate then."

I closed my eyes and slowly shook my head with unwelcome defeat. There would be no reasoning with Khalen and I knew it. No matter how much I begged him to allow me to help, he would deny my request. I felt destined to reside the rest of my pregnancy locked in this room with only the refuge of the balcony to sooth my desire for freedom.

"I'll send Khalen up right away upon their return," said Lenore.

"Thank you." I pulled her into me and wrapped my arms around her firmly. "For everything."

"We mums have to stick together, eh love?"

I nodded and smiled. "That we do, my friend."

"Sister," she corrected. "We are sisters, love, and dun't ye forget it."

Tears stung my eyes. "Thank you."

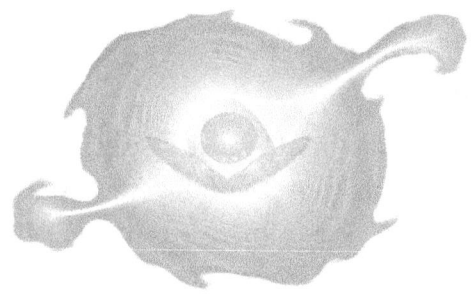

Chapter 12

When you allow the world to define your reality, you become a prisoner of the collected fate.

A COMMOTION OUTSIDE DREW MY attention. From the balcony, I saw Khalen and Darius riding two large horses. A third horse was packed with fresh meat and a large set of antlers. Men and children gathered around them, excited and eager to help with the bounty. Khalen easily dismounted, patted a young boy on the shoulders, and then headed toward the mansion with Darius.

The two of them behaved more like brothers than friends. I was still on the balcony when Khalen opened our bedroom door. The smile on his face was one I hadn't seen in quite some time. The recent burden of leadership had replaced that smile with frowns of anger. It was nice to see him happy again.

"Ah, there you are, my love. Did you see the beast we brought down?" He wrapped his arms around me so tightly, I had to wait to respond.

"I did. Judging by the points on his antlers, he must have been a magnificent sight."

"Ooh, that he was, love, that he was. Almost missed the shot after being entranced by his majesty."

His accent mimicked that of his friend's more and more each day. I liked it. "I can't imagine you missing anything you set your sights on."

He widened his stance before me and his eyes glowed with golden hues. "Yes, well right now, my sights are on you." He sealed that statement with a long, lingering kiss. It made me hunger for more but I knew that hunger wouldn't be sated any time soon. He smelled of sweat, horse, and wet leaves. My stomach reacted in kind with a mild threat to purge my last meal.

Khalen stepped back. "God, I must smell awful."

"A bit—wild is all."

He laughed. "I'll get cleaned up. I hear we have quite the crowd coming tonight." He started to undress. I figured since he was in such a good mood, it might be the perfect time to ask if I could help in the kitchen.

"I told Lenore I would like to help prepare the meal. Perhaps you can meet me in the kitchen when you're through?"

He tossed his soiled clothes in the hamper. "You're not feeling well as it is, love, do you think it wise to tire yourself?"

"I'm feeling fine," I said.

His dubious expression called my bluff.

"Please, Khalen. I'm going stir crazy here."

"I think you should rest until our guests arrive," he said, his mouth straight and firm.

"You know I cannot rest right now."

"I could always help you."

I backed away from him. "No, Khalen. I don't want to rest. I want to help—be useful."

"Right now, I need you to be useful to our young and do the right thing."

The twins kicked, indicating their displeasure. I bit back the pain.

"Come," he said, leading me over to our bed. Even standing naked, he was very commanding.

"I know I can't convince you that I'm fine, but perhaps you will grant me one request?"

He arched a brow.

"Let me be a part of this celebration. Since the moment we arrived, I have been a prisoner to this room."

His jaw clenched as I spoke. I walked up to him and began untying his braid. "I promise I will be all right, Khalen, please."

"Do not make promises you cannot keep," he growled, gripping my hands and bringing them to his lips. "Honestly, Skye, you test my patience."

"You'd do the same if the situation were reversed."

"I pray we never find out," he said with humor, though his jaw was still tight and ropey.

"I need a distraction."

His growl deepened. "I can rule many clans, but when it comes to my mate, I find I'm weak as a kitten caught in a river's rage."

"Not a kitten, my love, but a strong tiger struggling to stay afloat."

"Ha! As if I have a chance."

I stood on my toes and gave him a kiss. "Thank you."

He pulled me into him. "Don't push it, Skye. If you feel weak, tired, or anything of the sort, you will return to this bed. Understood?"

When I didn't answer right away, his grip tightened. "Yes," I said. "Understood."

"Good. I'll see you soon." He nodded and released his bind on the room.

Before he changed his mind, I hurried for the door as best I could in my burdened condition before realizing I had no idea how to find the kitchen. This castle was huge and there were so many corridors.

Khalen sent me a telepathic image of the kitchen's location, along with a reminder to take my cane. I rarely used my cane, but it was probably a good idea to use it now seeing I didn't know my way around and tripping or falling would not exactly gain his confidence in my choices.

Before I could reach the door, he willed it open and floated the cane into my hand. *Thank you*, I silently said.

You're welcome. I could hear the smile in his response, and then I knew that my stubbornness hadn't gotten him too upset. I was excited to be a part of something other than sitting and resting in my room. My feet couldn't carry me fast enough down the first hall. We were on the ground floor, thank God. Traversing stairs in my condition was scary enough without being blind.

I used the image that Khalen had sent me, following the commotion of banging pots, clanging utensils, and excited chatter to help me navigate the massive corridors.

"Skye!" Lenore shouted.

"Come sit," said Sunjia, as she led me to a table where several women and children sat peeling potatoes.

Lenore offered a warm embrace. "I see ye were able to sway yer man into havin' some freedom, eh?"

"It wasn't easy," I said. "Pray the twins behave themselves."

Lenore made the sign of the cross in front of her chest, closed her eyes then placed her warm palm on the top of my belly. "Behave, yerselves young," she quietly said. "Give yer mum a break."

One of them gave a defiant kick.

"Oh," Lenore gasped. "Feisty that one is, eh? Must be like her mum."

"No," I said. "That had Khalen written all over it."

Sunjia offered a brief introduction to the folks at the table then set a bunch of freshly-washed beets and greens in front of me. She pointed to a bowl on the left. "Diced beets in there, and sliced greens in there," she pointed to the other bowl on the right.

A young girl slid closer to me and propped her chin in her hands. "Are you really the legend?" she asked.

Heat immediately flushed my cheeks. The weight of too many eyes challenged my nerves. Conversations ceased.

"Yes," Khalen answered for me. "She truly is the legend."

Now I wanted to dive under the tall table and stay there for the duration of the evening. Khalen came up and pressed a kiss to my cheek. "How are you feeling, love?"

"Like a slug with salt poured over my body," I replied through clenched teeth.

Khalen leaned over and whispered to the little girl. "She's

a good healer, too." He gestured to her arm, wrapped in a bandage. "Do you want her to have a peek?"

The little girl glanced at me shyly then nodded and offered Khalen her arm. Khalen very gently removed the bandage. "She got a bit too close to the oven yesterday," he explained.

The arm was severely blistered and moist from the burn salve that coated her skin. My stomach churned at the sight of it, though I had seen much worse several times over. I connected with the earth and the Father, felt the hum throughout my body then hovered my trembling hand over her arm. First, I had to remove the heat from the area. I conjured the blue mist and directed it to lift the heat and return it to the Father for a more positive transformation. Then, I lifted the pain and prompted the cells to regenerate. The little girls eyes grew wide and a smile replaced her timid frown.

"Wow!" she said. "That's cool."

When I finished the healing, the girl rubbed her arm and rushed over to give me a hug. "Thank you," she squealed then ran off to show the crowd her newly-healed arm. The excitement her healing generated made me feel uncomfortable, even though I was surrounded by other Spirians who expected the phenomenon.

Three women started chanting in some foreign language, while others came to touch me. I looked over at Khalen, and begged for his help. He smiled, obviously feeling very proud.

Lenore finally came to my rescue. "Okay, ladies, we have a crowd of guests arrivin' in two hours and we have much to do." She clapped her hands to instigate a quick response.

"Thank you," I mouthed to her.

She nodded in response then gave Khalen a warning glare. "Dun't ye have somewhere to be?"

"That I do, m'lady, that I do." He leaned down and kissed the top of my head. "I'll check on you soon, love."

"Okay,"

"Men," said Lenore, shaking her head. "They can be as clueless as a new-born babe."

"He's just proud of his mate," said Sunjia. "And for good reason," she added.

"I don't want to be a legend," I quietly said, wanting the statement to only be audible to Sunjia and Lenore.

"Some things," Sunjia said, "are out of our control. Good or no, you have a contract to fulfill. The rhyme and reason of it will be revealed in time—trust me." The sly smile curling one side of her mouth convinced me that she knew something that was not quite ready to be revealed.

Her body stiffened. She wrung the towel she held in her hands then tossed it onto the table before bolting for the door. "He's here," she said, excitement sharpening her voice.

I knew, without asking, who "he" was. Aidan had arrived. I could feel his presence, along with Case and Eve. Arcadie's presence was oddly absent, though, and my heart grew heavy. Had he stayed behind?

Lenore laughed, having read my thoughts. "No worries, dear. Arcadie does not allow his presence to be sensed. Ye won't know about him until he's right in front of ye." Her eyes shifted. "Or behind ye." She smiled.

The rest of the ladies concentrated on their tasks and seemed to be disinterested in anything other than preparing the evening meal.

I turned to find a handsome, silver-haired man standing at my back. I started to stand, but his heavy hand fell on my shoulder and pressed me down. "No need, dear. Stay seated." His long arms wrapped around me like a familiar blanket. "Skye, you look absolutely radiant."

I glanced down then back up at him with doubt in my eyes, but gratitude in my heart. "Thank you, Arcadie. How are you?"

"Couldn't be better. I hear the young will make their appearance soon." He glanced down at my swollen belly.

I looked over at Lenore.

"Within the week," she confirmed.

Arcadie walked around me and lifted the large woman completely off the ground. "Lenore, y'beauty, it's good to see you."

She giggled. "Always the charmer, Arcadie. It's been too long. How is Kitta?"

He frowned then lowered his head slightly. "Hmm, not too good, I'm afraid. Her pa is sick. She wanted to come but I convinced her to go home instead."

"I'm sorry to hear that," said Lenore. "I'm sure Nitara is beside herself."

"Oh aye," he said. "It's never easy to lose your mate."

"Is there anything I can do to help?" I asked, hoping his illness was one I could cure.

"No, Skye. Patrone is being called home. There is nothing you can do, gifted as you are, I'm afraid."

A sadness filled my heart as I thought about Nitara and the loss she faced. The thought of losing Khalen was nearly unbearable. I could not imagine having to come face-to-face with it.

Arcadie placed his hand on my shoulder as if sensing my thoughts and pain. "Being called home is a reason for celebration, Skye, not a call for mourning."

"I mourn for Nitara."

"She's an old soul, Skye, and understands the Father's way. She will carry on with honor and pride, for she is the mate of a loved and well-respected man."

My soul must be in infancy, I thought, because I would not be able to do the same.

Arcadie squeezed my shoulder. "Young Khalen tells me that you found some papers that my father left?"

"Yes," I said, unable to hide the excitement in my voice. "They are written in old Gallic, Khalen thinks. He said you might be able to decipher them for us."

"Oh yes," he said. "I'm sure I can. My father was adamant about having his children learn the old language. Where is it?"

"It's in our room." I glanced over at Lenore.

"Go," she said. "Ye haven't been able to think of anythin' else. It'll be nice to have it off yer mind, dear."

I hopped off the stool then stumbled off balance. Both Arcadie and Lenore grabbed my arms.

"Lord, Skye. Ye can't be jumpin' off the stool like that," Lenore stated in a sharp tone of voice. "If ye fell, it would be my head on that platter, instead the rump of that beast yer mate brought in."

"Sorry," I said, fumbling for my cane. I sensed Lenore giving Arcadie a mental location of our room.

Arcadie gripped my arm. "Come, he said. Let's take a

look at those papers."

"Where is Case and Eve? I would like to say hi to them first."

"Waiting in your room with Khalen. I think we are all very interested in what those pages have to say."

My stomach twisted. With any stroke of luck, perhaps they will reveal who the real legend is and I will be relieved of that duty. I wondered if that fact would change Khalen's feelings toward me in any way. I didn't want to believe so, but the thought lingered in my mind like a dark storm cloud that could charge a fatal bolt of lightning straight to my heart.

"Khalen is in love with you, Skye, not the legend," Arcadie offered.

My brows knit together. "So, perhaps I'm not the legend?"

He looked at me questioningly. "Does it matter?"

I thought for a moment. In one sense, believing I was the legend offered me purpose in my life. In another, I didn't want the responsibility. I certainly didn't like the attention it drew. I also didn't want Shanuk to look like a fool for claiming I was, or the disappointment it might create within the clans. Either way, I decided, the matter was not in my hands. I was who I was and legend or no, I couldn't change a thing. "No," I finally answered. "It really doesn't."

He half smiled. "A legend, Skye, is nothing more than a ray of hope for those who have lost sight of the truth. If people believe there is one person in their lifetime who can turn things around, their collective spark of hope will invoke a positive change. The legend merely needs to exist and you're doing a fine job at that."

"But why me?"

"My father had been told of the legend by his grandfather who, in turn, had heard it from his grandfather. Shanuk obviously saw something in you that made him believe that you had what it took to fulfill the legendary role. Other than that, I honestly cannot say why you are the one."

We approached the door. It stood open and Eve rushed toward me with open arms. "Daughter," she sighed, pulling me tight against her.

I breathed in her scent of lilac and mint while relishing her warm and familiar embrace. "I'm glad you're here."

Case hugged me next and held me as if we had been separated for more than a mere month. "You're beautiful, my dear, simply radiant."

Heat colored my cheeks. "Thank you. I'm so happy you made it before the twins were born."

"Yes, well, Khalen said that your time was nearing and that we had to come quickly. Eve threatened to fly the plane herself if we didn't get our act together soon and leave."

We all laughed because we knew she was feisty enough to pull off such a threat if forced to do so.

Eve blushed slightly. "They were dragging their feet with trivial matters," she explained. "I had to do something to get their attention."

"Apparently it worked," said Khalen.

Arcadie wandered toward the desk where Shanuk's book lay waiting. He brushed the cover lightly with his hand as if touching something sacred. "Where did you find this?" he said, his voice somewhere between awe and disbelief.

"The basement," Khalen answered.

"I entered that basement years ago. Nothing was there

except empty shelves and an old desk. I'm not even sure where the key is anymore. It was lost long before Shanuk passed."

"I asked Darius about that room and he claims it hasn't been entered since the time he moved in. Shanuk had to have placed it there shortly after Calla died."

"Without anyone's notice?" Arcadie questioned.

"Father had his ways," Case said. "If he didn't want it found, he would have protected it."

"Until now," said Arcadie. His eyes shifted to me. "You say that Shanuk showed you its location in a dream?"

I nodded. "Yes, the night we found it."

We all sat at the table as Arcadie flipped through the pages of the large book.

"There is a letter written to Skye tucked in the back cover," said Khalen. "But it is written in the old language."

I refrained from showing them the paper I had written when I was young. At this point, it seemed irrelevant.

Arcadie pulled out the paper, carefully unfolded it then frowned. He flipped to a specific page of the book and ran his finger down the thick paper before tapping on what looked to be a family tree. "I'll be damned." His gaze honed in on my eyes. "Yes, I see it now. It had eluded me before."

"What?" said Eve, expressing her impatience.

Arcadie began reading the rest of the paper written in Shanuk's hand. He then handed the book and the paper to Case. Case read quickly then burst out laughing. "Praise the Father, he found you."

I tried reading their thoughts but had no success in gleaning any information. Eve, too, had come up with nothing. Only Khalen seemed to know what was going on. His expression was one of disbelief.

Case pointed to a name on the tree. Taezza Wallace, daughter of Shanti Graham and Renault Wallace. "This is you," he said, looking at me. "You are the granddaughter of Shanuk."

"Shanti," Arcadie explained, "was my twin. She was killed in the third war of our race, two days after you were born." The sadness in his voice was evident. He lifted the paper that Shanuk had written. "Renault, her mate, hid you away in the basement where you found this document. He died protecting you. Shanuk came for you shortly after your father passed. The appearance of your eyes confirmed his suspicions. That is why the Shadows were so adamant about trying to kill your parents before you were born. They breached our barriers and tried to steal you away. Shanuk was wise to hide you from them."

"You mentioned my eyes," I said. "What about them was different?"

"They were silver," Arcadie explained, as if I should have known. "Shanuk created a shield over them, making them appear gray. He also shielded your gifts until you reached an age when he could find and develop you properly."

I sat back, having a hard time taking in all that he told me. The connection I had with Shanuk was undeniably strong—stronger than just a mentor-like attraction. We were blood, actual blood. My chest felt oddly heavy with the realization. Who were my parents then, the people who raised me?

"Shanuk had chosen them for you," Arcadie answered, having read my jumbled thoughts. He read more of the document that Shanuk had written. "They had been trying for many years to have a child. Their daughter did not fare well during the birth and was whisked away for more intensive care. At the moment the baby girl died, Shanuk replaced her with you then reprogrammed the parents and the hospital staff to believe that you were the couple's daughter. No one knew the difference."

Now, I wanted to be sick and covered my mouth. Khalen rubbed my back and held my other hand so tightly, I thought he might crush it.

"For years," Arcadie continued, "the Shadows searched you out but did not find you until Shanuk found you in the hospital." He turned the document over and continued reading.

"Shanuk had lost track of you until you were injured. Your spirit called to him like a beacon in the night. When he came to you, your eyes glistened with silver specks. At that moment, he removed the shields that had protected you and guided you to Khalen."

"If he removed my shield," I said, "then why did the Shadows inject a chip in me?"

"You are still protected, Skye. The Shadows cannot track your energy. Once they found you, they needed a way to follow you. In some respects, you still carry Shanuk's protection."

"And my blindness?"

He finished reading the paper then carefully folded it and returned it to its location in the back of the book. I tried to read his thoughts about what the rest of it said, but he kept them from me.

"It is an anomaly," he explained. "Silver eyes are reserved

for those who see."

I had to laugh at that one. "Well, for someone who is supposed to see, I am certainly blind at times."

"If a human doctor were to examine you, Skye, you would appear completely blind. You see things in ways that humans cannot possibly understand."

I had experienced that more than once, I remembered. "Why does my vision fade?"

He glanced down at my belly. "The young take your strength. Without it, you cannot see."

"As I have explained to you earlier, love," said Khalen, "your gifts are strongest when you are healthy. If your immune system is compromised at all, either through stress, illness, or difficult pregnancies, your sight and ability to heal will fade."

I did remember him explaining that. I just didn't believe it. I was told I had Retinitis Pigmentosa and chose to believe that fallacy. Now it seemed my entire life had been a lie.

"Not a lie," said Case, "a necessary segregation."

"Did you know?" I asked him.

"No. None of us did."

Arcadie closed the book before him. "I was led to believe that my sister's child was killed along with her mate. Shanuk told no one."

"Is that why I was not gifted to Dirk, your son?" We were blood related and the union would not have been blessed.

"No," said Arcadie. "not entirely."

"Dirk said that he had been told stories of my existence."

"He heard stories of the legend, Skye. That legend had been told for thousands of years before you were born. When you were found, Shanuk kept the truth of your blood a secret. By all rights, my son had first rights to you, so he assumed you would be his."

"Shanuk brought me to Khalen's clan, instead," I said.

"You had to unite with a man of strong blood. Khalen is powerful. His gifts are strong and his blood is pure. It was a solid match."

Khalen squeezed my hand, indicating that he, too, believed the match was solid. There was so much for me to take in. I sat back and sighed, rubbing my hand over my aching belly. "So, what else are you not telling me," I asked Arcadie.

"The rest is for Case and I, only. My father knew the old language was understood by very few, save us. He knew that we would be the ones to tell you these things.

Despite my condition with the twins, my ability to read intentions endured. My eyes remained fixed on Arcadie.

His smile ensured me that whatever was written on that document would be revealed one way or the other. He had obviously shared the tidbit with his brother in thought, because Case, too, was smiling. The both of them resembled two children caught in mischief.

"Skye," Arcadie said, his voice irritably condescending. "You needn't concern yourself with trivial matters. You have much more important things to tend, do you not?" His glance fell to my abdomen.

"Not at this moment," I said.

Arcadie looked at Khalen. "Is she always this stubborn?"

"Yes," Khalen said, studying my expression. "She knows the information you read has to do with her and not just you and Case."

Arcadie laughed. "Ah, yes, intentions. A bloody nuisance at times like this."

"Tell her," said Case. "She will not rest until you do."

"Taezza Wallace was reported dead," Arcadie said. "You no longer exist as Shanuk's granddaughter."

"On paper," I said.

Arcadie nodded. "You're children will not be recoded in his line."

"Is that a problem?"

"Oh aye," said Arcadie. "On paper, you are the daughter of humans—a halfling."

"But I'm obviously not a halfling."

"Aye," he said "So how do you explain your birth certificate?"

"Well," I stammered. "I was adopted."

"Without adoption papers?"

Khalen leaned forward. "Why does this matter?"

"According to the new law," Case intervened. "Your children must be destroyed."

Khalen stood. "My mate is not a halfling," he growled, pounding his fist against the table.

"Prove it," Arcadie said, his voice low and calm.

Khalen started to pace, something he did when trying to control his anger.

A sharp pang gripped my belly.

Eve was the first to notice. "Skye." She jumped from her chair, but Khalen had me lifted in his arms before she could reach me.

"Be calm, my love. No one will hurt our young." His voice

held a reassuring promise in it.

"Shall I find Lenore?"

"I'm already here," a voice said at the door way. "It is time." She looked over at Khalen. "Bring her to the surgery," she said, hastily leaving the room.

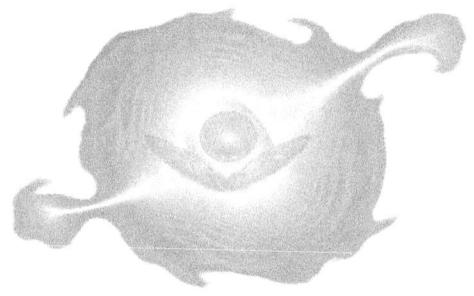

Chapter 13

*In our feeble attempt to understand the reasons behind
catastrophes, we label the culprit and cast it in stone.*

I PRESSED MY HEAD AGAINST Khalen's arm. "I'm not
ready."

"Be still," he replied. I could sense his tension and fear.
He was not ready for this either. His pace quickened and the
scent of him changed from his usual cedar and clove to one
more pungent—bitter.

"Khalen," I said, trying my best to sound reassuring. "We
will be all right."

He glanced down at me as if begging me to guarantee
that statement. We both knew that I couldn't.

"I want to birth them, Khalen. No surgery—please."

Tears welled in his eyes as he rushed me down the hall
and into a large room that felt sterile and cold. He gently laid
me down onto the exam table. His eyes glowed gold as he
peered into my womb. "Lenore, they are not in position."

"Then urge them there," she hissed.

I groaned as Khalen telekinetically rotated the first twin into position.

"Check the cord," said Lenore, as she scrubbed her hands and arms. "Make sure it is clear of the throat."

"It is," he replied.

"I want Eve and Sunjia here," I said, biting back the pain gripping my sides.

Khalen called them both in thought then continued to remove my clothes. "They will wait outside," he said.

"No, I want them here."

He hesitated for a moment, shook his head, and then continued with his task. His hands were shaking. I reached for them and held them to my lips. "Be calm, my love. We're going to be fine." His hands were cold and vibrating with so much energy that it made my heart palpate in response.

He squeezed my hands and closed his eyes as if in prayer. "God protect you," he whispered.

A sharp pain seized my breath. I felt my pupils contract and my sight instantly faded.

Khalen scrubbed his hands and arms as Lenore had done then hurried back to my side.

"Help her dilate," Lenore instructed. "Massage her cervix with yer fingers."

I heard Eve and Sunjia enter the room then felt Eve take my hand. Sunjia kept her distance from Khalen. "What can we do to help?" asked Eve.

"Keep her calm," Lenore said. "Sunjia, ye are to keep us well supplied with clean hot water and towels."

I heard Sunjia pad across the floor and the sound of water filling a vessel.

"Where is she at?" Lenore asked Khalen.

He measured my cervix with this fingers. "Three centimeters."

Another contraction gripped me.

"Don't push," Lenore commanded. "Listen to me, now, lass. Yer gonna want to bear down, but dunna do it until I say to. Understand?"

I nodded. Tears streamed down my face. A soft towel wiped them dry. I assumed it was Eve who held it.

"The contractions come too close," Khalen said. "She is not prepared."

"Sunjia, fill the tub," Lenore said. "Make the water warm but not hot."

I heard a rush of water filling a large porcelain tub.

I took a few deep breaths and tried to place my mind in a calmer state. I imagined the feel of the earth's core, slow and rhythmic as calm waters. A low hum vibrated in my head. It was instantly quenched with the next contraction. I felt as if my insides were fighting to escape and every organ had daggers with serrated edges.

"Get her in the tub," Lenore told Khalen.

He pulled my shirt off over my head, cradled me in his arms then effortlessly carried me over to the tub. The water enveloped my body like a soothing blanket.

"Keep the temperature of the water at 38 degrees Celsius," she told Sunjia. "No more, no less."

The warmth of the water eased the pains considerably. I deepened my breaths between contractions and tried to relax my muscles. Lenore explained that we had to wait now, and let nature proceed. I was offered hot tea, and small morsels of food. My skin was getting waterlogged and my sight was slowly returning. I could make out faint shapes meandering about me. Khalen never left my side. His hands remained on me always. When a contraction hit, he felt it, too. His grip on me tightened and I sensed his pain.

"Khalen, check the young's position," Lenore said.

He placed his hand over my belly. "She's dropped."

"Good. Check her dilation."

"It's better. She 100% effaced and at nine centimeters."

"Monitor her next contraction. Tell me if the babe is crowning."

So he wouldn't have to take his hands from mine, he used his gift to monitor the contraction.

"Dun't wear yerself down, lad. Yer gonna need your energy. I can't have ye weak."

"I'm fine," he barked back, his voice shaky and deep.

On the next contraction, I felt a burn then a rush of warmth around my thighs.

"God," Khalen roared. "She's torn. The babe's head is free."

The contraction ended. I felt numb with the exception of the burning pain through my center.

"On the next contraction, Skye, yer gonna push, do ye hear me?"

I nodded.

"Sunjia, do ye have the incubator prepared, lass?"

"Yes, everything's ready."

"Eve, darlin', I'm gonna hand the babe to you. Clean her nose and mouth just like I showed ye. When ye have her clean, give her to Sunjia."

"Okay."

"Khalen, help the babe out on the next contraction. Let Skye do most of the work, ye see."

When the pain hit me, I did as Lenore instructed and pushed. I remembered nothing after that. Everything happened too quickly. Lenore was barking out orders, Khalen's energy was humming in my head, and Eve and Sunjia tended to the babe. I was present in body only, but not in spirit. My mind was in another place.

"She's goin' into shock," Lenore said. "Khalen, help me lift her out."

~ Khalen ~

LENORE INSTRUCTED ME ON what to do, my body going through the motions, but my spirit lingering elsewhere. I imagined it was where Skye had gone, but I wasn't sure.

"Khalen!" Lenore barked sharply. "Come, lad, I need ye here now." She snapped her fingers to emphasize her point. "Stay focused, for God's sake."

There was so much blood. I couldn't stop the flow and the next babe was positioned for birthing. If she didn't come soon, Skye would lose far too much blood. Lenore didn't seem concerned with that now.

"Next contraction, Khalen, pull the babe out. Do it quickly."

I did as she said, handed the babe to Eve then turned my attention back to Skye. "She's bleeding out."

Lenore compressed Skye's abdomen to cause the uterus to contract. "Check for the afterbirth. Make sure she's clean."

"She's clean," I said, "but still bleeding too much."

Sunjia stepped in. "I can help you save her."

The sound of her words sent shivers down my spine. The devil, himself, could have been speaking to me. The tone in her voice was the same as if he were.

"Khalen," she said, trying to get me to look at her. "She will die if you don't trust me now."

"Khalen, please, listen to her," Eve said, still tending to the babe.

"You can heal her," Sunjia explained.

I shook my head. "Males cannot heal."

"You can heal her through me. Tap Skye's gift and push it through me."

"No," I roared. It was a trick, I could feel it. Once Sunjia was tapped into Skye and myself, she could do irreparable damage.

She touched my arm and my skin crawled. "Please," she said. "Trust me."

Khalen, Shanuk's voice rang in my head. *Trust her.*

"Don't do this to me," I roared. "Not now."

"You have no choice, Khalen," Eve chimed in. "Do it now!" I had never heard such a commanding tone in my mother's voice. It seemed oddly out of place and was enough to shock me back to rational thinking.

"Her pulse is fading," Lenore announced.

"Okay," I said, gripping Sunjia's arm. "Know this, woman. If you do harm, I will haunt you through all eternity."

She nodded. I felt her energy field open, a vulnerable place for her as well, I knew. I tapped Skye's gift of healing and pushed it over to Sunjia. The connection was jarring as a bolt of lightning. A small cry escaped her lips but she held firm to the connection.

The healing was slow, but productive. The bleeding lessened and Skye's pulse strengthened. I could feel the tear mend through Sunjia's touch. She glistened with perspiration, and her lips trembled as she held the connection. When Skye was healed, Sunjia broke free and collapsed onto the floor.

After checking my mate, I lifted Sunjia and carried her to another table. "Get me a warm blanket," I instructed Eve. She quickly retrieved one from the UV heater and handed it to me. I wrapped Sunjia up then moved to ground her feet. Her vibrations were up too high from the healing and she needed to be grounded. When I felt confident she would recover, I mentally called for Aidan then turned my attention back to Skye and Lenore.

"How is she?" I touched her forehead, still damp with perspiration but cool to the touch.

"Better." She had started the flow of blood and fluids that I had supplied over the past weeks. "She'll come around soon enough."

Eve finished cleaning up then dried her hands on a clean towel. "I'll tell the others. I'm sure they're all very worried."

I stopped her before she could leave. "Thank you," I said, meeting her strong, black eyes."

Her lips tightened. "You make me very proud, my son." She pulled away then quickly left the room with misty eyes.

Lenore refocused her attention to the young now resting in the incubators. They barely made a sound upon their arrival and their color was much too blue for my comfort. "Their lungs are weak, Khalen."

I lifted the eldest. She rested in my hand, so small and fragile, I feared I would crush her. She wiggled in my hand and turned her face toward my fingers. "Be still, young Kaili. Save your strength." Her tiny lips latched onto my little finger, barely making a connection.

"She hungers," Lenore explained. "That is a good sign."

I gently laid Kaili down, and then lifted her twin. She was slightly smaller than her sibling, but much more active. "I will call you, Shaiya," I said with a smile. She, too, searched for my finger. I kissed her tiny, warm head then set her down.

Aidan entered the room and immediately rushed to Sunjia's side. "What happened?"

"She saved Skye's life," I answered. "And I owe her an apology."

Aidan lifted the young woman's hand and gently kissed the back of it. "I'm sure she doesn't expect it."

"But," I said, "she will receive it, along with my utmost gratitude. I was wrong about her."

Aidan looked at me quizzically. "In what way?"

"I believed she had ulterior motives in wanting to join our clan."

"And now you don't?"

"Instead of saving my mate, she had the perfect opportunity to send both Skye and myself to oblivion. I would have been powerless to stop her. She didn't. Instead, she risked her own being to save another. That is not the act of a Shadow, my brother."

Aidan's eyes softened. "I told you she was special."

"And you were right."

Aidan lowered Sunjia's hand before wandering over to

Skye. "How is she and the young?"

"Alive."

Lenore busied herself with preparing a bed for Skye. When it came to midwifery, she was all business. It was one of the things I loved and respected most about her.

Aidan glanced down at the young squirming in their tiny, heated chambers. "God, they're so small."

"But feisty," Lenore added.

"Well, look at their parents, lass. Do ye expect anything less?"

"Oh Nay, they'll be a handful sure enough."

"Khalen," I heard a weak voice call out. I turned to find my lovely mate searching for me with glassy eyes. I came to her side and held her hand. It was so cold and weak.

"I'm here, love. It's over. The girls are fine and anxious to meet you."

A smile warmed her tired face. "I want to see them."

"Transfer her to the bed, Khalen." Lenore gestured toward the bed that she had adjusted so that Skye could sit up. She then gathered the IV bags and waited to follow me over.

"Come, love." I lifted her into my arms. She sagged against me like warm taffy. "Our young is hungry."

"I miss feeling them inside me," she said.

"That's normal," Lenore explained. "You'll appreciate their absence soon enough, believe me."

After lowering Skye down, I opened the gown that Lenore had draped over her, fastening the top to offer a semblance of privacy while still enabling her to feed the young.

Aidan politely turned his attention back to Sunjia.

"Aidan?" Skye called.

I wrapped a blanket around her to keep her warm and to keep Aidan honest. When it came to my mate, I felt uncontrollably possessive.

Aidan gave Skye a long and unnecessarily close hug. I felt my pulse quicken.

Both he and Skye chuckled. "Easy, lad. I'm just happy to see her is all."

"Where is Eve?" Skye asked.

"She left to update the others."

Lenore returned with the eldest twin in her arms. With a beaming smile, she lowered the infant down to Skye. "There ye go, love. Say hello to yer young."

Skye's smile erased the hours of long labor and pain that had passed only moments ago. "Have you named them yet?" she asked.

"This is Kaili," I said. "Angel of light."

Lenore returned with the youngest.

"And this is, Shaiya, spirit of Earth."

"Both strong names," Skye said, giving them each a tender kiss on their forehead.

Aidan reached out for Shaiya. "May I?" He accepted the young from Skye then looked at the tiny infant as if staring into the face of an angel. She was fast asleep and content to be wrapped up tight in a soft blanket. He carried her over to where Sunjia lay resting.

"Look, lass. See who's come into our world."

Sunjia was still listless and remained still.

Aidan walked around with the tiny bundle, singing a soft Irish lullaby while Skye fed Kaili.

An indescribable sense of peace filled my heart. The past

months had been occupied with so much worry and dread that the present moment seemed like a golden speck in time. I had known happiness before but never to this extent.

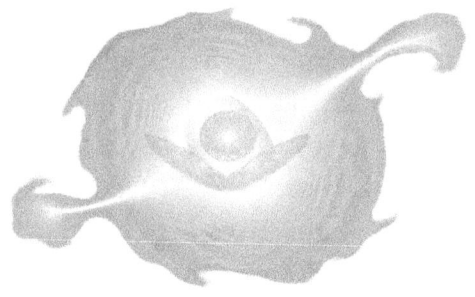

Chapter 14

The draw of duality is meek when the heart is strong.

~ S k y e ~

THE NEXT FEW WEEKS WERE filled with celebration and social gatherings. It felt good to feel strong again. Khalen and I took long walks around the lake while the twins napped. During these moments, it seemed that all time stood still. There were no issues to consider or quandaries to solve. In the back of my mind, however, there lingered the complication of my bloodlines.

Arcadie had not raised the issue, though it weighed heavily on his mind. Case, too, seemed preoccupied with what to do. The situation was sticky. My birth records clearly indicated that I was human, though, everyone knew them to be false. There was nothing human about me. Without accurate records, though, Arcadie would have to prove my blood. That involved consulting the High Council—

something Khalen avoided discussing with me.

He was silent this morning as we walked, my hand in his, his thoughts heavy and deep. I probed them but the snippets I received made little to no sense.

"What has you so occupied?" I finally asked, unable to hide the frustration from my voice.

"Drake Talo will be coming this evening."

I waited for him to say more, but he remained silent. "And, he is?"

Khalen's eyes darkened, a reaction that typically preceded a strong emotion. "My mother's younger sibling."

"That sounds like it should be a good thing."

His grip tightened against mine. "I killed her, remember?"

I hadn't remembered. Why would I choose to? "Does he know?"

"If not, he will soon enough."

"Because, you will tell him," I completed the thought. My mate was not one to harbor such truths, be them good or evil.

"I must. It is the right thing to do. He needs to know what happened to her. He deserves to know the truth."

"And you worry about his reaction?"

"Yes."

I thought about the various consequences, the emotions that could erupt, and Khalen's response to it all. None of it seemed worthy of concern. My brows knit with confusion.

"He has the right to challenge me," Khalen finally explained.

"Challenge you?"

"Yes, to honor the ill fate of his mother. If he wins, my soul will be destroyed and she will be avenged."

"Vengeance does not have a place in a Protected clan," I stated. "That is something that is craved and practiced by the Shadows."

Khalen shrugged. "The choice is his and I will be the one to offer it to him."

I looked at him with disbelief. "Do you honestly think he could beat you?"

"I am gifted, Skye, not invincible."

"And, what if you win? What will that prove?"

He picked up a stick and tossed it into the lake. It landed with a skip, and then a plunk. The geese that were wading peacefully there squawked with displeasure as if chastising a rude child. "That I truly am a ruthless bugger that killed an innocent woman for no reason whatsoever."

I stopped walking and looked at him. "Are you listening to yourself? You were nine years old when that happened. You don't even know the truth of it all, save what your father told you. I don't know your feelings but I'm pretty convinced that the man did not hold integrity high on his list of treasures."

"My blood taints my soul, Skye."

"Stop it!" I commanded, my voice much harsher than I had intended. "Your blood is pure as mine. If you choose to believe such nonsense then you have no right to govern a region of clans, Khalen Dunning. You need to decide right here and now what side you want to live in? Protected or Shadowed?"

His eyes glowed gold. He stepped back from me. "I may not have a choice that clear, Skye."

"Hogwash. We all have that choice, despite our blood. Do us both a favor and stay here to ponder that fact. When you have decided, return to the castle and tell me your answer. Once it is made, there is no turning back. I will not hear of this anymore, nor will you think of yourself unworthy. Agreed?"

He closed his eyes and pressed his brows together as if trying to keep himself contained. "Agreed," he seethed.

I turned and left him there to battle the demons that ruled his emotions. Part of me felt guilty for speaking to him in such a way, but another was utterly frustrated with his self-defeatist lack of esteem. He needed to think about his words and his destructive way of thinking.

My heart was heavy as I made my way back to the castle alone. He was my mate and what he felt, I felt. I started to run. It had been years since I had last done so and it felt good. My heart pumped, my bare feet thumped against the fallen leaves on the trail. I didn't need to see where I was going. Khalen and I had walked this path so many times, I could find my way back in the dark. For now, I just wanted to run, it didn't matter to where I was heading.

~ Khalen ~

DAMN MY EMOTIONS, I THOUGHT as I watched her run up the path, her golden hair flying behind her. I knew I had hurt her—something I had promised myself I'd never do. It was a feeble promise and a dishonest one. Relationships were not spared pain. I knew that.

My fears about who I was constantly battled who I am and want to be. She was right. I had to decide which part of me would rule my life and move on.

"What you know about yourself is a lie, Khalen," a voice said from behind. I turned to find Shanuk, faded but visible just the same. "If you had the heart of a Shadow, I would not have blessed you with my granddaughter. Do you hold so lightly that gift?"

"I do not," I replied.

"Then, perhaps you feel I have misjudged you?"

Agreeing to that would be like spitting into the wind. "I have never known you to misjudge anyone," I stated.

"Your actions and emotions do not back that claim, Khalen, and they dishonor me and your father, Case."

"I don't mean to dishonor either of you."

He faded away without another word. It was his way of making me look within, I knew it. There was nothing more to say about the matter. The final decision had to be mine and it had to be cast in stone.

~ S k y e ~

AFTER NURSING THE TWINS AND offering them a healing on their tiny lungs, I left them in Eve' and Sunjia's care. I needed to retreat to a hot bath with a glass of Pinot Noir. I wanted silence this time, no music or story to cloud my thoughts. I needed time to think and ponder the days ahead.

It didn't take long to reach a meditative state. I was greeted by an old spirit guide I had known as Tezhu, guardian of truth. I had not seen him for nearly fourteen years and believed he had moved on to teach a more worthy student. It was refreshing to see him again. He led me to a gate through which a bright and alluring light shone in golden hues. The gate, itself, was comprised of a dark and evil-looking dragon whose wings came together in the shape of a heart.

"Are you afraid," Tezhu asked.

"No," I answered.

"Will you walk through?"

I stepped forward before realizing he was not intending to follow me. I turned away and proceeded toward the gate. I checked and felt the Father's presence with me. So long as I felt that presence, I knew I would be protected for God will not enter where evil resides—or so I believed.

The light enveloped me like a shower of gold. I basked in the warmth of it then opened my eyes to find it all gone. Tezhu stood beside me.

"In all things," he explained. "There is good and evil. One cannot exist without the other. What is good can become evil, as evil can become good. It is an ever changing ebb and flow. Why were you not affected by the evil that lurked?"

"I was not focusing on the evil," I explained. "I was drawn toward the light."

"Just because your focus is on one thing does not mean the opposite can't claim you," he said.

"The Father was with me," I said. "I would have felt him fall away if evil were a threat. In that case, I would not have entered the gates."

Tezhu nodded, his bright opalescent face void of any features. His vision faded and I found myself back in the tub. The water was barely warm.

I reached for my glass of wine and took a lingering sip.

Tezhu was notorious for leaving me to ponder the lesson. I tapped my fingers against the glass and thought about Khalen. I told him to decide his position—a decision that was impossible to make, I realized. I was wrong and suddenly felt the urge to tell him so.

I released the plug to drain the tub and quickly got dressed. I sighed when I realized that it had grown dark outside. *Khalen,* I called to him in thought.

My love, he answered. Surprisingly, he opened our door and greeted me with a warm embrace. I couldn't help but wonder if he had been waiting for my call.

"I'm sorry," I whispered against his chest. "I was wrong."

"No," he said. "You were not."

He didn't explain, nor did he need to. Whatever had happened to him after I left was enough to draw him from his despair and for now, that was all that mattered.

"Come," he said, grabbing my coat from the peg by the door. "Eve has convinced the others that we should all gather and eat by a huge bonfire."

I had to laugh, trying to picture castle dwellers gathered around a fire, plates in hand and nowhere to set their insanely-expensive wine glass other than on the dusty ground. The past weeks had been occupied with fancy meals, fine china, long tables, and quiet conversations.

We stepped outside to the west-facing garden, on the opposite side the castle entrance. There, in the center of a fine-groomed lawn, was a blazing fire. Cooking near the fire was a side of beef. Eve was instructing the staff on the fine art of cooking over an open fire. From the looks of it, they were not enjoying the lesson. The head chef was obviously holding his tongue, knowing far better than to talk back to Case's mate.

Eve turned toward us and smiled. "What do you think?" she asked, hinting toward the fire.

"I think you're taking advantage of your status here—and I love it," I said. I held my arms out to take Kaili from her, but Eve held the sleeping babe as if giving her up would sever her soul. I decided it was best to leave the child right where she was.

Case approached us carrying Shaiya, who was also fast asleep. "This was Eve's idea," he said. "And a bloody good one, don't you think?" When Khalen offered to take the child, Case turned away.

Both Khalen and I exchanged glances as we realized that the twins were a rare commodity and would need to be shared for quite some time, especially when Case and Eve were around.

Khalen introduced me to other clan members then proceeded to tell me how they fit into our family tree. My head was spinning and I knew that the information would not be retained for any notable length of time. It was getting close to feeding time and I looked forward to the bit of quiet I could spend with my daughters. A tiny cry cut through the mingling conversations and my breasts immediately responded. I quickly excused myself and left to meet Eve with Shaiya.

"Right on schedule," said Eve, handing me the squirming bundle. I was sure that Sunjia would come with Kaili soon after she relieved Case of her. Even though the twins were fraternal, they seemed to be in sync with one another and constantly vying for the same nursing time.

As I nursed Shaiya on the patio swing, Eve kept me company. I could sense the longing in her eyes and the pang in her heart. "What's it like?" she asked.

I glanced up at her, confused.

"To nurse?" she clarified.

I smiled while pondering my answer. "Painful, awkward, calming, and strangely—magical."

Eve's eyes started to tear. I reached over and touched her hand. "Eve, please don't cry, you'll upset your granddaughter."

That cheered her up a bit. She forced a smile and dabbed at her eyes. "I'm just so happy for you and Khalen. Happy that everything turned out all right, happy that you are parents of two healthy little babes, and happy to be a part of it all.

A tiny cry sounded in the distance. Kaili was no doubt protesting her place in line for feeding. Khalen had been giving me plenty of fenugreek seed to increase my milk flow. I could only imagine what my breast would feel like two months from now. The twins were growing rapidly and their appetite increased as well. It seemed they were feeding every hour.

Aidan and Sunjia approached with my very unhappy daughter. Her screams were loud enough to drown the roaring bonfire not too far in the distance. Aidan bounced her, cooed to her, and even tried telling her ridiculous jokes. Nothing seemed to distract her.

Shaiya suddenly slowed her suckling as if taunting her sister all the more. I tried to free her but she was adamant about remaining latched. I uncovered my other breast and gestured for Kaili. Aidan quickly looked away as Sunjia lowered the babe to my free arm. I was getting used to having to feed the girls at the same time. When they grew larger, this would be much more difficult, I was sure.

Finally, the screams were replaced with blissful silence. Eve, Aidan, and Sunjia left to join the others by the fire, giving me some much-needed down time. I closed my eyes and took a deep breath. I heard someone approach.

"I thought ye could use this," Lenore said, holding a glass of wine.

I looked down at my occupied arms. "I already had one glass today."

She took a seat beside me. "Yer still thinkin' like a human, lass," she chuckled softly. "Spirians are not affected by alcohol like humans."

I looked at her with disbelief. "What do you mean?"

"Have you ever been drunk?"

"Heavens no," I said. "Nor would I want to be. I drink because I enjoy the experience, not to get plastered out of my mind."

"Have you ever seen any Spirian drunk?"

I thought for a moment then shook my head. "No, I don't suppose I have."

"Exactly," she said.

"You mean, I could have enjoyed wine throughout my pregnancy and it wouldn't have harmed my young?"

"Not in the least," she said.

My eyes narrowed. "Does Khalen know this?"

"Oh aye, he knows."

"Why didn't he tell me?"

"I suppose he didn't want to take any chances." She

shrugged. "Who really understands a man's actions?" she added.

She had a point. It really didn't matter anyway, not when I held two perfect little girls in my arms. Shaiya started squirming, indicating that she was now done feeding and in need of changing.

"I'll take her," Lenore said, lifting the infant from my arms.

"Thank you."

Again, I was left alone, with little Kaili taking her fill. She was the stronger of the two, but didn't have nearly the attitude of her younger sister. Kaili was more contemplative and observing. Shaiya, on the other hand, was vocal and never too shy to express her needs. If attention was to be had, it was hers for the offering. She reminded me of a puppy always vying for the best feeding position and the first petting. I determined that Kaili took more after me, while Shaiya took after Khalen who always seemed to get his way.

I'll remember that, he spoke in thought. I glanced out toward the crowd but my eyes only reported blurry colors that moved in the dark. I could typically detect his energy vibration from others, but he was nowhere in sight.

I felt a warm breath feather across my neck, and then a tender kiss that caused my sensitive hairs to raise. A low growl rumbled in my ear. "I grow impatient for you, my love."

I giggled and pressed into him. "Impatient? Have you forgotten about this morning?"

Another growl. "Absolutely not. It was satisfying but I hunger for more."

"You're insatiable."

"No, just making up for lost time." He walked around the swing bench to sit next to me. It's weathered chains squawked in protest as his weight settled.

"They feed so often," I said.

"Yes, that's a good sign."

Kaili fell asleep and her mouth released my nipple. I sighed with relief then did a quick healing on both my breasts to take the pain of nursing away.

"Are you using the olive oil on them?" asked Khalen.

I nodded. "Yes, it helps with the chafing, but does little to ease the ache of them."

"The ache will ease in time," he assured me. He reached over to take Kaili from me. She squirmed a little then quickly settled against the familiar warmth of his chest.

Eve came out to happily relieve us of her and put her to bed. Khalen kissed our young on her head then reluctantly handed her over. I smiled and squeezed his hand, knowing how frustrating it was to not have time with our girls. Knowing Eve and Case would return for England soon helped ease that frustration. Eve wanted to spend as much time with her grandchildren as possible. There was no telling when she would be out to see them again.

"Come," said Khalen. "There is someone I want you to meet." He stood and led me back to the crowd.

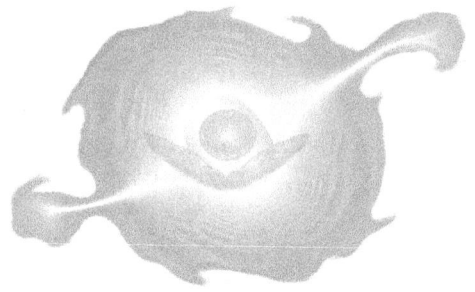

Chapter 15

Judging something is akin to describing detail as seen through clouded eyes.

BY THE TIME WE REACHED the crowd, we had been greeted by several people from neighboring clans. Some of them Khalen knew, while others simply knew him when he was young.

The night had grown darker, and the stars were bright and clear. The moon had not risen yet. The fire crackled loudly as two young men tossed a leafy branch into the flames. Children gasped as the leaves and small branches were devoured by the flames.

"Do it again," a young one called out. "Please."

Khalen continued to lead me past the fire and toward a small group of elders talking and laughing. Each of them held a drink of some sort. I assumed it was wine, but it could have been anything.

"Gentlemen," Khalen said, when the conversation lulled. "I'd like to introduce my mate, Skye."

I didn't have to see their eyes to feel them upon me. I felt like a rare painting in a gallery.

The tallest man reached for my hand then gently brought it to his lips. "It's an honor to meet you, lass. We have heard so much about you." He bowed his head. "I'm Swane, leader of the Galwan clan."

My hand remained in his. "It's a pleasure," I said, feeling a bit apprehensive. "Is the Galwan clan far from here?"

"On the other side of the mountains, it is," he said, as if that cleared up everything. I wasn't even sure what town we were in at present. I never thought to ask.

"Uig," Khalen whispered. "We're on the Northwest end of Skye Island. Swane's clan is a three-hour flight from here."

My eyes widened. "Did Arcadie fly you here?"

"Oh no, lass. I have me own plane."

My face flushed. For once I was grateful for the darkness. "It's a long way to come for dinner."

That earned a laugh from the four men, including my mate.

"I'm Tylee," another man said, gripping my hand as if I were about to fall off a cliff and he was preventing my fall. My bones crunched together. I tried not to wince.

A third man grabbed my hand next then pulled me into a rib-crushing hug. "Hi Skye. I'm Duncan, a distant cousin of Arcadie and Case. Welcome to the family, lass."

The fourth man stepped forward and took my hand. "M' nephew mated well—always knew he would. I'm Drake." He lowered his head.

His name made my heart flutter. I looked over at Khalen. His eyes were sparkling and there was not even a hint of concern in them. I wondered then, if it was the same Drake he had spoke of earlier.

The dinner chime rang, as Alice, the woman best known as the kitchen sergeant, aggressively pounded a triangular frame with an iron rod. It reminded me of something that rang at the old ranch I had worked on for most of my teenage years. I hadn't heard the sound of one since.

The four men hurried toward the dinner line as if they hadn't eaten all day. Drake turned back to address us. "We'll save you a spot near the fire," he said, indicating he wanted us to join him for dinner.

Khalen waved at him in acknowledgment then turned his attention to me. "I didn't know you worked on a ranch." He had obviously caught wind of my thoughts. We walked toward the line that was forming for dinner.

"It was a long time ago," I explained.

Khalen gestured to the long line we now stood in. "I have time to hear about it."

The memory felt like a different life ago. The details of it were lost to me so I started with the big picture. "My grandfather worked at a ranch in Wyoming somewhere near Casper. I worked with him during the summer for nine years until I left for college."

"What did you do?"

"In college?" I asked.

"No, on the ranch." He waved Case, Eve, Sunjia, and Aidan over to join us. They took their time coming, stopping to talk to others who also stood in line.

"We rescued wild horses," I said.

He humphed with disbelief. "I can't imagine you working

with horses," he said.

I looked up at him, finding it hard to take him seriously. "Why?"

"Well, for one, you'd have to wear shoes—boots no less."

I rolled my eyes. "It was a different time for me."

"In what way?"

"I had different dreams back then."

"That involved wearing shoes?"

I shoved him in the ribs. "No. About making a difference."

"I'd say you wearing shoes is one hell of a difference," he jibed.

When I became quiet, he wrapped his arms around me. "Sorry. I'll behave. Tell me about the difference you wanted to make."

"We tried to save the horses, but we only made it worse."

"There isn't much room for wild horses these days," he said.

"I know," I said, defeated.

"What happened?"

I looked up at him, trying to see his expression, but all I could see was the shape of his face and his alluring gold eyes. "Why do you want to know this, Khalen?"

He stopped moving forward and pulled me around to face him. He crooked a finger under my chin, forcing me to look up at him. "Because, it is a part of you, my mysterious mate. I want to know everything there is about you, including your past."

I closed my eyes and took a deep breath. He could easily read my thoughts, but he wanted me to voice this—go figure. "The ranch supported over thirteen separate herds. When the owner died, he left the land to his children. They decided it was best to parcel off the land."

"And the horses?"

My hands clenched. "They were slaughtered."

For a moment, his questions ceased and I was grateful for the silence. It didn't last long.

"Do you miss them? The horses?"

"I did. That was the main reason I trained in massage therapy. I wanted to massage horses."

"You did get your LAMP endorsement," he affirmed.

"Yes."

"And?"

I glanced over at Eve as if willing her to come to my rescue. Apparently, she was not interested in my thoughts at the moment. Aidan and Sunjia were definitely not interested, and Case was too busy talking.

"Answer my question," Khalen prompted. The persistence in his voice was alarming. Why was this so important to him?

"I worked at the race track for some time before volunteering at a rescue ranch in Maple Valley. When it became apparent that my lack of vision was a liability, I was forced to quit."

"Did you get injured?"

In a sense, I did, but I really didn't want to talk about it. "No." My answer was short and terse.

"Tell me about Keko," he pried, obviously having read the inner-most recesses of my darkened past.

I looked up at him with teary eyes. "Why are you doing this?"

"I have my reasons."

"You can read my thoughts, Khalen. You don't need to hear my words."

"Speak them anyway."

I tried to pull my hand from his, but his grip tightened, indicating that there was no escape from this now. I had to go through the door he was holding open. I took a deep breath and conjured the memory I had tucked away so long ago. "Keko was a two-year-old racetrack rebel. He was a disappointment to his breeder and trainer. His nickname was short stuff because he stood only 14.2 hands high—ridiculously small for a race horse. His sire was Keko's Medicine Man, a very successful racer and sire. Anyway, Keko was put out to a small pasture with a young mare. Neither of them were fed other than what they could graze from the ground. I met him the day he was sold to the butcher."

"The butcher?"

"Yes. If a horse can't make it on the track, they are often sold to the highest bidder. Keko's nasty attitude was a huge deterrent for any prospective pet owners. When it came time to load him up, he eluded their every attempt to halter him. They even tried loading his female companion into the trailer first, thinking he would want to follow. He was, indeed, distraught over loosing his mare, but his need for freedom drove him beyond everyone's expectations. He was a fast mover, and far smarter than any of the track hands." I had to laugh, remembering how he wore the crew out, all of them panting and leaning forward with exhaustion. Keko barely blew a visible breath.

"So what happened?"

"No one could catch him. The butcher thought about

putting a bullet through his head and cutting him up right there. As he entered the pasture, gun loaded and aimed for that magnificent colt's head, I pulled the barrel down and handed him my entire wages for that summer. It wasn't much for a nineteen-year old, but it was all that I had. I knew it was far more than he would have earned from Keko's flesh."

"And were you able to catch him?"

I laughed. "No. It took me three months just to get near enough to touch him. At the first sight of a halter, he bolted."

"So, what did you do?" he asked, sounding more like a child in the midst of a good story.

"I decided to change the rules on him. He really enjoyed the oats I brought him each day, but he would only eat them if I walked away from the bucket. This time, I decided that I would be the one to push him away. I made it very clear that he was not to come near me."

Khalen's expression changed from one of interest to one of confusion. "I don't understand. What would that prove?"

"Well, I watched far too many programs about wild horses and observed one very important aspect. The lead horse was always the one to push the others away. If you were allowed to eat beside the leader, it was considered an honor that none of the horses took lightly. Once you established that right to be near the lead horse, you fought to keep that right."

He nodded, as if understanding the concept, but not the entire technique.

"So," I continued. "When Keko began to approach me and the bucket, I lowered my head and charged him." A smile beamed across my face as I remembered the cartoon-like eyes that bulged from the colt's arrogant head.

"What did he do?"

"Turned tail and ran like the wind, snorting, bucking, and tossing his head. When he turned to face me, I walked away. This small action snagged his interest. Now he had a new goal to strive for. He had to find a way to earn my good graces, and I was not planning to make it easy. He would have to work for it."

Khalen stepped back, crossed his arms and grinned like a man about to be told the punch line of a joke. "And did he?"

"Oh yes," I said enthusiastically. "Just like the lead mare in the wild herds, he was only allowed to come into my space if his head was down, and his attitude was in check. If not, I chased him away."

"And how long did this take?" We moved up in line.

"Three days. He finally got the hint. He came up to me, head lowered and eyes soft. But, as soon as I showed him the halter, he bolted away. From that point forward, I walked into the pasture with the grain bucket in one hand, and the halter in another. By the fifth day, I stuck around for only ten minutes before leaving. On the sixth day, I stayed for only five minutes. On the seventh day. I got his attention as soon as I opened the gate. He saw the halter in my hand, trotted toward me then stopped about ten feet away."

"What did you do?"

"I left, taking the bucket of grain with me."

"What did he do?"

"Tossed his head, snorted then bucked away. He was beginning to understand that he needed me more than I needed him. On the next day, he was waiting for me at the gate. I shooed him away so that I could get through, set the bucket down on the ground then held the halter between him and the grain. Without much thought, he lowered his head, allowed me to slip the halter over his head then patiently waited for me to present the grain."

"Did he give you any troubles after that?"

"Oh, many," I said, "but they were quickly resolved. I just never gave into his attitude."

Again, we moved up in line. Things were flowing much more quickly now that a serving routine was established.

"So why were you so sad when I asked about him?"

The man had no boundaries when it came to finding answers. He just wouldn't let it lie. I breathed in deep and decided to just tell him everything so I could get some peace. "Keko and I became very close. He knew I couldn't see well and often stood between me and danger. You see, he was more like an over-protective dog than a horse. He followed me around all day, grazing here and there but never letting me out of his sight."

He waited for me to continue, but soon realized I wouldn't. The memory of my good friend choked the life from me. I found it hard to breathe. "Skye," he said, his voice silky as the evening breeze. "Please, tell me what happened."

I pressed my lips together, trying to control the anger that tempted me to shove him far away from me and storm into the house. No, I told myself. Face it. Stop running from the past. With a hearty groan, I continued. "One day, I had gotten a late start at feeding. I had to venture into the pasture where the stallion spent his days. We had several mares in season and his temper was on edge already. Having a late meal just added to his building tension. Keko must have known. He had tried to stop me from entering the pasture, but I callously pushed him away." I swallowed hard, as if continuing would consume my soul completely.

"Please," he whispered. "Continue."

I closed my eyes and shook my head slowly, willing the demons to flee my mind. "I entered the pasture with a large flake of alfalfa in my hands. When I heard the thunderous roar of the stallion's charge, I dropped the flake, but it was too late. The stallion was upon me, ears flat and hoofs raised high above my head. When I came to, I was surrounded by people. Blood trickled from my head. The stallion, I was told, had been killed—along with my beloved Keko. He had crashed through the fence, cutting himself to shreds then proceeded to veer the stud away from me. They engaged in battle," my voice choked and I had to swallow. "Keko kept the stallion from me, giving his life in return."

Khalen pulled me into him, and wrapped his arms around me. "And that is why you have stayed away from horses?" he proclaimed, knowing the answer.

"Yes," I sniffed.

I felt Khalen stiffen. His eyes were on Case who had his attention on a young teenage boy. Khalen grabbed my hand then hurried toward the young who was grabbing his own throat, eyes glistening with pain.

Khalen scanned the boy's throat. "A bone's caught," he explained.

"Can you remove it?" I asked.

Khalen tried to will the bone free. "No, it's caught. I'll tear his throat."

The boy thrashed around, his face becoming darker, his

skin cold. I placed my hands over his throat and conjured the blue mist. "Do it," I told Khalen. "I'll heal him and remove the pain. He won't feel it."

Khalen nodded then proceeded to will the bone free. I could feel the tear and immediately placed the blue mist there. When Khalen had the bone free and out of the boy, I continued my healing until the hum in my hands subsided.

The boy coughed and hacked a few times, his color slowly returning.

Khalen held the bone shard in his hand. "How did you manage to swallow this?" he asked the dazed teen.

"I thought it was cartilage," he replied. His legs shook as he tried to stand. Khalen helped him over to a chair. The boy's friends and family surrounded us.

Khalen looked at the boy's eyes and monitored his pulse. "You'll be all right, son. Chew your food more slowly next time, agreed?"

The boy nodded. "Thank you." He glanced over at me. "And you." It was obvious that I was a bit of a mystery to the young man. Healers were rare, even among Spirians. I was probably the first he had ever seen.

Through the murmurs, I heard the word, "Legend," whispered more than a few times and instantly felt uncomfortable. I almost willed my young to start screaming just to give me an excuse to leave, but I knew it was improbable. Once night fell, they slept too deep and sound to aid me.

A young woman came up to us and offered a crushing hug. "Thank you," she cried. "You saved my son. Thank you."

"Fabulous work," an older man said. "You two are quite gifted." He shook Khalen's hand firmly then lowered his lips to the back of my trembling hand. "It's an honor to meet the legend," he said, glancing up at me. "My family is indebted to you."

"No need," I choked out.

My reply caused the man to shift uncomfortably.

Khalen reached over and touched his arm. "Thank you," he said with great sincerity. He added something in thought, which caused the man to relax some. When it was clear that the teen would recover completely, Khalen took my hand and led me back to the line that had quickly reformed.

"When a family claims they are indebted to you, it is an honor," he explained. "You must always accept it with gratitude."

"Is that why my comment made him uncomfortable?"

"Yes. In a sense, you told him that his family was unworthy of such a claim and you chose to dismiss it."

I pulled back. "I must apologize," I said, feeling like a dolt whose rudeness breeched the barriers of no return.

"No need," he said, mirroring my same, cold words back to me. "I explained your intentions to him. He understands."

"What, that I'm an ignorant simpleton?"

Khalen stopped and shook my hand as if issuing a correction. "You must never say that," he said harshly. "My mate is not simple, nor is she ignorant."

"There is so much about the Spirian ways that I don't understand," I said. "I feel like a child in this mix."

"You are," he said. "Many of the people here are over 100 years old. They stick to the old ways. In America, we have grown quite lax in our traditions."

We stood in line, enduring the endless words of thanks

and feelings of honor. Sam would have loved all this attention. I, on the other hand, wanted to fade to the background.

"You need to get over this shyness, my love. You are my mate, and carry a very high status among the clans. Learn to hold your head high and know that you serve all who we govern."

I swallowed and forced myself to look into the eyes of those who approached us. The softness I saw there eased my discomfort, as well as Khalen's words. He did not view his position as leader to rule and mandate. He viewed it as a way of serving the whole. I liked that.

Case, Eve, Aidan, and Sunjia joined us in line. That seemed to draw even more attention. We were invited to sit with many families. Case was very gracious when he declined the offers, claiming we had prior invitations. In truth, he was looking forward to some quiet time, and for that, I was grateful.

When we had our plates of food, Arcadie waved us over to an area near the fire. There he sat with Lenore, Darius, and a few people I had not yet met. Several bottles of wine lingered between them, all resting on bricks that served as tables on the plush grass. Short garden benches had been arranged into a semi-circle, enabling us all to converse as we ate.

Arcadie introduced us to three men and a woman, all with unrecognizable, mixed accents. "Khalen, Skye, these are my dear friends, Zhenti, Kaarr, Tolite, and Grom." Each of them nodded as their name was spoken.

"That was quite a feat you two demonstrated," said the man called Kaarr. "Most impressive." He sounded South

African.

The woman, Zhenti had a pleasant smile. The wisdom that radiated from her made me wonder about her age. Her physical appearance, though, convinced me she was barely over 100. "Your father tells us you're a doctor, Khalen." She sounded more British, though there were hints of other accents mixed in.

"I am." He poured us each a glass of red wine, clicked my glass with his then planted a sweet kiss on my lips that caused the others to glance away.

"I knew your family," she said.

Khalen stiffened. "I'm sorry," he reply tersely, not meeting her gaze.

"I'm not," she replied. "They are good friends of mine. Your mother was like a sister to me."

That got his attention. "You knew my mother?"

"Oh yes," she said. "Nina came from a fine family. She was pure blooded Cherokee—quite a rarity these days."

We sat and ate as Zhenti recounted the days when she and Nina attended school at Harvard. Nina was studying finance, while Zhenti studied law and quantum science. Together they invested in many ventures, which explained why Khalen had so much money. Nina had willed everything she had to him and his brother.

"Do you know how she died?" he said, his voice guarded and low.

"Oh yes," she said. "Drake told me."

"And yet you still choose to sit with us?" The confusion in his words were evident.

Zhenti, in turn, matched his confusion. "Khalen, dear

boy, I am honored to be with you. Why wouldn't I be?"

Khalen said nothing. So many thoughts flooded his mind, it was like reading alphabet soup in the midst of a hurricane.

Case changed the subject. "Tolite, I hear your son has taken leadership of his own clan?"

Tolite took the bait and carried the conversation away. I lowered my unfinished dinner to the ground and wrapped my hands around Khalen's arm. His muscles were tight and heated. He ate in silence, no doubt pondering what Zhenti had said.

I nudged Sunjia. "Has Case spoken with Arcadie yet? About you and Dirk?"

She shook her head. "No, not yet."

"What are they waiting for?" I asked.

She shrugged. "The right time, I suppose."

"Tomorrow," Aidan said. "Arcadie wants to speak with Dirk first. He arrives tomorrow afternoon."

"Are you scared?" I asked her.

"No. Whatever happens will be for the best. I know that."

I patted her hand. She had the right attitude I supposed. If it were me, I doubted I would be so poised about the situation.

"The twins are doing well," she said, changing the subject.

"Yes, thanks to you and Khalen," I replied.

Eve picked up her tiny bench and came to join our conversation. The men's talk of war and hierarchy was not exactly engaging. Khalen was more interested in what Arcadie and Case discussed, so he moved closer to their side. Aidan left to find me a bottle of Pinot Noir. The bold red they had served was proving too harsh on my stomach. I needed something more calming. Lenore left with him and Zhenti wandered to another group of older women.

"What was it like?" I asked Sunjia. "Tapping into my gifts through Khalen."

"I don't remember," she said flatly. "When I'm in that space, I become like an empty vessel through which energy travels. I'm not really a part of the experience. My mind goes elsewhere."

"That must seem strange," Eve commented.

"In a sense, it is strange." Sunjia sipped her wine. "I suppose it is no different than the rest of us who are gifted."

"In what way?" I asked.

"Well," she said, setting her glass down on the brick beside her. "I am a seer, nothing more. I can see the gifts in others and can channel them, but have none of my own."

"Not true," I said. "You have the gift of making people believe what you want them to believe. You said so yourself."

"That is hardly a gift, Skye. It is merely a form of deep psychology. I sense what they want to hear and believe, and bring it to the surface. In truth, I simply manifest what they already want to happen."

Eve choked out a laugh. "I'd call that a gift, my dear. Far more than I could develop."

"Not true," Sunjia exclaimed.

Aidan returned with a beaming smile, holding two bottles of Pinot Noir and a bowl-shaped glass. "Straight from Darius' private cellar."

"Does Darius know?" I glanced over at the man, knowing he had heard his name. He nodded, affirming the knowledge.

Enjoy, my dear, he added in thought. *Those are two of my favorites.*

Thank you, I told him.

"Where is Lenore?"

"Instructing the staff," Aidan sighed. "That woman doesn't know the meaning of relax."

"Yes," I commented. "I've come to that same conclusion."

"So, which would you like me to open?" He held the two bottles for me to see, obviously forgetting that the labels looked the same to me in the dark.

"Open the Manos Negras," Khalen said. "She'll like that one."

"Very well," said Aidan, flipping open his corkscrew like a well-seasoned waiter. With finesse, he sliced the foil cap then carefully positioned the screw in the center of the cork before turning it clockwise.

Sunjia watched, enamored with his charm. Her love for him was apparent.

Aidan held the wine far above the glass and poured it with great skill and showmanship.

"Don't bruise it," Khalen barked. "Gently. Pour it gently for god's sakes."

Aidan sheepishly lowered the bottle closer to the glass and allowed it to trickle against the curved side. "Better?" he asked, directing the question to Khalen.

"Yes, much."

Aidan held the glass out to me. "M' lady,"

A wave of heat flushed my cheeks. "Thank you, Aidan."

He smiled down at me, set the bottle on the brick beside my chair then left to join the men in conversation.

"Your mate chose well when he assigned your templar,"

said Sunjia.

"That he did," I stated, wondering what it felt like to have the man you loved assigned to another woman as her templar. If Khalen were another woman's templar, I would think it rather odd.

"It is just a templar," Sunjia said, having read my thoughts. "Something akin to godparents."

I turned to Eve who sat quietly staring into the flames. "Who is your templar, Eve?"

"I am human, Skye. We are not assigned one."

"Why? Surely Case would want you cared for if he passed on."

Sunjia seemed to be in deep thought about something. "How long have you been mated to Case?" she asked.

"Thirty-three years," Eve replied.

Again, Sunjia slipped into her thoughts, deep and distant from the rest of us. I knew better than to disturb her. She was an odd woman, but one I trusted like a sister.

Drake came over and tapped Khalen's shoulder. "May I have a word with you?"

Khalen refilled his glass of wine before following the older man toward the lake.

"Are you not cold, dear?" a voice said. Zhenti stood by the fire, glancing down at my bare feet. I had not been able to see her before in the dark. Against the warm light of the fire, she resembled a tall, thin model manifested out of a Vogue magazine. She smoked a long, thin cigarette, held to her shiny lips with two slender fingers.

"No," I answered. "I guess I'm used to having my feet uncovered."

"Where are you from?"

Now that was a loaded question, I thought. I wasn't even sure what I believed. My life had been a facade, a planned scenario to keep me safe. How much of that should I reveal?

Arcadie, having heard the conversation, came and wrapped his arm around my shoulders. "Skye comes to us from California," he said. For some reason, he did not want to reveal my true heritage.

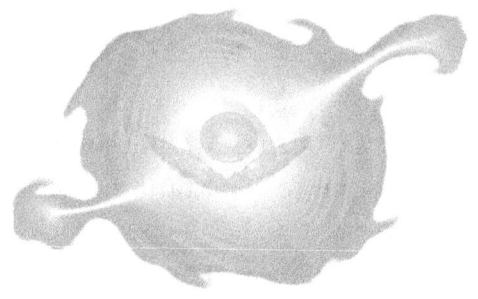

Chapter 16

What we believe today becomes our tomorrow.

ZHENTI'S EYES SPARKLED WITH NEW interest. "What are you hiding, Arcadie?" she almost purred.

"Always the lawyer, eh, Zhenti?" Arcadie replied. The hum between them grew stronger. I felt a shield go up around me, drawing the attention of Case and Aidan.

Khalen stood beside me now, having come from God knew where. The hum surrounding me was deafening—almost sickening.

"Enough, Zhenti," Grom commanded from the dark. He stood and placed his arm around her. "Forgive my mate," he said. "Since Nina's death, she has become rather protective of Khalen."

"For what reason?" Khalen demanded. "Skye is my mate, Zhenti. Her intentions are not to be questioned, ever." There was no warning in his statement, just a promise of retribution should his words be ignored.

The hum dissipated as she drew her hands up in retreat.

"Her origins seem to be a bit of mystery. I was merely curious, that's all."

Grom bowed to Khalen. "Forgive my mate, Khalen. She meant no harm." He offered Arcadie an apologetic glance then whisked his mate away for further discussion. Judging by the tone of his voice with her, it would not be a gentle one.

The ordeal drew the attention of several onlookers. Spirian conflicts rarely arose at social gatherings. Case assured the crowd that all was fine and encouraged everyone to continue their evening.

Despite Drake's persistence to get Khalen alone, he refused to leave my side.

"Go with him," I said. "I'll stay with Arcadie and Eve."

Khalen looked over at Drake, shoulders square and jaw held firm. I had grown to learn this as his peacock stance, one meant to intimate. "Whatever you have to say to me can be said before my mate," he said, almost as a growl.

Drake looked defeated and perhaps a bit hurt. "Very well," he said. "As you wish." He pulled a bench over and sat in front of Khalen and myself. Aidan had taken Sunjia away, and Eve left to stand beside Case and Arcadie. Khalen refilled my glass of wine as we waited for Drake to speak.

"What do you recall of your mother's death?" he finally blurted.

Khalen's muscles grew tense. "Not much," he replied. "I was told I killed her."

"Not intentionally," said Drake. "You see, I was there when it happened."

Khalen remained silent, waiting for Drake to continue. I sipped my wine, anticipating what was sure to be an enlightening story. The intentions of the older man were conflicting. It was hard to tell where he wanted to go with all this information.

In the background, I knew that Case was paying close attention and was ready to intervene should things turn ugly. Khalen felt it too.

"My sister, Nina, your mother," Drake began, "was taken by force during her visit here with our sister. The Shadows raided our camp and left with your mother. Our sister, Shara, was killed. Being only nine years old, I had turned myself into a field mouse."

"Into a field mouse?" I questioned.

"Drake is a shape shifter," Khalen explained. "He can change into the form of a creature."

"Why a field mouse?" I asked, wondering why he hadn't taken the shape of something far more formidable.

"Nina told me to stay hidden and inconspicuous. I promised her I would. A field mouse would not draw attention to itself and I knew nothing about the art of fighting other Spirians, especially Shadows." Drake took a long pull of his drink then set the empty glass down beside him.

"Damon raped Nina then proclaimed their union as if it were some honorable conquest. That was the day you and Treager were conceived. After destroying our camp, the women were taken. The men and children were destroyed." He shuddered with the horrid memories.

"I followed Nina, remaining hidden and in the shadows for so many years, I had almost forgotten what it was like to be in human form. The night she was killed, your father was punishing her for aborting their young four months after the babe's conception. It wasn't her fault, of course. It was his harsh sexual treatment of her." Drake started to shake and I could feel the rage building inside him.

Khalen, too, was feeling enraged. He hummed beside me like a freight train gearing for a long haul.

"Anyway," Drake continued. "You came into the room and witnessed your father's cruelness. Your mother read your intentions and tried to stop you, knowing your actions would bring you death. Your father was too powerful and she knew it. When she came between you and Damon, your will hit her square on, and just like that, she was gone."

Khalen frowned and forced himself to remember the details of that night, prying them from the darkest corner of his soul. "I remember his wrath," he said. "The sting of it plays sharp in my mind."

"Yes, he was cruel with you that night, and had every intention to kill you. If your brother would not have also died as a result, Damon would have, I'm sure of it."

"He was the one who placed me in that asylum," said Khalen. "He made me think I was crazy and out of control."

"And, for a time, it worked. He was not anticipating Case finding you. That was a huge disappointment."

"Did Case know the truth of it?"

Drake glanced over at Case. "No, he didn't."

Case came over and sat beside Khalen.

"So, why tell me now?" asked Khalen.

"I had to wait until Damon was gone. Traeger, too, was an issue. You were safer believing as you did until the two of them were gone."

"Very smart," Case agreed.

Drake started to stand. "I just wanted you to know."

Khalen stood and shook the man's hand. "Thank you."

Drake nodded then glanced over at me. "Don't be too harsh on Zhenti. She means no disrespect."

I nodded as he turned and walked away.

Aidan approached us with concern, his cell phone in hand. "I just spoke with Ian. The camp was attacked."

"When?" Khalen asked.

"Last night. The Shadows have taken Ember. Gregg and Ro are also missing."

Case's eyes narrowed. "Was it Sean's clan?"

"No, it was Greggorio's, from Westport. Sean and his clan have retreated to Canada."

"Why halflings and humans?" Khalen voiced. "It doesn't make sense."

"I'm returning with you," Case said. "My clan is stable. Could you use my help?"

"Yes, very much so." Khalen looked over at Aidan. "Tell Ian we will return in two days. Greggorio's clan is not a strong one, but if he joins forces with others, Ian and Caleb will be out numbered."

"Ian believes this is a trap."

"Yes," Case confirmed. "Of course. They will be expecting us to return immediately. They will be waiting."

"They know about the twins," Aidan added. "Ian believes they will ambush you at the airport. They want your young."

"Then, they will stay here with Skye."

Shivers tingled along my spine. The thought of Khalen returning home without me was unnerving. I wanted to scream no, but what he suggested made too much sense. The twins and I would be safer here.

"We're going to need help," said Case. He left before anyone could confirm or deny his statement.

"And I thought our return would be uneventful," Aidan remarked, a half smile distorting his face.

"What is it with Spirian men and battles?" Sunjia replied.

"Come now, lass," Aidan remarked. "It's in our blood, you see. Nothing gets it pumping like a good Spirian battle."

"It's dangerous," she retorted. "People die, Aidan. You are not exempt from that."

"Ah, you're worried for me, lass?"

"Yes, including the clan," she said.

He laughed in response.

"We will stay here with you," Eve assured me. "Right Sunjia?"

"Of course we will," she patted my arm.

"Will this ever end?" I asked. "Will my young ever have a life without threats?"

"None of us do," Eve replied. "Shanuk once said that every threat holds a blessing."

I smiled. "That sounds like something he'd say."

Eve shifted her voice to a deeper tone, trying to emulate Shanuk. "'Stay focused on the desired outcome', he told me, 'not on the possible threat.'"

"I wonder if that philosophy works on our mates as well," I said.

"It hasn't yet," Eve replied.

Chapter 17

Truth is revealed when deception is ignored.

IT WAS LATE AFTERNOON WHEN Dirk arrived. Time seemed to crawl as he greeted family and old friends. Arcadie had taken him to a private area where they could talk before our meeting. That had been several hours past. Khalen, and I sipped brandy on our balcony as we waited to be summoned. The twins had been fed and were now sleeping soundly.

"When do you leave for home?" I said, feeling an odd need to break the silence. He had a distance about him, as if he were lost in thought.

"Tomorrow," he said.

"How long will you be gone?"

The look in his tired eyes indicated that even one day was too long. He took a deep breath then sipped his drink. "I will come for you and the girls only when it is safe to do so."

The pain I felt must have been evident in my expression. He reached over and squeezed my hand. "Skye, it won't be long, I promise."

"You will keep your thoughts open to me?"

"Of course, when it is safe to do so. Besides, I will need you to offer healing when necessary."

"Yes, of course," I said, suddenly feeling part of the plan. It brightened my spirits knowing that I would be of some use, no matter how small the capacity.

"You are a binding part of me, love. When I go to battle, you are there by my side—always."

"Why do Spirian men love to fight?"

His lip started to curl. "Why do women crave to nurture?"

"Because it soothes another, making them feel better."

"To a man, fighting is akin to nurturing a soul."

"I don't understand."

He set his glass down and leaned forward as if about to reveal a deep secret. "When men fight, a camaraderie of sorts occurs. Like two stallions vying for a herd. Respect is earned for the victor."

"But lives are lost in the process," I added.

"Yes, the cost is high, but when a man dies in such a battle, he does so with honor."

"I don't want you to die, honor or no."

"Everyone dies, Skye. If it is my turn, I want to know I was protecting something of worth."

I looked him square in the eye. "And would you understand if I gave my life to save you?"

His silence proved my point—or so I thought.

"You are not a man."

My obvious expression of indignation did not phase him. "That has got to be the most asinine statement I have ever heard come out of your mouth, Khalen Dunning. Don't think for a moment that just because I'm not a man, I don't have protective instincts. Next time you're out in the woods and threaten the cubs of a mother bear, observe her reaction and never forget it."

He raised his hands in surrender. "Whoa, my love. Calm down."

I took a deep breath and downed a good portion of brandy. "You're not going to die—not yet."

"Okay," he laughed. "If it makes you feel better, know that we will have excellent backing. Arcadie' and Drake's clan will join us in pushing the Shadows back. They will think twice about attacking again, I assure you."

The news did little to ease the pang in my gut. "War and fighting," I murmured. "It all seems so pointless."

"Tell that to the mother bear who is protecting her cubs," he jibed with an irritating grin.

"Touche'," I said, raising my glass to him.

"It's time," he said, sitting up. "Case calls for us."

We walked down the long corridor, passing the myriad of tapestries and age-old photos that told stories of more difficult times. Even the Father engaged in war, I reminded myself. The war between good and evil was one that morphed and evolved for all eternity—always changing, but never ceasing.

We turned several corners before arriving in a room warmed by a small hearth, thick throw rugs, and plush couches. A tray of tea and biscuits occupied the long table in the center of the room. I immediately felt Dirk's eyes upon me as we entered.

He stood and took my hand before I could sit. "Skye,

you're looking lovely."

I glanced over at Khalen, reading his reaction to such a formal greeting. His eyes were peaceful and green, not a hint of aggression. That was good. "It's nice to see you again, Dirk."

Dirk nodded to Khalen, and extended his hand. "Khalen, Father tells me your twins are doing quite well." he said, taking a seat beside his father.

"They are," he agreed, glancing over at Sunjia. I could tell he wanted to give her credit, but held back that bit of knowledge.

Aidan sat beside Case, while Sunjia took the chair across from Arcadie. Both of them had their shields up, their expressions grim.

"I have had a chance to talk with my son," Arcadie began. "He did, indeed, agree to be Sunjia's templar."

"For what reason?" Case asked, his tone cool and collected.

"I was young and foolish," Dirk began. "Damon offered me territories if I agreed to be Sunjia's templar. At the time, I didn't fully understand the role I had vowed to keep."

"What territories were you granted?" Khalen asked, wondering what his father had been up to.

"English territories; Brighton, London," he said. "For years, the Protected clans have lived there without a single threat from the Shadows. It was a peaceful trade."

"Those are Rider's territories," Khalen explained. "What hand did my father have in them?"

I had no idea who Rider was but I assumed it was some Shadow leader. I listened quietly as the puzzle assembled.

"Rider's sacrifice was minimal," Arcadie said. "By creating

a bond between the clans, Rider could easily conquer the titles that Dirk inherited. Damon, of course, would allow Rider to take the territories before destroying him. If the plan had succeeded, Damon's status would escalate to the third most powerful Shadow."

"He would also be connected to Arcadie's clan through Dirk," Khalen said.

"Exactly," Arcadie confirmed. "It would have placed us in a very precarious position. In a sense, Damon was assuring his alliance with the most powerful clan on Earth. He would be untouchable."

"Traeger and I were pawns," Sunjia voiced.

"Not entirely, my dear," said Arcadie. "Pawns are expendable. You are far from that."

"What are your intentions?" Khalen asked Dirk.

"Originally, when you asked about Sunjia, I demanded her return," Dirk explained. "I was angry with you for having Skye and neglecting her health so recklessly. I wanted to give you nothing. My plan was to find her a mate and be done with it. I had no intention on claiming her for myself. She is a Shadow and—"

"Was a Shadow," Khalen interjected. "She is no more."

That remark earned him a genuine smile from Sunjia, and a gleam of respect from Aidan.

Dirk clenched his jaw while nodding his head. "I stand corrected. Truth be told, I have no interest in the woman. My father has shed some light as to why I was not gifted Skye for a mate. I can see for myself that she is alive and well and that your young now thrive. My original motive for keeping the female no longer exists. I release her to your care to do what you will."

His words sounded genuine, but his intent was forced. I concluded that Arcadie had given him options.

"And her children?" asked Khalen.

"I understand they are as giftless as she is. Having no placement for them, I leave them to you as well."

Arcadie had not told him about Sunjia—very clever. I found it odd, though, that he had mistrusted his son. I was sure he had his reasons.

"Then it is done," said Arcadie. "Khalen, the woman, Sunjia, is in your charge as well as her young." He stood and started to take his leave.

"Father?" Dirk added.

Arcadie turned to face his son. His expression worn and saddened. "Yes, my son?"

"I would like to join forces with you and others in defending Khalen's clan."

Arcadie's eyes reflected concern. "You have never engaged in such battles before."

Dirk lowered his gaze, a hint of shame etched in his features. "I would like to learn."

Case stood. "Dirk, these battles can be quite brutal. It is not a good place to start."

"I could stay with him," Aidan offered. "Keep him safe."

"I don't want to be kept safe," Dirk countered, his voice loud and edged. "I want to fight, even if it means dying in the process."

Arcadie shook his head then cast a debilitating blow toward his son. Dirk fell to the ground gasping for breath. "If dying is what you want, my son then do it here." With that, he turned and walked away.

Dirk struggled for a moment then reached out to Case. "Help me," he choked.

Case waved his hand, dispelling the charge then offered Dirk a hand up. "That was nothing compared to what you will face in battle," he said. "You are not prepared."

My stomach churned at the sight of the man's crushed spirit. He was nothing like his older brother, Darius; strong, bold, and incredibly gifted.

"We are never prepared," Dirk said, almost hissing the words.

Case's eyes grew dark in warning. "If lessons are what you are after, young Dirk, I will generously dole them out to you. Come to the barn after supper. I will be waiting." He did not wait for an answer before taking his leave.

"He is as arrogant as my father," Dirk spat.

Khalen patted his shoulder. "Good luck." He took my hand and we waited outside for Aidan and Sunjia to join us. After a few minutes, they emerged, hand-in-hand and both grinning like love-struck teens.

"Come," Khalen said. "Let's celebrate."

"Should we invite the lad?" Aidan asked, gesturing to the room.

"No," Khalen said. "He will need to think about a few things before his bout with my father."

We walked down the hall and headed upstairs toward the game room.

"I pity the lad," said Aidan.

"What is he trying to prove?" I asked. "He is not that gifted, from what I understand, and he does not have the heart of a leader."

"Dirk has been running from himself since the time he could stand," Khalen explained. "Now, he's trying to earn back his father's graces."

"By getting himself killed?"

Khalen shrugged. "He doesn't see it that way."

"Hmm," I said, glancing down at my aching breasts. "The twins must be fussing. It's close to feeding time."

I told Eve where we were heading. Happily, she agreed to bring the twins with her. The role of grandmother had sparked a new boost to her spirit that was refreshing to see. Khalen had noticed it as well. He thought she looked ten years younger.

When we reached the game room, Arcadie was engaged in a heated match of darts with Case, while Lenore sat upon Darius' lap, feeding him tidbits of food.

"It's about time you showed up," said Case. "I need your help here."

"Not yet, Brother," said Arcadie. "I'll wipe your clock first before we take up teams."

"It won't take long," Lenore whispered. "I took the liberty of makin' some snacks. I thought ye would be hungry."

The spread of chicken wings, fresh vegetables, cheese, fruit, and breads was more like a meal than a snack. Bottles of wine stood like gallant soldiers waiting to be served.

Eve soon entered the room with two screaming youngsters, one in each arm. I sat on a comfortable chair in the corner then took the twins from her. I was getting efficient at feeding them simultaneously.

Sunjia took a seat beside me while Eve pulled another

chair close by.

"I heard the good news," Eve said. "Congratulations."

Sunjia beamed a smile. "Thank you. I'm so happy."

Lenore came over with two glasses of wine and a plate of food. "Here ye go, my dear. Ye need yer strength to keep up with those babes." She set a glass down on the table next to my chair then placed the plate of cheese and fruit beside it. Eve scooted another chair over for her to sit upon.

"Thank you," I said, wishing I had a free hand to take a sip.

"I heard the men talking," Lenore said. "They leave tomorrow, bright and early."

My stomach felt hollow, my chest suddenly heavy.

"Worry not, lass," Lenore said, observing my expression. "The Shadows won't know what hit them when this is over. I'm just sorry I'll have to miss it this time."

"This time?"

"Oh, Aye. I've seen many a battle in my years. Have even taken a few of those Shadowy blokes down meself, I have."

"Really? Darius allowed you to do so?" I asked, my interest peaked.

She scoffed. "In the midst of battle, dear, there is no allowing or disallowing—just plain and simple survival."

"Uh oh," Eve retorted, giving me that look. "Get that idea right out of your head, Skye."

"What idea? I was merely asking out of interest, is all."

Lenore glanced over at Khalen, who was scowling like a cat being teased. She sighed. "Very well," she said audibly, still looking over at him.

"What's it like to battle them?" I asked.

"You know what's it's like," Eve responded, her lips firm and jaw clenched. "I nearly died, remember?"

"Yes, I remember." Kaili was the first to squirm away. Eve was quick to take her. Shaiya was still taking her fill. "Can a woman learn to fight?"

No, Khalen shouted in thought. *You cannot.* I ignored him and kept my focus on Lenore.

She glanced up at him and lowered her eyes. "No, my dear, you cannot."

"Yet, you were able to kill three Shadows? How is that possible without some sort of training?"

"I grew up in different times, my dear. Women had to fight to survive. Today, men by far outnumber us women."

"That doesn't mean we shouldn't know how to protect ourselves."

Shaiya opened her eyes and squirmed away. "Okay, little one," I said, lifting her against my shoulder. The soft scent of her filled my nostrils; lilac and jasmine. Her soft, black hair brushed against my cheek as she squirmed and cooed. I gently rubbed her back through the soft blanket that enveloped her, enjoying the weight of her against me.

"Who taught you to fight?"

"Me father," she said.

"Can you show me?"

"Perhaps later, dear." Nervously, she glanced over at Khalen. His scowl was evident, even from this distance.

"Excuse me," she said, making her way toward Khalen. They exchanged a few heated words then Lenore stormed away.

Eve rocked Kaili while witnessing the exchange. "She's

one of the few women, besides yourself, that can go head-to-head with him."

"He's being closed-minded," I said. "He, of all people, should know the value of women knowing self defense. His mother was abused and raped by her own mate. If she had known how to protect herself, she would have—"

"Been killed," Eve said. "Lenore had the element of surprise on her side. If she challenged a man outright, she would lose."

"There now, you see? That is precisely the information I need to know."

"Agh," she groaned, standing to walk the baby around. "All you need to know, Skye, is how to be the best possible mother to these babes. Leave the fighting to your mate."

"I don't want to fight, Eve. I just want to know enough to protect myself."

"No," Eve retorted. "That won't be enough for you and you know it. Khalen knows it. Standing on the sidelines has never satiated you. Learning how to fight will only gain you the confidence to get yourself killed." She started bouncing Kaili around now as if trying to work a marble loose from her lungs.

I had never seen Eve so agitated before. Even Case looked concerned as he called her to him. "Okay," I conceded, "I'll stop asking questions about it."

Sunjia quietly sipped her tea, obviously enjoying my plight.

"How do you do it?" I asked her. "Stay so calm when the water around you is so turbulent?"

"I lived among Shadows, Skye. Their tempers are flared

with the slighted breeze. It is best to not stir it up."

"How do we know that the Shadows don't anticipate Khalen's attack? What if they are counting on the men leaving us here? What if they attack once they're gone?"

"All very good questions," she said calmly. "Do you honestly think Khalen has not thought of that?"

"The men are leaving with him."

"Not all of them, Skye. Many of them will stay behind to ensure we are safe."

"Great," I said, feeling rather foolish. "Now I'm starting to sound paranoid."

She confirmed my statement with a grin.

Chapter 18

Knowledge is an asset until it is misapplied.

THAT EVENING, AFTER SUPPER, KHALEN left with Aidan and Arcadie to discuss plans for their return. The twins were sleeping, and I was on edge about the days to come. The bath I had taken did little to calm my thoughts. I needed to take a walk. I grabbed my coat and sight cane from the peg by the door then continued down the hall that led to the back gardens.

It was a clear evening, but very cold. I donned my coat and fastened the zipper. I made my way down the brick path, listening to the sounds of insects, chirping and buzzing in a chorus of discord. Creatures scampered away through the gardens as I walked past. I heard the sound of a thud then a disgruntled wheeze.

"Concentrate," I heard Case growl.

Quietly, I made my way to the barn, making sure to shield myself appropriately so that I would not be detected. I kept my thoughts guarded.

Dirk scampered around in a circle, keeping his gaze on Case. Energy blasts came at him from all directions. Case was teaching him how to detect and deflect their blows. I sat silent in the shadows, observing.

"Attack me," Case demanded. "Do it now!"

Dirk came at him, hands raised, and feet moving quickly forward. Case easily stepped out of his way before smashing his fist to the back of Dirk's head. He fell with another thump.

"Once you're down," Case explained. "You're dead." He circled around the man. "Why did you attack me with such momentum?"

"I was trying to make it quick," Dirk explained. "Like you said."

"You are fighting with Spirians. They can move in an instant, change shape, and make you see what is not really there. You cannot fight them with brawn. You must outthink them. Know my strengths, use them against me."

Dirk wiped his brow. Every move he made on Case was easily out maneuvered. I was feeling discouraged just watching the man. I could only imagine what he must be feeling.

After an hour, Dirk finally gave in. "You're right. I'm not prepared," he said huffing.

"There is much for you to learn, Dirk. It takes time and dedication. Your father is an excellent teacher. Learn from him. Don't be so damn proud all the time. You have much to offer this family. I know your father sees that as well." Case reached his hand out and pulled the man to a stand.

I quickly stood and turned to leave but stopped short

when Khalen suddenly appeared before me. I gasped, placing my hand over my chest. "Lord, you scared me."

"As well I should have. What are you doing out here?"

"Watching Case train Dirk."

Khalen's eyes narrowed to slits. "Why?"

"I'm curious is all. I'm fascinated by how Spirians fight and defend themselves."

His lips softened. "I will have to teach you, sometime."

"Really?"

"Really. I can see it is the only thing that will satiate your curiosity. And, if you are going to learn how to protect yourself, I'd rather it come from me."

I wrapped my arms around him. "Thank you."

"You will promise one thing in return," he added.

I stepped back, wondering what impossible vow he had in mind. "What?"

"You will only use the information I give you for self defense, nothing more. You must stay out of the fire line."

"Yes," I said, "I promise."

As we walked back to our room, I couldn't help wondering what had changed his mind. He seemed so adamant about my learning to fight in the game room. He and Lenore had even exchanged words on the matter.

"She was right," he answered, having read my thoughts. "I will have to admit that to her come morning. That should give her something to gloat about during our absence."

"What changed your mind?"

"More like who," he said. "Arcadie, Case, Aidan, and Darius all backed Lenore's argument. I was outnumbered."

"Oh," I said, trying to hide the disappointment from my

voice.

"Watching your eyes light up as Case demonstrated techniques to Dirk was enough to push me over the edge. You were happy, and I wanted to see more of that."

I stepped in front of him and wrapped my arms around his waist. "I know another way to make me happy."

He growled and lifted me up. My legs wrapped around him. "Tell me about it." His voice was husky now. "In detail."

I didn't have to tell him. When we reached our room, he proceeded to demonstrate the ways in which he pleased me. Typical—I was speechless, lost in the spell of his touch and numbing attention to detail. I eagerly returned that pleasure with delicious intent.

As we lay together, both spent and completely satiated, I thought about the coming days.

"Would the Shadows attack us here?" I asked.

"Quite possibly," he said in a sleepy tone. "No worries, love. The clans are on full alert. If an attack does commence, stay in the castle. I have placed a shield around it that will prevent any of them from entering."

"And if they try to drive us out?"

"Run to the cellar. Lenore knows this castle well. Stay by her side."

He seemed rather unaffected by my concerns, which was oddly reassuring. If he had had visions, he would never leave me, I was sure.

"Things will be all right?" I finally asked.

He pulled me close to him and sighed. "Yes, my love. Have no worries."

I laid my face against his chest and allowed his spicy scent and the rhythmic sway of his breath lull me to sleep.

T HE NEXT MORNING. LENORE HAD cooked a magnificent breakfast of fresh-baked breads, spicy sausage, duck eggs, and yams. The energy around the table was charged with excitement as the men discussed their plans. Listening to them, I would have believed they were planning a game of rugby in lieu of charging to war. The danger of it all seemed to elude them. In an odd way, I found comfort in that.

Dirk agreed to fly the other plane, but promised to stay out of the battle. It didn't take much to convince him after Case's shotgun lesson of War 101.

The airfield was on the opposite side of the lake. It took nearly twenty minutes to reach it by boat. I was glad to see that Eve and Sunjia looked about as pathetic as I felt, having a hard time saying good-bye. Lenore, on the other hand, slapped her man on the ass and bid him a good time.

"Plane's leaving in fifteen minutes," Arcadie announced, making his way to the jet.

I walked with Khalen to where his bags sat waiting by the shore. He had kissed the twins good-bye before they succumbed to their nap. Now it was my turn. "You'll keep yourself safe?" I said, fighting back the tears.

"You know I will. I won't be gone long, my love. I promise."

"You can't promise me that," I said.

He brushed my cheek with his thumb and his eyes glowed a bright yellow. "Through life or death, I will never leave your side." He leaned down to kiss me. "That is a promise."

The lump in my throat made it hard to swallow let alone talk. "Okay," I choked.

"I love you."

"I love you too," I replied, watching him carry his bags to the waiting plane. In a matter of minutes, both jets were in the air and bound for the States. I felt a part of me go with them.

"Come lassies, we have some preppin' to do," Lenore announced from the boat. Earlier, she had stated that she wanted to secure the lower windows and move everyone to the underground level. I didn't want to leave our room, but understood her reasons. If the castle did fall under attack, the basement was the safest place.

Khalen had told her about the shield he had placed on the castle, but Lenore did not want to take any chances. There could be some crazy bloke in a Shadow crowd that could annihilate a leader's shield. They were rare and often considered masochists, given their nature for craving pain.

If there was an attack planned, Khalen would have seen it. Then again, he never saw the one that hit the clan two nights ago. True, his mind had been on other matters, but visions weren't discriminate. Honestly, I could drive myself insane with the endless possibilities that flooded my thoughts.

Lenore docked the large flat-decked boat and secured it to the cleats.

"I'm getting a funny feeling," said Sunjia.

"Yeah," Eve confirmed. "Me too."

"Excitin' isn't it?" Lenore commented, her eyes sparkling with mischief. She was as bad as the men anticipating a battle.

We spent the rest of the day moving our things to the basement level and securing the first floor. The clan members who were charged with keeping us safe decided it was best if they occupied the upper floors. That would provide them with the best viewing, should an attack arise.

After supper, the ladies and I wandered back to the game room to enjoy some Madeira and a few games of cribbage. The conversations were shallow and endured many long pauses.

"Relax," Lenore suggested after winning the last game. "They won't be attackin' tonight, ye see. The Shadows are unscrupulous blokes. They'll wait until our guard is down and we get nice and comfortable." She carefully tucked the pegging pins in their notch before boxing the cards.

"Maybe they know that's what we think they're going to do, so they do the opposite?" I said.

The incredulous expression she flashed me tampered my boldness. "Pity, Skye," she said, ticking her tongue. "Ye should have been a writer, my dear, given that wild imagination and all."

"It sounds reasonable to me," said Eve. She was downing the sweet and spicy drink as if it were water. If she didn't slow down, she would be feeling that smooth and rapid stupor come morning. Unlike Spirians, humans were susceptible to the adverse affects of alcohol.

"Reasonable," said Lenore, "but not probable. Ye see, Shadows are patterned if not down-right predictable."

"You can read them?" Sunjia said.

"Oh Aye," Lenore admitted. "Like a bloody book."

"Why did I not see that earlier?" she asked, more of herself than of the rest of us.

Lenore winked. "I have other gifts as well."

"You can block a seer?"

"Oh, Aye, and anyone else who tries to pry into me business."

I scoffed. "That would be convenient."

"So you can tell what the Shadows are planning?" Eve asked, her words forming more slowly now.

"I could outside these walls. I doubt their plans have changed much since this afternoon." She looked around the room. "I can't sense anythin' past Khalen's cursed shield, though."

"But you're not sure they won't attack tonight?" I asked.

"No," she admitted. "Can we ever be sure of anything that's out of our control?"

"Death," Sunjia offered. "We can be sure of that."

All three of us gave her a, "You're not helping," look.

"I think we should all stick together tonight," Eve suggested. She had finished her drink and what was left of mine. It was odd hearing her words slow and slurred. I rarely saw her drink anything but tea.

"In one room?" Sunjia asked, knowing the rooms to be too small for all of us.

Lenore poured more wine then carried the spent bottle to the wet bar in the corner. "Our rooms are adjacent to one another. We'll be fine if we all stay put."

Eve downed her drink, her eyes looking glassy and distant. "I think I should stay with Skye and the babes," she slurred.

I placed my arm around her and helped her to stand. "I think I should get you to bed before you pass out here." She stumbled a bit then quickly caught her balance.

"I'm fine. Just a little—fuzzy is all."

Sunjia stood and supported Eve from the opposite side. "I'll help you."

"Honestly," Eve huffed. "I can walk there on my own." She took two steps and nearly fell on her face before we caught her. "I feel funny," she said.

Sunjia and I looked at each other, brows raised.

"Good night, lassies," Lenore called out.

"Good night, Lenore," I replied, grunting as Eve stepped on my bare foot with her hard-soled boots.

Sunjia and I wrestled her to bed, stripped her clothes then covered her with blankets. We stoked the fire before we left.

"She should become Spirian," Sunjia said.

I stopped and turned her to face me. "I was told that humans cannot become Spirians."

"Most of them can't, and some have died trying."

We continued to walk to our rooms. "What causes them to die?" I asked.

"The transition. It's too harsh for humans to withstand."

"But Eve could?"

Sunjia shrugged. "Possibly."

I shook her shoulders. "Sunjia, this is important. Could she survive it?"

Her dark eyes dilated. "I don't know, Skye."

My hope shattered with that confession. I closed my eyes and dropped my hands from her shoulders. "Sorry. I just thought—"

"No need. I understand." Sunjia turned to retreat into her room. "Good night, Skye."

"Good night." I walked to my room across the narrow corridor and closed the door. These accommodations were simple compared to the room we had earlier. The rooms in the basement were reserved for the staff and an overflow of guests. They had only a bed, a clothes cabinet, and a small hearth to warm the area.

Lenore explained that the hearths vented through pipes in the earth that rose up in the gardens. They served two purposes; they kept the room occupants warm while also providing heat for the garden. During the colder nights, the pipes had saved many a harvest from freezing. I thought it was a clever design.

The stone walls helped to retain the heat. The years had ingrained layers of history upon their rugged surface, hence the aroma of soot and oils. Unlike the upstairs rooms, the floors were stone cold and worn to a silky smoothness.

I padded my way to where the girls lay sleeping. Until now, they had slept in separate bassinets. Tonight, however, I thought it would be best if they shared each other's body heat. The room was warm enough, but it could get cold when the fire died down. I also felt better having them together if I needed to grab them quickly. They slept face-to-face. Kaili remained wrapped up tight in her blanket, but Shaiya had kicked hers free, leaving only her feet covered haphazardly. I covered her loosely with the blankets, tucked them under her feet then turned down the covers on my bed.

Sleep was the last thing on my mind and it was far too dark to journal or read. I thought about Khalen. He was sleeping on the plane, his thoughts distant and blurred. I laid back and began to meditate, slowing my breath, and centering my body between Heaven and Earth.

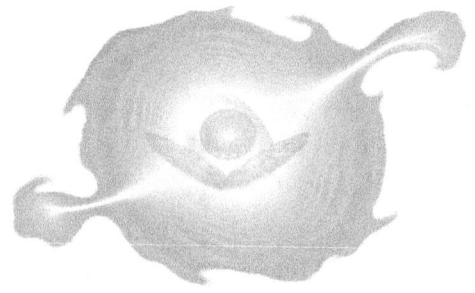

Chapter 19

Peace comes when all expectations are forgotten.

IAROSE WITH A JOLT, EVERY cell of my body alert and on guard. A scream sounded in the distance. "Everybody out," Lenore commanded. "Quickly now."

"Whatever happens," Khalen had said, "stay in the castle."

A series of pounds rattled my door. "Skye, come quickly. We must go outside."

I smelled smoke and heard distant screams. The twins lay sleeping. I walked toward them.

Don't leave, I reminded myself. Stay where you are.

I grabbed the twins and placed them onto the bed. They squirmed and cried but quickly settled back to sleep. I curled myself around them, trying to block the distant screams from my mind.

I heard Eve cry out in pain, calling for help. I sat up, looked at the twins then at the door. Eve needed help, but I couldn't leave the twins alone—I wouldn't.

Lenore pounded my door. "Skye, outside, now!" She

coughed, and then scurried away. More screams filled the halls.

The castle was made of stone, I reasoned. How could it burn? Still, I remained huddled with my girls. I saw flames lick beneath the door, the sound of them roaring and churning like an angry wind. Smoke filled my lungs. I picked the girls up and carried them to the floor. I grabbed a blanket and wrapped it around us. I heard Eve scream again. God, I couldn't just leave her.

The roar ceased and all was quiet. The smoke pulled away. I heard Eve scream in the distance. "Skye, help me." My heart compressed in my chest and felt torn between staying here with my young, or risk their safety helping Eve.

I picked up the girls and headed toward the door. The handle was oddly cold as I turned it. I padded toward Eve's room. The stone floor should have been warm from the flames, but it, too, was cold. Eve's door was open. Peering inside, I saw blood smeared over the bed and floor. I nearly dropped the twins.

"Oh God," I gasped, my stomach churning.

Eve screamed again. This time, she was upstairs and it sounded as if she were being dragged outside. The sound of it was clear—too clear.

I heard a noise behind me. A dark shadow of a man loomed near the door. He walked toward me. I backed away then quickly skirted around him, the twins wrapped securely in my arms. He caught the hem of my shirt and pulled me back. I screamed as he tried to pry the girls from my arms. "No!" I kicked out at him, but he didn't seem phased. I tried to form my shield but it wavered like volatile candle flame in the wind. I was trapped in an illusion.

The man released my arms and pulled the girls away. I was helpless to stop him. I grabbed his legs as he tried walking away. Despite the painful blows to my face and arms, I refused to release my grip. "You won't have them!" I roared. A solid kick to my face was enough to disengage my hold.

I gathered my wits and followed the man who now had my young. It seemed no matter how fast I ran, I could not keep pace with him. My heart pounded and my lungs ached for air, but still he remained ahead of me. He opened the door leading out to the rear gardens then slammed it shut behind him. I reached for the door, but something held me back. "Let me go!" I screamed.

"Skye, stop." It was Lenore who held me back.

"He has my girls, Lenore. Let me go."

"No, Skye, don't go out there."

I jerked away from her. "I have to." I reached for the handle then gasped as the air was driven from my lungs. Lenore had launched herself at me and was now sitting upon my chest.

I looked at her with disbelief. The illusion had been broken. "Where are the girls?" I asked, my voice raspy and deep.

Lenore wiped her forehead as she glanced upward. "Thank you, Lord," she whispered. "They are safe," she said, addressing my question. Her hand came down in an offer to help me stand.

My shirt was soaked, my arms cut and swollen. "I was in an illusion."

"Yes," she huffed, still trying to catch her breath. "I know."

"Where's Eve? Is she all right?"

"Yes, everyone's fine, lass."

We returned to my room to find Eve cooing and comforting my screaming twins, and Sunjia, horrified by the sight of me.

"What happened?" I asked.

Lenore rubbed her backside and winced when she found a bruise. "Well, let's just say that there is nothin' wrong with your fightin' skills, lass. Ye damn near killed me."

"We heard you scream," Sunjia explained. "When we came, it was like you were fighting some demon. Lenore tried to calm you down but you quickly thwarted her efforts then started to run down the hall."

"The girls were on the floor," Eve chimed in. "Both of them crying."

My hand covered my mouth in a weak attempt to dissuade my stomach from purging. "A man was trying to take them," I said. "There was a fire. People were screaming. Eve, you were hurt. Your room was covered in—blood." I dropped to my knees and started to shake.

"Easy now, lass. It's over. Ye and the girls are fine," Lenore said, her voice calming but concerned at the same time.

"How?" I asked. "Khalen has the place protected. "How can an illusionist get inside?"

"Can they project through Khalen's shield?" Eve asked.

Lenore shook her head. "No, lass, they can't. "The illusionist must be within the castle walls."

Khalen, I thought, desperate to hear his voice in my head.

What's wrong? He answered. *You don't feel right. What happened?*

In an instant, I filled him in on what had transpired. He

was silent.

Find the illusionist, he instructed me. Hold him until I return.

Are you all right? I asked him.

Yes, he replied. *We arrived and are standing with Ian now. Keep your thoughts open to me only.*

Okay, I thought back.

"Khalen wants us to find the illusionist and hold him until he gets back."

Lenore gave me a look. "Now how, pray tell, are we to do that?"

I shrugged then walked to where Eve held my young. I took Kaili from her and held her close. She was almost asleep already as I rubbed her back.

"If I can get close enough," said Sunjia, "I can sense the gifts of each of our guests."

"And then what?" Lenore asked. "We jump him, tie him up then toss him in the cellar?"

"Not likely," I said.

"How do we even know if he's still in the castle?" Eve chimed in. "With all the commotion, he has likely left."

"True," said Lenore.

I laid Kaili down in her crib. Eve followed suit with Shaiya. It was five o'clock in the morning.

"We'll start at breakfast," I said. "Sunjia, you can sense their gifts. When you find an illusionist, let me know, and I will start a conversation with them. Their intentions will let me know if something is amiss."

"It's a start," said Lenore. "I'll question the staff to determine if something is odd or out of place.

I glanced over at Eve and knew she must be feeling left out. "Eve," I said. "Would you mind staying with the girls? I don't feel comfortable leaving them alone."

"Of course," she said with a smile. "God help the poor soul who tries to come near them."

The seriousness in her tone concerned me. I prayed she wouldn't overreact should some innocent guest come by to say hello. Eve seemed a little more on edge lately than was typical for her.

"Are you all right?" I asked her.

"Yes, I'm fine. Just a bit tired is all."

"Get some rest then, all of ye. We'll sort this out come mornin'," said Lenore.

I was not relaxed enough to sleep. I waited for the three of them to file out of the room before closing the door. The strong sense of calm I felt seemed out of place given the event that just transpired. I should be anxious, disturbed, or even frightened, but I wasn't. It was as if I inherently knew that everything would be all right with Khalen, the others, and everyone here. The knowing of it was strong as if coming from my very core.

I sat on the bed and stared into the darkness. Who in the castle, I wondered, would betray us? It didn't make sense. Everyone here had agreed to stay behind to ensure our safety. I wanted to question Khalen but knew he was busy with the others. They were planning to attack immediately without taking time to rest. I knew their reasons, of course. They didn't want to give the Shadows any time to prepare and band together. The attack would be quick and deadly. Khalen wanted to annihilate Greggorio's clan but first he had to find out where they were keeping Gregg, Ro, and Ember. Were they holding them ransom?

My head spun with endless scenarios, none of which ended well. As I sensed the plan that Khalen and the others were scheming, I tuned them out, not wanting to hear any more. All I could do is pray that they all made it out safely.

I switched my thoughts to Maiyun and wondered if she missed me as much as I missed her. It had been months now since we left. Ian offered daily reports on her, and assured me that she was fine, but I wasn't completely convinced. He claimed that she refused to sleep in his yurt. She always snuck out during the night and returned to her own bed, despite the cold and loneliness of the space.

I sent loving thoughts, trying to assure her that I would return soon. I wasn't sure if she heard them or not. Now, I wished I had something that smelled like her. I had dressed a pillow in one of Khalen's shirts. It was silly, I know, but it always helped me sleep when he wasn't around. Next time, I would have to remember to bring something of Maiyun's.

Kaili squirmed a bit then began a soft cry. Not wanting her to wake her sister, I gently lifted my fussing young from the cradle and allowed her to feed. It was so much easier to nurse them one at a time. When they fed, nothing else seemed to matter at that moment, and I relished the peace.

Khalen's thoughts were still on strategizing and on an argument he had endured earlier with Aidan. Something about Ember. The emotions that clouded his thoughts made it difficult to read him. From what I could gather, Khalen wanted to ask Greggorio about our clansmen he had taken, but Aidan thought that would be a bad idea. Aidan wanted to raid the clan, kill everyone except Greggorio, and then question him when he was at his weakest.

Arcadie and Case had yet another idea. They wanted to position themselves and the others along the peninsula and prepare to off the Shadows one clan at a time until one of them revealed the location of our friends.

All of the ideas sounded horrid to me. I racked my mind for something better to offer. Why did they take our people? What purpose would it serve, or who?

An image of Sage entered my mind. Unlike his father, Victor, who stood confident and handsome as George Hamilton, Sage resembled more of a young and impetuous Ewan McGregor type. Could he be trying to make a statement? I offered the quick thought to my mate.

Brilliant, he replied. *Arcadie has the ability to summon the young leader. If he doesn't reply, Arcadie will summon Victor. Given Arcadie's status among Spirians, Victor will not have a choice but to reply.*

I breathed a peaceful breath knowing the plan was far more sound than the former ones. Kaili squirmed and pulled away, indicating she had her fill and was now ready for fresh diapers. I cleaned her up then allowed her to lay beside me on the bed while I fed her sister.

Eve came in just as Shaiya pulled away. It didn't take long for her to scream her demands. She needed to be walked around a bit after feeding, being far more prone to colic than her sister. Eve reached over and took her from me.

"Sleep well?" she asked.

"Not a wink," I replied. "How about you?"

"Surprisingly well," she said, "given how taxing these past

few days have been."

I half expected her to be hungover after last night, but she showed no signs of it. "Any ideas about who is behind this folly?"

Eve patted Shaiya's back and paced the floor between the bed and the doorway. "Not a clue. The only person who seems to have an issue with you is Zhenti, but women cannot be illusionists."

"Is her mate one?"

"Grom? No. He's an elementist."

Sunjia came into the room with a plate of food for Eve. "I thought you might be hungry?" she said, placing the tray on the table by the bed.

"No," I said. "I want Eve to join us. We'll bring the girls."

We quickly changed Shaiya, gathered the bassinet and carted the lot upstairs and into the dining hall. Many eyes looked upon us as we entered the room. Lenore offered a leery glance toward Zhenti. I took the seat across from her. When I met her gaze, she looked away. Her mate, Grom, noticed the exchange and curiosity lit his eyes.

"I'm grateful that you and your clan have chosen to stay to ensure our safety," I said to him.

"I hear there was some excitement this morning," he said.

"Yes, I was caught in an illusion of sorts," I blurted, observing Zhenti's reaction. Her energy fluctuated as if briefly angered then forced to calm.

"Odd," Grom stated, his energy calm and extended. "We don't have an illusionist among us. They all left with Khalen and the others." He glanced at his mate, and then at me. "Do you have any ideas on the matter, my dear?" he asked her.

Immediately, her energy closed in around her. She was keeping him and everyone else out of her thoughts. That fact did not go unnoticed by Grom.

"No," she choked out. "I do not." Her hand shook as she took a bite of her buttered toast.

Lenore served me a healthy portion of scrambled eggs, sausage cakes, and potato pancakes. "It was strange, really," Lenore recounted. "It was as if Skye were sleep walking."

This gained Grom's notice. Still, I could not read his thoughts. He remained silent.

"Sounds like the work of a visionist," Sunjia commented, staring directly at Zhenti.

She started to stand. "Excuse me for a moment."

Grom grabbed her arm and forced her to sit. "Did you have a hand in this?" he asked point blank.

She shook her head and I knew she was lying. Apparently Grom knew it as well. He slowly released her arm and allowed her to leave. His energy quivered more from embarrassment than fear.

"Again," he said folding his napkin and tucking it under his plate. "I apologize for my mate's actions." He slid his chair out and left his half-eaten breakfast.

The rest of the table remained quiet as if politely trying to mind their own business. Everyone knew the implications of Zhenti's actions. She would have to face Khalen. The decision of her fate remained with him. An attack on his mate would not be forgiven nor dealt with lightly.

"Tetris," Sunjia addressed the older gentleman across the table. He was the second in charge of Case's clan in England. "Can you offer Skye protection from visions and such?" She already knew he could. He was a wizard and often practiced the old school magic of sacred spells and charms.

"Of course," he answered in a charming British accent. "I would be honored." He bowed to me and caused my cheeks to heat up and redden.

"Thank you," I said. I quickly flashed Khalen a thought of what had just happened, but ensured him that Zhenti did not confess. Mostly, I wanted him to know that I would be all right. The danger had been identified and a solution was in the works.

His reply was a guarded one. Zhenti was his mother's closest friend. Dealing with her actions would not be easy. He told me to thank Tetris in his stead.

"Khalen extends his gratitude," I told Tetris.

The silver-haired man nodded and smiled. "Like I said, it is my honor."

The remainder of our breakfast was accompanied by light conversation, mostly about raising young teens, and dealing with clan drama. Afterward, I helped clear the plates and planned to spend the day with Eve and Sunjia. Lenore wanted to head into town and stock up on supplies. She had a full staff who could take care of such matters, but she said she enjoyed shopping and needed some time to herself.

Sunjia, Eve, the twins, and I retired to the game room where we could talk over a cup of tea. Our typical walk in the gardens was not advised. It was safer for us all to stay indoors. Lenore, I assumed, was an exception.

Shortly after we settled. Grom and Zhenti entered the room, both with grim expressions.

"May we speak with you?" he asked me.

I gestured for them to pull up two chairs. He nervously glanced at Eve and Sunjia, expecting them to leave, I supposed. Neither of them moved.

He and his mate sat across from us, closing the circle. "My mate has a confession to make," he said, his tone guarded and laced with disappointment.

I looked at Zhenti. In the dim light of the room, I could only make out her shape and the vibration of her energy. She was nervous, but had no ill intent.

"It was I who gave you the vision," she admitted.

"Why?" I asked. "What did you have to gain by it?"

She wrung her hands together and forced herself to look into my eyes. "I was only supposed to get you outside," she said, "nothing more."

"For what purpose?" Eve chimed in.

"I don't know," she said honestly. "A man approached me the other night and told me he had some papers that belonged to Nina—papers that Nina had addressed to me."

"What are these papers?" I asked.

She looked away, a tear glistening in the corner of her eye. "They are the plans for making a battery that could power a car for 500 miles without a charge. We had just perfected the prototype when our workshop was vandalized. The plans were stolen and we had been issued a threat to never speak of them again. The plans also included the design of a chip that could be used to track the vehicle in the event it was stolen. The Shadows used that technology to their advantage. They learned how to embed the chip in the body of a Spirian they wanted to track—which is how they found me."

I remembered when I had received a similar chip that

nearly killed me. "If you cannot use the information that is in those papers then why is it important to get them back? Don't they already have the originals?"

"The plans that Nina had locked away would enable a Spirian to leap through time—transport from one location to another in less than a nano second. I had the visions, and Nina recorded them. She had a photographic memory. After our other plans had been stolen, she had decided to encrypt the plans. Only I or another visionist can decode them. If the Shadows understand what those papers are, they will gain a huge advantage over us. At present, the papers look like ordinary letters, nothing more. Nina must have known her life was in danger, so she decided to mail them to me. One of Damon's minions must have intercepted them. Damon, of course, thought his mate had a lover."

"Which may be why he tried to kill her," I added.

"Yes."

"So, if you were able to get me outside, the Shadows would exchange me for the papers?"

She nodded.

"Oh no," said Eve. "What are you thinking, Skye?"

"If they believe that the papers are only letters to Nina's supposed lover, why do they think they're important to you? It doesn't make sense. Why would you want the letters?"

Zhenti shrugged.

"Unless they know the letters are something more," I deduced. "And you are the key."

"I thought that if I showed Khalen how to travel through time, he could get you back. I knew they wouldn't hurt you or I never would have agreed to the plan."

"You shouldn't have agreed to it in the first place, woman!" Grom roared. "If Khalen bans us from the clan for life, I wouldn't blame him."

I wanted to ensure him that my mate would never deem such a thing, but I knew I couldn't keep that promise. "It seems we have a dilemma. The Shadows expected you to succeed this morning. Are you planning on meeting with them again?"

"No. They said they would leave the letters in the north barn after they captured you. We were not to speak again."

"Did they give you a time frame?"

"Like you said, they were expecting you this morning. I'm not sure what they expect now."

"When Lenore returns, she will be able to tell us if the Shadows are still here. Grom, do we have any shape shifters among us?"

"Oh, yes, a few. What are you thinking?"

"If one of them shifts to look like me. He can allow himself to be taken. Later, after the papers are retrieved, he can shift into something that enables him to escape and return to us. Perhaps he can learn more about what the Shadows are intending?"

Grom shrugged one shoulder and lifted a brow with skepticism. "That might work providing they don't have a seer with them."

"Sunjia, can you sense if they do?"

She shook her head. "Not through Khalen's shield and not from this distance."

"What are the chances?" I asked.

"Good as any," said Grom. Shadows like diversity. They

tend to band with others with various gifts. Male seers are not that rare."

I rested my face in my hands, suddenly feeling the effects of fatigue. "It's not worth the risk then," I said. "If our man is found out, they will kill him."

"Tetris can place a shield around him," said Sunjia. "Block the seer's ability to see into his gifts."

"That won't work," I said. "They know about my gifts. They will seek confirmation. Can he make them see my gifts instead?"

She thought for a moment. "Theoretically, yes. He's a wizard. Whether he knows how to do it is another matter."

"I'll find him," said Eve, laying my very tired young down to rest.

"I'm sorry," Zhenti said, her voice low and laced with regret.

I wanted to tell her it was all right, but instead, my eyes softened on her. "Right now, I'm more interested in solving this issue. I'm sure your intentions were pure, but you have placed this entire clan in serious trouble."

"If the Shadows are out there," said Grom, "I could make their position unbearable in the face of a storm."

"Not until Lenore comes home. We'll decide what to do then," I said.

His face displayed an expression of knowing as the corners of his lips curled upward. "You truly are the mate of a leader, Skye, and live up to your legend beautifully."

"Thank you," I stumbled out, having been caught off guard. I wasn't used to receiving such compliments and still didn't know how to handle it with any amount of grace, the way Khalen said I should. "Would you like some tea?" I asked, trying to keep the trembling from my voice.

"That would be lovely," he said. "Thank you."

I poured both him and his mate a cup of tea then offered a warmer to Sunjia.

Eve returned with Tetris. Crystals draped around his neck like precious stones, while his wrists and ankles bore an impressive display of silver and gold cuffs. His long, grey hair was tied in a queue with a thick leather thong that dangled with beads on the ends.

He bowed before me to lower his lips to the back of my hands. I wanted to pull them away, but then remembered what Khalen had said about dishonoring the people's gratitude. I was still very uncomfortable with it but held my hands firm.

"Thank you for coming," I said. "We need your assistance."

He sat cross-legged before me, his eyes waiting for my explanation.

I cleared my throat and gathered my thoughts. I briefly recounted the situation, all the while watching his expression turn from confusion to concern. The deep lines etched between his brows indicated that he displayed this intense expression of thought far too often. "Have you conjured such a shield as this before?"

"No, nor do I know of anyone who has."

"Sunjia, can you tap into his gifts and see what you can find?"

"Gifts, yes, the proper spell, no."

"To access this information," said Tetris, "I must consult with the Star Council."

"The Star Council?" I questioned.

"Yes," he explained, "they govern all forms of magic, alchemy, and the likes. If anyone knows, it will be them." He stood. "I will return." With a wave of his hand, he disappeared causing a wake of wind to whip our faces.

"Bloody wizards," Grom muttered, wiping the tea from his lap.

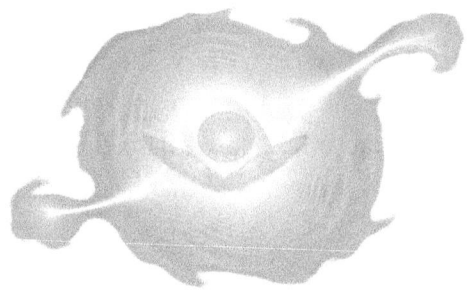

Chapter 20

A drop of water is complete within itself, yet when it rejoins its source, it knows the strength of the ocean.

IT WAS CLOSE TO FIVE PM before Lenore returned home. There was still no word from Tetris. I updated Khalen, fed the girls, enjoyed a hot bath then joined the others in the dining hall.

"The Shadows are still lurkin' about out there," Lenore reported. "Like bloody sharks preluding a massacre."

Lena, one of the servants, placed a rare slice of roast beef on my plate. It was followed with a generous portion of creamed corn and steamed kale. Another servant delicately placed a steaming yeast roll onto my bread plate, along with a dollop of whipped honey butter. Having skipped lunch, my stomach roared with eager anticipation. Spinach salad with warm goat cheese medallions would follow the meal. For dessert, Lenore had something special planned: bananas flambe´ served with a rich dark chocolate sauce and a glass of twenty-year tawny port from Portugal. Khalen would have loved that part, I was sure.

My heart suddenly felt the void of his presence. His thoughts had been closed to me for several hours now, and I knew it was because he had contacted Sage for council. I sensed he was safe, though, and that was all that mattered at the moment. I kept myself open to him in case I was needed for healing.

To help me see what was on my plate, Lenore had the staff install full-spectrum lightbulbs in the fixtures. It didn't do much for the atmosphere. Many people grumbled about the unbearable brightness but after Lenore explained things, they calmed down. She had gone to such an effort to ensure I would have ample light to see, I didn't have the heart to tell her that a candle in front of my plate would have sufficed.

Tetris returned just in time for dessert. The expression on his aged face hadn't softened any. He said a soft prayer to the Father then silently began eating the cold meal before him.

The conversations grew quiet and all eyes trained on him. When he glanced up and noticed that he was the center of our attention, he cleared his throat before taking a long sip of his wine. Disregarding our silent inquiries, he continued eating his meal.

"What did you find out?" I finally asked.

"More than I bargained for," he replied, wiping a speck of food from his lips with his napkin.

I waited for him to say more, but he continued to eat. "Can it be done?"

"Yes, but the possible consequences must be considered."

"Consequences?" I questioned.

He glanced up at me, and then sipped his wine. "Yes."

Again, I waited for him to say more. The man's mysterious nature was grating on my nerves. I took a deep breath and decided to wait for him to volunteer the information as opposed to wrenching it out of him. It would have been easier to extract a molar from a raging bull, I determined.

"For God's sake, Tetris, speak your thoughts," Lenore demanded.

The wizard pushed his plate away, wiped his mouth then carefully refolded his napkin before setting it by his plate. He finished his wine in one lengthy gulp, gesturing for more to be poured.

"The problem lies with the gender of the shape shifter and healer," he explained. "Only males have been known to shift shapes, and it is well documented that only chosen females can heal. To merge the two would be changing the universal laws. The council advises against such action."

"Did they give you the spell?" Lenore asked.

He snorted with disgust. "This takes more than a mere spell, dear woman. This requires the cooperation of the Angels and God, Himself."

"Tetris," she barked. "Can it be done?"

"Yes, you bloody termagant, it can be done."

"What are the consequences?" I asked again.

His steely-blue eyes glowed with hints of polished pewter. "Death."

"Oh," I said, sitting back in my chair.

"I'm thinking Khalen won't approve," he added.

"No," I confirmed. "He most certainly won't."

A young man named Jez stood from the table. He couldn't have been more than twenty years old. "It's fine," he said. "I am willing to take the risk. If they do happen to have a seer among them, I will simply change shape and disappear."

The old wizard's face softened then brightened with hope. "I can offer a shield of protection, young man. If a seer scans you, my spell will provoke an instant change, giving you a chance to escape."

"Tonight," I said. "Be ready."

Jez and Tetris nodded.

We waited until the staff retired and the house fell silent. Khalen had not communicated his status but I sent him regular updates. I knew he was listening. I could also feel his trepidation.

Stay in the castle, he said in thought. *No matter what happens, understand?*

I confirmed.

Jez transformed to look like my double. It was like staring into a magical mirror where my reflection took on a life of its own.

"Like we discussed," said Zhenti. "Run from the house, screaming for help." She sent him an image of her vision and he jolted back in response before nodding apprehensively.

"Shield your fear, Jez," Grom added. "You stink like a ruddy possum."

Jez took a few breaths, trying to ease his fears.

Tetris drizzled a light dusting of blue corn meal around Jez's feet while chanting indistinct words that sounded like a series of grunts and hums. Then, with a dramatic wave of his hand, he sent Jez into motion.

The young man ran from the house, screaming with genuine fear. What happened next was nothing short of a nightmare. Jez immediately turned into a white falcon then exploded in a cloud of ash.

At the time he ran from the house, a gust of cold wind blew into the castle.

"Necromancer!" Tetris yelled. "God helps us."

Screams and darkness quickly filled the mud room where we stood. I felt Lenore's hand grip my arm as she led me down the corridor. Sunjia followed close behind. Eve had remained with the twins in my room. I prayed she had the sense to stay there. Lightning lit the sky, while unearthly roars filled the darkened walls that surrounded us.

Something grabbed Sunjia and she screamed. Lenore stopped, and shoved me behind her. "Go to the game room, now," she barked.

I could feel Sunjia's pain as she was being dragged down the hall. Closing my eyes, I concentrated on projecting a shield toward her. The scuffling was silent now. I heard grunts and Lenore cursing before delivering a lethal blow. My sight faded with the adrenaline filling my veins. I had to rely completely on my instincts now and the telltale sounds around me.

I could feel a cold presence behind me, but before it could reach for me, the coldness suddenly faded. Khalen's energy was strong around me. He was tapped into my thoughts.

"Game room," Lenore shouted. "Hurry. I have weapons there."

"It's so dark," Sunjia stated. "I can't see a thing."

I grabbed her hand. "Follow me." I relied on my memory to negotiate the long corridors, turns, and doorways leading to the game room. With Sunjia in Lenore's capable care, I left to find Eve. Lenore ordered me to stay, but it was an order I refused to obey. Eve had no protection. I had to ensure she was all right.

I easily negotiated the darkened corridors and stairs. Khalen's shield hummed strong around me. The door to my room was locked. I banged on the solid surface. "Eve, let me in."

There was no answer.

"Eve, please, let me in."

In a rage of panic, I projected my energy at the door. The frame exploded in a flurry of splinters as the lock lost its hold.

Eve lay unconscious on the floor. A blue haze surrounded the area where the twins had been. They were gone. I struggled to stay focused. For my daughters' sake, I had to. We were connected just as Khalen and I were. I could feel them. They were still in the castle.

Khalen, I thought, *place a shield around the castle. Don't let anyone leave.*

I wasn't sure if he heard me, I just had to trust that he had. I knelt down and scanned Eve's body. She had been hit with a blast of energy. Her body was shattered. I conjured the blue mist and prayed for the Father's help. My lack of concentration made the healing take longer than it should have. Chastising myself about it now, however, would be counterproductive. I had to stay focused and calm.

Eve slowly came to. I helped her stand then quickly led her to the game room where Lenore had made quick work of two unfortunate Shadows.

"Stay here," I told her. "I'm going to find the twins."

Lenore objected, but I left her words to linger among the

rising smoke and battle screams.

Following my instincts, I ventured down the corridors that led to the east yard. I had only traversed them once, when Khalen was here. There was no shield around the castle. Despite Khalen's command for me not to venture outside, I had to go. The twins were out here and I was determined to find them.

They were there, in front of the barn, in the arms of a man who had no business holding a baby let alone two of them.

"Ye can't take em on alone, lass," Lenore said from behind. Eve and Sunjia were with her, backed by half of our clansmen. In the dark, I could not tell which of them were there.

"Come here, Skye," one of the Shadows said from across the lawn. He was standing between me and the man who held my twins. I moved forward. "Alone," he clarified, as Lenore and the others moved ahead with me.

"Don't do it, lass," a man said. It sounded like Grom but his voice was much more hoarse.

I continued to move forward. "I'm not afraid of you," I boldly stated. It was true, I was not afraid of him, but I was afraid of what I thought about doing to him for taking my young. My goal, of course, was to walk right up to the man holding the girls and wrenching them out of his miserable arms. Then, I thought about crushing the man's trachea. I was a healer, I reminded myself, not a killer.

I approached the man who had commanded me forward. "Give me my young," I said calmly. The vibration around my body made my ears ache and my heart pound in cadence.

The man slowly reached for me then jerked his hand back as if touching fire. I continued to stride past him where the man stood with my young. I felt as if there were a tracking beam between me and the twins, pulling us closer. The man's eyes widened as I reached for the babes.

"Don't just stand there," the first man yelled. "Someone take her." I heard several of them try then fall back, clutching their hands in pain. The man holding my young tried to move away but his feet held firm as if bound by roots buried deep into the earth. I felt my will holding him, paralyzing his legs. I reached out and plucked my young from his arms as if taking them from a friend. Both girls were fussing, but not screaming in fear or anger. When they were safe in my arms, the man dropped to the ground and didn't move.

Still in my trance, I walked back to where the clan stood waiting. The hum surrounding me was deafening. If there were people talking, I would not have been able to hear them.

Return to the castle, I heard Khalen say. *Don't look back.*

My only concern at the moment was the safety of my young. I walked past the clansmen, Lenore, Eve, and Sunjia without even offering them a reassuring glance. It took all that I had to continue moving and not look back. I heard the thuds as one Shadow fell after another. Lightning brightened the sky as the clansmen engaged in battle. The women followed me back to the castle. I continued to walk to the game room, a path with which I was very familiar. As if sensing every obstacle, I carefully negotiated my way around the battle debris, broken furniture and rumpled rugs. The women behind me were not as fortunate. I could hear their cries of pain as they banged their legs, or tripped over an unseen obstacle. Oddly, I didn't care. I only wanted to reach the game room.

"Skye, slow down," Eve huffed. "We cannot see."

I waited until I felt her hand on my shoulder before continuing. It was more challenging negotiating with three others following my lead, but we managed to make it to the game room without any major mishaps.

My trance completely diminished now, I was able to take a full breath and clear my head. Not much of what had happened made sense. It was akin to waking from a deep sleep and trying to remember a dream.

Eve took one of the girls, while Sunjia took the other. Lenore lit several candles before pouring us all a glass of brandy. She didn't wait on ceremony to down her first portion.

I sat down with my drink in hand. My head was pounding as if it had been slammed against a rock. Instinctively, I placed my hand over my temples until the pain faded.

"What happened out there, lass?" Lenore asked. "No one could touch ye."

"I don't know," I honestly admitted. "Part of it was me, another part was Khalen. My mind and body were separate, or so it seemed."

"Aye, it was bloody odd. Never seen anythin' like it." She downed another swallow.

"You drink that stuff as if it will have an effect," Eve stated, gesturing to the near-empty bottle.

"Sometimes, I wish it did," Lenore admitted. "For now, it just gives me somethin' to do until our clan reports the outcome."

"I believe we have the advantage," I said.

The clansmen clambered down the hall, screaming our names.

"In here, ye big lugs," Lenore shouted back. "Quit yer shoutin' or you'll wake the young."

Both girls were deep asleep in the women's arms.

Five men filed into the game room, all huffing and smelling of blood and sweat. I projected my healing to them all.

"Blimey," one of them said. "Me cut is healed!"

Another one shoved him hard. "She's a healer, you vapid bloke."

Lenore began pouring whiskey for them. "Where's Grom and the others?" she asked.

"Cleanin' up the mess, missy. It's bloody awful."

"Who did we lose beside Jez?" she asked.

The largest man scratched his head. "Quite a few, lass. We took a beatin' out there."

Tetris wandered in with Grom and four others in tow. Grom was limping. His face looked as if it had weathered a thousand storms. Lenore poured them both a drink then set it down before them.

"We lost Zhenti," he said solemnly.

My chest caved, and my head throbbed with renewed force. "How?"

"She went after the papers. They cut her down like a discarded paper doll." He bent over and released a howl of pain. "I killed the bastard who did it, but it does nothing to bring her back to me."

I walked over and placed my hands on the back of his shoulders. I could remove some of his pain, but not the mourning. He needed to feel that now. We all sat in silence and allowed him to cry. To a Spirian, losing your mate was akin to losing half your soul. I couldn't even imagine losing Khalen.

When Grom was feeling better and his wails tapered to quiet sobs, I sat down across from Tetris. "When Jez was killed, you yelled something like, 'Necromancer.' What is that?"

"A black magician; the worst possible kind of soul you'd ever want to encounter." He took a sip of whiskey, scrunched his face then set the glass down. "He blasted Khalen's shield on the castle as if it were a paper bag. Jez never had a chance. As soon as he walked out to the gardens, he was pegged. My spell was dispersed and poof—no more Jez."

"Ye didn't sense him?" Lenore asked.

"No, but I should have." He ran his long fingers through his silver mane, thin and scattered by the wind.

"Tell me you got him?" Eve said, sitting with Shaiya held close to her chest.

Tetris shook his head with defeat. "No. He and at least five of his lot fled to the woods."

"Will they be back?" Sunjia asked, her voice shy and laced with apprehension.

"Oh, most definitely, and in greater numbers."

"It's me, they're after," I said. "If I leave, they won't come back."

"No, lass," one of the older men stated. "This war is long in comin'. The tides been shiftin' for quite some time. Ye see, when odds weigh too heavy in one's favor, the other must act to restore balance. You have much to do with this, aye, but you are not the only freckle on the Spirian whole."

Lenore leaned forward toward the old wizard. "Tetris, are

you any match at all for this necromancer?"

"If we went at it, one-to-one, you bet I am. By birth, on both sides of my blood, I'm a third generation wizard. I am his opposing equal. There is one difference, however."

"What's that?" I asked.

"He doesn't comply with the laws that have been set forth by the Council. He's a rebel, a black demon with no integrity."

"Why doesn't the Council stop him?" asked Sunjia.

"For the same reason God does not eliminate Lucifer. It is the law of the universe, my dear. For every good, there is an equal and opposite evil. If Baru, the necromancer, is destroyed, another will take his place. It is the indisputable law of balance that we are facing right now. The Shadows are seeking power. When they believe they have taken enough from us, things will settle. Such has been the ebb and flow of our race for thousands of years."

"Was Baru born into the Shadows?" I asked.

The old wizard frowned. "No. He was turned, my dear, like many of us Spirians. They, no doubt, want to turn you and your young as well."

Now it was my turn to frown. The twins were too young to reveal their gifts, and I was a healer. "What good is a healer to them?" I asked.

"If turned, Skye, they will use you to cause harm, not heal. You have the ability to remove pain and heal wounds. On the darker side, you also have the ability to cause pain and create injuries. You are a perfect weapon."

My stomach wrenched. How many times had I imagined myself causing harm to those Shadows? Too many, for my comfort. "Why didn't Baru stop me from retrieving my young from that Shadow who held them?"

"Oh, he tried. For some odd reason, no one could blast through that shield that surrounded you."

"Yet they blasted through Khalen's bind on the castle?"

Tetris scratched his head. "All I can say is that you had some help, may it be from the Father, his Angels, or a combination of all that is good. Unless it is your will, the Shadows cannot turn a legend."

"Choosing to be a Shadow will never be my will," I stated defiantly.

"Never is a powerful word," said Tetris, "even for a legend."

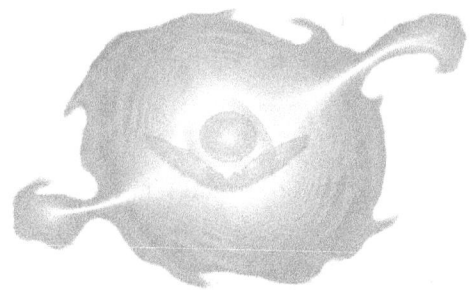

Chapter 21

Fear is the gateway through which evil enters.

~ K h a l e n ~

MY MIND WAS SPLIT BETWEEN my present business with Sage and my mate. Aidan stood with me, while the others waited in Union. When I felt the blast of my bind on the castle erupt, something inside me snapped like a tendon being stretched too thin. With Shanuk's help, I was able to protect her enough to retrieve our young.

Sage agreed to meet us in Hoodsport at an old abandoned shed in the woods. It was a vile place, but private and far from civilization.

He played dumb about our missing friends, but his intentions betrayed his lie. Taking lessons from my father, I demonstrated my disapproval with several painful shocks. The young leader screamed and jittered on the ground like a stunned sparrow with a broken wing.

"Where are my clansmen?" I asked again.

"If I tell you, they'll kill me," he stammered.

"If you don't, I'll kill you." My voice was calm but solid as steel.

"You know what that means if you do," he said.

"I warned you once, Sage. You chose not to listen. Now, your clans are out of control. You leave me no choice but to act. Now, I will ask one more time before I end your miserable life. Where are my clansmen?"

Sage writhed in agony, tears streaming down his pale face. "God, please stop."

"You have five minutes of this agony before I end it. It will soon feel like an hour, I assure you."

"Ahg," Sage yelled. He curled into a ball and gnashed his teeth. After three minutes had passed, he sucked in a deep breath, and blurted, almost indistinguishably, "Okay, okay. I'll tell you. Make it stop, please."

I pulled my energy back a bit, offering him a slight tingle that was just enough to keep him down. "Start talking."

"They're in a hold in Sequim. Carter's clan has them."

"And they're waiting for me?"

"No."

I hit him with another blast of energy. His screams echoed off the solid walls. "Something tells me you're lying again, Sage. Care to try again?"

"They're in cohorts with the clans in Scotland. If all goes well, your friends will be released."

"You have failed to control your clans, Sage. There will be repercussions." I pulled my energy back and left with Aidan in close pursuit.

"He'll warn the others," Aidan said. "Ye can't let him walk."

This was the one part about my status as a leader that churned my gut. Aidan was right. Sage was a loose cannon on a fragile deck. With a quick and lethal thought, I dropped the young leader where he stood. He never knew what hit him. I Immediately felt the drain on my energy and nearly collapsed.

"Come on," Aidan said. "Just make it to the car. You'll have time to rest in Union."

Case and Arcadie met us in the driveway after receiving an update from Aidan. Maiyun fell close in line. I was ushered inside then Case held my feet while Arcadie held my shoulders. Slowly, my energy returned. Ian handed me a glass of water. Maiyun laid her head on my lap. Since I had returned home, she had not left my side. I was sure she wondered where Skye was. I had no way of telling her. My telepathic communication seemed just as ambiguous to her as my words. Instead, I rubbed the space between her eyes the way I had seen Skye do multiple times. It seemed to calm her.

"Victor won't be pleased," Case mentioned.

Arcadie sat across from me and kicked his feet up. "His son was out of line. I say young Sage had it coming."

"I'm not arguing that point, dear brother, I'm merely stating the obvious."

I gulped a few swallows of water, the coolness of it calming my gut. "We need to keep pushing them back until they realize that we are not an amenable foe. If they begin to lose too many men, they will realize that their feeble attacks cost far too much to continue."

Arcadie sat up and poured himself a cup of tea. "From what I understand, the real battle is happing in Scotland. I hear they took a painful hit." His steely eyes rested on me. "Zhenti was killed."

I lowered my head and said a heartfelt prayer for her and her mate. "We need to get back." I looked over at Ian. "Can you handle releasing our friends?"

"Of course," he said. "I'll have them back home by evening's end." He glanced over at Caleb and Drew. "Come on," he gestured toward the door, "let's have some fun."

"Ian," I called out. He turned. "They're expecting me. Be mindful."

He nodded, grabbed his coat then called Maiyun to come. "Come on Maiyun, you cannot stay here."

Maiyun groaned then laid on top of my feet. When Ian came to get her, she released a low growl.

"Fine then, you ungrateful mongrel. Stay with Khalen." He scratched her under her chin then winked up at me. "She's all yours, Brother."

"I'll take care of her."

I looked to Arcadie. "How soon can we leave?"

Dirk answered in his father's stead. "I'll have the jets fueled and prepped in an hour. The young man had stayed out of the line of fire, but had proven himself useful in the periphery of the action. He had a good sense of what to expect and managed to always stay two steps ahead. His father was not disappointed, nor was I.

"Thank you," I said. "Take your brother Darius and the others with you."

The hurt on his face was evident, but there was a layer of understanding etched in the corner of his lips as well.

"Dirk," I said as he and the men were leaving. He turned. "You will make a fine warrior one day."

He bowed in response. "If it's my path," he replied then left.

As he had promised, the jets were ready to leave when we arrived. The men were grateful to return home. It had been an exhausting hunt that was laden with disappointment and little action. The clan was primed and ready for battle, only to find petty brawls that led to nowhere. The real action was back in Scotland. We were all anxious to return to our families, especially me.

Darius met us at the plane. He was about to say something when my phone rang.

It was Victor—what a surprise. "Hello, Victor," I answered.

"How dare you take my only son," he roared. "You had no right!"

"I had every right. He lost control of his clans. They've taken my people, attacked my clan, and have threatened my family. Know this, if it does not cease, more lives will be lost."

"I don't take well to petty threats, young man."

"I don't make threats, Victor. Your son would attest to that—if he could speak."

"Take care on your journey home, Khalen. I hear the wind kicks up all sorts of nasty things." The phone clicked then beeped twice, indicating the call had been terminated.

I had a vision of birds swarming. "Arcadie, I suggest you place a bird shield around your engines."

"Why?"

"I have a feeling we are about to encounter a massive flock of them in our flight."

"Oh, I don't like your feelings," Darius said. "I think I'll be ridin' with Dirk and the others."

"Perfect," Aidan muttered, as he sauntered toward our plane. "What's one more adventure, I suppose."

A FLOCK OF BIRDS WAS AN understatement. Before we reached altitude, a swarm of seagulls came at us, thick and black as a locus storm.

"Hang on," Arcadie shouted. "It's about to get rough."

The plane lurched left then shimmied. The right engined choked, sputtered then died. It looked as if the bird shield had been pried apart.

"God, I can't see a thing through this mess," Arcadie grumbled.

I willed the window clean of blood and feathers. "Can you take us up?"

"I need you to remove the obstruction from the right engine?"

I looked out the window and used my gift to peer through the steel hull of the engine. There were pieces of bird everywhere. Bit by bit, I began removing them telekinetically, grateful for the gift more than I had ever been.

"Try it now," I yelled.

The right engine whirred, sparked, and then coughed back to life.

Case had placed an energetic shield around the left engine, and now moved to place one on the right.

"I'm taking her up," Arcadie explained.

An explosion of conversation flooded the radio, asking why we had veered off course. Arcadie keyed the mic and announced our situation. What came back as a reply was almost comical.

"There can't be birds at that altitude. Are you sure you're seeing right?"

"Bloody hell," Arcadie roared. "Of course I know what I'm seeing, you dolt, I have enough seagull carcasses on my hull to feed an entire ocean. Now how high can I go?"

The man on the radio voiced a series of numbers then ended the conversation with a few choice words.

"Dirk," Arcadie called. "Come in, Son."

"Do you miss me already?" Dirk replied.

Arcadie's shoulders visibly dropped. "We had a run in with a slew of seagulls. What's your location?"

Dirk read off his coordinates.

"You're heading straight for them. You'd better change altitude."

"Father, there's nothing here. The sky is clear for miles. Are you sure you saw birds this high up?"

Arcadie looked up, took a deep breath then keyed the mic. "We'll discuss it later. Just be aware."

"Uh—all right."

"An illusion, perhaps?" Case muttered.

"Look at my bloody plane, lad. This is not an illusion."

"Definitely not an illusion," Aidan confirmed.

I peered out the windows in search of anything odd. "Skye mentioned that they were attacked by a necromancer named Baru."

"Ah, old Baru," Arcadie chimed.

"You know him?" Case inquired.

"Far too well, I'm afraid. He's a member of Canis' clan. I wonder what he's doing teaming with Victor."

"Perhaps Canis has designs on gaining territories in the States?" said Aidan.

Arcadie shrugged one shoulder. "Perhaps. Most likely, though, he has his sights on Victor's territories—all of them."

"No," Case countered, "Victor is too smart for that. He would know if Canis had ill intentions."

Arcadie spun his captain's chair around to face us. "Canis' clan is strong. If he had ill intentions, Victor would not be able to stop him."

"True," Case admitted. "Then what would bring Victor to join forces with the man?"

Something caught my eye. I stood and peered out the windows.

"What is it?" Case asked.

"Khalen," Arcadie said, staring out his front window. "Contact your mate. Have her send Tetris to our location. We are going to need his help."

A blue wing caught my attention as a huge dragon glided past.

I contacted Skye and quickly filled her in.

"Khalen, help me place a shield around the plane," Case ordered.

As we projected our energies outward to include the plane, we felt the bolt of the dragon's opposition.

"Khalen, give him something else to think about," Aidan suggested.

I reached out with my energy and grabbed the dragon's

tail. He whipped around and I grabbed his wing. In his moment of confusion, Case was able to form a solid shield.

"Is that Baru?" I asked, still having fun with my telekinetic game of tag.

"No doubt," Arcadie answered.

Baru slammed into the plane then screeched and drew back as the shock of Case's shield delivered a powerful blast.

Case continued to strengthen the shield as I distracted the dragon. A wall of flame draped over the plane but the shield held firm.

"I suppose the tower doesn't see this on their radar either?" Arcadie announced.

"I don't believe they would," said Aidan.

In the distance, I saw another dragon approaching, white with gold-tipped wings.

"Ah," Case said. "My good friend, Tetris." He stood and arranged himself for a better view. "This isn't something you see in a lifetime."

"You almost look like you're enjoying this," I said.

"Wizards are rare among Spirians. Seeing two of them at odds is even rarer. Of course I'm excited."

As Baru made the first attack. The plane pitched to the right. I fell back against wall before tumbling to the floor and into Aidan. Maiyun scrambled out of the way, hiding behind Arcadie.

"Whoa," Arcadie said. "That was too close." He righted our course and the right engine rumbled in protest.

Case pierced Baru with a stinging blow. "Ha, ha, did you see that?"

I peeled myself off the floor. "I don't suppose you see this as a dangerous situation?"

"Perhaps just a bit," Case replied, looking like a kid at an underwater park gaping at hungry, leering sharks.

Tetris didn't waste time countering the attack. He moved in like a bird of prey going after a tasty meal, his dark eyes sparkling. Apparently, he was enjoying the challenge as much as my father.

Sparks flashed in the sky as the two beasts brawled with claws and razor-edged tails. Fire spewed between them. Again, Case projected a painful blow and Baru wailed. Tetris bit the blue dragon, tearing its wing. Baru howled, shook himself free then descended below the clouds. Tetris followed.

Moments later, Tetris flew beside the plane, his scales scorched and clawed, but in fair shape considering. In a flash, he appeared in the cabin.

Maiyun growled, ears flat and eyes focused on the old man. I smoothed down her hackles.

"Easy, girl. He's a friend."

Tetris walked by the growling dog without a care then slumped down in a chair.

"You're getting old, my friend," Case chuckled, pouring the old wizard a drink.

Tetris looked up at him with steely eyes. "Who's the bitch?"

"Maiyun," I answered. "Skye's service dog."

The old man offered the back of his hand for Maiyun to smell. Once she deemed him worthy, he scratched under her chin and behind her ears. "Now what would you have done if I had growled back, my friend," he asked her, not really expecting an answer.

"I hear you had some excitement in our absence," Case inquired.

"Oh, a sad site of it, my friend. We suffered a painful loss." His eyes shifted to me. "Your mate nearly shocked the life from us, my boy."

"Yes, she has that effect," I replied.

"A true leader, that one." He stood and walked over to Arcadie. "That was a mighty display of flying skills, young man."

"I consider that a compliment coming from an old dragon."

"Ha," Tetris howled, slapping Arcadie on the shoulder.

Case glanced out the window. "Where's our old friend, Baru?"

Tetris laughed. "Licking his wounds and running tail-tucked for home, I imagine."

"Any reason why Canis has teamed up with Victor?" Case asked him.

Tetris took a hardy drink then pinched his thick silver brows in deep thought. "None that I can think of."

While the two men caught each other up, Aidan slept using Maiyun as a pillow while I contacted Skye to ensure her that we were all right. I didn't tell her that Maiyun was with me. I wanted it to be a surprise.

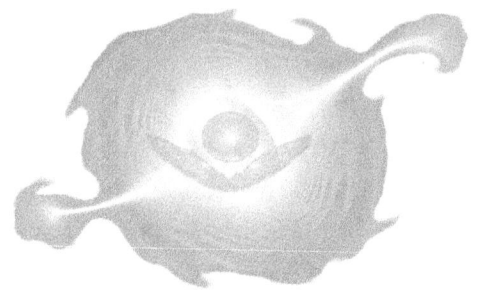

Chapter 22

*To understand a tree, you must grow roots and bare the
weight of your own branches.*

~ S k y e ~

KHALEN WAS SAFE FOR NOW and Tetris was with him.
I wondered if the necromancer's attack was just a ploy
to distract the old wizard then thought better of it. Tetris
could return with a mere thought. It was a gift granted only
to wizards, I was told.

I was holding Kaili in the dark, rocking her gently to
sleep when a thunderous sound of boot steps shattered my
candle-lit stillness.

"Skye, Skye!" Sunjia shouted as she whipped through the
door.

"What is it," I whispered.

"It's Ian. He's injured and needs your help."

I didn't take the time to ask her how she knew this. I

tapped into him and sensed his injury. He had been sliced through the stomach. There was no damage to his organs, but his artery had been cut and he was bleeding severely. I mended that first before sealing the wound. There was nothing I could do about the blood loss.

Caleb was with him. He knew enough about doctoring to help Ian further. For now, he was out of immediate danger. I breathed deep and released the connection.

"Is he all right?" Sunjia asked, panic sharpening her voice.

"Yes, for now. He's lost a lot of blood. Knowing Ian, though, he's stubborn enough to pull through."

"Oh," Sunjia plopped onto the bed. "Thank God." With hesitance, she asked her next question. "Any word from Khalen?"

"Yes. They're on their way home. Aidan is with him." I left out the part about Baru, not wanting to give the poor woman more to fret over. She had been a nervous wreck since the attack. I wasn't sure how much more she could take.

I laid Kaili down beside her sister. It seemed all they did was eat and sleep at this age. Like me, both of them enjoyed their baths. I made it a point to rub plenty of extra-virgin olive oil over their delicate skin before drying them off. After miserably failing at the task of cutting their tiny fingernails, I gladly gave that task to Eve.

I glanced over at Sunjia, who bore a solemn expression. "Do you miss your children?" I asked.

"Yes, I wasn't expecting to be away from them for so long."

"I'm sure Ian is taking good care of them."

"And how does Ian define 'good care?'" she asked, a sly smile curing her lips.

"Plenty of sweets, late nights, dangerously large bonfires—"

"And ice cream and cheerios for breakfast," she finished for me.

Both of us laughed.

"Do you think he will ever find a mate?" she asked.

"Yes, I do."

"Eve and Lenore are waiting for us in the game room. Did you want to join them?"

I glanced down at my soundly-sleeping young and sighed. Sleeping sounded like such a splendid idea, but I was too amped up to calm my mind enough to rest. "Sure," I said. "Let's go." A glass of Pinot Noir sounded perfect.

As if having read my thoughts, Lenore, bless her heart, had a glass of the mild red wine primed and waiting for me. She and Eve were in a heated game of cribbage. Eve was twenty-three points in the lead.

"Bollocks!" Lenore exclaimed. "I'm finally dealt a decent hand and I'm givin' me points away."

"Well, I do appreciate the gift, my dear," Eve chimed.

"Aye, I bet ye do." She laid her cards down then cut the deck.

"Our men will be home soon," I said.

"Aye. Darius said they'll be here by mornin'"

"Are there any Shadows lurking?" Sunjia asked hesitantly.

"No, lass. There will be no excitement tonight, rest assured."

Sunjia rocked forward, her hands clasped together. "How do you know?"

Lenore laid down a card. "Seven," she announced then

reached over to touch Sunjia's hand. "Because we hit'em where it hurts, lass. It will take them some time to recover."

"Fifteen," Eve said victoriously then moved her peg two holes forward.

"Bloody figures," Lenore grumbled. She laid another card down. "Twenty-five."

"Ha," Eve chirped. "Thirty-one." She moved her peg to the finishing hole. "I believe you've been skunked, my dear."

"That I have, lass. That I have." Lenore folded her cards then proceeded to fill her glass with something much stronger than wine.

"How did you find out about Ian?" I finally asked Sunjia.

"Caleb called here." She pointed to the phone on the wall. "He said you weren't answering your cell phone."

I thought for a moment then remembered that I had left my phone in our original room. "Oh, it must still be upstairs."

"It's probably safe for you all to move up there again," said Lenore. "The initial danger is over."

"How can you be so sure?" asked Sunjia. "You seem eerily calm about all this."

Lenore rolled her eyes. "I've been through enough of these skirmishes to know how the Shadows think, m'dear."

"Do they happen here a lot?" Eve asked.

"They seem to every ten years or so."

I sipped my wine, savoring the fruity flavor on my tongue. "Well I, for one, am planning to move my things upstairs tonight. I'm ready for a hot bath, a good book, and candle light."

"Mmm," Eve hummed. "Sounds lovely."

Lenore picked up the phone, issued a slurry of orders

then came back to join us. "I've asked the staff to move your things back to your rooms."

"Oh, Lenore, they must be exhausted after having to clean up the battle mess. They shouldn't have to do more," I explained.

"That's what I pay them for," she countered. "And they get paid very well, I assure ye. Besides, the women did most of the clean up. The men are the ones who are movin' your stuff."

Eve stood. "Not the young." She rushed out of the game room and headed toward the basement.

"A little over protective, that one," said Lenore, gesturing toward the exit that Eve had taken.

"Just a little," I replied.

I wondered how Maiyun would take to the young. Would she be just as protective of them as Eve? I highly doubted it. Visions of the young climbing over Maiyun's strong back filled my head with playful thoughts, making me smile.

After three hours of cribbage, idle talk, and watching the men play darts, I was ready to retire for the night. My bath would have to wait for morning. I didn't want to ruin the welcoming fatigue any more than necessary. I needed a good night's sleep. With Lenore so confident that there wouldn't be another attack, I was determined to rest deep and long.

The twins squirmed a bit as I gave them both a kiss good night. Feeling Khalen's absence, I dressed a pillow in one of his Shirts. With a sigh, I snuggled up against it, closing my eyes.

This room was much warmer than the one in the basement. It was a welcoming change. The bed was firmer as well. Without much prompting, I breathed deep and drifted into blissful oblivion.

As promised, the men arrived mid-morning. When Maiyun trotted down the ramp by Khalen's side, tears welled in my eyes. I wasn't sure who to hug first. Khalen made the decision for me while Maiyun protested with verbal howls and grunts.

"Fine," Khalen grunted. "I'll share her, but only for an instant."

Reluctantly, he let me go. Maiyun plowed into me with such force, I was knocked to the ground. She took full advantage and gave my face a drenching tongue bath. She wouldn't stand still long enough for me to hug her. She danced around the way she did as a puppy—too eager to stay in her own skin.

Khalen held our young as he beamed me a smile. "Happy?"

"Oh yes, very." I managed to get Maiyun to stay still long enough to give her a hug. Her scent was a tonic to my senses; sweet, sharp, and delightfully familiar. I smiled back at Khalen. "Thank you."

"You're very welcome, my love."

With everyone home, a large brunch was served. Monte Christos, cooked to perfection, towered on our plates, drizzled with fine powdered sugar, cinnamon, and fresh strawberry jam. A warm apple crisp was served with it. Champagne circulated about the table, but I was more interested in coffee than the sweet bubbly drink. Khalen held onto my hand as if I would slip away should he let go. I had to admit, I loved the display of possession he showed. It felt strange admitting that truth, but it was, indeed, the truth.

Stories about the battles drifted through the air, mingled with the sadness of loss. Khalen reported that Ian had found the missing clansmen and brought them home. He had been attacked by a lucky bloke wielding a machete of all things. Ian caught it square in the gut. Caleb reported that he was doing fine, but refuses to rest until his strength has returned.

Aidan laughed at that one, knowing his brother far too well. "Just wave a bottle of Irish Scotch in front of him and a plump little blonde. His strength will return in no time."

A roar of laugher resounded through the room. It was a sound my soul had been hungry for. Despite my aching sides, I didn't want it to end.

Tetris and Case recounted the battle of the dragons, while Arcadie stood by to exploit their exaggerations. By the time brunch had ended, our bellies were blissfully full and sore from all the laughter that ensued. I had to relieve myself but I was surrounded by the twins, Maiyun, and Khalen. I didn't want to disturb that, no matter how uncomfortable I felt.

Later that morning, we had a ceremony for the loved-ones who were lost in battle. The bodies were burned and scattered to the four winds with a blessing. Khalen, Arcadie, and Case were planning to pay Canis a visit. They had promised to return by nightfall. Aidan chose to remain with Sunjia.

I spent the afternoon helping Lenore tend the gardens. The twins laid on a blanket in the sun, cooing and enjoying the sights and sounds around them. Children engaged themselves in a mild game of rugby near the lake, while Eve helped bake bread in the kitchen. Aidan and Sunjia had gone for a long walk. I wasn't expecting to see either of them soon. Tetris and the others returned home. He was eager to see his mate and family.

With Maiyun by my side, my young happy and healthy, and my mate home and safe, I was content. I did miss our clan and the gatherings by the fire, but in a strange sense, this also seemed like home. I had been born here, and had returned. The circle was complete. What the future would bring was anyone's guess.

Eve had told me that Case wanted to return to our clan in Washington. He could see how miserable she was back in England, separate from her son and family. She had also agreed to return to England with him every six months.

The castle here, on the beautiful Island of Skye, was mine, I was told. Lenore and Darius, of course, promised to keep the place in pristine condition, as they had for the past fifty years.

I left the documents that Shanuk had given to me in Arcadie's care. He promised to visit the high council to address the matter of my blood and name. Before the twins could be officially documented as full-blooded Spirians of Shanuk's prestigious line, my own origins had to be proven and documented. Arcadie assured me that Shanuk had consulted with the council previously and that what Arcadie had to do was a mere formality, nothing more.

Eve was planning another dinner by the fire this evening. It was a rare day in fall when the sky was clear and the weather was amiable. I figured Grom had something to do with that. The sky seemed to clear as he was leaving.

I imagined he wanted to take the gloom with him to

share his grief. He and Khalen had exchanged words later this morning. Grom wanted to explain his mate's ill-actions, but Khalen dismissed them, stating that what happened was over. No repercussions would incur. Khalen offered his full forgiveness to Grom, setting the man free from all guilt and remorse for what had transpired as a result.

I could sense the relief in the old man, but there was still something amiss in his manner. I credited it to the loss of his mate.

Lenore held up a thick stalk of brussels sprouts. "Would ye look at this dandy stock of sprouts."

"Save the leaves," I told her. "They're fabulous in soups."

"Really?" She looked at the sturdy plant with new wonder. "I've never tried them."

I pointed to the garlic sprouts to the left. "Those, too, are good in vegetable dishes. They give the food a garlic-flavored onion zeal."

"Do you cut the entire stalk?" she asked.

"No, just the ones on the outside. The inner ones you leave alone. And only cut them half way down, not too close to the dirt."

Lenore harvested the greens with revived enthusiasm. "I'm glad you're here," she said. "I'll sorely miss you when you go."

"Oh, we'll return on a regular basis, I'm sure of it. I want the girls to know their aunt and uncle."

Lenore blushed for the first time since I met her. For my eyes to pick up the color, even in bright sunlight, it must have been a rare sight. Darius was true blood to the family now, but not through Khalen, through me. Darius and I were cousins.

She dropped her bounty and offered me a dirt-laden hug. "Thank you," she whispered. "I will miss those babes of yours."

"Well, if Khalen has his wish, which I'm sure you know he will, there will many more to follow in their wake."

"No wonder the Shadows are worried," she laughed. "A brood of Khalen's and a powerful healer are something to consider for sure."

"God help us all," I added.

"Amen." She drew the sign of the cross over her ample chest.

Khalen, Arcadie, and Case returned shortly before the sun fell past the horizon. The bonfire was already blazing as the food cooked slowly in a large cast-iron kettle over a bed of glowing embers. Lamb stew was on the menu, served with Eve's fresh bread and herbed goat butter. The wafting aroma caused my stomach to voice its approval.

I had taken my bath with my young, and was dressed in a white cotton shirt and pants that flowed on my body like a summer breeze. Lenore said it nearly screamed my name as she walked past it in the store. The colorful stitching that adorned the front of the shirt and pant hems gave the garment a Native American flare. My stomach had not yet returned to its original size, but it had firmed up quite a bit since the birth of my twins. I had even managed to lose a few pounds, due to breast feeding, I was sure.

Khalen stepped from the boat that took him across the lake and immediately cast his eyes upon me. I could feel the warmth of their golden glow as he looked beyond the garment. My face blushed.

Without a word, he lifted me effortlessly into his arms, carried me across the courtyard, into the castle, and straight to our room. He told Maiyun to stay outside with the others. She reluctantly obeyed.

Two hours later, we continued to lay in each other's arms, hair tangled and damp. He smelled of sweat and sex and I loved it.

He drizzled soft kisses over my shoulders and neck then worked his way up to my ardent lips. Time stood still when he loved me and nothing else seemed to matter. I was lost in the way of his touch, the feel of his body merging with mine. I hungered for him.

"I love you, mate," he said, his voice husky and low.

We managed to join the others several hours later. We were lucky there was still some stew left. Eve saved a loaf of bread for us and Case approached with two glasses of Barolo, a perfect choice for the meal.

"Nice that you could join us," he said with a knowing smile.

"Well," Khalen admitted, "I did have other ideas, but Skye insisted that we join the family."

Maiyun greeted us briefly then quickly returned to a group of teenagers who were generously sharing their meals with her.

Eve gave her son a lingering hug. "Well, I'm glad that you're here. This is our last night and I wanted it to be special."

My eyes widened. "We're going home?"

"Yes, I didn't get a chance to tell you, my love."

Truth be told, he had plenty of chances to tell me, he just

chose to spend them making sweet love, instead. I was not complaining—not in the least.

Chapter 23

*Love is like fire, it melts your inhibitions, warms your soul,
and singes with its absence.*

WHEN WE RETURNED HOME, IT was like stepping
through a time warp. The camp had been completely
revamped, including the many huts that housed our families,
the pens that sheltered our livestock, and the gardens that
flourished with color.

I wanted to settle into our yurt, but kept getting distracted.
One of the young boys, named Abel, took our bags, while his
older brother, Graham, ushered me to see the new homes
that had gone up in our absence. All I really wanted was a hot
bath and a glass of wine. Eve scampered away with the twins,
while Maiyun was smart. She followed Abel into our yurt and
stayed there. I should have done the same.

Caleb's mate, Dania, had prepared a fabulous meal of
spaghetti with fat meatballs, and raspberry spinach salad. We
would all be able to enjoy it by the fires in a few hours. I was
hoping to rest some before the meal, but that didn't look too

promising.

Khalen and I visited Ember. She looked worse for the wear and was currently sleeping. I offered a general healing to her then let her rest.

Next we paid Gregg and Ro a visit. They too were sleeping and looked to have aged at least ten years. I gave them a general healing as well then left.

"Will they be all right?" I asked Khalen.

He shrugged. "Ian said their spirits had been broken. Neither of them said much on the way home. They'll heal soon enough. For now, they need food and rest."

Ian approached us with a mischievous smile etched on his face. He was up to something; I doubted it was any good.

"Come," said Khalen, taking my hand. "We have something to show you before it gets dark."

I allowed him to lead me back to the pasture. I saw small herds of goats, sheep, and two calves. Another pen housed turkeys and other variations of fowl. Then, something caught my attention. A young mare, barely a Paint with only a single white spot on her belly. She looked at us through large, brown eyes. The white blaze that dominated her face was stained with green and mud. Her color was a rich liver chestnut.

As if quite bored with our presence, she kept her tail turned toward us and stared out at the distant trees.

"Where did you find her?" I asked, curious about her indifference.

Ian shoved Khalen, prompting him to tell the story.

"No," said Khalen, "this is yours to tell."

"This little mare is how we were able to find our missing clansmen," Ian said with pride. "She's a bit temperamental, but smart beyond measure. You see, she was a prisoner, too. I'm not sure how she was captured, because the poor bloke who kept her died shortly after attacking Drew. Unfortunately, he was the only one who knew where our friends were kept."

"Where were they?" I asked, my curiosity peaked.

"This little lass," he said, gesturing to the stand-offish mare, "was wildly running along the far fence line. It was Caleb's idea to set her free, so we did. She led us to a large rock then bolted to keep her distance. Confused, we walked away. Again, she ran to the large rock, snorted and pawed the ground. I suggested that we try to move the boulder. For Caleb, that was an easy feat. With a wave of his hand, the boulder rolled to the side and revealed a long and narrow cave. Our friends were found in the belly of it, cold, starving, and barely conscious. We helped them from their damp hell hole and brought them to the truck. The mare was gone when we emerged from the cave, or so we thought."

She must have known we were talking about her but feigned indifference. She swished her tail and stood with one leg relaxed.

"She looks like she's in pain," I said. "She won't put weight on that leg."

"Aye, it's injured. You see, as we were loading our friends into the truck, some crazy bloke comes out of nowhere and slices me in the belly with a machete. Caleb and Drew made quick work of him. After helping me into the truck, Caleb made the call to you. While on the phone, this mare comes running up and charges him from behind. Drew sees her coming, jumps out of the car, and creates a shield around us. The mare runs into the shield, gets royally miffed after receiving a very confusing shock then proceeds to kick the truck. In the process, she injures her leg."

"So you brought her here." I stated the obvious. "What are we going to do with her after I heal her?"

"I was kind of hoping we could keep her."

I looked at Khalen who now stood with both hands in the air. "Hey, don't look at me. This was his idea."

"I bet it was," I said. "So how did you get her here?"

"Caleb borrowed the horse trailer that was parked nearby. Drew used his powers of persuasion to guide her in, and here she is."

"She doesn't look too happy about it," I said. I opened the gate and ventured toward her.

"Easy lass, I'm not sure you want to get too close to that one. She's not too fond of people."

"Perfect," I muttered. This was all I needed; a rogue mare with an attitude. I continued to walk toward her then felt the hum of a shield forming around me. "I'll be okay, Khalen. Remove your shield." The mare would be able to feel the hum, I was sure, and she already knew the pain it could cause. I didn't want to give her more reason to fear me. If she did try to attack, I knew Khalen would fell her where she stood with absolutely no regrets.

She immediately pinned her ears and shook her head. I ignored the gesture and gathered the rope that hung from a nail outside her shed. I walked around to meet her head on, the way a lead mare would in the wild. If she attempted to turn away, I was prepared to swing the rope in a lazy fashion and tap her on the rump. Turning her rump to me was rude and I wanted her to know that I knew that. If I had been a lead mare, I would simply bite her for displaying such behavior. Lacking a long neck and large incisors, however, I was forced to use a rope to make my point.

Again, the mare pinned her ears in mock warning. I could sense the pain in her eyes and her intention was not to harm me. She didn't trust humans. That was obvious. God knew what had happened to her in the past.

When she started to turn away, I began swinging the rope. This got her attention. She turned to face me and I lowered the rope. Now we were speaking the same language. I took another step toward her. When I got close enough, I held out the back of my hand and allowed her to smell it. Then, I waited for her to lower her head with acceptance. I knew better than to touch her face. She would have considered the gesture rude and would retract the small amount of respect she had offered me. Instead, I lightly rubbed her neck then gave her a gentle scratch on her withers. Her skin shimmied in response as if averting a fly. Keeping an eye on her head in case she decided to take a chunk out of me, I began healing her leg.

She lowered her head further then chanced a bit of weight on her leg. Feeling no pain, she tucked her back legs under her then lunged away from the shed, squealing and kicking up her heels. I didn't expect any gratitude, which was good, because she wasn't about to show any. I picked up the rope and carried it out of the pasture.

"Khalen's right," said Ian. "You're good with horses."

I gave my mate a speculative glance. "Don't expect miracles," I said. "She's obviously been through a lot."

"Well," said Khalen. "If anyone can heal her spirit, it'll be you, my love."

"Right now, I'm exhausted and ready for a hot bath."

His lips curled into a devious smile. "I have another surprise for you."

"Does it involve putting my feet up and soaking in hot water?"

Ian raised both his hands. "I have chores to do," he said then hastened his way toward the feed shed.

"Perhaps," Khalen replied. "Come." He took my hand and led me back to our yurt.

The front door had been replaced by a sturdier one made from cherry wood. On the top was a stained window in the shape of the setting sun.

"Oh, I like this," I said, admiring the smooth surface.

"There's more," he said, opening the door. He slid a panel on what used to be a wall and revealed a private bathroom, fully equipped with a sunken tub and an open shower with no walls. Five shower heads protruded from the wall, all adjustable. The bath was already filled with hot water. Several candles surrounded the tub, and a glass of red wine sat waiting on the corner. He reached over and pressed a button. The book I had been listening to on my iPhone began to play.

I turned and wrapped my arms around his thick shoulders. "This," I said, kissing his neck and chest, "is perfect."

He stepped back and kissed the back of my hand. "Enjoy, my love. I expect to be properly thanked when you are done." His brows raised as he closed the door.

So there I was, in blissful darkness with only the sound of my book to fill the space of time. I shed my clothes, allowed them to drift to the floor then carefully stepped into the steaming water. There were two floating candles in the tub.

I TOOK LONGER THAN AN HOUR to emerge. Wrapped in a plush lavender towel, I gathered my clothes from the floor, and then padded my way across the room. Khalen lay waiting on the bed, naked and alluring. As I approached, he sat up and wasted no time in removing my towel. A deep, throaty growl rumbled in his chest. "How do you command my body so completely?" he purred.

I gently pushed him back onto the bed. "I will show you." As promised, I thanked him royally for the gift. Or did he thank me? It didn't matter. When he loved me, everything made sense.

Maiyun looked up from her cozy bed and collection of bones, groaned loudly as if asking us to keep it down, and then drifted back to sleep.

Hours later, a knock sounded on our door. Khalen covered us up while clearing his throat. "Come in."

"Come join us for dinner, Son," Case said. "The clan is waiting."

"Give us a minute," he groaned.

I swung my legs out of bed, but he pulled me back and kissed me. "We'll continue this later," he said.

"Perhaps we can eat quickly and retire?" I suggested.

His expression reflected my own thoughts. Not a chance. When the clan ate together, nothing finished quickly. It was guaranteed to be a long night of food, drink and conversation. I loved it and had missed it for far too long. Khalen did as well, despite his sluggishness to leave our bed and get dressed.

Brushing damp hair is synonymous to untangling silk

threads in the wind. It seemed the more I brushed, the more tangled my hair became. I groaned with frustration. Khalen took the brush from my hand and gestured for me to sit on a stool. I did, grateful for all the help I could get.

"It'll be cold out there," he said. "Did you want one of my sweaters?"

Odd question, seeing I had plenty of sweaters of my own. Still, the thought of having his scent wrapped around me did sound rather enticing.

"Sure," I said. "I'd like that."

After managing to tame my stubborn tangles, he draped a large white cable-knit sweater over my head. "I like having your scent on my clothes," he said.

I laughed. "Even when it competes with fire smoke and salty air?"

He nuzzled my neck with his face and breathed in a hefty breath. "Yes."

"Okay," I said, gently pushing him back. "At this rate, my love, Case will be banging down our door."

"Ugh," he moaned. "Very well."

Maiyun, having found a new surge of enthusiasm for life, jumped up and met us at the door. She had grown to learn that when food and kids mingle, there was sure to be a bounty of treats. It didn't take long for her to find where the kids were gathered.

As Khalen and I made our way to the fire, Aidan came and pulled him aside. "Brother, may I have a word with you?"

Khalen kissed my hand. "I'll meet you over there," he said, pointing to where Eve and Sunjia were sitting.

"Okay." I gave Aidan a smile as I left.

Arcadie and Case came over to guide me toward the ladies. "Where's your mate?" Case asked.

"With Aidan."

Case groaned.

"What's wrong?" I asked him.

"I was hoping for a peaceful evening, is all."

I looked around at the clan who sat around the fire, happily engaged in conversation. The children were already eating. "It looks fairly peaceful to me."

"Well, if Aidan is asking what I think he's asking, I fear this peace will be short lived."

I frowned. "Why?"

Eve intervened. "Case, stop it."

Sunjia sat, wringing her hands in her lap.

"What's going on?" I asked.

Sunjia stood. "Aidan is asking Khalen to bless our union," she said.

"Oh, God help us," Case muttered.

All three of us women shot him a glance that must have stung like a thousand bee stings.

"I'll pour us some wine," he said, slinking away.

"So why are you so nervous?" I asked Sunjia. "Khalen loves you both. There is no reason for him to not bless your union."

"But if he refuses, I will have to leave."

"He won't," I assured her.

I had already finished a full glass of wine by the time he and Aidan returned. Both had sullen looks on their faces.

Aidan returned to Sunjia's side, his eyes filled with the kind of sorrow that only a puppy could master. A tear formed in her eyes.

Khalen lifted his wine glass in the air then banged the side of it with a spoon. "Attention, everyone. I have an announcement to make."

My back stiffened. Surely he would not announce his denial of their union so publicly?

He waited for an uncomfortable amount of time before speaking again. Only the soft crackle of the fire and the songs of the night critters communed with the silence. Even the children were silent and waiting.

"Aidan, my brother, has come to me with a request." Khalen glanced over at the sullen man with a look that clearly stated that his decision was not to be challenged.

My stomach twisted inside, extinguishing all traces of appetite. I wanted to place a hand on my mate's arm to remind him to be kind. I held back.

He wishes to join with this woman, Sunjia," Khalen now gestured to her, ignoring the tears in her eyes. "Now, most of you know how I feel about this matter. It has never been a secret."

Murmurs filtered through the crowd like hushed whispers meant only for select ears. I wanted to kick my mate. Instead, I swallowed the rest of my wine and started to walk away. His vice-like grip held me firm.

"This woman, as you well know, was joined with my late brother, Treager. This makes her a Shadow, a soul not to be trusted."

Now it was Sunjia who attempted to leave. Aidan held her at his side.

"I'm here to offer you testimony to the contrary. Not

only has she saved my life, and the life of my beautiful mate, she saved the lives of my children when she had every opportunity to betray us. If it were not for this wonderful soul, my mate and I would not be able to bless and witness this perfect union."

He now turned to Sunjia, who stood speechless, mouth hung open, and hands shaking. "Sunjia," he bowed, something a leader of a clan rarely did. "I welcome you to our family, and completely and unconditionally bless your union with Aidan with my God-given soul. May your lives together be long and prolific. Congratulations!" He raised his glass then drank, sealing the blessing.

The clan roared so loud that it echoed off the surrounding trees. Khalen and Aidan embraced each other in a bone-crushing hug, while Sunjia sank to the log, releasing the tears she could no longer restrain.

Eve and I wrapped our arms around her. "Hey," I said. "We're sisters now."

Sunjia laughed then released another dose of tears. She shook as we held her.

Seth and Tria ran up to us, kicking up dust as they slid to a stop. "Does this mean we can stay?"

Khalen slapped Seth's back. "Yes, if Aidan will have you."

Aidan looked skeptically. "I don't know. You two might be trouble."

Seth and Tria wrapped their arms around him as if he were a soft and squishy bear. They never waited for an answer, they bolted away and joined the other kids who were just as happy about the news.

"I knew this night would not be peaceful," Case said,

extending his hand to Aidan. "Congratulations, young man. It's about time."

"Brother," Ian said from behind. "I never thought I'd see the day." He and Aidan embraced.

"I want you to be Sunjia's templar," he said.

Ian stepped back then looked at Khalen questioningly. "I thought Khalen was her templar?"

"Aye, and a good choice he is, too. But I'm asking you to stand in his stead, my brother. Will you do it?"

Khalen raised his glass to Ian, who for the first time since I'd known him, stammered his words. "Aye—uh—yes, of course." He then sunk to his knees. "Oh boy," he muttered.

Sunjia offered him a hand up. "It's all right, Ian. I'll be an easy keeper."

"Is it the honor that has you so shaken, lad, or is it the responsibility?" Arcadie asked.

"A bit of both, I presume."

"Ha." Arcadie placed a glass of whiskey in his hands then slapped him on the back. He then raised his drink in the air. "Congratulations to everyone."

WITH OUR BELLIES FULL OF fresh-made pasta, and hearty meatballs, I was ready to take a nap. I fed the twins by the fire as the clan gathered in conversation. Khalen opened a bottle of Madeira and passed it around.

Maiyun laid by my side, wedged between me and Khalen. For once, he didn't seem to mind it. He held Kaili as Shaiya continued to feed, always the last to get her fill. Between Khalen and I, and the women in camp, the girls were not shy of attention. They had spent most of the day being passed around from one clan member to another. I only saw them when it was time to feed, and finally concluded that things were not going to change anytime soon.

Content and well rested, they seemed to marvel at the sight of fire, and drew comfort from the sound of conversation. Sunjia came to sit beside me, smiling as I rubbed the soft black hair on Shaiya's head.

"Can you tell what their gifts are?" I asked her.

"No, it's too early. Spirian gifts take time to manifest. Sometimes, they don't display them until they are nearly twenty years."

"Two years ago, that would have seemed like a long time. Now, it seems like only a moment."

Sunjia laughed. "Spoken like a true mother," she sighed. "The years do seem to go by quickly." She glanced over at Seth and Tria, laughing and talking with the other kids. "It's nice to see them so happy."

"Have you and Aidan set a date for your union?"

Again, she laughed. The sound of it was like chimes in the breeze. "Aidan wanted to take me tonight, but Khalen said no, 'not without ceremony,'" she mocked in a low voice.

"Yeah, that sounds like something he'd say."

"Eve said she would need a few days to prepare."

I smiled. "Can you wait that long?"

"According to your stubborn mate, I have no choice. So yes, I can wait."

Chapter 24

A gift and a curse are inseparable. One cannot exist without the other.

KHALEN AND I FINALLY RETIRED with the girls who were both too excited to sleep. We sat on the bed playing with them while sipping a hot cup of cocoa.

"I liked your announcement," I admitted.

"Just not at first."

"No. At first, I wanted to wrap your mouth with duct tape and set you on fire."

He chuckled. "That's a little dark."

"Well, I was angry at the time."

"Did you honestly think I would deny their union?" Kaili's hand wrapped around his little finger barely able to make it around. She cooed and kicked her feet.

"Deep down, no. On the surface, it certainly seemed possible." I rubbed Shaiya's tiny feet until she could no longer open her eyes.

"I think the union is a solid one."

"Me too," I admitted and refrained from reminding him that I had thought so all along. "Arcadie must miss his family. He's been away from them so long."

"He meets with the High Council tomorrow. Dirk has agreed to bring Kitta here so that she can enjoy the wedding."

"This will be quite a change for her, don't you think?"

"Oh, yes. So far as I know, she's never traveled outside of Brazil."

I picked Shaiya up and gently lowered her into her bed by the fire. "That seems hard to believe, given her age."

Kaili was still wide awake. It didn't help that Khalen kept playing with her. "Rub her feet," I suggested.

He tried and Kaili kicked his hands away. "Hmm," he groaned. "I seem to lack the magic touch."

I placed one of her feet in his hand and held the other in mine. "Do it softly, like this." I demonstrated long, slow strokes along the tiny arch of her foot. Before too long, Kaili gave into the rhythmic caresses and surrendered to sleep.

"There, see? You have the magic touch."

"I think I need more practice," he jibed. "Come here."

"Are you sure you want to lull me to sleep?"

"Right. Good point." He sipped his cocoa and smiled as I tucked Kaili in bed.

I returned to his side. "Are you going to perform the ceremony for Aidan and Sunjia?"

"He has asked me to, yes."

I touched his face. "Your first one?" I felt heat flush his cheeks.

"Yes. It should be quite interesting."

"I'm sure Case will offer some enlightening instruction." I

started to peel the shirt away from his shoulders.

"Perhaps," he said, suddenly losing interest in the conversation. He tossed his shirt aside then began removing my clothes with a growl.

Once his engine was revved, Khalen was an unstoppable freight train in high gear. I loved the way he took control and made me crave more of him. It seemed every time we made love, it was new and fresh. I had never hungered for anything the way I hungered for him.

Afterward, we laid there hot, damp, and exhausted in each other's arms.

"It frightens me how much I love you," he said.

I propped myself up onto one elbow, my hair damp and limp over his chest. "Because you fear you will lose me?"

He nodded. "I do."

"If you truly have me, Khalen, you can never lose me. I will always be bonded to you—forever."

He rolled me onto my back. "Then, my angel, I will have to make sure that our union is renewed each time we make love."

"Are you sure you have the strength?"

Again, he growled, a deep, throaty sound that caused my body to pulse in anticipation.

Smiling, I said, "Am I ever going to grow tired of you?"

"No," he whispered, nibbling my ear. "I won't allow it."

WE AWOKE TO THE SOUND OF Kaili, screaming as if her world were about to end. I leapt out of bed and stubbed my toe on the bed frame. Functioning on only two hours of solid sleep, I lost my bearings and banged into the wall.

"Skye, sit before you hurt yourself," Khalen said as he lovingly lifted our screaming babe from her bed. I stumbled to the couch, propped a pillow behind my back, and then accepted Kaili from his arms. It didn't take long for her to latch on and settle into a state of contentment.

Khalen returned with a blanket. Reluctantly, he draped it around me and the babe before stoking the fire. He added a few more logs before padding into the kitchen to brew some coffee, all without a stitch of clothing—fabulous.

"I thought I might work with the mare a bit today."

I saw a smile soften his face. "That sounds like a good idea."

"I just don't want the kids getting hurt, should they decide to play with her."

"Good thinking," he said.

"I wish I had some brushes for her. She could use a good cleaning, and her hooves are a mess. Did you see the cracks in them?"

"I believe you'll find all that you need in the shed next to the feed barn. There is even a grooming area set up for you."

"And how, pray tell, did you manage all this in a day, Khalen Dunning?"

"I didn't," he said. "I had Drew start the work shortly after we left. Ian ordered the grooming supplies."

"Why?"

"I was going to buy you a horse, but when Ian told me the story about the mare, I thought she would be the perfect project for you."

"I told you I didn't want another horse."

He shrugged. "Very well. I'll have Ian haul her to a rescue facility after breakfast."

"You will not!"

Kaili cried a protest to my abrupt movement. I settled her down, shifting my position on the couch.

"What, so now you want her?"

"She's not ready to go anywhere," I said. "She's been through too much to cart her to yet another unknown."

He looked up at me and flashed that annoying smirk of his. The one that screamed, victory in the face of defeat. "Very well then. Just let me know when she's ready to go and I will have her taken away."

I bit at my lower lip. "That's a deal. It shouldn't take long."

"Do you have a name for her yet?"

"Why would I need to name her if she will soon be leaving?"

"Just asking. No need to get your hair in a fluff."

The smell of fresh-brewed coffee wafted toward me, mingling with the spicy scent of cinnamon and chocolate. Khalen liked to shave dark chocolate in the press as the coffee brewed.

Shaiya awoke with a whimper that soon escalated to a full-out holler. Khalen lifted her up, changed her diaper, and then exchanged her for Kaili who was also ready for a change. He hummed a sweet little tune as he tended their needs. Looking at him, one would believe he had done this all his life.

"You're a natural," I said.

He smiled. "Thank you. I have a feeling I'll be getting quite a bit of practice."

I blushed slightly. "At the rate you're going, it will be sooner rather than later."

"I can make it happen now if you're ready, love," he boasted while setting Kaili down on the rug to play. She kicked her feet and thrust her arms with squeals of pure contentment.

"These two are a lot of work. Are you sure you want to have another so soon?" I asked.

He played with Kaili for a moment, rubbing her tummy and allowing her to grip his finger with her hands before heading back to the kitchen. "If it were up to me, you'd be pregnant all the time." A sly smile shone on his face.

In a sense, it was up to him, but I wasn't about to highlight that fact. "Let's wait another few months," I said.

He became silent as he prepared our coffees.

"Khalen?"

He carried mine over to me, and laid a nibble of dark chocolate beside it, fresh from the freezer. I popped the nibble into my mouth and allowed it to slowly melt onto my tongue.

My mate was silent as he sat beside me on the couch. He remained that way for quite some time.

"Is there something you want to tell me?" I prodded.

He sipped his coffee while staring into the flames in the circular fireplace. "We have a larger clan now," he casually mentioned. "Caleb and Drew have combined their families with ours. Case and Eve also plan to stay."

"Yes, I've noticed. I like it." There were more children than before, and many more elders. The camp felt complete and whole again.

"There are more elders to care for the young."

"Yes, there are," I agreed, sipping my coffee and savoring

the flavor on my tongue.

Shaiya pulled away and yawned with satisfaction. I lifted her against my shoulder and patted her back before setting her down beside her sister. They both had thick, black hair and dark eyes with long lashes. Kaili's nose was a bit more round than Shaiya's and her lips were fuller. Shaiya displayed more of her father's looks. Her face was longer and her eyes were set wider apart.

I returned to my place on the couch, tucked my feet beneath me, and covered myself with the blanket.

Khalen urged my feet out from under me and placed them onto his lap so he could rub them. "Your feet are cold," he said.

"You've given me a son," I blurted, having read his thoughts. My hand instinctively went to my belly, still slightly swollen from carrying the twins. I wondered if I would ever have a flat stomach again.

"Last night," he said. "It just felt right, and I let it happen." He almost sounded disappointed.

I smiled. "Well then, it is right."

"Know this, my love. If you have twins, I will take one of them. We will not repeat our last mistake."

When I opened my mouth to speak, he claimed it with his own then whispered in a gruff voice, "No exceptions."

I swallowed hard, knowing the finality of those words. No amount of pleading would dissuade him. "I don't want to know about it," I said. "If you take our young, I don't want to know."

"You have access to my thoughts. How can I keep that from you?"

"Please, Khalen. Try."

"Perhaps this might help you accept things better. If you chance carrying twins again, they will be much larger than your first. I don't have to remind you of the pain you endured toward the end of your term, do I?"

"No, you most certainly do not." I sipped my coffee and focused my thoughts on the fire." This conversation was disturbing. It was time to change it.

"Do you have a name in mind for our son?"

"Names are not given until the young is born. It is his spirit that chooses the name, not I."

I sighed. "Will I ever learn all the Spirian ways?"

He chuckled and held my hand, bringing it to his soft lips. "Not even Shanuk knew all the ways, and he lived beyond three-hundred years."

"Thank you," I said, caressing the back of his hand with my thumb.

"For what?"

"Giving me another child. Ready for it or not, I love the idea of carrying our young."

His expression changed with the light that only shines from within. It is a look that words cannot describe—an image of pure emotion. It can only be felt and shared soul-to-soul.

"It's funny," he said. "I often prayed to stay free of the emotion and ties of a female. Now, I thank the Father for ignoring those foolish pleas."

"To understand the wisdom of the Father is to know not to profess to having such understanding."

"Shanuk?" he said.

I nodded. "It didn't make much sense when he said it, but for some reason, now it does. For us to declare that we understand our creator is as absurd as claiming that we are his equal, which is impossible."

"Why's that?"

"Can you ever be both your mother and your father?"

His brows furrowed in thought. "I'm not following you."

"To claim to be the Creator's equal, you would have to be equal with the entire universe. To do that, you would have to shed your own soul and become the Father."

"What's wrong with that?"

"Imagine if every cell of your body, decided to morph into one, to change their DNA to match the whole. What would we become?"

"Ameba," he blurted. "One giant cell."

"But the Father created each of us individually, to carry a unique strand of DNA, to function as individuals that serve the whole. So, in a sense, we are like a cell in the body of the Creator. It takes the collection of us to enable that body to function."

"So to claim that one is equal to the Father, is mute, because to be equal to Him is to annihilate Him by annihilating ourselves?"

"Exactly!"

"I think you have too much of Shanuk's blood."

"It makes sense, that's all." I stood and padded across the room to where my comfy sweats lay waiting on the bench at the foot of the bed. I put them on before tossing Khalen his robe.

He caught it with a frown, obviously disappointed at

having to don clothes.

"What sounds good for breakfast?" I asked, opening the blinds.

"You," he said playfully, tying his robe and walking toward me.

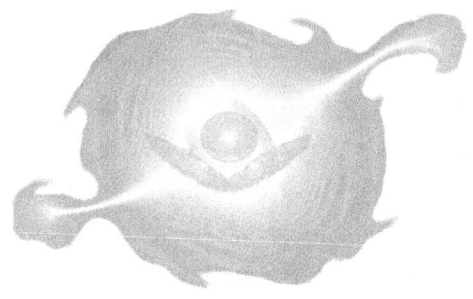

Chapter 25

Wisdom comes with knowing that few things are truly understood.

AFTER EATING BREAKFAST, AND BATHING the girls, I was ready to visit the mare. Eve and Sunjia eagerly took possession of the twins. Maiyun walked beside me, happy to be outside.

Ian was busy cleaning the pens and scattering hay scraps to the goats and calves. I continued my way to the grooming shed where Khalen said I would find all that I needed. Ian beat me there, flipped the light switch then reveled in my gawking response.

Full-spectrum lights had been installed and the place lit up like a white-sanded beach in Miami. Rubber mats covered the center aisle while the walls were amply equipped with tie rings, ropes, and hooks. A white nylon halter hung with a matching 12' lead rope.

Next to the cross ties, hung a cleverly-designed grooming caddy made of canvas. In it was a collection of curry combs, soft and hard brushes, a hoof pick, and a mane and tail brush.

Stored in another cubby was a light-weight hoof jack, a hoof file, and a variety of nippers and knives. There was even a step stool.

Khalen was right, everything I needed was here. I strangely felt comfortable with these things and the smell of the barn invoked memories of days long forgotten.

Ian flipped another switch and soft music began to play. "Khalen thought it might calm the horse."

I smiled. "This is amazing," I said. "I love all of it."

Ian beamed a smile.

"Is there a pen where I can turn the horse out and work her?"

He wiggled his finger, gesturing that I follow him outside. "Will this do?"

A 20-foot round pen constructed of pipe panels spanned across a leveled area filled with black sand. It took a horse person to know the value of using black sand. "How did you know?" I asked, gesturing at the sparkling ground.

"Caleb and his family farmed horses several years ago until their land was absorbed by the government. He said that the sand was best for barefooted horses. It helped keep their hooves firm and tough."

"That it does," I said. "It's good for muscle conditioning as well."

The mare looked at me from over the fence. When our eyes made contact, she flattened her ears and turned away.

"She looks happy to see you," he said.

I raised a brow, wondering if he was serious.

"When I looked at her this morning, she charged the

fence and snorted."

"Great," I muttered. I returned to the grooming shed and fetched the halter and short lead. "This should be fun." I looked around for anything I could use as a treat. "Do we have any horse treats or carrots?

"No carrots that are ready to eat. There is grain in the feed room."

"How about honey?"

"Will molasses do?"

"Yes."

"Feed room," he said, leading the way.

"Do we have any gloves?"

He disappeared, and then came back with two pairs of gloves, hinting, I assumed, that he wanted to help.

With gloved hands, I put two handfuls of oats in a bucket, added molasses then stirred it all together. Ian watched with child-like curiosity. It made me smile. "Put more oats in that container there," I instructed, gesturing to a smaller quart-sized container on the shelf.

"Now take a peanut-sized amount of the mixture and roll it into an oblong shape." I demonstrated the action. "Drop it into the container of oats. Get it nice and coated then place them here." I dropped the makeshift horse cookie into another quart-sized container.

"Won't these amp her up even more?" he asked, knowing the effects that oats had on horses.

"Does valerian root always make people calm?" I asked.

He shrugged. "That's more your specialty than mine," he said.

We worked together forming the mixture and coating it.

"In homeopathy, like cures like. If a patient has a bee sting, you offer him apis, made from the bee's venom. The same can hold true for food. In traditional medicine, you look at the horse in a symptomatic way. The horse is obviously displaying a hot temperament, therefore, you treat that symptom. From a holistic approach, we look at the cause of the symptom. In this case, fear, abandonment, and mistrust causes this mare to display a facade of belligerence to ward off those who threaten her."

"So, her hot-blooded nature is a fraud?"

"Yes. In fact, I would bet that her passion in life is peacefully grazing in a pasture and soaking up the sun. Her favorite gear is whoa, and she thrives on affection."

"Ha," Ian laughed. "You're kidding, right?"

"No." With the mixture gone, and the container filled with cookies, I removed my gloves and tossed them into the covered trash barrel. Ian followed suit.

"I'll keep an eye on you," he said. "If this mare happens to injure you, it will be my head on Khalen's chopping block, right next to the mare's."

"She won't injure me," I assured him. With the cookies, rope, and halter in hand, I walked into the pasture.

"Maiyun, you stay here," I said. She had been around livestock before, but never felt comfortable with me in their presence.

Not surprisingly, the mare trotted toward the far end of the pasture as I entered. It wasn't very large, only fifty by sixty feet or so. I walked out to the center of it, placed the cookies at my feet, and held the rope and halter where she could see it. I played back the many films I had seen so long ago about wild horses and their behaviors.

If I were a lead mare, I recalled, the horses would approach me with respect. If not, I would demand that respect with an adverse response. It was a game of chicken, really. Only she had about 1200 pounds on me, a longer neck, stronger teeth, and four powerful legs. I, on the other hand, had knowledge of her language—a huge plus.

She glanced at me and pinned her ears. When that didn't dissuade me from occupying her space, she gnashed her teeth. My lack of response both intrigued the mare and fueled her anger. Now, she faced me head on, sizing me up. I continued to hold the rope and halter where she could see it.

She trotted toward me, ears flat, teeth bared, and head low in mock warning.

I swung the rope around me, allowing it to slap against the ground. She slid to a halt, spun then galloped back to the fence line, snorting and pawing the ground. Horses did that when they had something to consider.

This time, she decided to circle around and charge me from behind. Maiyun barked a warning. I used my ears to listen to the advancing hoofbeats then turned at the last moment to face her. She reared and struck at me with her front legs. I stood my ground and countered her threat with one of my own. I swung the coiled rope in my hands and tossed it toward her back legs. The mare squealed, kicked the rope free then bounded back to the fence.

It took nearly twenty minutes before she tried again. This time, she approached me more in curiosity than threat. When she did, I turned my back to her, indicating that she was not worthy of my notice. This intrigued her even more.

When she got within 12 feet of me. I picked up the container of cookies and walked away from her. She followed. By now, she had caught wind of the tasty treats and started licking her lips. This is also a sign that she was beginning to understand my position.

Again, I allowed her to get close then walked away. Now, she was trotting toward me, ears up and eyes soft with longing. The table had been turned. Before, it was she who played hard-to-get. Now, it was my turn.

We played this game for some time before I allowed her to approach me. When she did, I offered my hand for scenting then presented a cookie. She jerked back, but didn't run. Again, her action prompted me to turn my back and walk away.

I heard her approach from behind. There was no anger in her steps, only curiosity. I felt the warm breath from her nostrils as she pushed her muzzle past my head. With gentleness, she lowered her chin and pressed my shoulder against her chest as if asking me to stop.

Maiyun growled but stayed with Ian. I could hear him trying to comfort her.

With the mare's head still draped over my shoulder, I presented the cookie again. She sniffed it then turned it around in my hand with her nimble lips. Satisfied that the cookie was harmless, she ventured a taste. Her head bobbed up and down, gesturing an exuberant yes. I turned and noticed the softness in her gentle brown eyes. She allowed me to scratch her neck and withers then pressed her hips toward me for further attention.

Slowly, I lifted the halter and lead rope and rubbed her

body with it. She eyed the contraption warily, but stood for the attention.

Before unbuckling the halter, I walked away from her. If I had stayed, she would have seen the action as a threat and may have bolted. I wanted to keep her curiosity peaked.

I turned slowly to face her, presenting the rope. She stopped, snorted and pawed the ground. Again, I turned and walked away, showing her that my intention was not to alarm her. If I had meant harm, I would have approached her. As it was, I was the one walking away.

She followed. This time, when I raised the rope, she stood quiet but cautious. I formed a circle with the rope, dangled it in front of my other hand that held a cookie. If she wanted the cookie, she would have to reach through the rope. This required considerable thought on her end.

Slowly, she reached her lips as far as they could stretch, being careful not to touch the rope. I started walking backward. If I could get her feet moving, her thoughts would not be on the rope, it would be on the cookie that was now getting away.

She trotted toward me, her eyes on the goodie. I stopped. Without thought, she slipped her head through the rope and nibbled the cookie from my hand. We repeated this exercise a few times until the rope became an afterthought. While scratching her neck, I slowly draped the rope around her withers. This made her jump a bit, but she didn't bolt. I walked away and the rope fell off her withers. She followed.

This time, I draped the rope around her neck, just behind her ears. She shook and the rope fell to her withers. Next time, I created a loose loop. When she seemed okay with that, I began leading her around, being careful not to pull on the rope. I merely allowed her to follow. The lesson of course is to instill a sense of freedom around the rope. I was not trying to control her and I didn't want her to feel trapped.

I then used the rope to create a mock halter. She had obviously worn one before and did not act alarmed. Next came the web halter. I showed it to her, allowed her to smell it then waited. I slipped the nose band up, held it there until her eyes softened again, and then removed it and gave her a treat. We repeated this several times until she grew comfortable with it.

Satisfied with the progress, I decided that it was time to leave—she had other plans. As I made my way toward the gate, she trotted and stood before me. This time, I approached her with the halter and fastened the buckle. She didn't flinch. Showing comfort with being led around, I asked Ian to open the gate.

"Unbelievable," he said, keeping a wide berth between him and the mare. She pinned her ears at Maiyun and I jiggled the rope, telling her that the action was unacceptable. She backed up and raised her head as if expecting a fight. I offered none. I followed her retreat, confident that my action was a fair and just correction. I gave her more lead then waited for her to walk forward.

She did and we continued our way to the grooming shed. The confinement of the walls and ceiling was another challenge for her but I wanted her to enter on her own terms. "Ian, fetch me the lunge line on the wall."

Ian grabbed the 25-foot line and carefully handed it to me. The mare pinned her ears and lunged her teeth toward him. Again, I wiggled the rope and forced her back. She reared in response so I wiggled the rope again. When she turned her shoulders away, I tossed the end of the lunge line toward her hind legs, letting her know that her challenge was noted and addressed.

"Stand beside me," I told Ian. I placed a cookie in his hand.

The mare stood at the end of the lead rope, assessing her options. It was clear that she had been overcorrected for inappropriate actions, and she was expecting the same from me. I only demanded respect, nothing more.

It took her some time, but she finally decided that Ian was not a monster and that he might be trustworthy. "Let her approach you," I told him. "Hold the cookie close to your body, don't present her with it."

I looked over at his shaking hand. "Don't be scared. She can sense it."

I stepped away from the shed and started walking backward. "Stay by my side," I told Ian. Maiyun followed suit and backed up with us. The mare followed being familiar now with this game. As her pace quickened, ours did too. I led her behind to the other end of the shed. "Keep walking with me."

As the mare approached the shed's entrance, she stopped. "Okay, now we take one step toward her."

"Why?" Ian asked.

"Just watch."

The mare backed up. I tied the end of the lunge line to the end of the lead rope and took two steps backward. The mare stepped forward. We, in turn stepped forward and waited.

The mare stepped forward again. We did too. She backed up and tossed her head. We backed up as well, but twice as far this time.

"What are we doing?" Ian asked.

"She wants to be close to us, but battles the confinement of the shed. Every time she backs up, we get further away, the opposite of what she wants. When she makes an effort to come closer, we do the same, thus giving her what she wants."

"Do you think she'll figure that out, lass?"

"Yes, I do."

Maiyun, having grown bored of the game, laid down on the soft mats and panted nervously.

"Turn your back to her."

"Um, I'm not sure that's a good idea," he said, remembering Caleb's experience with the mare.

"Trust me," I said, trying to mimic his mischievous smile.

We turned. "Now, start walking slowly toward the center of the barn."

Through the rope in my hand, I could feel the mare's movements. Her head was bobbing up and down as she pawed the ground. She released a squeal as if to say, "Don't leave me."

We stopped and faced her.

"Now what?" Ian said, clearly perplexed with all this.

"We wait." I gave Maiyun one of the cookies which provided the mare with a new sense of urgency.

Hesitantly, she stepped forward. Her front feet were now on the mat. We, too, stepped forward. Again, she bobbed her head and took another step. That brought us closer as well. Her body stiffened, fighting her mind's will to back out. Her front feet held firm. Another step closer. We matched it. She stretched her nose out as far as her neck would allow, lips reaching as well. We waited. She took another step forward, so did we.

"Offer her a cookie," I told Ian. "Keep your hand flat and your fingers together."

He did. The mare sniffed him then carefully took the treat that he offered.

"Excellent," I said. "Congratulations. You just made a new friend."

"Will she let me pet her?"

"Not yet," I said. "Slowly, walk backward. We are going to lead her out of the barn. Now, she's going to want to bolt, so be alert. Watch her body language. Once her sympathetic response clicks into gear, I won't be able to stop her. That will have to be another lesson once she gains more confidence. If she does bolt, stay with me. Do not push to the other side, it will make her feel trapped.

The mare continued to follow, snorting and fighting the demons that ruled her emotions, eyes wide with fear. The skin below her withers started to quiver.

"Okay, stay close to me, Ian. We're going to press closer to the wall. Let her run past if she needs to, okay. Just stay pressed against the wall."

"What if she kicks us?"

"Don't give her any reason to."

Maiyun started to follow the mare. "No, Maiyun," I said. "Down, stay." Maiyun groaned, but obeyed.

The mare's feet started to pace, her breathing increased. Five feet from the door, she bolted past us, ran to the end of the line then spun to face us.

"Blimey! You know horses," said Ian.

"They're easier to read than humans," I said. "Their intentions are not masked with lies."

"Now what?"

"She may have had enough for one day, but if we put her away now, she will associate bad behavior with the reward of release."

"Should we take her around again?" The look of eagerness on his face was endearing. It was difficult to see the man past the youthful enthusiasm he now expressed.

"You look like you're having fun."

"Oh, Aye. I am. I've always been a bit leery of horses."

"Smart man," I said. "You should be."

I lunged the mare around a bit, offering her something else to think about. I pushed her into a leisurely trot then asked her to change directions. It was an easy exercise for her and seemed to leave her calm and collected. With renewed confidence, she approached Ian and I, ears up and eyes soft and alert. Ian enjoyed feeding her treats and was quickly becoming too quick to offer them.

"Not so many," I said. "They're treats, not appetizers."

"I think she likes me now."

I smiled. "What's not to like?"

"Shall we take her around to the barn again?" His hands gently and slowly brushed the soft fur on her neck. The mare seemed to enjoy the attention.

"Yes, we'll give it another try."

After the fifth attempt, Ian took the lead and coaxed the mare to follow him. She was much calmer with the exercise and no longer bolted from the shed. On the sixth attempt, I asked Ian to hold her while I brushed her down and cleaned her hooves.

AN HOUR HAD PASSED. It was the twins' feeding time, and Ian had chores to attend. He thanked me for the experience, gave the mare a gentle pat then walked away.

"Beautiful Belle," I muttered, leading her back to the pasture. I removed her halter, gave her one last treat then closed the gate. She gave her body a hearty shake then proceeded to roll in the dirt. "Figures," I said, "No gratitude."

Maiyun groaned in agreement.

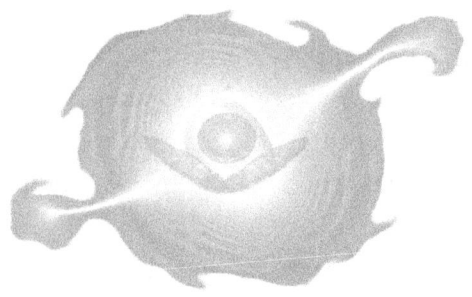

Chapter 26

The voice of God drifts like a whisper of a breeze through the pitch of silence.

Arcadie had returned later that evening to report the decision of the High Council. Not surprisingly, Shanuk had cleared everything with them before placing me with the humans. All they needed from Arcadie were the papers that Shanuk had left. The documents had been changed along with my birth name. In the family tree, my name now read Taezza Skye Taylor Wallace.

Taezza, I was told, means, "She who brings dreams." I wasn't sure about that. Arcadie explained that Taezza was the name of the rare purple dragonfly, a symbol of dreams from the spirit world. Shanuk was the one who named me Skye, after the Island on which I was born. As pretty as the name Taezza was, I decided to stick with Skye, "The winged one."

The next two days flew by with the busy activities of preparing for the upcoming union. The ceremony was scheduled for tomorrow night. Eve, of course, was in her glory. She helped plan the meal, while Sunjia and Dania tailored the dress and organized the decorations. I helped more with mundane tasks and busy work.

Arcadie's wife, Kitta, adapted well to the clan. She had never had the pleasure of eating by a large open fire while sitting on a log and using the earth as a table. At first, she felt awkward, but it didn't take her long to relax into it and enjoy the simple pleasure of casual conversation and fresh air.

Her attire this evening consisted of blue jeans and a frumpy sweater—a far cry from her typical long dress and sheer leggings. Arcadie seemed to like the change as well. It sparked a new kind of friskiness in the old man, one that seemed oddly out of place. He had made Kitta blush more than once, adding to her new-found charm.

Drinking Madeira from a bottle was a huge social faux pas, but she quickly got over it and joined in the fun. She sat with Kaili against her shoulder, nuzzling her soft hair and marveling at the tiny hands and long fingers. She kept a leery eye on her oldest daughter, Erika, as she and Ian laughed by the fire.

"He's a good man," I assured her.

"She's too young for him."

Erika was only thirty-three years compared to Ian's fifty, but in Spirian age, that was hardly something to fret over. I believed the true issue was that Ian lived here, which was too far from Brazil.

"You look good with a young one draped over your shoulder," Arcadie said. "Perhaps we should think about having another?" He nuzzled his wife's neck, making her giggle.

"Honestly, Arcadie, what has gotten into you?"

"You," he said, "and this new look you've adopted. It suits you and I like it." He growled at the end, making her giggle and cover her face.

"Oh, you're terrible," she jibed.

Arcadie lifted my sleepy babe and handed her to me. "I would like to dance with my mate," he said.

"To what music," she countered.

"Our own." He lifted her to her feet then ushered her away like a man who was guaranteed to get lucky.

Eve smiled at the sleeping babe in her arms "I think it's time for bed."

"Yes, for this one too." I stood and followed her back to our yurt. Maiyun stayed by my side, nudging me when I started to stray from the path.

Eve and I laid the girls down. I noticed a glum look on her face. "What's wrong?"

"I long for a babe of my own, Skye. I really do."

A sharp pang of empathy stung at my chest. I had known that feeling when I was with Derrick. I remembered how disheartened I felt each time I saw a child. I had learned to distance myself from them, convincing myself that I was not the motherly type. "Come sit," I told her, gesturing toward the couch.

"I know Case doesn't want to take the risk of me getting pregnant, but I do."

"It's not just that, Eve, it's the ill fate of your young that also deters him. Sunjia said that there was a chance that Case could change you into a Spirian, remember?"

Eve laughed, "Oh, the High Council would have a field

day with that one."

"With the Spirian race at risk, I doubt they would refuse him."

"Providing he could convince them about the possibility."

"Sunjia could."

I stood and offered my hand to Eve. "Come, let's talk to Case and Sunjia and see what can be done."

Maiyun stayed with the twins. She had made it her personal duty to alert me at the slightest whimper. I didn't have the heart to tell her that a Spirian mother is tapped into her young and didn't need a monitor. Like all jobs, Maiyun took it seriously and it was important for her to know that I did too.

Sunjia and I explained the possibility to Case while Eve sat beside him.

"Absolutely not!" Case roared. "It's too risky."

"Why?" asked Sunjia. "At worst, you will hurt Eve. Skye will stand by to heal her, and you have Khalen to tend to other matters. The risk is low."

"I will not hurt my mate."

"You are hurting me by not trying," Eve chimed in. "Like Sunjia said, the risk is low."

Khalen and Arcadie heard the conversation grow louder and came to investigate.

"Three women to one man," Arcadie said. "Looks like harsh odds."

"They're talking crazy," Case explained. "I've heard enough." He started to stand.

Sunjia touched his arm. "She's stronger than you know. Why not give her a chance?"

Khalen stepped in. "What's this about?"

"There is a chance for Eve to become a Spirian," I said.

Arcadie laughed. "Impossible, child. It has never been done."

"It's not impossible," Sunjia retorted. "Case is a strong leader. He and Eve have been together for a long while. She is more Spirian than human, just not completely."

"The High Council will never agree to this," Case said.

"Have you asked them?" I asked. I felt the hum of his anger. Apparently so did everyone else. Khalen stepped between us.

"Father, calm down."

"I will not allow you to raise my mate's hopes for something that will never happen."

"You're not thinking of her," I carelessly stated.

Case's eyes glowed against the evening sky. I had crossed the line. The hum surrounding us grew to a deafening frequency as a mild shock tingled up my spine. Khalen absorbed most of it.

"Wait," Eve cried, coming between us and her mate. "I want this, Case. I want to be given the chance."

The hum calmed. The tingles faded. Case looked defeated at the sound of his mate's plea. He sat down on the log and buried his face in his hands. "You don't know what you're asking."

"I do," said Eve. "I want this. Please let me try."

"Eve, you could die," Arcadie explained. "It has been the fate of every human who's tried."

"I don't care! Don't you see I'm dying already? My spirit longs for something it cannot have. If I'm going to die anyway, please let me die for something I believe in."

"Sunjia," Khalen said. "How sure are you about this?"

She raised her chin to meet his eyes. "Very sure. If something goes wrong, you and Skye can step in."

By now, other clan members had gained interest in the conversation and were now chanting, "Let her try, let her try."

"Enough!" Case roared. He pointed to Sunjia. "Come with me."

Sunjia glanced over at Khalen and Aidan then hesitantly followed Case away from the crowd where they engaged in quiet conversation.

I looked over at Arcadie. "Will the council approve?"

"Getting them to believe is more the question, child."

"What if they are successful?"

Arcadie's eyes grew cold. "They may choose to kill her."

Kitta wrapped her arm around Arcadie's waist. "Surely you can talk with them first and gain their approval."

"Case will have to make that call, my dear, not I."

Aidan paced before the fire. "What is he asking her, for Christ's sake?"

Case and Sunjia returned, her face slightly blushed. Aidan wrapped a protective arm around her and whispered something into her ear. She smiled.

Case took a deep breath and looked down at his mate. "Eve, my love," his voice sounded almost pleading. "If it is your will, I will speak with the High Council tomorrow."

"It is," she said. "Thank you."

He walked away, signaling the other men to follow.

Sunjia, Kitta, and I wrapped our arms around Eve.

Eve looked to Sunjia. "What did he ask you?"

"How to make it happen," she answered matter of factly.

"Do we want to know?" I asked.

Sunjia shrugged. "He must join with you the way he would with any other Spirian woman he unites with."

"But we're already united."

"Not as Spirians," Sunjia explained. "If he had joined with you the same way he would join with a Spirian, you would not be here to talk about it."

Eve folded her hands. "Explain."

Sunjia looked around as if asking me and Kitta for help. We smiled and allowed her to explain. "When a Spirian man claims a Spirian woman, he unites with her soul. This occurs on a very deep level. He must claim your body as well—completely."

The blank look on Eve's face betrayed her confusion and innocence. "Um, we have done that, several times," she said shyly.

"He has held back—considerably," said Sunjia.

"Impossible," Eve admitted. "I cannot believe that."

All three of us were silent.

Eve brought her hand to her mouth. "Good God, he is going to kill me."

"No," I said. "You're strong, you will survive, Eve, I know it."

Eve stood and started to pace. "What do I do when he's—you know?"

Sunjia stifled a giggle. Kitta and I were not so subtle.

"Just accept him. Open your body and spirit to him. He will do the rest."

"Well, what in blue blazes have I been doing thus far?"

she asked, now sounding slightly perturbed.

"Relax, Eve. You can always call it off."

"I will not!"

I raised my hand in submission. "Okay, okay. I'm just saying that Case will stop if you ask him to."

"After you risked your lives convincing him to try? Not a chance."

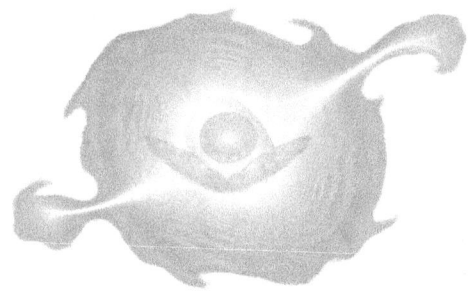

Chapter 27

Taking a risk is the purest display of faith but often demands a hefty price.

KHALEN CLOSED THE DOOR TO our yurt. "Don't ever do that again," he growled.

"Do what?" I inquired, wondering what had him in such a foul mood.

"Challenge an elder, especially when he's my father."

"He was being narrow-minded," I countered. "I had to make him see that."

"If he wanted to send you into oblivion, Skye, I would not have been able to stop him."

I walked to the kitchen and set the kettle to boil. "He would not have done that."

"You were not the one absorbing his wrath," he roared, nearly waking the twins and alerting Maiyun. He jammed his coat on the peg by the door. "You are lucky that Eve stepped in."

"Do you think I was wrong in making him see?" The

hurt in my eyes caused him to look away and growl with frustration.

"You do not corner a mountain lion and expect to escape unscathed."

"That is not an answer."

He poured himself a snifter of brandy then took a long, slow sip with a shaky hand. He closed his eyes as if praying for patience. I knew that look of his too well. Anger had a way of making his body look rigid and harsh. Even his jawline looked to be chiseled from stone.

I turned off the kettle then walked out the door, leaving him to wallow in his mood. Right now, I didn't want to be anywhere near him. The fires had died down and everyone had retired to their homes. It was dark and quiet, with only the insects to keep me company. I followed the path that led to the barn.

Belle nickered to me in greeting. "Hey, girl." I reached over the fence and rubbed her soft nose. The barn was a welcoming sanctuary for nights such as this. I was grateful to have somewhere to go while my mate cooled his temper. There was no reasoning with rage, no matter how gently you chose your words. It was best to just give it space to dissipate.

I turned on the barn lights, flicked on the music then grabbed the halter and lead by the door. Belle was more than eager to come in from the cold and receive a good brushing. She was beginning to look forward to these sessions. I tried to work with her at least twice a day. It was really starting to pay off.

I grabbed the soft curry and started with slow circular motions over her neck. Beethoven's *Moonlight Sonata*, played in the background, complimenting the songs of the insects outside.

I followed the curry with a soft brush that I used to flick the dust away from her fur. Now that her coat was getting some attention, the coppery highlights were starting to shine through.

Her hooves were still in sad shape, but everyday, I trimmed them more, making sure to round the toes and edges. If I had trimmed them short right away, I would have made her too sore to work. Between using the file and working her in the black sand, her feet were shaping up nicely.

In her feed, I increased her biotin and added a bit of soaked beet pulp to put some weight on her. In another week or two, I planned to replace the beet pulp with something more substantial.

I picked up the medium brush and continued to clean her coat. After that, I used the soft finishing brush and ayate cloth to remove the loose dust. She didn't require such a thorough grooming, but I had nothing better to do, so I took my time and enjoyed the process.

A soft guitar solo started to play. I cleaned Belle's hooves then used the file to shape them better. I saved brushing the mane and tail for last. I rubbed a good amount of extra-virgin olive oil onto my hands then distributed it through her long, thick tail. It consisted of white, black, brown, and copper strands, giving it a soft chestnut color throughout. I started brushing from the tip of her tail and worked my way up to the base. By the time I was done, she looked like a show horse. There was not much to her mane. It was short and sparse from having been rubbed on trees and fences. I rubbed a bit of olive oil into the crest and brushed what little she had. Her forelock was soft and had almost a fur-like feel; not at all like her tail. It was a milk-chocolate brown, and offered a lovely contrast to her stark-white blaze.

"There," I said, stepping back. "You now resemble your name, Beautiful Belle."

I cleaned my brushes then carefully put them away. "I had a horse that was similar to you, once," I told her. "His name was Keko. You would have liked him. He had an attitude, and judging by the way the mares treated him, he was not a bad lo—never mind. I shouldn't be telling you that."

Belle snorted as if laughing. I swept the rubber mat beneath her until I had a nice pile formed. She stood relaxed with one leg bent and perched on her toe. We had gotten so comfortable with one another, I never thought about how she would react around a broom near her legs. Obviously it wasn't an issue.

"Anyway," I continued. "Keko was a handsome Appaloosa. He was chestnut in color, similar to yours, only not as dark and coppery. A white blanket splashed across his rump with large brown spots that looked like they had shadows. It was very unique. On his face, he had one small star right here." I pointed to the center of her forehead, right between her eyes. "And a snippet of white here." I brushed the tip of her nose. She licked my hand.

"You'll meet him one day in heaven, I'm sure." I rubbed her face. "When you do, tell him I love him."

Khalen stepped around the corner. His face was softer now and his eyes were apologetic. "Beautiful Belle, huh? I thought you weren't going to name her?"

Belle's ears perked up when she noticed he had something in his hand. Peppermint candies, no doubt. When he had discovered that she liked them, he bought a pound of the bite-sized mints.

"You're going to rot her teeth," I exclaimed with disgust.

"She doesn't seem to mind," he said, rubbing the mare's nose.

"She will when she's older and has to eat mush out of a pan."

"Well, she'll have a new home by then and new owners who won't feed her peppermint candy."

The thought, realistic as it was, turned my gut.

"That is, of course, if you're still planning on getting rid of her," he said. Mock laced his words like thick Marmite.

"When she's ready," I said.

"Well, at least she's not trying to kill people anymore."

"Yes, that is an improvement. She still has a lot to learn." I unclipped her from the cross ties before leading her back to the paddock. "Good night, Belle," I said then hung the halter near the door.

When I tried to walk past him to turn off the music, he pulled me into him. "Wait, I want to talk to you." The softness in his voice made me want to listen. "I'm sorry for snapping at you. I was wrong."

"Not completely," I said. "I was a bit more harsh on Case than was necessary. I allowed my emotions to rule my mouth, as always." I smiled up at him.

"Yes, you did, but I still did not have to react with anger. I just wanted you to know how dangerous it is to speak to an elder with such disrespect."

"I'll apologize to him tomorrow."

He flipped the switch to the music then turned out the light. "And now, my little rebel, I'm going to apologize to you properly."

He lifted me into his arms, and carried me back to our yurt. Candles were lit all around the room, the fire was warm, and there were two glasses of wine by the bed, accompanied by an impressive display of what looked to be cheeses and fruit.

"Hmm," I said, as he lowered me down. "Your apology is very persuasive."

He stripped me down, removed his own clothes then escorted me into the shower. "No offense, love, but you smell like Belle."

"Yeah," I said. "Isn't it great?"

Hot water poured from the five shower heads, soaking the tile and steaming the room. Khalen proceeded to lather me up with plenty of soap, probably more than he needed. The experience was enough to make me love showers far more than baths, especially when Khalen was involved.

Afterward, even though I had accepted his apology multiple times over, he still felt compelled to continue. He fed me thin slices of cheese, grapes, blueberries, and melon. We polished off a bottle of Pinot Noir before he brought out the port. A 40-year tawny, and a tray of dark-chocolate truffles. My stomach felt ready to burst.

"No more," I finally said. "I'm calling uncle." I placed my hand over my aching belly.

"I can help you work some of that off." He took the drink from my hands, laid me down, and then demonstrated with utmost precision, how to work off the equivalent of a pound of cheese and two truffles.

By two a.m., I was ready to surrender to the deepest sleep I had experienced in over five months.

The morning brought with it, a rush of activity, conversation, and a bit of chaos. Case had left to speak with the high council, while the rest of the camp prepared for the union ceremony at sunset.

Sunjia was a nervous wreck as Ember worked quickly at hemming her dress. It was a simple design; one that Sunjia had chosen from a photo in People Magazine. She wanted the hem to fall just above her ankle, so that she could show off the fancy pair of boots that fastened up her legs with pearl buttons and silk lace. Their rich brown color played nicely against the beige of her dress.

I heard the annoying click of her fingers toying at her newly-polished nails. I gently held her hands. "You have been through this before, remember?"

"I know, I'm just—" she wrung her hands together, a trait she often displayed when her emotions ran high.

Again, I wrapped my hands around hers. "Breathe," I told her. "It'll be all right. You want to do this, don't you?"

"Oh yes," she said. "Very much." She bobbed up and down like a young girl about to greet her date for the prom.

"Hold still," Ember scolded. "You're going to end up with one side higher than the other."

Ro came in holding a tangled wad of chains and beads. "This is what happens when men are in charge of putting things away." She laid them on the table and diligently worked them free.

"Where is the crystal pendant?" I asked.

"Gregg is still looking for it."

"What if he can't find it?" Sunjia panicked.

"Calm down," I assured her. "It can't be too far. Khalen gave it to him only yesterday. How far could it have gone?"

"Then again," Ro said, "we are talking about Gregg."

"I'll go help him look for it," I said.

"Um, Skye. You're blind, remember?"

"But Maiyun's not. She knows Khalen's scent. If the pendant is in your cabin, she will find it." I motioned for Maiyun to follow me back to our yurt where I could pick up something of Khalen's.

"Good luck," Ember called.

The ceremony circle was in place with rocks and candles forming the boundary. A group of young men were setting up tiki torches and bringing wood for the fire. Groups of giggling girls were stringing flowers together to set around the circle.

On the spit, a huge rack of lamb slowly turned beside several Dutch ovens filled with bread, potatoes, and other goodies. My stomach growled, having missed breakfast this morning. Maiyun's nose worked double time trying to identify all the wonderful smells.

"Save it," I told her. "I need you to find something for me."

When we entered Gregg and Ro's cabin, Gregg had the place torn apart. Clothes, books, and drawers littered the bed and floor.

He looked up at Maiyun and me. "Hi."

"Let me guess. You can't find the pendant?"

"I put it somewhere safe."

"Uh, yeah, I can see that. Did you need some help?"

He sighed. "All I can get."

I pulled Khalen's hair tie from my pocket and allowed Skye to sniff it. "Find it," I told her. Finding lost items was a game she and I used to play when she was young. I wasn't sure if she would remember the game. It took her a moment to fully understand what I asked, but once she caught on, her nose went into high gear.

She approached Gregg and sniffed his pocket.

Gregg put his hand in his pocket then removed the pendant. "You've got to be kidding me."

I reached out my hand. "I'll take that to Ro for you." I glanced around at the mess. "I recommend that you clean this up before she returns."

"Yeah, good idea," he agreed, still perplexed at how he missed checking his own pockets. That was Gregg, though. If younger, he would be the poster child for attention deficit disorder.

By the time I returned to Eve's yurt, Ro had the chains and beads untangled and neatly laid out on the table. Ember was finishing the hem on the dress, and Sunjia was sipping a cup of tea. I hoped it was chamomile and not black tea.

"You found it!" she chimed.

"Where was it?" Ro asked.

"His pocket."

"Which pocket?"

"The one on the pants he was wearing."

Everyone laughed, including Sunjia.

Eve came in to beat down the dough she had rising. "What's so funny?"

We happily shared Gregg's embarrassing plight.

"Oh," she said, laughing. "That is funny. Typical of him, but funny none the less."

"My poor husband," Ro said. "He just can't help himself."

It took two hours to get Sunjia ready. With her hair done up so elegantly, she looked like a model about to stride along a cat walk at some fancy designer hall. I gave her a hug.

"We'll see you out there," I whispered.

She nodded, twisting her hands as we left to join the others.

Case, having barely returned from seeing the council, sat in the ceremonial circle quietly beating on the drums that were used only for special occasions. Khalen held various herbs in his hand and offered them to the four directions, asking the Father and other Protected spirits to honor the ceremony with their presence. I could feel Shanuk by my side. His massive presence was undeniable.

"I'm glad you could make it, Grandfather," I said, a hint of pride in my voice.

He did not answer, but I felt him all around me as if he were giving me a hug. Case explained to me that the longer you're in the spirit world, the harder it is to manifest in the physical. I guess that explained why my birth parents had not made an appearance. Somehow, though, I knew they were with me.

Everyone had taken their seats now and the dusk grew silent, with only the rhythmic beat of the drum to fill it. The fire flickered in competition with the setting sun. The union circle glimmered with crystals and other gemstones that Aidan had been collecting for years.

He stood there now, across from Khalen who was dressed in white robes with gold sash and embellishments. It was the same gown worn by Case during our ceremony. Khalen looked confident. The red sash draped over his right arm, the pendant draped over his left.

With three distinct beats of the drum, Case signaled for everyone to be silent. Then after a quiet pause, he began a slow, even beat as Sunjia appeared just outside the circle. The clan looked to where she stood, her beige gown flowing all around her. The scent of slow-cooking food laced the air, mingling with the burning cedar and fir. As she passed, the aroma of jasmine dominated the other scents. She wore her hair up and simply adorned with a delicate dragonfly barrette. She smiled at me as she passed.

She stood to the right of Aidan. He claimed her hand, and then they both turned to face Khalen. The sacred words that opened the ceremony with the presence of God were spoken in old Gaelic. After that, Khalen nodded to Aidan.

"Aidan O'Dougherty, son of Francis and Dorothy, do you claim this woman, Sunjia Shepherd, daughter of Shamar and Keisha, to be your lifetime mate?"

Aidan looked down at Sunjia with a glimmer of pride and appreciation in his emerald-green eyes. It was the happiest I had ever seen him. "I do." He held up his left hand.

Khalen pressed his right hand against Aidan's. "Repeat these words to bind your commitment before God and family. I, Aidan, vow to claim you, Sunjia, in the name of God, protect you, and stand by your side throughout our life together. My love for you comes from pure spirit and is blessed by our Father."

Aidan repeated the words, and then kissed Sunjia's hand.

Khalen lowered his hand, nodding to Sunjia. Her delicate legs were visibly shaking under her flowing skirt. She still feared my mate, though she had earned his devout respect over the last few months.

"Sunjia, do you agree to unite with this man, Aidan, for the remainder of your lives together?"

Sunjia looked up at Aidan, her dark eyes filled with joy and indescribable adoration. "I do." She raised her trembling right hand.

With utmost gentleness, Khalen pressed his left hand against hers and smiled. "Repeat these words to bind your commitment before God and family. I, Sunjia, willingly offer myself to you, Aidan, to be your lifetime mate, to honor your status among the clan, stand beside you, and contribute to the strength of this clan."

Sunjia repeated the vow with a shaky but confident voice. Her chin was held high as she kept her soft gaze focused on her mate.

Khalen released her hand. He gestured for the two of them to present their wrists to him. With the binding Herkimer crystal, he cut a shallow incision through their skin. He pressed the wounds together then bound their wrists with the red sash. "I, Khalen Dunning, leader of the Grahdun clan, bless this union with all my heart." He turned the couple to face the clan. "As clan leader, I proudly announce this union of Aidan and Sunjia O'Dougherty." He raised their bound wrists.

The clan stood and cheered. Aidan removed the sash and proudly presented it to his brother. With a bow, he placed the sash in Ian's hand. "Will you accept the honor of being my mate's templar?"

Ian returned the bow, brought the sash to his lips then joined the new couple in prayer to seal the bond.

Khalen had left to remove his ceremonial garb then quickly returned to dance the Union dance with me. It reminded me of an erotic tango of sorts with its slow moves, hypnotic eye contact, and physical touch. Three very talented young men provided the live music, playing instruments I had never seen nor heard before. By the end, I could understand why the dance had been associated with sacred unions. By the end of it, I was ready to lie down right there in the presence of God and the clan and let Khalen have his way with me. The night air had a sudden heat to it and my body's response had a wanton edge.

Sometime during the dance, Aidan and Sunjia had disappeared—to consummate their union, I was sure, especially after that dance. Knowing Aidan, he had probably conjured an alluring illusion of a sunny deserted island in the Caribbean. How fabulous to have that gift, I mused.

Khalen lifted me in his arms, obviously feeling the effects of the dance himself. It would be rude, however, to leave the party so soon, so he settled for a long, slow kiss and a promise of proper fulfillment later that evening.

Dinner was casual and self-served by those who were ready to eat. Khalen and I joined Case and Eve by the fire.

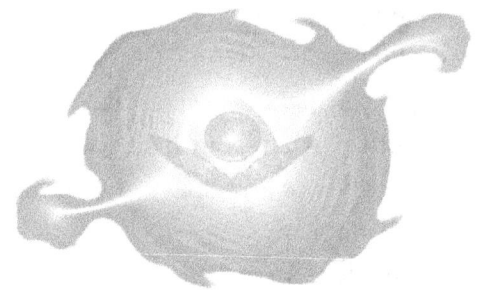

Chapter 28

Impossibilities are conquered by faith, intention, and
unwavering love.

PLACING MY HANDS OVER CASE'S, I said, "I owe you a
sincere and overdue apology."

He squeezed my hand as if to say the apology was
unnecessary.

"I should not have spoken to you so harshly last night. It
was not my place to judge you. It won't happen again."

"I appreciate your understanding, Skye, but know this.
Even an elder leader must be questioned at times. Your
approach was disrespectful, true, but your message was on
the mark." He bowed. "I accept your apology." He released
my hand and offered Khalen an approving nod.

Khalen met his obsidian eyes. "What did the council
have to say?"

"They claim that converting a human has never been
done and were surprised that a seer said that it was possible.
I believe their curiosity was peaked."

"Will they honor the outcome?" I asked.

"Yes, they will."

Eve grabbed my arm with obvious excitement.

Case took both her hands in his. "Eve, I need to know that this decision is yours and that you want this to happen for yourself, and not for me."

Her eyes were clear and focused on her mate's. "I want this for both of us, not just me. If you are not comfortable with this decision then I respect your choice."

"But you will not be happy about it?"

She glanced away. "I will be disappointed, of course."

Now it was Case's turn to look away. He did so with a growl of indecision. "Lord, woman, you ask for so little from me, but when you do, must it be the impossible?"

"Improbable," she said, "not impossible."

Another low growl rumbled the air. "Every cell of my being screams against this insanity."

Eve said nothing. She kept her gaze on him.

"Know this," he said, his voice deep and authoritative. "If things go wrong, I will not try it again. Agreed?"

She nodded. "Agreed." Her voice was shaky.

Case looked at me and Khalen. "Tonight, keep your minds open. If I call, do not hesitate."

"Of course," Khalen agreed.

Case stood. "I need some brandy."

Eve reached over and hugged me so tight, my neck cracked and threatened to snap. "Skye, tell me this is possible," she whispered.

"It is."

Case returned with four snifters of brandy. "This is the

good stuff, so enjoy it for all it's worth." He handed us each a glass, before raising his own. "To new beginnings, miracles, and the faith to make them happen."

We all clinked our glasses then took a long, appreciative sip. The fiery liquid heated my throat and coated my stomach with liquid fervor. He was right, this was a drink to be savored. The spicy finish of cinnamon and clove lingered on my tongue like a gingersnap fresh from the oven.

"What's all this?" Arcadie said from behind. He and Kitta stood hand-in-hand, looking exhilarated from hours of dancing.

Case gestured that they join us. "I intend to achieve the improbable tonight," he explained.

Having known what this issue was about, Arcadie poured his mate and himself a drink then clinked Case and Eve's glass with genuine approval. "God's spirit be with you, my brother, my sister."

"Congratulations," Kitta said, looking over at Eve. "I know this is what you have wanted."

"It is," Eve admitted. "More than words can express." She held Case's hand and gave it an affirming squeeze.

Khalen and I looked at each other moments before the cries of our young could be heard. He hopped up and headed toward our yurt. Soon later, he returned with two babes screaming and kicking against his hold. "They are clean," he said, "but still edged with hunger."

As my young fed, I started to think about Eve and her soon-to-be Spirian self. "I wonder what gifts you will have?"

Eve chuckled. "I don't think I have any."

"Oh, you do, my dear, believe me," Case bantered.

Her face turned a shade darker in the firelight.

I looked down at my young and thought about my unborn son. "What determines the gifts you develop?"

"The Father," Arcadie replied.

"Tetris said that he was a third-generation wizard. Is that gift only promoted by birth?"

Arcadie shook his head. "Not always. There are instances of first-generation wizards."

Of course, I thought. There would have to be. "So, gifts are not always handed down through blood?"

"No," he said, "but your blood determines the strengths of your gifts. For example, there are others like your mate, Khalen, who can claim life. Very few are able to do it and remain standing. Khalen's blood is strong, and therefore, his gifts are strong."

Eve frowned. "What determines if your gifts are good or bad?"

"Good and bad are one in the same," Case said. "One cannot exist without the other."

"But Skye uses her gifts to heal. How is that bad?"

"She also has the ability to cause harm, remember?"

Eve nodded, remembering our earlier conversations.

"If Khalen can take a life," I said, "can he also restore it?"

"To do that," Arcadie answered, "he would be spitting in the face of God. Restoring life is the darkest of all gifts. When Khalen takes a life, he releases the soul. The soul can be reborn and is able to transform into something better than what it was. To bring back a life would be no different than claiming that soul. That kind of work is often practiced by the Father's adversaries."

"It seems odd that taking a life is the work of the light, and restoring a life is the work of the dark," I said.

Arcadie chuckled. "That is why the lines between good and evil are often distorted. It is also the reason that God gives everyone the gift of discernment, the inherent ability to know right from wrong, good from evil, and so on. When you invite the light into your heart, you feel good and at peace. When you invite the dark, you feel fear, worry, doubt, pain, sadness, guilt, and a myriad of other negative emotions. Peace is God's way of letting us know we are living in the light."

"So, living in the dark is bad?" I asked.

This time, both Arcadie and Case laughed.

"Dumb question," I said, lowering my eyes and feeling rather foolish.

"No," Case interjected. "Not dumb, my dear; right on the mark."

I pressed my lips together, while my mind tried to fit that square peg into my round hole of understanding.

"You see," Arcadie explained, leaning forward and clasping his hands together like a wise professor. "If a person thrives on negative feelings, meaning they feed one's soul then the dark is a place of familiarity. It is good for that soul because it provides comfort. Imagine, if you will, a world where sadness does not exist."

"I imagine a world of happy people," I countered.

"How would you know?"

"Know what?"

"That they are happy? How would they know what happy was if its opposite did not exist? There would be nothing to compare it to; nothing to define its edges of truth."

The twins wriggled away, having filled their need and replacing it with another. I handed Shaiya to Khalen and lifted Kaili to my chest. She squirmed wanting to face the fire and conversation. I sat her on my knee and supported her with my arms and body. She settled, finding contentment.

Case set his glass down. "I want you to step on my glass," he said.

My eyes widened. "Why?"

"To demonstrate a point."

"If I do that, the glass will break and cut my foot."

"How do you know? Have you done it before?"

I thought about that for a moment. I had broken a glass before and knew about the dangers. "I have cut myself before, yes."

"So," he said, "was that a good experience or a bad one?"

"It was a painful one."

"And that was bad?"

My brows knit together. "Yes, it was bad."

"But it was also good," he added, "because it made you wiser. If you never had that experience, you would have trusted me and stepped on my glass."

"I think I understand now. Without the balance of opposites, nothing can be defined."

"In the physical," Arcadie added. "But that, my dear, is another discussion all together."

My head was spinning as it was. So much to learn. It hardly seemed possible to gain such understanding in one lifetime. No wonder Spirians lived so long.

Khalen leaned forward. "You have plenty of time to learn

these things, my love."

"I think I'm going to need it," I said.

Case laughed, finished his drink then offered his hand to Eve. "Never lose your innocence, Skye. It becomes you—adds to your charm."

I cocked my head, wondering if he was being facetious. My expression made him laugh some more.

"Come, my mate" he said to Eve. "We have some preparing to do."

Eve jumped up and followed him back to their yurt. I could feel her anxiety and fear. It was an emotion I was clearly familiar with.

Arcadie and Kitta also left for their yurt, leaving Khalen and I by the fire. Sometime, during our conversation, the music had ceased, and people had retired for the night.

"Are you ready for bed?"

I nodded. "Yes, more than ready, really. I'm exhausted." The twins were sleeping now.

"Hopefully not too exhausted," he said, handing me Shaiya and lifting all three of us into his arms. The girls slumped against me like two warm, limp teddy bears, wrapped in soft blankets. I kissed the tops of their heads wondering how things would be five years from now. They smelled like corn flowers, sweet and tangy.

They would soon be too big to carry, and we would have other babes to consider. I imagined our young playing with Sunjia' and Eve's children. Our families would grow together, strengthening the race and would form clans of their own. The thought made me smile.

Khalen smiled too, obviously reading my thoughts. "You

like being a mother?"

"Yes," I said, kissing the tops of our daughters' heads. "Very much."

"The other pregnancies will be better," he said. "The first is the hardest."

"Seems to be the case for everything in a Spirian's world."

"In most cases, yes," he said.

We were quiet as he carried me up the steps, Maiyun close on his heels. He sat me down on the bed. "Glass of wine?"

"Do we have spiced rum?

He searched the cabinet and held up a bottle of Captain Morgan's Private Stock. "Will this do?"

I nodded. "Do we have apple cider in the fridge?"

He looked. "No, just cranberry juice."

"That'll do. Can you warm it up, and then add the rum to it?"

He looked at me speculatively. "Cravings all ready, love?"

I laid the twins down in their beds, kissed them, and then covered them with a soft blanket by the fire. "It just sounds good, that's all."

"Hmm, okay," he mumbled, preparing the drink. He took a sip before handing it to me. "Oh, God. It's awful." He held the drink out as if it were a dead rat.

I took a sip. The tart cranberry juice played rather nicely with the spicy rum. "I like it."

He shook his head. "I'll never understand female hormones."

I rolled my eyes, knowing that my taste had nothing to do with hormones. I just wanted something warm and spicy. It was time to change the subject. "The girls are going to need a room of their own, soon."

"Yes," he said, pouring himself a glass of wine. "I have thought about that. I have three small yurts on order. Caleb and Drew are going to build the foundations for them in Spring, and then extend our yurt to access them through short corridors."

"Would it not be wiser to just build ourselves a house?"

His expression almost looked hurtful. "Is that what you want?"

"I'm just trying to be practical."

"We have many houses, love. Any one of them would do for a family."

"But they're not here," I said.

"No, they are not."

"I like our yurt."

His eyes brightened. "As do I."

"Very good then," I said. "Let's add on." I sipped my hot cranberry drink and walked over to sit on the couch, thinking about Eve and Case.

"You're worried?" he asked.

"Yes, a bit."

He came and sat beside me, lifting my foot onto his lap. With slow, deliberate strokes, he rubbed my toes, working his way up to my ankles. "They haven't even started yet," he said, having tapped Case's thoughts.

I tried taping Eve's mind, but it was jumbled and vague. It felt wrong, anyway, I told myself. They should have privacy.

"Don't worry. When Case begins, no one can tap either one of them—trust me."

"That's good." I thought about it, wondering how Case

could keep his mind closed when he was concentrating on other things.

Khalen smiled. "When a man claims a woman, the energy he emits is like a huge electromagnetic force that scrambles anything that comes near it."

"Including thoughts," I laughed, remembering how intense Khalen could be when we made love. Often times, I felt detached from this world and part of another where physical bodies didn't exist.

He lifted my other foot onto his lap and lavished the same loving attention on it as he had the other.

"Careful," I warned him. "You don't want to start something you cannot finish."

He growled. "Oh, I'll finish, my love, when Case is done."

My face burned with the intensity of his voice. It was odd how quickly he could excite me. I took a long drink from my glass, trying to think of something else. "This is going to be a long night," I sighed.

"Yes it is," he agreed. His eyes sparkled with golden hues.

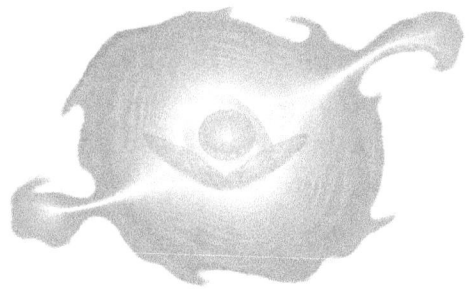

Chapter 29

*True power is not defined by one's ability to destroy. It is
defined by our intention to neutralize and restore balance.*

~ E v e ~

I WATCHED AS CASE BOILED A concoction of white sage,
feverfew, and red peony root. He was very deep in thought
and his hands were shaking.

I sipped the glass of brandy he had poured me. "What are
you doing?" I finally asked.

"I am to bathe you in this," he said, "inside and out."

I choked on the fiery drink, burning my nose in the
process. "Per Sunjia's instructions?" I asked, my voice still
hampered with shock.

"Yes." He pulled the concoction from the heat then
strained the liquid into a container sitting in cold water.

"Case, are you all right with this?"

He turned to face me, his obsidian eyes rich with rainbow

hues. "No, my dear, I'm most certainly not all right with this."
He filled an odd looking syringe with some of the liquid. "I
do this, because it is important to you."

I stood and took his hands. "I want this to be important
to you as well." I studied his prismatic eyes with probing
depth. "Do not do this just for me."

"What we attempt is highly dangerous. I don't believe you
fully comprehend what you are about to endure."

"Do we ever? Life is paved with challenges, pain, and
dangers. If I must die, at least allow me the dignity of knowing
I had done all that I could."

He slammed his hand upon the counter, making me
flinch. "All you could do about what?"

"Becoming a part of you; part of this clan, this life. I want
to have your child and see your eyes in their faces. Do you
not understand how worthless I feel among other Spirians?"

He grabbed my arms and shook them. "You are a part of
this clan like any other Spirian and you mean far more to me
than any young you could bear. What you ask of me is to sign
your death sentence."

"No," I roared back, in a tone I had never used with him
before, "not a death sentence, my love; a life sentence, with
you, as a Spirian female."

He stepped back and shook his head as if not believing
my words. "This is crazy, utterly insane."

I walked over to the tea he had poured into the syringe.
"So, what am I to do with this?"

He told me with an endearing shyness to his voice.
"When you are done, come back here and I will bathe you
with the tea."

"You don't have to," I said. "I can do it myself."

"No, I want to do it." There was a gentleness to his words that was hard to deny.

I took the syringe and did as he instructed. When I returned, the entire room was lit with candles. A melodic piano concerto played in the background while the fire crackled in the hearth.

"Come here," he said. His voice sultry.

My heart pounded in my chest as if this were the first time we had ever been together. It was hard to breathe.

"This is our first time," he whispered. "Until this night, I have never loved you as a Spirian female." He stood me by the warm fire and removed my robe.

My skin tingled as he dipped a soft cloth into the warm tea and smoothed it over my body. He performed the ritual with such love, I felt the warmth of his touch through the cloth and beyond the heat of the tea.

"You mean everything to me, Eve," he whispered, kneeling before me. He left the cloth in the bowl then pressed his head against my stomach. "Father," he spoke clearly, "you know my heart and the heart of my mate. If this union is your will, I beg you to shroud her in your light—protect her with all your Angels, and bless her soul this night." He bowed his head and held me in silence for what seemed like minutes.

He stood then carefully, effortlessly, carried me to our bed. How a man so powerful could be so gentle amazed me. It was one of the many things I loved most about him.

"Listen to me," he said. "I want you to focus on my eyes at all times. Understand?"

I nodded.

His eyes began to glow like rainbow obsidian in bright sunlight. It was easy to get lost in their gaze, lost in him. He brushed the hair from my face then kissed me slow and hard, his rising excitement driving mine over the edge.

This was different, I thought. Nothing, however could prepare me for what was to come.

"Look at me," he groaned. "Your eyes will tell me if it's too much."

"It won't be," I assured him. God, don't let it be too much, I added in thought.

I felt as if my core had been opened and filled with such intense heat, it almost felt cold. I kept my gaze on him, drinking the love that captured my soul. For the first time, I felt his spirit penetrate mine, merging us together. The pain shot deep through my abdomen. I wanted to scream, but choked it back, knowing it would cause him to stop.

"It's too much," he growled.

"No. Don't stop." My voiced sounded odd, as if it were not my own. I felt light flood my body. The hum of it was deafening. Still, I felt the heat of my mate, his love, and the intensity of his actions. The light spread out, encompassing us both. It was blinding. I could no longer see his beautiful eyes before me. In the distance, I heard him roar, deep and guttural like that of a lion in mourning.

Silence and numbness suspended me in a state of utter peace. Case was inside me, a part of me in a way I had never felt before. I didn't want to think. I just wanted to feel this surreal sensation that held me weightless.

Shanuk's gallant form manifested like blue mist moving toward me. "Eve," he called. "Welcome to the family." He touched the center of my forehead and something inside me exploded—it died.

I felt the gentle caress of my lover, my mate. His soft words bringing me back. "It's over," he whispered. "Open your eyes."

I did, blinking back the omniscient glow of the candles.

"My God," he exclaimed. "Your eyes are the color of labradorite. They're beautiful." He leaned down to kiss me then covered my left wrist with his hand.

The scorching pain shot up my arm and pierced my heart like liquid flame. I suppressed my cry.

"This night, Eve Graham, I claim you as my mate."

Tears welled in my eyes. They felt like those of a newborn, soft, weak, and ultra sensitive. Everything felt new, as if I were experiencing them for the first time.

"How do you feel?" He asked, dabbing the sweat from my forehead.

"Odd," I replied. "My voice sounds strange. Everything feels strange, even my skin."

"It will pass, my love."

I looked down at the mark he had left on my wrist. It was his, the mark of my mate.

He removed the ring from my left hand. "You won't be needing this anymore."

~ S k y e ~

I WAS WRONG. IT WASN'T A long night. It was a very long night. Sometime during the odd hours of the morning, I had fallen asleep on the couch. Khalen carried me to our bed then made love to me as if it were our night of union.

We didn't awaken until the sun was high. The sound of laughing children startled me out of my deep slumber. Khalen wrapped his arms around me and pulled me back down.

"What time is it?" I asked.

"I don't care," he groaned.

I wriggled out from under his heavy hold before checking on the twins. They were both sound asleep. I frowned. They always woke up at around seven. Never had they slept so late. I checked them both to see if they were warm and breathing. They were, thank God.

"Come back to bed," said Khalen.

I hesitated, knowing that the girls would scream the moment my head hit the pillow. I looked back at my mate. His eyes were glowing and intently focused on me. The next thing I knew, I was lifted off my feet and pulled back to the bed as if I weighed no more than a paper doll.

"Ah, that's better," he purred, wrapping his arms around me.

"Khalen, I really should get up."

"Why?"

"Because I'm wide awake and ready to start my day."

He rolled on top of me and demonstrated the proper way to start any day. The twins were gracious enough to sleep through the ruckus, waking only when I had drifted back to sleep. I rolled from under the weight of Khalen's arms and out of bed. My comfy pair of sweats laid sprawled over the trunk at the foot of our bed. I quickly donned them, and then lifted Shaiya from her crib to change her. Kaili was next, and then it was feeding time.

Khalen eased himself out of bed, glared over at the twins who were now content and taking their fill before padding his way to the kitchen. He donned the robe that was hanging near the bathroom.

He later joined me with two cups of coffee in his hands. "I think it's time to start them on solid foods," he said, setting my mug down beside me. "Now that you're pregnant, your milk will soon dry up."

The thought made me sad. Feeding the twins was something I had grown to enjoy. I never thought about the day it would end.

"We should start introducing them to goat milk."

"Well, Eve will like to hear that," I said, trying to keep the sadness from my voice.

He lifted my chin with his hand. "You will have many more young, my love, trust me."

I smiled down at Kaili and Shaiya. "Yes, but these two are my first." I handed Kaili to Khalen, and held Shaiya against my shoulder. Both of them could sit up now and they were starting to explore the possibility of crawling.

"I will make them rice cereal with goat milk today," he said, allowing Kaili to play with his massive hands. "Soon, they will be able to play with the other children."

"Khalen, they are only seven months old."

"Yes, they'll be walking soon."

"They grow so fast as it is. Don't make them advance any sooner."

He laughed. "Spoken like a true mother."

I sat Shaiya down on the rug, and then handed her a ring

of shiny stones and bells that Aidan had made for her. Kaili had one similar to it. They liked the sound it made when they shook it in their tiny fists.

Khalen sat Kaili beside her sister then lifted me into his arms to carry me to the breakfast counter.

"I can walk, you know," I said, trailing my finger down his widely-exposed chest.

"I promise you won't walk for quite some time if you continue your powerful teasing."

I adjusted myself on the chair he lowered me into. He quickly returned with my coffee in hand. "I'm anxious to talk with Eve."

He smiled. "She and Case are still sleeping."

"Is everything all right?" I asked, hesitantly.

"Yes," he said. "Case assured me we would all hear about it today."

"Is he happy?"

Khalen's smiled broadened. "Ecstatic."

I clasped my hands together and offered a heart-felt thanks to our Father. "I bet Eve is ecstatic as well."

"Case has her thoughts shrouded. He wants her to be able to share them when she's ready."

Khalen started a pot of brown rice, adding far more water than necessary. I assumed he wanted the finished product to be soft and mushy for the girls. He added coconut oil, himalayan sea salt, and a dash of fresh parsley before closing the lid and reducing the flame.

"When this is done," he said. "I'll whip up a portion of fresh goat milk, and then fold it into the rice mixture. It gives it a soft texture."

"Such a good father."

He smiled. "Well, you can contribute that to my mother," he said. "She was a good woman." His brows pinched together as if the words had caused some deep emotional pain.

"Are you happy to know more about her now?"

"In some respect, yes. In another, no."

I sipped my coffee, waiting for him to explain.

"I don't like knowing she was abused by my father, though the reminder of it all did not surprise me. Damon was an evil man with anger and lust in his heart. There was no room for love, not even for his sons." The last of his words held sadness but not regret. His lips pressed into a firm line.

"All of that is behind you now, love."

"But, it is also a part of me; one that I cannot shed." He placed a cast-iron pan on a burner over a low flame.

"Then don't try. Transform that darker negative part into its opposite positive light. Neutralize it, per se. Shanuk once told me that true power is revealed in one's ability to calm the storm with a peaceful breeze."

"Yes, he told me the same thing once, when I was young and wild with anger. He said, 'Khalen, young lad, you cannot extinguish a fire with the fuel of anger. Simply offer it nothing to consume, and the fire extinguishes itself.' He then demonstrated his point by setting my couch on fire and extinguishing it by removing its source of oxygen. The couch was remarkably unscathed."

I laughed. "That doesn't surprise me."

He added bacon to the hot iron pan then cracked eggs in a bowl. "I tried controlling fire the way he did. It ended in disaster."

I walked around the counter to start another press of coffee. "What happened?"

"I gathered a few sticks, some kindling, and placed them within a circle of rocks. I was very careful to build this fire away from anything that could burn."

I rinsed the press out and added fresh coffee. "Sounds like a good idea."

"Right, that's what I thought. Anyway, I concentrated on the pile, willing it to burn."

"And did it?"

"Well, yes. The entire pile went up in flames along with the neighboring trees, and Shanuk's wood shed."

"Too much oomph?"

"A bit, yes." He chopped fresh vegetables and poured them into the egg mixture.

"How did you extinguish it?"

"I tried removing the oxygen like Shanuk had done, but nothing happened. The blaze grew stronger and hotter. It jumped nearly twenty feet and ignited the roof of a cottage."

The kettle whistled and I pulled it off the flame. The smell of fresh coffee wafted up as I poured the water over the grounds. "That's scary. Did the cottage burn down?"

Khalen served us each an omelet and two strips of bacon. "No. Shanuk waved his hand and the flames dwindled to harmless plumes of smoke."

I pressed the coffee down to fill our cups. The twins were playing with toys scattered over the rug. "I'm guessing he wasn't too happy with you?"

"No, not at all." He walked around the counter and joined me in prayer before continuing. "We spent that evening working on controlling my will." He shook his head and laughed. "God, I thought I'd never survive that night. By the time Shanuk was done with me, I was so exhausted. Even the mere thought of experimenting with new gifts made my legs weak. I spent the next several weeks cleaning up the mess, rebuilding his shed, and repairing the damaged roof. All done without the use of gifts, mind you. Shanuk said he wanted me to fully comprehend the ramifications of my actions. Until my work was done, he had bound me from using any of my gifts. Honestly, I felt like a bird in a cage."

"Did you learn your lesson?"

He carefully sliced a bite of omelet and impaled it with his fork. "Yes, until the next time."

"Not another fire?"

"No. Anger-related issues, mostly. Between Case and Shanuk, I didn't stand a chance at getting too far out of line. I did, however, develop an unusual tolerance to pain."

"For survival purposes, I'm sure."

"Something like that."

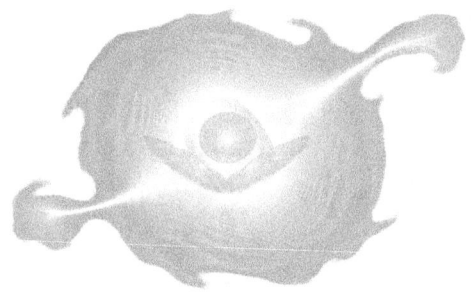

Chapter 30

Physical objects have only the power that we bestow in them.
Without intention, they are merely part of the whole.

THERE WAS NO SIGN OF Eve or Sunjia when I walked toward the barn. I assumed I would not see them until late afternoon. Khalen left for the Wellness Center with Gregg and Ro to see if the business could be revived after being neglected for so long. Our temporary help did their best to run things smoothly, but our practitioners were complaining that their clients were unhappy with the situation.

I had planned to work three days a week until my last quarter of pregnancy, but Khalen was against it. He had hired another doctor to take his place and did not like the idea of me going into Belfair alone. His leadership role was too time consuming to continue his practice, he explained, and he wanted me to be home with our young. It made sense, really, and I didn't like the idea of leaving my girls. I would miss my clients, however, and giving massages. Khalen assured me that the clan would keep me busy enough in that area.

I carried the twins to meet Belle for the first time. She reached her head over the fence and greeted me with a series of soft nickers. Khalen had made her a batch of peppermint oat cookies using a recipe that Ian had supplied.

I walked into the barn and lowered the girls into the play pen that Khalen had carried down earlier. I switched on the music and lights before retrieving the halter and lead from the hook by the door.

Belle was eager for her grooming, but when she entered the barn, she bulked at the sight of the twins in the playpen. I gave her all the lead she wanted, and allowed her to approach the girls on her own terms. If she wanted a cookie, however, she would have to choose to approach the pen and overcome her fears.

As she typically did when facing a difficult decision, she pawed the ground, tossed her head and snorted. With hesitance, she entered the grooming area then backed away when the twins made cooing sounds.

Shaiya peered through the netted walls at Belle as if she were a magical fairy with shiny wings. Kaili feigned disinterest, content with playing with the shape puzzle in the pen. I picked Shaiya up and showed her to Belle.

The mare responded with a loud snort and wide eyes. Eventually, she ventured toward us with shaky legs and wide nostrils. Shaiya reached her hand out toward Belle's nose. Belle stretched her neck and began sniffing the tiny hand stretched out toward her. I offered her a cookie for her bravery. She nibbled it from my hand then tossed her head as she ate the treat, making Shaiya laugh.

"You like that, huh?" I said, combing the soft plume of

hair that stood straight from her head.

Belle ventured closer, taking in more of Shaiya's strange scent. Shaiya touched the soft nose and squealed with delight.

When she had her fill of exploration, I put her back in the pen. Belle stood between the cross-ties and waited for another cookie. She curled her lip the way she did when the peppermint candies reached the back of her throat. I secured her to the ties then began currying her coat.

Belle kept a leery eye on the girls in the pen, but seemed more comfortable as time went by.

I heard a knock sound against the wall and looked behind me. Eve stood there with a beaming smile stretched across her face. "Can I come in?"

"Of course. I greeted her with a warm, lengthy hug. "You look radiant."

She eased away from our embrace then proudly showed me her marked left wrist. "I'm one of you now."

I smiled and traced the mark with my finger. "You've always been one of us, Eve." Her mark was similar to mine, only with slight variations on the design. "Do you feel any different?"

"A little," she said. "Kind of sensitive like a snake that has just shed its skin. My eyes are clearer, my hearing is more keen, and the noise of the clan is deafening."

I laughed. "I know what you mean. It tapers down eventually."

Belle nickered and nudged Eve's hand. She jumped back, startled.

"Here," I said, placing a cookie in her hand. "I think she wants one of these."

"How do I give it to her?"

I opened her hand flat and placed the cookie in the middle. "Keep your fingers together and flat."

Belle gently nibbled the cookie from Eve's hand. Eve rubbed the bridge of Belle's nose. "Wow, she's come a long way,"

"Yes, but I fear I've created a monster by having everyone feed her goodies. Now she just expects it."

Eve ran her hand down Belle's long and slender neck. "Nothing wrong with that, right girl?"

Belle shook her head, making us laugh.

Eve walked over and gave each of the twins a hug before letting them continue to play. "They look happy."

"Khalen started them on real food today. It seems to satisfy them longer."

"They'll be walking and playing with the other children in no time."

I frowned, not really wanting to think about my babies growing up. "Yeah, that's what Khalen said."

"Would you like to help me brush Belle?"

"I'm not sure I know how."

I placed a bristle brush in her hand and showed her how to flick the dirt out from under the coat. "Short, flicking strokes," I said. "Got it?"

"I think so." She gave it a try, her motions a bit choppy at first.

I started brushing the other side. "I'm going to try riding her today."

Eve peeked over Belle's back. "Are you sure you want to do that?"

"Yes, I think she's ready." Maiyun trotted into the barn, her face covered in mud. "Oh, Maiyun. Where have you been?"

"Down by the lake would be my guess," said Eve.

I cleaned Belle's feet and brushed her mane and tail. Eve held the twins and watched as I led Belle out to the round pen to warm her up a bit. I put her through our typical paces, walking, trotting, loping then changing directions. We did some stops, backs, and moving away from pressure exercises. When I felt she had a good idea of what I wanted. I led her toward the fence where I could get high enough to drape my leg over her back.

"Aren't you going to use a saddle or something in her mouth?" Eve asked.

"No. I prefer bareback. If I did my job correctly, I don't really need a bridle. The halter and lead should suffice."

I cued Belle to come closer to the fence. She was apprehensive, but her trust in me was evident. I rubbed her neck then slowly lowered my leg over her back. She jumped a bit, but didn't bolt, even though I gave her more than enough lead rope to get away. Slowly, I lowered myself onto her back. Her muscles tensed beneath me. I gathered the rope in my hands, along with a tuft of mane. Gently, I squeezed my legs. She bolted, shaking her head and squealing as if calling me a traitor. I held on, allowing her to express her grief. When she calmed, I relaxed the pressure of my legs and gently rubbed her neck.

We sat there for quite some time before I squeezed my legs again. This time, she trotted forward, bucked a few times then calmed to an easy walk. I relaxed my grip and flowed with the motion of her shoulders and hips.

"You ride very well," Eve said. "I would have been on the ground by now."

"I learned a long time ago that staying on was a lot less painful than falling off."

Belle licked her lips, indicating that she understood what I wanted. I sat back and pushed my feet forward a bit, cuing her to stop. She slowed, but didn't quite come to a complete halt. I gently pulled on the lead, reaffirming my request. When she stood still, I rewarded her with a cookie and a rub over her withers.

In another twenty minutes, I had her performing all the actions she knew so well when I was on the ground. I saved trotting and loping for another day. For now, I just wanted her to respond to the pressure of my legs. We ended the session with a good rub down then time out in the grassy meadow for grazing.

Eve sat beside me on a log under a tree. "You're amazing with her," she said. "I had no idea you knew so much about horses."

We set the girls down on the grass. They took turns crawling over Maiyun. She rolled over and exposed her belly to the twins' eager grasps. I cringed every time they pulled her fur. Maiyun didn't seem to care much.

"I wanted to be a trainer once," I said. "A long time ago."

"Why didn't you?"

I shrugged. "No money in it—and, I kind of lost interest."

She looked at me with a questioning yearn in her eyes. "Do you mind if I ask why?"

"I lost a horse that was very dear to me. After that, my

interest in horses faded. It never re-engaged."

"Until now?"

I shook my head. "I'm just getting Belle to the point where we can find her a good home. I'm not keeping her."

Eve stared out at the mare. "That's too bad. I kind of like having her here."

It was time to change the subject. "Is Case happy, now that it's over?

"Yes, more happy than I have ever seen him.

We were silent again, both lost in our own thoughts. I watched as the girls tumbled around Maiyun as she laid sprawled on the grass, her tongue hanging wet and loose out of her mouth. She had taken to the young very well. It surprised me, seeing she hadn't been raised around kids. The clan children played with her from time to time, but they were much older. The young ones stayed away.

"Have you seen Aidan and Sunjia?" I asked.

Eve shook her head. "No. Ian said they left camp early this morning. Khalen may know where they went."

Some kids ran up, chasing a soccer ball that had been kicked off field. Belle flinched at the sudden rush then quickly settled back into grazing.

"Can we pet her?" a young girl named Lita asked, her brown eyes sparkling against the reflection in the lake.

"Sure," I said, standing. I wasn't sure how Belle would take to so many young crowding around her, so I walked with the group of three girls and four boys to where Belle stood grazing.

I released her ground tie and held her as the children approached. She stood amazingly calm as each of them patted her gently around her belly and legs. They soon became bored then left to continue their game.

Lita ventured to kiss the tip of Belle's nose, making a squeaky sound with her lips. Belle raised her head, eyes wide, but standing calm despite the unexpected noise. It was the same queue I used to ask her to canter. "That noise is a command to her," I explained to the confused girl. "It means you want her to run."

"Oh," Lita said, a hint of sadness in her voice.

"Do you want to feed her a cookie?" I asked, pulling a crunchy tidbit from my pocket.

"Yeah!" She held out her hand and I placed the goodie in the center of it, helping her hold her hand flat and still.

Belle gently took the cookie from her hand then nodded her head.

Lita giggled. "She's funny." She rubbed Belle's nose. "Can I sit on her?"

I frowned, not really sure that Belle was ready for that yet. "What do you think, girl?" I asked her. "Can Lita sit on your back?" The young girl was only six years old and weighed no more than 30 pounds. Belle would hardly notice her.

"Okay, we'll try it," I told Lita. "If Belle seems uncomfortable, I want you to hold on to me and slide off, okay?"

Lita nodded, wide eyed and eager. I lifted her into my arms and walked to Belle's side. She turned her head. Her eyes were soft and inviting. Slowly, I lifted Lita's leg over Belle's back and softly set her down. "Keep your legs very still," I told her.

"Okay."

Belle lowered her head and began grazing again, not in the least bit concerned with the child on her back.

"You want me to walk her around a bit?" I asked.

Lita nodded.

"Okay, hold onto her mane here," I instructed, placing a tuft of mane in her tiny hand.

I cued Belle to raise her head then began leading her around. Lita squealed with excitement. "Eve, look, I'm riding a real horse."

Eve laughed. "Yes, I see that. You look great."

I completed a huge circle then helped the girl down.

"Can I ride her again tomorrow?" she asked.

"Of course you can," I answered. "Did you want to help brush her as well?"

Lita's eyes grew wide, her mouth hung open. "Can I?"

"Yes, I'll come get you tomorrow."

The little girl ran back to the group of children, her thin, dark braids flying behind her.

"I think you made her day," said Eve.

"She reminds me of myself at that age. There was an old draft horse who lived in a field across from our school. I would feed her carrots and apples every day. When the farmer invited me over to pet the old mare, I was in heaven. She was the first horse I ever sat on and it was magical, just like this was for Lita."

Eve looked at me as if I were a stranger with a familiar face. "I feel as if there is a lifetime about you that I don't know."

I smiled. "There is."

Epilogue

Power belongs to those who wield it wisely. It is not the demonstration of strength to destroy, but to build and unite with the unfathomable balance in all things.

~ 5 Years Later ~

I SAT AND WATCHED AS MY children played in the field with other young. Their laughter energized the peaceful silence. Kaili and Shaiya were nearly six years old, while my boys Gabrihen was four and Zhentu, three. Gabrihen already showed signs of gifts. He could will things toward him, while his younger brother seemed rather apt at communicating with creatures. Khalen said he would probably develop into a shapeshifter someday.

Shaiya had a talent to heal, while Kaili displayed an ability to calm those around her. When tension was high at home, Kaili eased the deafening hum. It seemed she had a balancing gift to her father's anger.

Eve birthed three lovely daughters and now carried a son, due to birth in three months. Sunjia, after birthing two beautiful sons, asked Aidan for a little girl. Unable to deny her sweet request, he blessed her with the seed of a daughter. We looked forward to her birth in 10 more months.

My hands were busy tying a rope halter for Belle. She had so many and really didn't need another, but it gave me something to do while I watched the children play. Eve was in the gardens, while Sunjia played along with the young.

Belle stood in the center of the field, grazing on the fresh spring grass. Lita braided her tail, while three young boys sat on her back. Her coat glistened in the sun, dark and rich with coppery hues. Her bones no longer protruded under her skin and her muscle tone gave her twice the girth she had three years past. Her mane had grown in thick and long, nearly covering her neck. Her forelock feathered over her face like a silky veil. She was a beautiful mare and had taken well to the children.

I heard my mate approach from behind. He leaned over and kissed my neck, sending cool shivers down my spine. His touch still had the same effect on me as it had the week we met.

"How do you do that?" he asked, gesturing at my hands. He knew my vision was fading and I could no longer see detail. I didn't even try anymore.

"I see better with my hands than with my eyes," I said.

He lifted the length of knots and soft cotton twine from my fingers and inspected my work. "How do you get the lengths between the knots right?"

He knew that if the spacing was incorrect, it would not fit

properly over the horse's face. "I have made so many of them for her, I know what works best for her delicate head."

He sat beside me on the log, and stoked the small fire Aidan had built to keep me warm. Maiyun lifted her head for Khalen's affection then lowered her head with a groan. She was nine years old now, and unable to keep up with the kids and younger dogs.

"She gets tired," I commented. "I find her curled in her bed for most of the day."

Khalen scratched behind Maiyun's ear. "Well, her health is good, and she is not in pain. That's better than most dogs her age."

"Her sire is thirteen years old and still going strong," I said. "I expect nothing less from her."

Khalen sat up and gestured toward Belle. "And what about that one. Is she ready to find a new home?"

I shook my head. "No, she is still very unpredictable and won't take to a saddle."

Khalen laughed, witnessing the young sprawled over the mare's back, and the girls fussing with her mane and tail, as she grazed peacefully amid the boys playing soccer. "Oh yes, she's a real spitfire, that one. And Skye, you don't even own a saddle."

"Well, if I did, I'm certain she wouldn't want to carry it."

He laughed some more. "Are you ever going to admit how much you love her and cannot stand the idea of parting with her?"

"No," I said, matter of factly. "I'm merely doing the responsible thing for her and her future owner."

"Right."

I finished tying the last knot in the halter then set it down beside me. "Did you speak with Kitta and Arcadie about Ian and Erika?"

"I did."

"And?"

"Kitta will not change her mind."

"What about Arcadie?"

"He agrees that the two of them make a good match."

I pressed my brows together with confusion. "I wonder why Kitta cannot see that?"

"Erika is her eldest daughter. Kitta knows that she will choose to live here with Ian, should they unite."

"Well, it's not as if she'll never see her daughter again," I said.

He smiled. "Can you imagine Shaiya or Kaili uniting with a man in Brazil?"

My stomach lurched with the thought. "Absolutely not! They are only six years old."

"What about when they turn thirty or fifty?"

Several years ago, that would have seemed like a long time, and that age would seem far too old to find a mate. Today, it seemed like hours. I shook my head. "I don't want to think about it."

He laughed. "Now you understand Kitta's reasons."

I rolled my eyes. "And what does Ian plan to do?"

"He wants to learn to fly, purchase a small jet, and plan to see Erika every chance he gets."

Now it was my turn to laugh. "Yeah, I can see that happening. Ian is not one to let go of something so easily."

"He courts her everyday on the phone."

"Poor man. He certainly likes a challenge."

Khalen brought my hand up to his lips. "I think that's what he likes so much about that girl. She doesn't make it easy for him, nor does her mother."

Eve came bounding toward us, despite her enormous size. A smiled beamed across her face. "Are you busy?" she asked me.

"I was just about ready to put Belle up for the night and get the kids cleaned up for dinner. Did you need me for something?"

"I could use your help packing the vegetables I just harvested."

Since Eve discovered her innate ability to grow things rapidly and rise dough in a matter of minutes, she had been slightly over the top with her gifts. I could only imagine what I would find in that cart of hers. We had enough vegetables packed away to last us through three winters. We had since been giving the produce away to neighboring clans. Case had to build a separate shed just to store the jars of pickled and canned goods.

Khalen stood. "I'll take care of Belle and the kids," he said. "You help my dear mother with her bounty."

I kissed him on the lips. "You're an angel."

He winked. "You can make it up to me tonight."

I felt my face redden, knowing he would make good on that promise. I turned and joined Eve.

She had harvested two carts full of peas, corn, beans, tomatoes, herbs, and other greens. I could smell the pungent aroma of their life force, packed with chlorophyll and minerals. "Good Lord, Eve. What are we going to do with all this?"

"Sell it to the produce stand in Belfair. They're having a hard time competing right now and things are bound to get better if we can supply them with enough fresh produce."

I had never seen such enthusiasm in her eyes. They literally glowed as she spoke. "I've also been giving some to the food banks in town."

"I'm sure they appreciate it," I said.

We both took a cart and hauled it back to the shower hut where we could clean the bounty and sort it out. What we didn't save for our meals this week was packed and loaded in Ian's truck. He didn't seem too surprised to hear that he had another truckload to deliver this week.

Dinner had been served outdoors as it typically was when the weather cooperated. The kids had eaten and were tucked into bed. As promised, Khalen had added a few smaller yurts to our large one. Each child had their own room, and there was ample room to spare for future young. When they were fast asleep, Khalen and I joined the others by the fire.

Eve and Case were in the middle of a conversation. Eve looked frustrated. "I just feel more valuable now that I have a gift," she said.

"Like I said," Case interjected. "You always had those gifts, my dear. You just didn't believe in them."

"I wasn't a Spirian."

"You've always been a Spirian, Eve."

Her brows pinched together in confusion. "So you've been saying, but yet I had no gifts before our union and I never bared your mark." She held up her left wrist with obvious pride.

Case leaned over and kissed it. "You have always had the gift of growing the garden, my love. And your dough has never failed to rise."

"How do you explain the children?"

Case looked over at me and Sunjia. "It proves that with faith and the Father's will, all things are possible."

Khalen served us each a portion of lamb stew then poured two glasses of red wine. "For the first time," he said, "I see hope for our kind." He raised his glass.

"Aye," Case agreed, raising his own glass.

The toast was soon followed by others in the circle.

Since Victor had been stripped of his territories, peace had soon followed. The past few years had been rather dull, but delightful all the same. The council assured us that another would take his place and to keep our guard. The rise of the Shadows was as certain as the ebbing of the tides. History had proven that truth time and again. For now, however, the calm before the storm was well appreciated.

My life had come full circle. As a human, I was born, had lived through trials and triumphs, had loved, and had known lost. That life ended when I met Khalen. In that death, I was reborn into a role of a legend. A legend that consisted of nothing more than pure hope. Perhaps that was what legends really were—simple manifestations of what was meant to be, nothing more. Legends are not the magic. It is the faith in them that is so—the belief in knowing that miracles happen.

The power behind my legend was the pure belief that the Spirian race would once again thrive on this Earth.

My legend, and the very small part in which I played, was fulfilled—only to be replaced by another:

Legend

The meek shall inherit the earth; and shall delight themselves in the abundance of peace.

~Psalms 37:11

A Note From the Author

I hope you have enjoyed reading Legend. The Spirian Saga continues with new characters that are introduced into Khalen's clan.

Many people have asked where the quotes at the beginning of each chapter came from. They are quotes I have conjured throughout my life. I kept them recorded in a journal since I was a young teen. It was fun to finally be able to use them.

Many of us have a story to tell but are afraid tell it for one reason or another. My goal is to encourage and inspire you all to tell your story, be it as a memoir or as a fictional tale based on fact, such as this one.

About the Author

Rowena started writing at a young age, feeling an inherent need to tell stories that inspire and reflect aspects of life that are rarely considered.

Being a descendant of James Hudson Taylor, author and founder of the China Inland Mission, Rowena comes from a long line of story tellers, including her mother and father. The tradition of writing continues through her daughter, Erika.

Rowena's goal is to inspire others to tell their stories and share the wonderful gift and adventure of life. She often speaks before groups, sharing her experiences of writing and telling stories. It is a passion of hers that she shares with her mate, Gregg.

Together, they are writing a book entitled, *Finding Peace Among Chaos*, due to be released in Spring 2013.

Though she is over seventy-five percent blind, she doesn't allow that to derail her ambitions. Her husband is deaf, so they make the perfect pair. They live on the Olympic Peninsula in Washington with her guide dog Skye-Bear.

Other Books by Rowena

Protected
Union
Aeon Pneuma
Illusions
Fealty

www.Rowena-Portch.com

Book a Speaking Engagement with Rowena and Gregg

Rowena and Gregg love to inspire people to tell their story and to follow their passion no matter how unobtainable it may seem.

Both of them have been on their own since age fourteen and have some incredible stories to share. Though both of them are disabled—she's blind and he's deaf—neither of them allow their impairments to deter them from their dreams.

If you want Rowena and Gregg to speak at your next event, please email them at:

Rowena@Rowena-Portch.com

www.ingramcontent.com/pod-product-compliance
Lightning Source LLC
Chambersburg PA
CBHW060345260626
47160CB00006B/2210